Rushed

Evancurt

Brian Harmon

Rushed: Evancurt

ISBN: 1-945559-15-2
ISBN-13: 978-1-945559-15-0

This is book 8!
Want to start at the beginning?
Be sure to check out all the books in this series:

And don't miss these other great books by Brian Harmon:

The Temple of the Blind series:

Hands of the Architects trilogy:

For Guinevere

Chapter One

Everything was darkness, pain and fog. Eric drifted through an icy, black void, lost in the crushing depths of a vast, stinging ocean, his thoughts tossed in the strange currents, scattered and broken, grasping at desperate fragments of confused questions churning in the murky waves.

What happened to him? Where was he? Why was he in so much pain?

Slowly, he clawed his way back to consciousness and struggled to open his eyes. He was lying on the cold, damp ground, his face pressed against the bare earth, the smell of dirt, dead leaves and blood filling his nose.

This wasn't how he usually started his morning. Call him a pessimist, but this felt like it was going to be one of those days.

He tried to move his arms and felt a sharp, jarring pain in his left shoulder that jolted him a little more awake. His eyes fluttered open, but they didn't want to focus. The world around him was a cloudy blur of mottled shadow and churning light. Again, he felt as if he were deep underwater, peering up through murky fathoms.

His head was pounding. There was a throbbing in his left knee. It even hurt to breathe. With a painful grunt, he lifted his head and blinked away the tears in his eyes. Some of the haze peeled away, revealing those imagined deep-sea lights to really be a canopy of bare tree branches looming over him and swaying in the cold breeze.

A forest... But why was he in the woods? He *hated* the woods. Bad things tended to happen to him in the woods.

He blinked again, trying to clear away more of that haze, but not all of it was in his head. The day, itself, was gray and gloomy. There was a cold and haunting mist hanging in the air.

A crow was perched on one of the branches, staring down at him like a tired cliché of an ill omen, its head tilted to one side as if it were as baffled about how he'd ended up here as he was.

What the hell happened to him? The last thing he remembered was…

He closed his eyes and groaned. What *was* the last thing he remembered?

Again, he moved his arms. Again, his shoulder cried out in pain. But he managed to plant the palms of his hands against the ground and push himself up.

Above him, the crow spread its wings and took off into the sky.

The conference. He was at the teacher's conference. In Oshkosh.

He drew his knees up beneath him, grimacing at the pain in the left one as he settled his weight onto it. Then he coughed and the motion sent shockwaves of pain through his chest and left side.

This wasn't the sort of thing that usually happened at teachers' conferences. He was fairly sure he was missing something here.

Reaching up with a shaky hand, he felt a shallow gash on the side of his forehead. That was where the blood was coming from. It'd run down his face, matting his eyebrow and covering his cheek. But it didn't seem to be gushing. Hopefully he wouldn't need stitches.

He sat up and looked around, trying to blink away more of that confusing haze.

He was on his way home. He remembered that much. It wasn't morning at all, but late afternoon or early evening. But…how did he end up *out here*? And for that matter, where was his *vehicle*?

He blinked hard and then turned and looked behind him.

His silver PT Cruiser was there. It was mangled up among the tree trunks, utterly totaled.

His heart sank at the sight. He'd had it for six years now. It might not have been the coolest of rides. Karen was the one who picked it out. She thought it was cute. But they brought it home brand-new from the dealer with only twelve miles on it. And he'd taken good care of it, too.

Now it was gone.

It felt a little like losing an old friend...

He closed his eyes again and lowered his head. Was it his fault? Did he fall asleep? Did a deer run out in front of him? He didn't see any other vehicles. He hoped to God no one else was involved.

With a loud and painful grunt, he rose to his feet and staggered a few steps toward the destroyed Chrysler. It was funny, he was never quite sure what to call the thing. The dealer told them it was technically classified as a truck. But calling it a truck seemed a bit pretentious. The same with just calling it the "Cruiser." Like he was trying to lump it in with those souped-up Chargers the police used. But it didn't feel like just a "car," either. And it certainly wasn't a van or an SUV.

He stood there a moment, his eyes closed, swaying a little on his feet, just letting himself breathe. His head was still foggy. It was difficult to think straight.

Forget the stupid car. (Or truck or whatever it was...like it really mattered anymore...) Right now, he needed to clear his mind and focus. It was getting late. And the sky was gray and dreary, as it'd been all day, meaning it'd be dark early. It was a rather warm day for late January, much warmer than it'd been the past few days, but it was still cold, only a few degrees above freezing. And it was only going to get colder as the night dragged on.

He opened his eyes and stared at the remains of the vehicle. Then he frowned. He turned and looked back at the place where he woke up. It was at least fifty feet away. Was he thrown that far in the crash? No... That wouldn't be possible. He knew he was wearing his seatbelt. He *always* wore his seatbelt.

Again, he turned and looked at the mangled wreck in front of him. It was crumpled and folded against the trees. Between the impact and being thrown fifty feet, how was he not dead?

That couldn't be right. Maybe he'd climbed out of the car,

dazed from the crash, and collapsed over there. It made more sense than being thrown clear of the crash in spite of being properly buckled in.

He started walking toward the wreck again, his mind racing. Then something caught his eye, something hanging out of the open door. He paused, confused. Was that a *sleeve*? Was someone there?

But no one was with him when he left the conference…

He was startled by the sudden and ridiculous idea of walking up and finding *himself* still in the car, his body mangled along with the wreckage, his eyes lifeless and glazed.

Was it possible? *Could* he be dead?

No. That was stupid. He wouldn't have such a headache if he were dead.

Right?

He walked up to the crumpled door and peered inside. It *was* his sleeve. More specifically, it was the sleeve of his jacket, which he'd taken off before leaving Oshkosh.

"Get it together…" he muttered, running his hand through his hair.

He reached through the broken window and grabbed the jacket. Then he shook off the broken bits of safety glass and put it on.

His chest still hurt on the left side. He felt it when he raised his arms. Had he cracked a rib? He hoped he didn't end up spending the night in a hospital somewhere. That'd be annoying. Fortunately, the pain in his shoulder and knee seemed to ease a bit as he moved around and loosened his joints. His hand hurt, too, he realized, although there weren't any injuries that he could see.

Glancing back through the broken window, he saw that the airbags had deployed. Maybe those had hurt his hand. At the very least, they probably explained how he survived such a grue-some-looking impact.

The fuzziness in his aching head was starting to clear up. But with this clarity came another bizarre realization.

He turned all the way around, scanning his surroundings.

Where was the road?

He turned around again, scanning those same surroundings a second time, and then a third, as if he were merely missing it. There was nothing but hazy forest in every direction. He couldn't hear any traffic.

How could he have run off the road if there wasn't a road?

There wasn't even any clear path by which he could've driven to this spot, much less fast enough to have done this kind of damage. He saw no tire tracks. How did he end up here? It didn't make any sense.

None of this made any sense.

He leaned against the mangled fender and closed his eyes again, trying to think through the headache.

Then he looked up, his senses finally returning to him. "Isabelle!" he gasped. She'd know what happened. He reached for his phone in his front pants pocket, but it was gone. "What...? No!" He checked his other front pocket. His back pockets. His jacket pockets. He leaned into the driver's window and searched the seats, the console and the cupholders. Then he pried the door all the way open, wincing at the awful sound of grinding metal and cracking fiberglass, and looked in the floorboards and under the seats. Finally, he turned and scanned the ground between here and where he awoke.

He had it when he left the conference. He was certain of that. He'd called Karen from the parking lot to let her know he was on his way home. He was fairly sure he remembered returning it to his pants pocket.

But the rational part of his mind told him that if it was here and it still worked, he'd hear it ringing. Isabelle would've heard him and called before now. In fact, thinking more clearly about it, she should've been calling him from the start, trying to wake him up while he was lying unconscious on the ground.

But then where had it gone? It couldn't have just disappeared.

He turned and searched the vehicle again. He wanted to believe that it was just turned off. Or maybe the battery had died. He only had to find where it fell and plug it into the travel charger. The car battery would probably still be good for that. But he knew better. He always kept it on when he was traveling. Karen insisted. And it was fully charged when he left the house that morning. *And* he'd kept it off all during the conference. It was either gone or broken. Those were the only possibilities that made any sense.

And he hadn't even begun to process the fact that his wallet seemed to have gone missing as well. Had he been robbed? Maybe someone witnessed the accident, pulled him out of the wreckage and then relieved him of his valuables. It'd be a dick move, to be sure, but it was a scenario that at least made some sort of sense, he supposed.

He stood there a moment, still leaning over the driver's seat, still trying to make sense of it all. Then he glanced up at the darkening sky above. There was a flashlight, spare batteries and a first aid kit in the glove box. He reached over and retrieved them, then stepped away from the wreck and filled the empty pockets of his jacket.

This was bad. The PT Cruiser was destroyed. He had no idea where he was, or even where the *road* was. He'd lost his phone, so he wasn't going to be able to talk to Isabelle or call for help or to look up where he was. *And* he had several injuries that seemed minor, but probably should be looked at.

Absently, he dabbed at the gash on his forehead again.

"What the hell happened?" he muttered to himself.

The forest, not surprisingly, offered him no answer.

He wandered off a few steps and then sat down on the cold ground again, wincing at the pain in his ribs and rubbing at his aching hand. Then he withdrew a disinfecting wipe from the first aid supplies he'd stuffed in his pocket and began cleaning the blood off his face while he went over the facts in his head, one by one.

An accident was one thing. It happened. And the phone could've fallen somewhere and broke. Or he might've dropped it while stumbling around in whatever unremembered haze carried him to the place on the ground where he eventually awoke. Or it could've been stolen with his wallet. Even some memory loss wasn't unexpected, given that he'd hit his head somewhere along the way. (He should probably have that looked at sooner than later.)

It was the road. That was the part that didn't add up, no matter how he approached it.

He tried to remember the events leading up to the accident, but it was pointless. His last clear memory was of driving down the highway. He recalled nothing odd at all. Traffic was fairly light. The roads were damp, but clear of ice. It'd been drizzling off and on all day. Given the current light, that must've been at least an hour or two ago.

He glanced down to check his watch, as he'd been doing all day, only to remember that it was still at home. The battery had gone dead on him the day before and he hadn't had time to buy a new one.

Just his luck...

He was starting to have a bad feeling about all this. Or, more precisely, he'd been having that bad feeling this whole time and was starting to run out of excuses to keep trying to rationalize it away.

Something *weird* was going on. And if he could talk to Isabelle, she'd probably confirm it for him.

What happened during that missing time? And what was he supposed to do now that he was here? Wandering around blind didn't seem like a good idea. With no idea which way the nearest road might be, he'd only end up more lost.

Maybe he should stay close to the vehicle for now. He'd have the best chance of being found that way. Isabelle would've informed Karen of his accident as soon as it happened. And Karen would've dispatched his brother, Paul, to come searching for him. By now, he'd almost certainly be following Isabelle's directions to the last place she knew him to be.

At the very least, he could just take a moment and rest and let his head clear a little more.

But then something strange happened. Stranger, even, than waking up in the middle of the forest without his phone, wallet, memories or even the road that brought him here. Strange, even by Eric's warped standards.

The wind abruptly died away and every branch and twig became unnaturally still. An eerie silence fell across the forest, leaving not a single sound but the pounding of his own pulse in his ears. At the same time, an intense and irresistible panic began to rise from deep inside him. Inside his bruised chest, his heart was suddenly racing. He jumped to his feet and turned around, his eyes wide, convinced that he wasn't alone.

Something was here. He was immediately and absolutely sure of it. Something was watching him. Something in the forest. Something *dangerous*.

He turned the other way, scanning his surroundings, trying to find the source of this awful feeling. Beneath his shoes, the crunching of the leaves sounded as loud as gunshots in the eerie silence, and the noise he made only intensified this bizarre terror.

He needed to get out of here right now.

He didn't think about which way he should go.

He just ran.

Chapter Two

Somewhere in the depths of his frightened mind, he knew this made no sense. He was blindly running through a hazy, unfamiliar forest, probably getting himself hopelessly lost, and he didn't even know what he was so deathly afraid of. He didn't *see* anything. He looked back over his shoulder as he scrambled up the side of a rocky hill, but there was nothing chasing him. The only sound he could hear was footsteps and they were his own. And yet no amount of logical reasoning could diminish the utter terror that filled his racing heart. If anything, he was only growing more panicked with each passing second. His every instinct was screaming at him that he was in danger. Regardless of what that stubbornly logical part of his brain might say, he could feel the weight of dangerous, unseen eyes bearing down on him as he dashed through the trees, watching his every move, stalking him, waiting for the perfect moment to strike.

As he crested the top of the hill and stumbled down the other side, it occurred to him that it was no longer silent. A strange sort of sound was slowly rising, an indescribable noise that didn't seem to have a name because it was a sound that hadn't existed until this very moment. The closest he could come to describing it was an ominous *buzzing* sort of sound, as if a swarm of deadly insects were rapidly approaching. But that wasn't quite the right description for it. Nor was the idea of a vast, flesh-eating swarm of alien bugs even remotely terrifying enough to adequately describe this sound. Deep down, somewhere in some primitive part of his mind, he *recognized* this sound as something awful, as if it were hardwired directly into the evolutionary coding of his very instincts. He was in unimaginable danger. Something *terrible* was coming!

He was certain of it.

It grew louder and louder, and yet he couldn't seem to tell which direction it was coming from. It was all around him. Or perhaps, he suddenly thought, it was *within* him, inside his head, where there was no escape.

He tripped and fell. A bolt of pain tore through his injured knee, but he ignored it. He jumped back to his feet and turned around, searching the trees. Something was here. He couldn't see it, but he could *feel* it. A terrible and overwhelming presence bearing down on him. It was right on top of him!

Then, as quickly as it all started, the buzzing noise suddenly vanished.

The wind picked up. The branches above him seemed to sigh with relief. Somewhere, a crow cried out. That feeling of intense dread drained away as quickly as it'd come upon him.

He stood there, looking back the way he came, confused. What *was* that? Why did he react so intensely to it? His heart was still pounding in his chest. He was gasping for breath and wincing at the pain in his ribs with each gulp of air he took.

His fingers crept toward his pocket where the phone was supposed to be. He wanted to talk to Isabelle. He wanted to know if she felt the same thing, if she'd ever heard of anything like this before. But Isabelle wasn't here. *No one* was here.

He was alone in these mysterious woods.

He turned and leaned against the trunk of a tall pine and closed his eyes, willing himself to calm down. He needed to think clearly.

He reached up and touched the gash on his forehead again. It didn't seem all that bad, but you just never knew about head injuries until you had yourself checked out. There was a very real possibility that he'd suffered a concussion. If that were true, then there was always a chance that the bizarre panic attack he'd just experienced was nothing more than a very vivid hallucination.

Four years ago, that would've been all the explanation he needed. But there was another fact that he needed to acknowledge and that was that unexplainable things like this were *real*. He'd found that out on numerous occasions now. Alternate universes were real. Ghosts were real. Magic and witches were real. Monsters and maniacs with terrifying supernatural powers were real.

Why *not* an eerie, terror-inducing, invisible presence in a forest?

He needed to find a phone. He needed to talk to Isabelle.

He rubbed at his aching hand. It didn't hurt quite as much as the freshly-awakened pain in his knee, but it was distracting. He hoped it didn't get worse as the night drew on. He was probably going to need that hand to defend himself from something scary.

When he opened his eyes, he found that it was snowing.

He stood up straight and looked around. Everything seemed to be normal now. He felt none of the intense panic that had swept through him a moment ago. It felt as unreal as a dream looking back on it, as if he'd only imagined the entire ordeal.

Strange...

But he didn't have time to dwell on it now. The light was fading. And he had no way of knowing which way he should go. These woods could stretch for miles. If he wandered blindly he could easily become lost. Should he make his way back to the scene of the crash and wait for help? Or would that only invite another of those terrifying encounters?

Before he could decide, he caught sight of a protruding length of pipe sticking up out of the ground a few yards away, half hidden behind a tree. He walked closer, curious. It was a very thick, very sturdy pipe. Lead, he thought, about six inches in diameter and three feet tall, ending in a U-shaped bend, presumably to prevent it from being clogged by rain and falling leaves.

What was this for? Was there something buried here?

He held his hand under the opening and felt a very faint passing of warm air against his palm. Was it an exhaust pipe of some sort? Was there something under the ground? A heated room? Maybe some sort of bunker? Whatever its purpose, it was a sign of civilization. If there were people around somewhere, he could find help. He could get in out of the cold. He could find a phone.

He looked around, but there didn't appear to be any sort of entrance nearby.

Instead, he caught sight of another pipe, exactly like this one, about fifteen yards away, jutting up from the side of the next hill. He made his way over to it and passed his hand under the end of it. More warm air. Faint, but definitely there.

A tunnel, perhaps?

He continued past it, to the top of the hill and looked down the other side. There were two more pipes, evenly spaced in a straight line, leading...*where*? Leading out of these woods? To safety? Or only deeper into the forest?

He turned and looked back the other way. He couldn't see any more of these pipes in that direction, but the trees were thicker over there and they didn't exactly stand out.

He glanced out into the woods, distracted. Was that a voice calling out? He tilted his head to one side, then the other, trying to hear over the gusting wind and falling snow. It was probably nothing. Only the very wind and snow he was trying to listen through. He was jumpy. That was all. He'd feel better once he was able to talk to Isabelle.

Probably.

But for a moment, he continued to listen.

His gaze drifted back to the pipe jutting from the ground next to him. Could it have come from there? A voice carried up from somewhere below?

No. His imagination. Nothing more.

He'd always had something of an overactive imagination. Sometimes it was a good thing, like when he was settled in with a good book. But when dealing with things like this, it had a nasty habit of only making every frightful situation he found himself in considerably worse. Before long it would have him convinced that he could hear hell, itself, howling up from every rabbit hole and hollow tree in the forest.

He decided to continue following the pipes in this direction and see where they led him, since he'd already started walking this way and saw no reason to retrace his steps. But he'd barely begun his descent down the other side of the hill when he was distracted by something moving in the corner of his eye. He turned, startled, to see a small shape dart behind a cluster of trees and out of sight.

Was that a person? He was fairly sure it was too small to be an adult, but a child, perhaps? The source of the voice he thought he heard a moment ago? "Hello?" he called out. "Is someone there?"

But no one answered.

"I've had an accident. And I'm lost. I could use some help."

But the forest remained silent.

It slowly dawned on him that it was late January and it was getting dark. Why would a child be out here in the woods at such a time?

Again, his hand crept toward his pocket, his fingers itching to close around the cell phone that wasn't there.

Another voice carried across the wind, but again, he couldn't be sure he wasn't imagining it.

He turned back, intending to continue following the pipes, but was startled by someone standing right behind him, someone that loomed much larger than the child-sized shape he thought he saw a moment before. Someone *reaching out for him.*

He cried out and jumped back while turning to face this person, stumbling and slipping down the hill, barely managing to stay on his feet.

But whoever—or *whatever*—was there was already gone. He was alone again. Sort of…

This time, he was sure he heard a voice. Several voices, in fact. All around him. Barely audible murmurings filled his ears.

He ran his hand through his hair and took a calming breath. This was nothing. Darting shapes. Flitting shadows. Disembodied voices. This wasn't the first time he'd encountered things like this.

He was becoming more and more convinced that he didn't wake up in these woods by chance.

He closed his eyes for a moment and focused on the thumping of his heart. Whatever these things were, they hadn't actually attacked him. They'd only startled him. Whether they were real or only in his head, they were so far harmless. Until something physically touched him, he decided it'd be best to simply ignore them.

When he opened his eyes, he caught a glimpse of someone in the trees far off to his left, mostly obscured in the foliage of the forest and the haze of the snow, little more than a pale figure, visible for only a fleeting second.

He stood there a moment, staring after it. Something about it gave him an uneasy sort of feeling, but he couldn't explain exactly why.

He pushed it from his mind and turned his attention back to the pipes.

He stuffed his hands into his jacket pockets, lowered his head and continued on, shouldering his way through the naked branches. This time, when something darted between the trees far to his left, he didn't bother turning his head. When he felt something following in his footsteps, he didn't look back. When whispered voices washed over him with the wind, he pretended he didn't hear them. Even when something heavy settled into the branches above him, making them bow toward the earth, he didn't bother lifting his head.

Let them play their games.

He pushed through a dense cluster of naked brush and found a much larger pipe protruding from the earth. This one was only about two feet high, but almost three feet in diameter, with a heavy iron grate preventing anything much larger than a rat from entering or leaving.

He bent over it and peered inside, but it was far too dark to see. It was just a black, round hole descending deep into the earth. A dank, cellar-like smell was rising up from it. And something else, as well. A strange and subtle stench that was a little bit like the sulfurous reek of a sewer, but mostly it was a different sort of foul that he didn't think was like anything he'd ever smelled before.

Again, he reached for the phone that wasn't there, this time thinking to use the flashlight to peer into that darkness, only to remember that it was gone.

Then he remembered the actual flashlight he took from the glovebox. He pulled it out and aimed it through the grate. But the only thing it showed him was that the hole was much deeper than he expected.

Still, there must be a reason why this was here. It looked to him like part of a sewer or storm drain of some sort, but there weren't any streets or buildings of any kind within sight. Why would a forest need something like this?

Was it possible that he was near a town of some sort?

He turned and looked behind him as he pondered it, and saw that there was an old woman standing there, staring at him.

He stared back at her, surprised. There was no way he simply didn't notice her there as he walked up. She didn't blend in with her surroundings at all. She was standing right out in the open, her posture straight and prim, dressed in a long, modest skirt and a heavy, knitted shawl. Her chin was raised, her chest pushed out. Her hair was tied back into a tidy and rather humorless bun. She looked dreadfully unfriendly. And rather *pretentious*, he thought. As if she were judging him. If this were his first experience with the weird, he might've felt the need to apologize for his rough appearance and his uninvited presence. But he was older and wiser than he used to be, and even from here he saw that her eyes were strangely empty and that her feet didn't quite touch the ground.

He said nothing. He turned and looked ahead of him again, ignoring her. The row of pipes continued on the other side of the grate. There was something under the ground here. A passageway or a culvert or something. The grate suggested it was something fairly large. Hopefully that meant it was all the more likely to lead him to some sort of civilization.

When he glanced back at the old woman, he expected her to have vanished, but she was still there, still staring at him with those empty, judging eyes. Was she a ghost? Or was she something else? He was quite certain she was more than just a woman. And he really didn't think he was merely imagining her, either.

The wind picked up, tossing the falling snow. He didn't

have time to linger here. Again, he turned away from the woman and continued following the pipes. But as he walked, a whispered voice drifted through the wind, carrying a single word to his ears: "Bones…"

He turned, surprised and looked back at the woman again. But this time, she *was* gone.

He frowned. Bones? What did that mean?

He glanced around at the forest, but again he was alone out here. Nothing moved in the trees.

Bones…

It was just a word. He wasn't even entirely sure if he heard it right. It was just a whisper and the wind was gusting. But somehow it sent a creepy shudder through his body.

He continued on, the word hanging over him like a bad omen.

Chapter Three

Just over the next hill, he discovered a small, rectangular box, about the size of an outhouse, but made entirely of thick, rusty metal and lacking any sort of door.

The row of pipes ended here, leaving nothing to follow and no indication whatsoever of which way he should go next.

He stood there a moment, confused. Then he walked all the way around it, examining it from every angle. There was a short length of that same lead pipe protruding from the top of one side like some sort of exhaust pipe. In the center of another side there was a small panel held in place with six badly rusted screws. And there were three much smaller copper pipes running from the lower half of the third side to the ground. The fourth side was entirely blank.

It was just a box. There was no way to open it and nothing around it. A dead end.

He looked back the way he came. Maybe he went the wrong direction after all. Maybe this was the far end of whatever was buried here and there were more pipes that he didn't see leading back the other way.

But before he could start walking again, he was startled by a loud, metallic banging from somewhere behind him. The noise only lasted a few brief seconds, but it was definitely not a nature sound.

The snow was blowing harder now. He squinted into it and took a few steps in that direction.

There was something there, he realized. A large shape loomed behind the naked, swaying branches, almost hidden in the darkening haze. A building! His heart leapt at the sight. He ran toward it, shoving his way through the naked underbrush.

It was a fairly small structure, less than a thousand square feet at its foundation, he estimated, but was curiously tall, towering four or five stories above him. There was a garage door on one side and a smaller, man-sized door on another, both of them heavy and sturdy and bound with large padlocks.

He circled around the building, but there was no way in. And knocking seemed like a waste of time. It was obvious that no one was in there because it was locked from the outside. Even if there was, for some reason, someone inside, they wouldn't be able to let him in if they wanted to.

There weren't even any windows. The only other opening was a third doorway way up near the top of the far side. Unlike the other two doors, it didn't have a padlock holding it shut, but it didn't need one. There was no way to get up to it. There were no steps. And there wasn't any sort of balcony to step out onto from the inside. It opened into empty space, at least four stories above the ground. He had no idea what such a door might be used for. It looked like nothing more than a serious safety hazard.

There was no way inside this building. He'd be wasting his time trying.

There *was*, however, a road.

A narrow, washed-out, gravel road passed very close to the structure, almost directly under the mysterious door to nowhere. He walked out into the middle of it and looked both ways. There was nothing in sight, but unlike the pipes he'd been following, this was almost certain to lead somewhere. That was the whole purpose of a road, after all, to lead from one place to another.

But again, which way did he go?

As he stood there, pondering the question, a voice drifted to him on the wind. And unlike most of the voices he'd heard until now, this one spoke clearly: "Find what was lost…"

He turned all the way around, searching his surroundings, but there was no one here. "Hello?" he called.

But the voice didn't come again.

Was it that old woman? The one who was there when he heard the word "bones"? Was *she* the one speaking to him on the wind?

He cocked his head to one side and listened hard, trying to hear if there were any more voices hidden in the wind. But no more words came to him. Instead, he was startled by that loud banging noise. He turned and faced the mysterious building. The sound was coming from inside it. It reminded him of the noise the washing machine made when he put too much laundry in and it became unbalanced.

Again, it wound down to silence.

Some sort of machine was running in there. Something that seemed to be cycling on and off.

Something tugged at the tail of his jacket. But when he turned around, no one was there. Was it only his imagination? Or was it another of the forest's ghosts? Experience had taught him that it was foolish to assume the former. But if what he felt was an actual encounter, then the spirits of these woods weren't limited to disembodied voices and spooky manifestations. If they could tug on his jacket, then they could touch him. And if they could touch him, then they could hurt him.

He needed to keep moving.

But an unsettling feeling came over him. He turned and looked out into the forest on the other side of the road. It was strange, but he felt like something was out there, something hidden in the haze of the falling snow. Something dangerous.

He squinted into the snow, his heart beating faster. It wasn't anything like that weird panic that drove him from the site of the accident, but it was still strong.

Movement drew his gaze upward. The very top of one of the trees was bowing, as if something high up were pulling down on it.

Birds, he told himself. *Big* birds. Fat ones.

But no amount of logical thinking eased that unsettling feeling in his gut. He felt very strongly that it wasn't safe to stay here.

He chose a direction at random and followed the road, hoping it would lead him to a phone.

More voices called out to him, only half-heard over the wind and snow. Brief, incomprehensible mutterings, mostly.

Murmurings. Whispered nothings.

After a few minutes, these mumbling voices gave way to the sound of someone crying. It wasn't the first time he'd heard ghostly weeping in a haunted forest, but there was something about this particular sound that seemed to grab him, making him stop and listen for a moment. Something about the sound of it...the deep, agonizing sadness of it...made his heart ache. It made him want to follow it, to seek out whoever it was, to try to help. But he resisted the urge. He'd fallen for that trick before.

He'd met some nice ghosts in his weird travels, but for the most part, he'd learned to mind his own damn business when dealing with the dead. Some of them simply didn't play well with others.

A crow cawed in the trees above him. He squinted up into the falling snow, but he couldn't see where it was perched. The same one that greeted him when he first awoke, he wondered? Or another one?

Birds...

The birds were there when all this started, he suddenly recalled. Way back in the beginning, *all* the way back to that first extraordinary dream that sent him fleeing out into the night, convinced that there was somewhere he desperately needed to be, even though the only thing he could remember was something about *birds*.

He stood there for a moment, watching the crows, his thoughts drifting back to that ordeal in the fissure. He still wasn't entirely sure what happened back there. Those final moments inside that hellish cathedral were a blur. He couldn't even remember what it was he found down there. Only that it was something so incredibly profound and important that he couldn't handle the very memory of it. Now he carried it only in the deepest depths of his subconscious mind, where only his dreams could reach it. Or so said the little gas station attendant who put it there for him.

It was such a strange journey. He'd discovered terrors he'd never known were real. Golems. Corn creeps. Strange and monstrous creatures from another world. And the first in a long line of nameless agents of a terrible, unknown organization. He'd met Isabelle there. And he'd witnessed his own death, too, in a way. It was only a dream. But it was a very powerful dream. It showed him things as they would've happened if he'd arrived two days sooner than he did. In that dream, he never ran into any golems or corn creeps. He never met the foggy man. But he'd also run into worse things. A monstrous cat-like thing had bitten off half his right hand. And unlike the real version of him that arrived two days late, Dream Eric had not survived the ordeal inside the cathedral.

He lowered his eyes and shivered against a gust of wind. It was getting colder. And he doubted that he'd get to warm up any time soon.

There were leather gloves in one of his jacket pockets. He took them out and slipped them on. Then he lifted his hood and drew the strings tight against the wind.

He moved on, leaving the weeping spirit to its creepy, heartbreaking misery.

I hope you're still with me, he thought. Isabelle was always connected to him, whether he had a phone or not. She was in his head. She could always hear him. The phone was only so *he* could hear *her*. She should be following along right now, aware of his every thought, able to perceive the world around him, even things he couldn't feel himself, like the strange, exotic energies that he often came across in the weird. By now, she'd probably mobilized the whole team. She'd be keeping an open line with Karen, probably on speaker so Holly and Paige could listen in while they sat over a bowl of steaming water, using their curious magic to find a way to unravel this mystery and bring him home. And Paul was almost certainly on his way here right now.

Hopefully, he'd be here soon.

Unless, of course, Paul was still mad about that incident last year...

Everyone had apologized over and over again. They didn't *mean* to forget about him and leave him stranded in that frigid Canadian wilderness... And it was still well before noon when Ella finally located him and blipped him back home.

You could barely see any frostbite at all.

Thinking about it now, he couldn't help but realize that this was a pretty fitting revenge.

Paul would still come. He was sure of it. Although Eric suspected that he might not be opposed to stopping for a leisurely cup of coffee along the way...

But without a phone or other device for Isabelle to let him know that she was still there, he couldn't be certain. There were places in the world, after all, where their connection had been severed. For all he knew, this could be one of those places and he could truly be on his own out here. She could've lost contact with him before whatever strange, forgotten events took place to bring him to these woods, with no idea where he'd gone or what he was doing, perhaps with no idea whether he was still alive.

She probably still would've contacted Karen and Holly, though. And Holly's magic could probably tell them he was still okay. (Unless something here blocked that, too...because that had also happened before...)

He pushed the thoughts out of his head. It was pointless to dwell on it. Even if Isabelle *was* with him, it did him little good. Unless he found a phone, she couldn't tell him anything about the energy of this place. She couldn't warn him of any dangers. She couldn't tell him if she felt anything unseen. He had no access to her vast knowledge of the weird. And any information Holly and Paige might be able to scry from the water spell would do him no good if they couldn't pass it on to him.

Ahead of him, the forest around the road began to thin. He could see a gate up ahead. An old, wooden archway. There was a larger road on the other side of it. Not a highway, by any definition. It wasn't much bigger than the one he was on. It was paved, at least, just wide enough for two lanes and riddled with potholes, but even a neglected road like that had to go *somewhere*.

He expected something to stop him. A monster would appear, blocking his path. Or ghostly hands would grab him and drag him back into the depths of the forest again. Or perhaps there'd simply be a big, invisible wall blocking the way.

When it came to the weird, he didn't usually have a choice

in the matter.

But nothing stopped him. He walked through the gate and stepped onto the cracked asphalt.

Was he really free to go? The weird wasn't going to try to stop him?

He wanted to breathe a sigh of relief, but it was far too soon. For all he knew, the gate wasn't the exit. He could still be standing in the very middle of the weird. And even if he *was* free to go, there was no guarantee that he was out of danger. It could be *miles* to the nearest house. He still had no idea where he was.

And in truth, he'd been lying to himself the whole time. There *were* roads out there that didn't go anywhere, roads that went on forever. And there were roads that went one way, but not the other. And those who chose the wrong way tended to never be seen again.

He should've just picked a direction and started walking. That would've been the smart thing to do. He should've walked away and never looked back.

But that wasn't what he did.

Maybe there was something wrong with him. Maybe that's why he was always getting into these kinds of situations. Because he simply couldn't stop himself from looking back.

She was right there on the other side of the gate, in the middle of the road that he'd just walked down. A lovely girl with long, brown hair. She looked to be about fifteen. She wore a summery dress and was barefoot, even though the ground beneath her was harsh gravel and the snow was coming down all around her.

She was dancing.

She twirled around, slowly, gracefully, as if it were the most natural thing in the world.

He stood there, watching her. She was incredibly lovely. Her movements were nothing short of angelic. She was *perfect*...and yet, she was entirely *wrong*.

Like the old woman back in the forest, her feet didn't quite seem to touch the ground. And she seemed strangely *fractured*, as if she were nothing more than a fragile illusion. She sort of glitched, like a poorly-rendered video game character. She pulled apart from herself and then came back together again. It was as if he were watching her dance through a broken mirror. Her movements were smooth and graceful, but her body twisted and bent in impossible ways.

He couldn't quite comprehend what he was seeing. For a moment, he thought he'd suffered more head trauma in that accident than he first thought. But then he remembered something another ghost once said to him.

When you see the broken girl dancing in the snow… he thought, and an icy chill that had nothing to do with the cold blew through him.

This wasn't random at all. He was always meant to come here.

When you see the broken girl dancing in the snow, follow the bones and you will find her.

These words were spoken to him months ago, in the basement of a small bungalow on the outskirts of his home town of Creek Bend, the words of the ghost of a brutally murdered witch that had lingered in that awful place for more than six decades before being set free by Holly's magic.

And now that he was thinking about it…

…follow the bones and you will find her.

"Bones…" he whispered. That was the word the old woman spoke to him on the wind just a little while ago.

Slowly, he lifted his head, pushed back his hood and looked up at the archway he'd just walked under. Another crow was perched atop it, he saw, staring down at him. But he barely noticed the bird. His eyes were fixed on the old beam beneath its talons, on the name that was carved into that rotten wood. And as he read those eight ominous letters, the chill he'd felt at the sight of the broken girl settled all the way into his veins.

EVANCURT

Chapter Four

He couldn't walk away. He knew that now.

He'd heard the name Evancurt only twice before in his life, spoken to him on both occasions by less-than-friendly spirits. One was an ancient and monstrous hag with kitchen knife fingers who chased him down and then randomly whispered it into his ear like some kind of curse. The second was a recently-departed, antisocial witch trainer who much less subtly screamed it into his face.

He stared at the sign, his whole body numb. Evancurt... *And* the broken girl... Another message delivered by a ghost...

He lowered his gaze to the overgrown road in front of him, but the girl was gone. He was alone again. Everything was quiet but for the soft pattering of falling snow. Even the wind had died down for the moment.

It was as if the entire forest were waiting for him to make a decision.

But it wasn't much of a decision. He stared back into those trees, a sick dread wriggling around in his gut. A haunted forest that shared a name with a message from beyond the grave... A broken girl dancing in the snow... No memory of how he came to be stranded here... The word "bones" whispered on the frigid wind...

The dead have business with you, Eric, he thought, remembering the words of the beautiful toll collector he met the previous year.

Darn. He was really hoping it was just a serious head injury.

He turned and looked down the road in one direction, then the other. Nothing seemed to be stopping him from just turning away. But it wasn't really a choice. He knew how these things worked. The weird didn't give him options. Not really. He could turn his back and walk away, he could try to find his way home, but he had no guarantee that he'd find any aid on that road. He could freeze to death out there searching for help. And even if he did manage to find his way home, what would be the cost? More than once, the weird had tasked him with saving lives, sometimes a great many. Who knew what might've happened if he hadn't stopped that conqueror worm from gnawing a hole through reality in Hedge Lake?

What if he found his way home only to find disturbing news reports of some grand disaster? What if people died? What if *children* had died?

He couldn't risk it. Whatever was happening here was important. The dead had all but told him so.

He glanced up at the ominous sign hanging over him once more and met the gaze of that lone, staring crow. "Well...?" it seemed to ask him. "What will you do?"

With a deep, defeated sort of sigh, he stepped through the gate and trudged back up the overgrown road.

Whatever grand task awaited him in these woods, he was certain it wasn't going to be easy. He was utterly blind without Isabelle. He didn't have Holly's spells. He didn't have Paul.

He was alone.

And yet he wasn't alone at all.

"Find what is lost," whispered the wind again.

He didn't bother looking around this time. He knew no one was going to be there.

"Follow the bones," he sighed. "Find what's lost. I heard you."

He ran his gloved hand through his hair and took a deep breath. It wasn't as if it were hopeless. All he really needed was a phone. Once he was able to talk to Isabelle again, things would get easier. There had to be one *somewhere* on this property. Didn't there? It only made sense. There was machinery running inside that building he found. If there was machinery running, then there were people around and if there were people around, there were cell phones. In this day and age, it was practically guaranteed.

But he was only trying to make himself feel better. Running machinery didn't necessarily mean there was anyone around. It was probably automated, especially considering that the building containing the machine was tightly locked. And then there was the time. The sun had already set. The last of the day's light was already fading. What if everyone had gone home for the night?

Yet even if that turned out to be true and there were no people to be found here, there should be at least a few landlines. Even if they weren't working anymore, Isabelle might still be able to use them. She didn't need him to have a working signal to call him on his cell phone, after all. In fact, *she* didn't need a phone at all. When she first contacted him, she did so using one she found, but she quickly learned that the phone had nothing to do with it. She now communicated with him directly from her head, simply by *imagining* that she was holding a phone.

He didn't pretend to understand it, but that was how it worked.

He made his way to the top of the hill and around the bend in the road. The ghostly voices had calmed for the time being, it seemed. Even the eerie, heart-wrenching sobbing had stopped. But as he approached the tall, locked structure again, he glanced out into the forest and saw something moving among the trees.

More than a shadow, it was a distinct, pale shape, like the one he glimpsed earlier disappearing over the hillside. Again, there was something unsettling about the sight. Although he'd already seen a number of ghostly figures since he awoke in these woods, there was something about this one that made him uneasy, something about the slow way it was moving, its head down and its shoulders slack... There was something strangely familiar about it.

And now that he was looking at it, he realized that he could hear it. The sounds of crunching leaves and snapping branches carried across the white noise of the falling snow.

None of the other spirits had made any noise, except for their various creepy voices. The small shape that he glimpsed darting between the trees. That big shadow that crept up right behind him. The prim old woman. Even the broken girl. They'd all been silent.

Was it a ghost?

He squinted at it, trying to get a better look, but it passed behind a clump of trees and vanished.

He stopped walking and stared after it for a moment.

A memory seemed to be twitching somewhere deep in his mind. Something about a dark corridor… A creeping shadow on the floor… But it wouldn't quite surface.

He continued walking, his eyes lingering on the place where the shape was when it disappeared. Whatever it was, it'd eventually show itself. These sorts of things always did.

When he looked forward again, that high, unreachable doorway of the building was suddenly wide open and there was someone standing in it.

He stopped, surprised.

There was just enough light left in the day to see that she was a teenage girl, different from the broken girl. This one had long, black hair that blew about her face in the wind. She wore a short, black, pleated skirt, sneakers and a light gray sweater. She was older, too, between seventeen and nineteen, whereas the broken girl had looked to be only twelve or thirteen, taller, awkwardly skinny. Even from this distance, there was something odd about her. She looked strangely *haunted*.

He opened his mouth to call out to her, to tell her to be careful up there, but before any words could escape him, the girl leaned forward, stepped from the doorway and plummeted toward the earth.

Eric cried out, startled, and ran toward her, but there was nothing he could do. She dropped like a stone toward the hard gravel surface beneath her, far too quickly for him to reach her in time. And really, looking back afterward, he had no idea what he thought he was going to be able to do anyway. Catch her? He could barely catch a football! He watched, horrified as the girl sped silently toward the earth, her arms outstretched, her long hair trailing behind her. It seemed like a long time as it was happening, although it couldn't have been more than a second or two. He stopped and turned away at the last instant, not wanting to see the awful thing that was about to happen, cringing against the anticipation of the awful sound of her body striking the cold, unyielding ground.

But no sound came.

He opened his eyes and dared a peek…but there was nothing there.

His heart still pounding, he looked back up at the empty doorway. Slowly, the door was swinging closed. He watched as it latched itself, returning everything back to the way it was before, as if the entire, frightful ordeal had only taken place inside his disturbed head.

Another ghost?

That was terrifying. For a moment, he really thought…

He took a breath and turned around.

A woman was standing right in front of him. Like the two girls, she was dressed for warmer weather, but less casually. She wore a knee-length, gray skirt, a white, ruffled blouse and black high-heels. Her hair was shoulder-length and blonde and her gaze was piercing.

Before he could think of anything to say to her, she reached out and slapped him hard across his face.

There was nothing ghostly about the slap. It felt as real as any slap across the face could feel. He stared wide-eyed into the forest, his mouth agape. "*Ow!*"

The woman turned and stomped away.

He stared after her, bewildered, and watched as she faded away in the falling snow.

He blinked hard, trying to clear his head.

What the hell was *that* for? Did he *know* that woman? He was fairly certain he didn't deserve that.

"Black…" said a creaky sort of voice from right behind him.

He turned around to find a very sickly-looking man in filthy clothes standing there, looking as if he might collapse at any second. He was deathly thin. His hair was limp, his eyes sunken and bruised. His skin was pale.

"They're all turning black…"

Eric took a step back. "What?"

"The *sounds*..." said the man, taking a trembling step toward him. "All the sounds are turning black..."

Eric took another step back. "Are they?" was all he could think to say.

A hand fell on his shoulder, freezing him in place, and a gruff voice whispered into his ear: "So pretty..."

With a terrified, "*Whoa!*" he spun around and backed away.

A large brute of a man in dirty coveralls was standing there, his face smudged with grease, his bald head slick with sweat. His eyes were red and puffy. Tears streamed down his cheeks. "She was so pretty..." he moaned.

"Black..." sighed the sickly man.

The weeping brute turned, sniffling, and gazed out into the woods. "I've looked everywhere, but I can't find her..."

"Why are all the sounds black?"

"Please... I just want to see her again..."

Eric looked back and forth between the two men, confused. What the hell was going on here?

Then a third voice spoke, again from behind him, but this time from a reasonable distance: "It wasn't me."

He turned to find a man dressed in jeans and a leather jacket staring back at him with desperate eyes. He was shaking his head in a strangely twitchy sort of manner.

"I don't know who was standing in the mirror, but it wasn't me. I don't know who it was. And I don't know how he got in there."

Eric stared at him. What was this? What was happening? Who were these people?

That loud banging began again. He turned and faced the building. The sickly man and the weeping brute were gone. He turned back to the man in the leather jacket and found that he'd gone, too. There was no one around. He was alone.

The banging wound down again, leaving only silence.

He reached for his phone, but remembered that it was gone. Instead, he ran his gloved hand through his hair and sighed.

He could already tell that this was going to be a very long night.

Chapter Five

Eric walked on, following the overgrown gravel.

Night had fully arrived. He took the flashlight from his pocket and switched it on as the gloom deepened to black around him. There was comfort in the extra light it provided, but he couldn't help feeling more vulnerable as he shined it into the endless shadows of the forest and wondered what might be looking back at him now that he was basically a shining beacon in the dark. It was too easy to imagine countless terrible things turning their slobbering jaws toward a dangerously conspicuous bright light.

The forest had fallen silent except for the gusting wind and the falling snow. But he didn't dare let his guard down. Any minute now, he was sure another ghostly weirdo was going to appear out of nowhere and start talking crazy again.

Were they really ghosts? Or were they something else? In the past, many of the spirits he'd encountered had appeared so natural that he didn't realize he was dealing with a ghost at first. They looked solid, spoke normally and even interacted effortlessly with their surroundings, but they always avoided physical contact with him, leaving him to later wonder if a simple handshake would've revealed them sooner for what they were. And later, when he met the dead witch who told him about the broken girl, she'd grabbed his arm with a hand that felt as cold as ice, supporting that theory. But the blonde woman and the weeping brute had each laid a hand on him and both had felt as real as living people.

Isabelle had told him before that there were no set rules governing spirits, as far as she knew. There seemed to be as many kinds of ghosts as there were people in the world. But there were also things out there besides ghosts. And without her to read the energy, he had no way to be certain what he was really dealing with. She, herself, was a living person trapped in a strange state of being outside the normal flow of time, after all. These could be people just like her. Or they could be something else entirely, only mimicking the appearance of people. It wouldn't be the first time he mistook something otherworldly for a ghost.

A light in the darkness of the surrounding forest caught his eye and he paused to watch as it moved through the trees. It looked like another flashlight. Or maybe a lantern. But although he could see the light, he couldn't get a glimpse of who was holding it. Nor could he hear anyone stomping around out there. Before he could decide whether he should wander off the road to investigate it, the light receded deeper into the woods and then vanished altogether.

Could it be that there was someone else wandering these woods? He had his doubts. It seemed far more likely that it was just another of Evancurt's ghosts.

He turned his attention to the road in front of him again and stopped as he found his path blocked by a boy in tattered jeans and a black hoodie. He had a strange sort of scowl on his face, as if Eric had done something to offend him.

Before he could think of anything to say, the boy thrust both middle fingers out at him, then stooped down, snatched up a rock and threw it at him.

Eric blocked it with his arm. "*Hey!*"

But the boy turned and ran off, disappearing into the woods.

He stared after him, confused. Then he glanced around, waiting there a moment to see if anyone else wanted to file a grievance with him. When no one appeared, he continued onward.

Again, everything fell still but the wind and the snow.

Ahead of him, on the left side of the road, a small building stood half-hidden in the trees. It was far too small to be any kind of home, but maybe a hunting cabin? There weren't any lights in the windows, no sign of anyone inside who might be able to help him. But it was the ideal place to begin looking for a telephone.

He hurried to the cabin and shined his flashlight into the window, but the glass was too dirty to see anything clearly. He knocked on the door. "Hello? Is anybody in there?"

When no one answered, he tried the knob. It was unlocked. But he hesitated. He turned and glanced around. This was just the sort of place where something scary was likely to jump out at him and he wasn't looking forward to being called pretty again. But every second he lingered was another second he had to spend in these damned woods, so he pushed the door all the way open and stepped inside.

It appeared to be an office of some sort. There were three desks crammed into the space. And it was immediately clear that no one had sat at any of them in a very long time. The entire room was hoary with dust and cobwebs.

His first thought was that an office should be the ideal place to find a phone, but this one didn't seem to have one. In fact, looking around, it occurred to him that there was no modern technology in here at all. The desks were covered in books and folders and loose, yellowed papers. There were no laptops or monitors, not even any typewriters.

It looked as if no one had been here in years. And as he turned and swept the room behind him with his light, he found an old calendar hanging on the wall, turned to the page for April 1971.

He stared at it, amazed. Had this place really been sitting here like this, collecting dust and cobwebs for almost forty-seven years?

That didn't seem right. The place was clearly in disuse, but it wasn't exactly *rotting*. After five decades of neglect, it seemed to him that the entire roof should be caving in. Maybe they just moved to a new office that year and no one ever bothered with the calendar again. Things like that probably happened all the time.

He shined his light over the rest of the walls. They were covered in an ugly, dark wood paneling that reminded him of his grandparents' house way back when he was little, before Grandpa remodeled everything.

There was a single, rather odd-looking light fixture in the center of the ceiling. It was sort of saucer-shaped, like a flattened ball, made of white, frosted glass. There was no pull chain, and a quick look around revealed no visible light switches, which struck him as particularly odd. There must be one. If there was a light, there should be a way to turn it on and off. Was it located behind one of the desks? That seemed unnecessarily inconvenient.

Not that it mattered, he supposed. There probably wasn't any power anyway.

As he turned his light to the back wall of the room, something new caught his attention. There was a large, metal box sitting there, about the size of an old luggage chest. It looked strangely out of place in this room, more like a tool box than a piece of office equipment.

He brushed aside the cobwebs and walked over to it, curious. Closer up, it looked a lot like the box those strange pipes led him to in the woods, but considerably smaller and less rusted. It was made of the same dull, welded metal. But while that one had no door of any sort, only that small panel held on with those rusty screws, this one had an easily-accessible, hinged top.

He knelt beside the box, grasped the lid and lifted it open, then he stared down into it, surprised. It wasn't just a box sitting on the floor. It was the top portion of a deep, metal shaft extending down *into* the floor. There was a ladder mounted to the front side, leading down into an unsettling darkness.

He turned and looked behind him, still expecting someone or something to be sneaking up on him. Then he shined his light back down into the shaft again.

What was he looking at?

He stood up, contemplating the decision before him. Did he leave the cabin and continue on? Or did he dare descend into that cobweb-filled darkness and see what was hiding down there?

There might be a phone at the bottom, he told himself. There might also be a billion dollars in gold bars. Chances were probably about equal. After all, why would there be a phone down there but not up here where people actually *worked*? Given the creepy stuff that was going on up here, there was a far better chance he'd find something frightful at the bottom.

And then there was the box, itself. The shaft. Why was it made of metal? It didn't seem to be for keeping people out. There was no lock. There wasn't anywhere to *put* a lock.

His morbid imagination, always eager to offer up terrifying possibilities to any strange new situation, immediately suggested that the metal was to keep out deadly, skin-melting radiation.

He ran his hand through his hair again. He always did that when he felt anxious. It was surprising he had any hair left. And he wasn't entirely sure what he was going to do when the radiation made it all fall out after stupidly climbing down the wrong ladder.

Like an ill omen, his flashlight began to flicker.

He bumped it gently against the palm of his hand and it stopped at once, but the incident, as minor as it may have been, left him unsettled. This whole experience was bad enough, but just the *thought* of doing all this without a light was more frightful than all the ghosts in the world.

But it seemed okay now.

Maybe the batteries were just a bit loose.

He turned and glanced around at the empty room one last time, making sure there were no weirdo ghosts waiting to give him a well-deserved shove as he started down, and then carefully stepped over the side of the box and onto the ladder.

If this had been an ordinary accident, if he'd awakened in his car on the side of the road instead of on the ground fifty feet from the car to find that the road was simply *gone*... If he hadn't been scared out of his mind by a mysterious, unseen presence... If he hadn't found himself surrounded by ghosts... If he hadn't seen the broken girl dancing in the snow... If the property didn't bear the name *Evancurt*... Maybe then he wouldn't be snooping around. It'd be none of his business. He'd just move along and keep looking for a phone. But this wasn't ordinary by any definition. This was the weird. At some point before this was over, he was probably going to have to climb down into the cobweb-filled darkness and see what was hidden there. He might as well do it now and get it over with.

It was a good thing he wasn't deathly afraid of spiders. He had that going for him at least. And yet the deeper down he went, the less webs he encountered, until there were none left. That awful imagination of his wondered loudly and obnoxiously what sort of place even a spider would refuse to go, and some more reasonable part of his mind wondered why he was still moving down instead of getting the hell out of this hole.

The shaft descended thirty feet into the earth and then opened up onto a pitch-black room that was twice as big as the room above. It had a strange stench about it. There was that dank, earthy smell of underground places, of course. And there was a subtle, swampy stench of mold and decay that also wasn't unexpected. But there was something else in the air down here, too, something he couldn't identify. Something foul, with a hint of sulfur and a twinge of something metallic.

It was like the storm grate he found in the woods, he realized. It wasn't *exactly* the same stench he detected wafting up from that darkness, but it was too similar not to be related.

He decided at once that he didn't like it down here.

The dirt floor squelched beneath his shoe as he stepped off the ladder and shined his light around. The walls weren't painted black, he saw. They were bare concrete. Instead, they were covered in what appeared to be a thick, black mold. There were several mossy-looking metal boxes mounted to the walls. The rest of the room was completely empty except for an odd-looking window in the far wall.

He turned his light on this window, curious of exactly *why* there was a window in a room thirty feet underground. It certainly wasn't to admire the view. Maybe there used to be something there? A wall safe, perhaps? A medicine cabinet?

He took a step toward it, prodding the darkness with his light, trying to see into the empty space, and felt the sole of his shoe sink deeper into the mud.

The floor on that side of the room was completely covered.

He wasn't dressed for this kind of activity. If he went any farther, he was going to get his feet wet. And he couldn't go wandering around the woods at night in the snow with wet feet. His mother would've told him that he'd catch his death for sure like that. And like Karen, Sharon Fortrell had always had a frightening tendency to almost never be wrong.

So he leaned forward instead, inching the light closer, hoping his foot didn't sink any deeper. There was something in there. A dark lump of a shape, wrapped in a darkness that resisted his light.

It was no use. He realized that the thing must've become covered in that black mold that blanketed the walls. Even if he waded all the way over to it, he might not be able to see what it was.

He stood there a moment, trying to decide what he should do.

Then the thing at the end of his flashlight beam *moved*.

He jumped, startled, and took an involuntary step back. As a result, his foot slipped in the mud, threatening to spill him onto the filthy floor, but he grabbed the ladder and steadied himself.

Was something *living* in there? A *nest* of some kind?

His heart thumping again, he stood with his flashlight aimed at it, wondering again what he should do.

Then the inky darkness inside that window split apart and a huge, bulging eyeball rolled into view and stared back at him, its great, black pupil shrinking in the bright beam of his flashlight.

Chapter Six

Eric decided that finding out what was in the opening in the wall *wasn't* important. He should just leave the freaky thing where it was. He was obviously disturbing its sleep and he really didn't want to be rude.

He grabbed the ladder and tried to flee back up the way he came. But it wasn't as easy as going down. Twice, he slipped. The mud on his shoes was slick. But the ladder, itself, was slippery, too. As he climbed, he realized that there was more of that black mold growing on it. Going down wasn't too bad because he'd taken his time, uncertain of what awaited him down there, but in his rush to get back up it, he was having more difficulty. And the second time his foot slipped, he was terrifyingly convinced for a moment that he wasn't going to be able to get back up, that he was going to be trapped down there in that darkness forever with the huge, monster eyeball and the probably-toxic black mold.

But he found his footing and finally managed to climb back up out of the shaft. And as soon as his muddy feet were firmly on the cabin floor, he turned and slammed the box shut.

Do not disturb, he thought as he backed away from it.

That was freaky. But even freakier, he realized, was the fact that it wasn't the first time he'd found a mutant body part inside a wall. What the hell had become of his life, anyway? There was a time when it was normal. He was sure of it. He could almost remember it.

He turned and started back toward the door, but again, his foot slipped from under him, nearly sending him sprawling onto the floor.

He paused to scrape the bottoms of his shoes. He wished he had his good snow boots. But then again, he wished he had a lot of things that he didn't. He was just going to have to deal with it.

He stared down at the floor, distracted.

It wasn't the mud that made his shoes so slick. It was that mold. It was like a thick, black slime. And looking down at himself, he realized that it was on his clothes as well. It was smeared on the front of his jeans and jacket. It was on his sleeves. It was on his gloves. He lifted his hands and looked at them. When he touched his fingers together and then pulled them apart, long, slimy strands stretched between the leather.

Gross.

He considered smelling it, but decided better of it. He'd already been exposed to more of the stuff than he was strictly comfortable with. Besides, he could smell it well enough from here. That strange, metallic stench seasoned with a generous amount of sulfur.

He turned and wiped his gloves on the corner of the nearest desk and made a mental note to try not to touch his face while he was wearing them.

It was at this moment that he first felt it. An unnatural presence in the room with him. Something dark. Something *sinister*. His heart pounding again, he turned, expecting to see the box opening as the owner of the huge, grotesque eyeball pursued him out of that slimy, black pit.

But the box remained closed. The eyeball and whatever it was attached to inside its strange little hole in the wall wasn't looking back at him. Instead, there was a different kind of blackness oozing down from the ceiling above the box.

He shined the flashlight onto it, chasing away the natural shadows and leaving only the one that was crawling down the wall. It was mostly a formless blackness, but with strange, oozing blotches of bloody red that blossomed like flower petals and then faded into the surrounding blackness again.

Something about the sight sent a violent shiver through his body.

He didn't need Isabelle to tell him that the churning, blackish thing before him was giving off some sort of terrible energy.

It seemed to fill the air around him, charging it with an other-worldly sort of static that made his skin feel cold and filled him with unspeakable dread.

Still keeping the flashlight aimed at the thing, not daring to take his eyes off it, he backed toward the cabin door and groped blindly for the knob behind him.

A blackish tendril reached out from the mass as it neared the floor and split apart, forming a long, skeletal hand that clutched at the metal box as his own fingers brushed the cob-web-covered surface of the old, wooden door behind him.

Where the hell was the knob?

Two more churning, oozing tendrils bubbled out of the shadow. One became a second hand and arm that reached to-ward the metal box, while the other swelled into something that resembled a vaguely human head.

What kind of new hell was this thing? Where did it come from? And what did it want?

So far, it only seemed interested in the box, in spite of the fact that he was standing in plain sight and shining a flashlight right at the thing's horror movie face. But he had no intention of relaxing. He needed to get out of here before the thing turned its attention to him.

If he could only find the damned doorknob!

Those strange, shadowy fingers grew longer and longer, splitting apart from the arm, becoming less like fingers than like long, spidery legs. The tips of each one oozed into the crack in the box's lid and began to lift it.

That astoundingly unhelpful imagination of his was quick to offer that in another moment, he'd have to deal with both the nightmare shadow man *and* the eyeball thing.

Finally, his hand closed around the cold metal of the knob. He turned it and pulled, cringing at the noise the door made as it scraped across the threshold.

The shadow thing finally seemed to notice him. Slowly, it turned its awful face toward him.

He slipped through the door and pulled it closed behind him. It probably wasn't going to do him a lot of good. If the thing could open the box housing the ladder down to that moldy eyeball pit, then it could probably work a doorknob. But any little obstacle for the thing to overcome made him feel better.

He turned around, ready to leave this freaky place behind and continue his search for a phone, only to find that he still wasn't alone.

This time, it was a woman. She was standing in the middle of the road, staring back at him. She wasn't one of the women he'd encountered before. Not unless she'd been through quite an ordeal since the last time he saw her. She was stripped down to her underwear. She was drenched, as if she'd just dragged herself out of a lake somewhere. Her hair hung over her face, limp and black and dripping down her body. She was dreadfully thin, even more so than the sickly man with his black sounds. Her flesh was stretched tight over her bones like a living corpse and covered in cuts and bruises, as if someone had beaten her. And she was filthy. Leaves and twigs and dirt were clinging to her body, especially her legs and feet, as if she'd trudged a great distance through the forest just to stand here facing him.

Yet in spite of the frigid wind and the falling snow that had already begun to cover the ground, she didn't look cold at all. She wasn't shivering. In fact, she looked *sweaty*. Her skin was damp and flushed. There was *steam* rising from her body.

He stood there a moment, uncertain what he should do. He wanted to get far away from here before the shadow thing and its pet eyeball walked out of the cabin to take a closer look at him. But he managed enough patience to ask, "Are you okay? Do you need some help?"

It seemed like the polite thing to offer, far less rude than running off and leaving a soaking-wet, half-naked, battered woman at the mercy of the elements. He was only trying to be considerate. The woman, however, seemed greatly offended at the suggestion that she needed any kind of help, because she immediately let out a furious shriek and ran at him, her bony hands curled into threatening claws.

With a shrill yelp and a flurry of curses, Eric turned and fled, retaining just enough of his senses to make sure he'd pointed himself in the direction of the road so he wouldn't risk getting lost.

He wasn't sure what it was he did wrong, but he was confident that Karen, and indeed every woman he knew, would take the overly-sensitive, soaking-wet, half-naked woman's side. They'd call him an inconsiderate ass and no one would explain it to him, just like all those other times. It wasn't *his* idea to bring home the stripper! He didn't *want* to let that psycho woman smear her lipstick all over his face! He didn't *ask* to be haunted by the naked ghost! And yet it was always *his* fault and his alone.

It'd probably be his fault that she was half-naked, too. Why did they always have to be in some various state of undress?

He risked a glance over his shoulder and found that the woman had vanished.

He stopped running and turned to face the cabin again. That seemed too easy, but sometimes that was simply the way it happened.

And sometimes it really was too easy. When he looked forward again, the woman was right in front of him, her ghastly, shrieking face only inches from his own.

When recalling the story later, he'd leave out the part about the shrill, girlish scream that escaped him in that terrible moment. Nobody needed to know about that.

He stumbled backward, the scream having turned into a flurry of mangled and half-stuttered curses, and fell hard on his butt. She was on top of him in an instant, knocking him all the way onto his back and slashing at him with inhuman claws, tearing at the front of his jacket as if she meant to dig out his very heart. He tried to shove her back, but she was strong for someone so thin. Though he seized her arms, he couldn't hold her back. And she was *heavy*. She sat straddling him, her bony butt crushing down on his hips as if her body were made of lead, grinding him into the dirt beneath him, making it hard for him to breathe. He was helpless to move her.

This was another one of those things he was going to get in trouble for. He just knew it.

He cried out, frustrated, and thrust his hands at the woman's face, desperate. Not hard. He didn't want to hurt the woman, but he was frightened and desperate. Maybe if he could simply distract her, make her flinch, it would be enough to allow him a chance at escape. But his fingers never touched anything. The weight holding him down suddenly lifted. Her final scream trailed away into the distance, following her as she vanished into the woods.

He lay there on the damp ground, his eyes wide, uncertain what had just happened.

Had she made her point? Did she remember an important engagement? Maybe she was scheduled to crawl out of someone's television set and was running late.

He didn't lay there contemplating it. He rose to his feet and brushed himself off as he scanned the forest around him, unconvinced that she hadn't simply remembered that she'd left her straightening iron on and would come racing back as soon as she was done turning it off.

Or maybe she went to fetch the angry blonde woman and the hateful little brat in the black hoodie so they could beat him senseless together.

He glanced down at his jacket. She'd really done a number on it. There were several tears in the fabric over his chest and shoulders. Another few seconds and he was pretty sure she would've struck flesh and bone.

First he'd felt a tug on his jacket. Then the weeping brute's hand on his shoulder. The angry blonde's slap. The rock-throwing kid. And now claws. These ghosts were different from the ones in Hedge Lake. These were far more *physical*. That woman in particular... She reminded him of the Hosler hag back in Creek Bend, the one with the kitchen-knife claws.

But before he could ponder the thought any further, he became aware of a strange trembling sensation beneath his feet. It was subtle, but it was growing more intense with each passing second.

An earthquake? In Wisconsin?

No... This was something else. He knew it in his gut.

Then, just as quickly, it was over. Everything seemed normal again. For a moment. Then a noise at his back startled him and he turned around, ready to defend himself. But it was neither the moody, half-naked woman nor the black and crimson shadow monster from the cabin. Instead, there was a great, silvery beast galloping toward him.

It wasn't anything as common as a deer. It had two rows of backward-curling horns running down its back and a long, whip-like tail. Its legs were long and lean, horse-like, but with strange, tripod-like feet.

He stumbled backward, surprised, and the beast shot past him, barely sparing him a passing glance. He turned and watched it as it disappeared into the mist.

As he stood there, he saw a small, bristly-looking creature run past him on the other side of the road. It looked like a large hedgehog, but with a long neck and even longer, peacock-like tail that dragged the ground behind it.

Behind him, someone started crying. He turned again and found a small boy sitting on the ground, his face buried in his hands, seemingly terrified.

In the forest behind the boy, a light was moving through the haze of the snow, illuminating the trees and casting eerie shadows across the ground. It looked like the light he saw before, like someone wandering around with a flashlight or a lantern, but again he couldn't make out the source of the light.

As he watched it, the pale figure of a naked man sprinted across his line of sight, his muscular arms pumping at his sides.

The footsteps of something he couldn't see rushed past him as he shined his light around at the chaos that was breaking out all around him.

Somewhere in the forest, a woman screamed.

He heard a loud "caw" and looked up in time to see several crows fly overhead, followed by what appeared to be a giant centipede slithering through the air, gliding on huge, outstretched wings like an elaborate kite.

And now that he was looking up, he saw that the treetops were moving again. This time, he could see a dark, ominous shape pushing its way through them, bending them, sending heavy branches crashing to the ground, as if to prove that it wasn't just his eyes playing tricks on him.

He stood there, staring up at the mysterious giant, his brain numb from the shock of it all.

"What is this place?" he breathed.

He didn't expect an answer when he asked the question, and yet, to his surprise, he got one: "This is Evancurt."

The voice didn't come from any one particular direction. And it had a strange, warbling quality about it, like a warped record.

"This is where they broke the world."

Chapter Seven

Eric turned around, a fresh chill washing over him at the words he'd just heard.

The words…but not the voice. The voice was the first familiar thing he'd encountered since he awoke in this nightmare forest.

"You…"

Her smile was warm and familiar, a drastic contrast to her tangled hair, the dark bruises that encircled her wrists and ankles and those ghastly, bloody eyes.

He wasn't sure why he didn't think of her before. Without his phone, he couldn't communicate with Isabelle, or with *any* living person for that matter. But *Tessa* wasn't bound by any form of technology. She came and went as she pleased, like all ghosts.

"Boy, am I glad to see *you*," he sighed.

Tessa's smile spread. She practically beamed at him, as if it'd absolutely made her day that he was happy she was there.

She once gave him some of her spiritual power in order to enable him to fight a demonic rat beast—because that was the sort of life he was living, apparently—and in the process she gave him a glimpse of her memories. He didn't know if that was an intentional part of the exchange or merely an unexpected side-effect, but it'd allowed him to understand a little better both the person she used to be and the consciousness that she was now. Her mortal life had been a terribly unhappy one. She was abused, neglected and exploited. She never knew genuine kindness or real love in any form, only the darker natures of humanity. And yet somehow, she managed to stay a good person deep inside until the day she died, even spending the last of her energy in an attempt to save an innocent boy from her murderers. She deserved more than anyone to move on and find a better world beyond this one, but she'd taken a strong liking to Eric, and helping him on his weird travels was, for some reason, the first thing in her unfortunate existence that seemed to make her feel true joy. He didn't understand it in the least, but she'd helped him out of a few predicaments and he was always thankful.

"Do you know what's going on here?" he asked.

She nodded, still smiling, but said nothing. Communication wasn't exactly Tessa's strongest skill set. He wasn't entirely sure why, but she seemed to have trouble speaking. He'd met plenty of other wayward spirits that could speak just fine, many of them without any indication that they weren't still living, breathing people. But unlike them, she couldn't seem to sync her voice with the physical movement of her lips. She was like watching a video with a broken soundtrack. Isabelle had theorized that the horrific torture she'd endured at the tragic end of her life had damaged her vocal cords and her inability to produce natural sounds was the same as her bloody eyes and the bruises around her wrists and ankles. It was sort of disorienting to witness. Perhaps because of this, she seemed to avoid speaking needlessly. She mostly communicated through expressions and gestures, which could be rather endearing, once you got past those creepy eyes.

"Can you tell me what I'm supposed to do?" he pressed.

She gestured for him to follow her and began walking down the overgrown road.

He stood there for a moment, staring after her, his mind still a little sluggish from all that he'd seen. "Aren't you cold?" he asked her. She was, after all, stark naked.

She was *always* naked. He wasn't sure if it was because she'd died naked or if she just liked being that way. But he wished she'd put some clothes on. *She* might not be able to feel the cold, but seeing her like that in this weather was giving *him* a wicked chill.

Other ghosts manifested fully clothed. Even the soggy, easily-offended woman was wearing *underwear*. Would it kill her again to put on a *bathing suit*, at least?

But Tessa didn't answer him. She didn't look back at him. She continued walking, her bare feet not even disturbing the snow that was beginning to gather on the ground.

He dropped the pointless subject and followed after her.

Around them, the mysterious creatures and odd anomalies had mostly disappeared back into the forest. Even the weeping boy had vanished again.

The giant, however, was still there. He could hear tree branches snapping and crashing to the ground somewhere nearby. But it'd moved away some distance. And Tessa didn't seem concerned by the thing.

Still, his gaze lingered on those woods for a moment. Like so many other crazy things, he'd encountered giants before. Although those other giants had turned out to be nothing more than extremely advanced projections created by a mad, power-drunk witch.

He turned his attention back to Tessa again. She always turned up when he needed her on his weird adventures, sometimes just to help him get through a locked door, sometimes to help him with a powerful enemy, but she'd never shown herself on a normal day. She never appeared to him at home. He had no idea where she went or how she spent her time between these episodes of weirdness.

"You told me about the broken girl," he recalled as he caught up to her. "When we first met. You told me to follow the bones. You were talking about this place, weren't you?"

She glanced over at him. That smile never faltered. She always smiled at him like that. It was the sort of smile she shouldn't have, given the horrific way that she died and the many years she spent trapped in that horrid basement. He couldn't understand how she could suffer something like that, an end of her life so gruesome that her eyes remained bloody to this day, and always smile at him like he was a dear friend.

"You knew I was going to end up here. Even way back then. You knew I'd come here one day. You knew I'd see that girl. But how?"

She smiled back at him for a moment longer, then she simply turned and looked ahead of her again.

Apparently, that was a secret.

He looked back over his shoulder to make sure nothing was creeping up behind them. It was strange seeing only one set of tracks in the snow. "You said something about this being where they...'broke the world,' was it?"

Ahead of him, Tessa nodded. This, it seemed, was a topic worthy of her broken voice, because it drifted to him across the wind, disconnected, haunting: "A long time ago, some people found something they weren't meant to find. They built something they weren't supposed to build."

"Something that broke the world," said Eric. It sounded like the plot of a science fiction novel.

Again, Tessa nodded.

"And all these people I keep seeing?"

"Spirits," she replied. "Lingering souls of the dead. It lures them here. Draws them from miles around. Trapping them here."

Trapped... That probably explained why many of them seemed so confused. They probably didn't know where they were or why. Death was probably a fairly traumatizing experience by itself, but to find yourself in a place like this, with no idea where you were...or why you were here...or even *how*?

"Other things, too," said Tessa in her warped-record voice.

He glanced back at the woods behind them, at the slowly receding sounds of the lumbering giant. "Right. Those creatures." Those animals that were fleeing the giant's path. Those weren't of this world, but they certainly weren't wayward spirits. Those were just animals. *Alien* animals, like the things he encountered in the fissure, and in that freaky facility on Weapony Island.

"It's eating through the boundaries," she explained, "letting things pass back and forth."

He nodded. Just like in Hedge Lake.

Ahead of them, a building emerged from the gloom, much larger than the previous two. It looked like some kind of warehouse, a stout, concrete structure with a shallow tin roof that stretched back and out of sight into the dense and hazy forest.

He squinted into the snow, then he looked around. For the first time, it occurred to him how peculiar this weather was. It was *too* hazy, now that he was really thinking about it. It was almost foggy, in spite of the snow. It looked *unnatural*.

It was like it was in Hedge Lake, he realized, when he descended into the triangle, deeper into the anomaly, where the fabric of the universe was blistering and reality was peeling apart. That place was hazy, too.

Like Hedge Lake, this was a place that overlapped other worlds.

Tessa was right. This was a *broken* place.

She stopped walking and pointed into the forest.

He turned to look. For a moment, he didn't see anything. But then he did. There was a shadow creeping through the gloom of the forest, oozing from tree to tree. It was the same thing he saw in the cabin just now. Or at least the same *sort* of thing. He couldn't say for certain how many might be lurking here. This one had separated itself from the surfaces of the forest and was walking among the trees, its long, spider-like fingers probing at its surroundings. "What is it?" he asked.

"They're the sentinels of Evancurt. They're neither alive nor dead, but they're incredibly dangerous. They've already noticed you. They know you're different, that you don't belong here. If they discover your purpose, they *will* destroy you. You can't let them know why you're here."

"*I* don't know why I'm here," he retorted. "You haven't told me *what* I'm supposed to find."

She gave him another of those sad smiles and said, "I still don't know it all myself. I'm sorry."

He sighed. "It's fine. I get it." He couldn't get mad at Tessa. For one thing, it wasn't her fault. Being dead didn't make her all-knowing. For another, he kind of had a soft spot for her. Something about the joyless life she showed him that day at Bellylaugh Playland... He just wanted to do everything he could to make sure she never had to feel that way again, not even for a moment.

"They are tied to the thing that was built in this place," she went on, "and to the lingering things left behind in the wake of the first process."

First process? What did that mean?

But she didn't pause to let him ask more questions. "They have the power to pierce your *soul*. You can't let them catch you."

Eric nodded. "Got it." He looked at the creeping shadow as it slunk through the forest, at those many thin, spider-like fingers that sliced through the air like long, curved blades. "Avoid the...uh...*reapers*."

Tessa shrugged. It was as good a name for them as any, she supposed. "But there will be other dangers in this place, too," she warned him. "Not all the spirits will be friendly."

"Yeah, I deduced that for myself," he grumbled, glancing down at his ripped jacket.

"And not all creatures from the other worlds will be docile. Even the land, itself, will be hostile. The things the sinners built here. And the pale things that walk between worlds."

"So a whole lot of crap," he grumbled. "Got it."

She gave him another sad smile. "Please be careful. I can only do so much to protect you."

"Of course. I understand." Although the truth was that he understood very little. But that was how it always was in the weird. Again, he looked out into the haze of the forest, at the creeping shadow.

"Find what the sinners built," said Tessa. "Destroy it. Before it's too late."

Eric nodded as he watched the shadow slip out of sight again. "What happens after it's too late?" he wondered. But when he looked back at her, she was gone.

He was alone again.

Well, not actually *alone*. He heard the loud crack of a breaking tree branch and glanced back to see a dark shape bending the treetops behind him. It was moving toward him again. Could it be attracted by his flashlight?

Given the circumstances, the building right in front of him seemed as good a place to start as any. He hurried on to the door, hoping the giant hadn't noticed him and wouldn't flatten the building with him inside it.

But he still didn't know what he was supposed to do. *Find what the sinners built,* he thought. *Destroy it. Before it's too late.* But what was it they built? He didn't know what he was looking for.

When you see the broken girl dancing in the snow, he thought, remembering the first words Tessa ever spoke to him, *follow the bones and you will find her.*

He took hold of the door handle and paused, frowning. *Her?* Was he looking for a thing or a person? Or did he have to find a person in order to find the thing?

The door was unlocked.

He opened it and stepped into the darkness that awaited him within.

Chapter Eight

It soon became clear that this was no warehouse. In fact, he wasn't sure *what* the place was. The inside was drastically different from the stark concrete and rusting tin of its outside. This looked like something from the set of a science fiction movie. He was standing in a small, empty room with glass walls and a shiny, copper-colored floor. Fifteen feet above him, the ceiling was a strange, translucent-white material. In front of him, a twelve-foot-long, white tunnel extended deeper into the darkness.

Unlike in the cabin with the moldy eyeball basement and the reaper, this place was entirely free of cobwebs and covered in only a light layer of collected dust. Did that mean that this building was recently still in use? He dared to let himself hope that he might actually find a phone in here somewhere. But as he looked around, he wasn't so sure about that. There were no furnishings of any kind, not so much as a desk or a chair.

And again, there weren't any light switches. Or even any lights, as far as he could see.

His eyes were drawn to the glass walls and the mysterious shadows looming behind them. He couldn't see what was there. The glass was warped and distorted, preventing him from peering through it. Nothing seemed to be moving at the moment, but given the things he'd already encountered here, he was sure that nightmarish faces would be appearing there any moment now, staring back at him with dead and hungry eyes.

Something bad was going to happen in here. He just knew it.

He glanced back at the door behind him. Going back out wasn't an option. There was a giant wandering around out there. And while Tessa hadn't specifically told him to enter this building, she'd practically walked him to the door. It was possible that there was something in here she wanted him to find.

When he looked forward again, he caught just a glimpse of something darting past the end of the tunnel, startling him.

He sighed. There was simply no doubt about it. This was definitely going to suck.

He walked through the tunnel, his flashlight sliding over every surface. He didn't have to duck. It was seven feet in diameter, a large, cylindrical tube laid on its side. Its interior was as smooth as glass, made of a translucent material, like the ceiling, but with countless flecks of shiny, crystal-like stones frozen inside. He didn't think he'd ever seen anything like it before.

The bottom of the tube, however, had a slip-resistant coating painted over it to prevent any accidents. That was a considerate touch, he thought. Very responsible.

He kept wanting to reach for his phone, to talk to Isabelle, to see if any of this strangeness sounded familiar to her. Or if she sensed any dangerous energies. But of course that was impossible. And it was looking as if he wasn't going to find a phone anytime soon.

He wished he could at least be certain she was still with him. He wished he had some way to know she was watching over him, even if she couldn't speak to him.

At the end of the tunnel was a small, open area enclosed by more of those strange, glass walls. Twelve three-inch-thick, gold-colored cables protruded from various holes around the blunt end of the white tube. They bent to either side, parting away from the opening and allowing space to step out, then curved down and disappeared into the floor. He paused as he passed between them, curious. They definitely weren't copper. He was fairly sure that was real gold. Probably gold plating, but as strange as this place was, he couldn't help but wonder.

The fact that they were bare was curious, too. If they were meant to carry electricity, shouldn't they be insulated?

What else would cables like that be for?

But he pushed all these questions from his mind and moved on. Even if there were someone here to explain it to him, he wouldn't understand. He barely understood how the coffee pot worked. He turned his attention to the rest of his surroundings, instead.

On either side of the protruding tunnel was a large, glass cylinder that ran from the floor to the ceiling. Both appeared to be filled with some kind of clear, thick liquid, visible only because of a steady trickle of slowly-rising bubbles. Above him was a round hole, leading up through the strange, white surface and into the darkness above, with no visible purpose. And there was a two-foot cylinder sticking straight up from the floor, about ten inches in diameter. It wasn't a pipe of any sort. It appeared to be a solid piece of shiny, black metal, just standing there, with no apparent purpose.

What the hell was this place? It looked like something from *Star Trek*. Was this stuff supposed to be some kind of machinery? He'd never seen anything like it before. And he didn't hear anything running. The entire place was utterly silent.

Was it abandoned or merely offline for the night? It didn't *look* abandoned. It didn't resemble that first building he entered at all. That office was covered in dust and curtained in cobwebs. This place was surprisingly clean. It looked almost *sterile*. There was only the slightest coating of dust to be found.

Something tugged at the tail of his jacket again.

He turned and looked around, but there was no one there.

For a moment, he didn't move. He stood silently, listening, wondering if anything else was going to happen.

He used to love the idea of ghosts and haunted places. He used to be a big fan of those popular ghost hunting shows on television. But it'd been a while now since he'd sat down and watched one. His favorite ones were off the air now, anyway, but the fact was that they just didn't fascinate him like they used to. And was it any wonder? What was the point in watching people pour over barely-audible EVPs and blurry, shaking video recordings, trying to glimpse some fleeting proof of the supernatural when the supernatural had, on multiple occasions, grabbed him by the shoulders and literally screamed right into his face?

It seemed to him that those "professional" investigators

were doing something wrong.

Maybe they were looking for these things in all the wrong places. He'd never seen them investigate a place like this before, after all.

Whatever the reason, he was well beyond their level of investigating. He didn't stand there wondering if the tug he felt on his jacket tail was real. He stood there wondering whether whatever had tugged on it wanted to toy with him or to drag him into a dark corner and rip his still-beating heart out.

He dismissed it for the time being and turned his attention to the narrow passageways on either side of him.

When he looked left, he caught another glimpse of something darting past, heading for the front corner of the building.

He went that way, ducking under a large bundle of those gold cables and stepping into the next passage. He expected whatever he saw to be gone, and he wasn't wrong. There was no one here. Nor was there anywhere for anyone to have gone. The area was entirely closed in with those strange glass walls.

In front of him was something that sort of resembled a backyard hot tub, except it was made of the same translucent-white material as that tunnel he walked through and filled with an odd, reddish liquid.

There were several more of those thick, gold-colored cables rising out of the tub and disappearing into a metal box mounted to the ceiling above it.

Time machine? he wondered jokingly, then frowned as he caught himself unconsciously reaching for the cell phone that wasn't there again. He didn't even have anyone to comment on his lame jokes... How disappointing.

He turned to try the other way, but paused as a light appeared somewhere on the other side of the warped glass.

It drifted along, moving slowly. It seemed to be the same light he'd seen in the woods, the one he'd thought was a flashlight. Or maybe a lantern. This light seemed smaller and dimmer, more like a candle, but that was probably because he was looking at it through several of these warped-glass walls.

Was it someone else like him, he wondered? Or was it only

another wandering spirit?

He was holding a light, too. He should be every bit as visible as the other guy. If it *was* just another lost soul wandering around in the dark, shouldn't they try to investigate the other light? But then again, who was he to talk? He wasn't exactly calling out to them. He wasn't nearly confident enough about what might answer.

As he watched, the light drifted farther away and then winked out again.

He watched for a moment to make sure it was gone, then turned his attention back to the task before him and started back the way he came. But he immediately stopped again. There, at the far end of the glass passage, was a man. He was wearing an expensive-looking business suit and crawling around on the floor.

Eric walked toward the man, curious. He could hear him muttering to himself.

"Where is it? Where'd it go?"

"You okay?" he asked.

The man didn't seem to hear him. He turned and crawled in the other direction, his nose hovering only a few inches off the ground. "Come on… Where is it?"

"Hey," said Eric, raising his voice. "Do you need some help?"

But the well-dressed man either couldn't hear him or wouldn't. He crawled off, deeper into the darkness, still searching for whatever it was he'd lost.

Eric wasn't sure how he expected to find anything anyway. He didn't have a light. And he wasn't searching like someone who'd lost something in the dark. He wasn't searching with his hands. He was literally *looking* for something.

He watched the man for a moment, curious, then he turned his attention to his surroundings. There were more of those glass walls over here, as well as another of those vertical glass tubes filled with bubbling liquid. There was also a large, stainless-steel tank, like something you might find in a brewery, but with more of those fat, gold cables sticking out of it.

Still, none of these cables were insulated. He was no electrician, but he was fairly certain that any wire that size carrying electricity would be deadly to touch. Maybe they were more like grounding wires?

He shook his head. He was wasting his time trying to understand anything here.

"Where is it?" groaned the man crawling around on the floor.

Eric felt bad for him, but he wasn't sure what he was supposed to do about it. He'd already asked if he needed help. And if the man *had* accepted his help, he had a feeling that whatever he'd lost wasn't going to be found here.

"You there!" said a gruff voice.

Eric looked up to see an older man in a brightly-colored, Hawaiian shirt, khaki shorts and what looked like a brand-new Panama hat strolling toward him from the darkness. He was waving a handful of papers at him.

"Do you work here?" he asked.

Eric stared back at him, confused. "What? Me?"

But the old man walked right up to him, almost close enough to stick his nose in his face. "Which way is it to gate five?"

Eric leaned back. What was it with some people and their total disregard for personal space? "Gate five?" Did this guy think he was in an airport? "Um…"

The old man jabbed a stubby finger at the tickets in his hand. "I'm in a helluva hurry and I can't find this danged gate *anywhere.*"

He looked around, but he didn't think there were any gates here. "I…don't think you're in the right building."

But the old man didn't seem to be listening to him. He was holding his wrist up to his face, squinting hard at his watch as if he'd forgotten his bifocals. "I've only got five minutes!"

"I'm sorry, but…"

The old man hurried on past him, as if he'd forgotten that he'd stopped to ask for directions. "Gate five…" he muttered as he vanished back into the darkness. "Gate five… Why the heck do they have to make these places so danged *complicated?*"

Eric stared after him, confused.

"Where is it?" groaned the crawling, nicely-dressed man. He still didn't know what this guy was looking for, but it didn't seem to be gate five. It seemed to be something a lot smaller than any kind of gate he could think of.

He left the men to their business and carried on.

He walked past the metal tank, turned the corner and found himself standing in front of another of those strange hot tub things filled with that odd, reddish liquid.

Was this some sort of bizarre *laboratory?* He felt like he was going to turn a corner any minute and find a square-headed monster lying under a tarp.

He found a narrow passageway on the other side of the tub and followed it to another open space beyond, where he nearly collided with an old woman.

"Hey, *you!*" she shouted at him, poking him in the chest with the bottle in her hand. "Don' even *think* about it!"

Eric stumbled backward, surprised.

This lady looked to be at least eighty, with thin, white hair that was sticking out in every direction. Her wrinkled cheeks were flushed red. She seemed to be having trouble focusing her eyes. And she positively *reeked* of vodka.

She staggered toward him, trying to poke him in the chest with the bottle again, but she kept missing. "Jus' 'cause I get a *teeny* bit *tipsy*, you think I'm gonna be an easy target, huh?"

He frowned at her. "Huh?" Target? Did she think he was trying to mug her or something? And what the hell was this "teeny bit tipsy" nonsense? She was as drunk as Paul at an open bar wedding reception. "I wasn't..."

She took another staggering step toward him, tipped dangerously to one side, then somehow recovered and stood up straight again. "Yer gon' hafta work jus'uz hard as all the *udder* boys if you wan' summa *this!*" she informed him as she pulled open the collar of her shirt and flashed him the most unsexy cleavage he'd ever seen in his life.

Eric stumbled backward again, horrified. "That's not

what…uh…"

The woman took a swig from the bottle and then squinted at him again. "Then again…" she said, leaning toward him. "Now th' I had a *lookit* ya… Maybe ya won' hafta work all *that* hard after all… Yer kinda *cute!*"

"Sorry," he said, revolted. "Wrong room." Then he turned and fled down the next passageway, ducking under several large, heavy pipes.

"You'll be back!" she called after him, cackling. "Ev'ryone knows the *shriveled* fruits're the *sweetest!*"

Well, there went *his* appetite for the rest of the week.

He stepped into the next room and glanced back to make sure he wasn't being followed. But the perverted old drunk seemed to be staying put.

That was unpleasant.

Was she a ghost, too? That bottle she jabbed him with sure felt real. And she certainly *smelled* real. Were ghosts supposed to be able to get drunk? Were drunk ghosts supposed to smell like alcohol?

Not that he cared enough to go back and ask her, of course.

Relaxing a little, he turned to see where he was, but his flashlight flickered and then went dark, plunging him into utter blackness.

He cursed and banged it against his palm. His obnoxious imagination, of course, leapt into action, wasting no time gleefully describing all the horrors that were probably already closing in around him.

He really didn't know what was wrong with his brain. It couldn't possibly be normal.

The flashlight flickered twice, then came back on, revealing a ghastly, corpse-like face rushing at him.

He cried out, terrified, and thrust out his arms to shield himself, but the thing seemed to pass right through his outstretched hands. In an instant it was in his face, empty, cataract eyes staring back at him, shriveled lips peeled back from rotten teeth in a hateful snarl. A furious, rasping shriek filled his ears and a foul breath washed over him like a cold, fetid wind.

He stumbled backward, still trying to push the thing away, but although he could feel cold, dead hands grasping at his chest, his own hands found nothing tangible. Even when he struck out at that corpse-like face, there didn't seem to be anything in front of him but empty air.

He leaned back, still crying out in horror, and the thing moved with him so that it remained constantly a bare inch from his nose.

Still flailing at it, desperate to get away, he fell backward, dropping the flashlight, and *still* that awful, shrieking face stared back at him.

Something tore at his jacket. Something cold drew itself across the left side of his chest, leaving a hot pain painted in its wake. Hard, bony hands closed around his face, clawing at his flesh. And still, he couldn't find any part of this thing that his hands could push against.

He crossed his arms in front of his face and tried to roll away, but those hands pulled at him, holding him down.

It seemed to have lots of hands. More hands than anything had any business having. Hundreds of them, with countless fingers, grasping and clawing and gouging, pulling at his clothes and his hair.

A new horrible thought filled his head then, not of hands and fingers at all, but the countless, grotesque, wriggling legs of some enormous bug, and he cried out again as a horrid, blinding panic overwhelmed him.

Then, like the soaking-wet, half-naked woman before it, the deathly, shrieking thing simply vanished.

Eric rolled across the floor, snatched up the flashlight and jumped to his feet, still gasping with fright. He shined his light around the cramped space, expecting to be attacked again, but he was alone once more.

"What the hell was *that?*" he gasped, reaching for his phone again.

But his phone still hadn't magically appeared in his pocket while he was being assaulted by whatever that angry, handsy thing was. For better *and* worse, he was alone here.

Or so he thought.

As he stood there, shining his light back and forth, trying to calm his racing heart, something slammed against the other side of the glass wall next to him, startling another undignified scream from him.

He stumbled backward, shining his light at it. The warped glass made it impossible to see clearly what was there. It was only a shadowy, distorted outline of what appeared to be a person, but probably wasn't anymore. And perhaps it never *was* a person. There was something distinctly wrong with the shape, something beyond the warping of the glass. He didn't think this was the same thing that attacked him a moment ago. This thing looked bigger. And it was oddly proportioned, more monstrous.

Like the thing he glimpsed moving in the forest, it immediately filled him with an unsettling dread. Again, there was something familiar about the shape.

It banged its fists against the glass, as if it meant to crash through it to get at him.

Eric, having no reason to believe that the thing on the other side just *really* needed a hug, opted to turn and flee in the other direction, hoping to put as many glass walls between him and it as possible.

Chapter Nine

He wove through the glass labyrinth, past several more of those strange, vertical tubes filled with slowly-rising bubbles and dozens more of those fat, gold cables until he was fairly certain that the monster behind the glass wouldn't be able to easily follow him, hoping the whole time that he didn't simply end up circling around and running right into the thing.

Hopefully the flashlight trouble wouldn't turn out to be a main theme of the night. Especially with things like that shrieking, hundred-handed corpse-thing waiting around to take advantage of it. He was stressed-out enough as it was. His heart was still pounding and his nerves were shot. He kept jumping at shadows and shapes in the gloom, expecting at any moment to be attacked again.

When he found himself in a dead-end, his path blocked by another of those huge, stainless-steel tanks, he turned back, only to find himself standing before another woman.

She didn't look anything like a corpse, fortunately. She looked every bit as alive as he was. And she didn't appear to be drunk, either, which was also good. She was young, in her early or mid-twenties, he thought. She had brown, shoulder-length hair and, like a lot of the people he'd encountered here, was dressed for warmer weather. She had denim capris pants, sandals and a light, summery blouse.

"There you are!" she gasped. Then she threw herself at him, hugging him.

"Uh...?" was all he could think to say. Like the angry blonde, he didn't think he knew this woman.

"Where in the world have you been?"

"I...uh..."

"Oh, it doesn't matter!" She pulled away from him and, before he could react, kissed him firmly on the lips.

"Whoa! Hold on!" This was clearly a very confused woman. She was going to be *super* embarrassed when she realized he wasn't who she thought he was.

She seized one of his arms in both of hers and pulled on him, leading him back the way he came. "Come on!"

"I think you're mistaking me for someone else," he told her.

But the confused woman didn't seem to be listening to him. "We have to go! We're going to be late!"

Eric tried to pull his arm free, but she wouldn't let go. "I'm telling you, I don't know you."

"Hurry up!"

He didn't understand what was going on here. Why wasn't she listening to him? Could she not hear him? Was she trapped in some kind of delusion?

Tessa said that all the people here were spirits, trapped here in this place where they "broke the world," whatever that meant. Was this woman really one of them? She certainly *felt* real. She had a very real grip on his arm. He could feel her pressed against him. He could feel strands of her hair licking at his cheek as she pulled him along. He could even smell her perfume.

Not to mention that *kiss* a moment ago…

How real could a ghost be?

He couldn't help but think that this woman couldn't be one of them. She must've just wandered in here somehow, not unlike he did. Maybe she'd had an accident, too. Maybe she was delirious.

Another of those strange, white tunnels appeared from the darkness, about half the length of the first one, and she dragged him through it, into an area with dozens of those thick, golden cables crisscrossing overhead.

He shined his light up at them. Unlike the previous cables, each of these appeared to be encased in a shiny coating of clear glass, seemingly to insulate them from each other.

The woman paused here and looked around. "The door should be around here somewhere," she told him. "I just saw it a little while ago."

Eric shined his light around. There didn't appear to be any doors. Maybe she was confusing the tunnel they just came from with the one at the front of the building. If she didn't know whose arm she was clinging to, she probably didn't know the way out. "Could you let go of me, please?"

Instead, the strange, clingy woman turned and snuggled against his shoulder. "I was so worried about you."

"You don't even know me!"

Then she lifted her head and slapped his shoulder. "Why would you leave me alone like that?"

"What're you talking about? I keep telling you—"

But then a man in a Milwaukee Brewers jacket and very thick glasses was suddenly standing next to him, his eyes huge behind those magnifying lenses. "They'll come with the first ca-lamity," he said in a conspiratorial whisper, "descending in the final hours of the fourth age! All the worthy will receive the mark… Show them! And we'll sail the endless seas of the stars together!"

Eric stared at him for a moment. When it was clear that the man had nothing else to add, he simply nodded and said, "Okay."

The man nodded back, seemingly satisfied, and said, "Pass it on." Then he turned and fled back into the darkness from which he came.

He watched him go, then turned and looked at the confused woman still clinging to his arm. "I keep telling you, I don't know you."

"I can't wait 'til we get to the hotel," she sighed, as if she hadn't heard a word of it. "It feels like I've been waiting *forever*."

Hotel? Did she think this was a vacation? He had no inten-tion of going to any hotel room with this woman. Karen would kill them both.

He glanced down at her hand. She was wearing a wedding band. Did she think he was her *husband*?

He pulled at his arm, but she still refused to let go. And she was strong for her size.

Why did she suddenly have time to stand around *cuddling*? Didn't she just say they were running late? "Let go, already! Who *are* you?" He glanced around again, uncomfortable, and immediately caught sight of another person standing in the dark, this one a broad-shouldered, teenage boy with long, tousled hair. He stared back at him with haunted eyes.

"There's something *wrong* with this place!" he whispered.

"No kidding," replied Eric. It was the understatement of the year.

The woman gasped. "This way!" she suddenly decided. She let go of his arm and took his hand instead, pulling at him. "Hurry!"

This time, he managed to pull his hand free of her grip and stand his ground.

He expected her to turn and seize his arm again, but she continued hurrying into the darkness, her hand still held out behind her, as if she didn't realize she'd lost him.

"That was awkward," he grumbled as he reached for his phone again.

But of course it wasn't there.

He'd gotten used to talking to Isabelle on these adventures. It was strange not being able to see her replies.

He missed her.

He sighed and turned his attention back to his surroundings. For the moment, at least, he seemed to be alone again.

Except he wasn't. As he swept his flashlight across the room, it came to rest on a small girl.

She looked to be only about seven. She had long, brown hair that hid much of her face, and like many of the people he'd encountered, was dressed for much warmer weather. She wore shorts, sandals and a bright, pink tee shirt with a picture of a cupcake on the front. She was backed into a corner, her hands clasped in front of her, staring back at him with big, blue eyes.

"Are you okay?" he asked her. "Do you need help?"

He didn't think she'd respond, but she abruptly darted forward and grabbed his hand.

"Oh. Okay." He glanced around, uncomfortable. "Sure. I

guess…"

The little girl said nothing. She stood there, clinging to his hand and looking around at the darkness that surrounded them.

"What's your name?"

But she didn't respond. If she had a name, it was a secret. He could handle that. It wasn't the first time someone refused to share their name with him. There were a lot of people in the world like that. There was an entire mysterious organization filled with strange and powerful agents who were discouraged from sharing their names, forcing him to give them silly nicknames like "the cowboy" and "pink shirt" and "steampunk monk" to keep them straight. He'd also met a blood witch once who told him that sharing your name with people was the same as giving them power over you, as if the simple act of introducing yourself was the same as signing over your soul.

This girl didn't look like an evil, nameless agent *or* a blood witch. She just looked like a frightened little girl.

He stared down at her. Her hand felt real enough… It was so warm. She couldn't be…like those other people… Could she?

He was immediately reluctant to accept that this girl wasn't among the living. He couldn't even think the words. He hated the thought of ghostly children. If she were a ghost, like those other people, then that meant that there was someone out there who'd had to put their little girl in the ground, and that was a thought that he'd always found unbearably disturbing.

"My name's Eric," he told her.

She lifted her face and looked up at him, but still said nothing.

He nodded. "Right. Well…" He glanced around at these strange surroundings, considering where he should go next. But then he paused as Tessa's words came back to him: *Follow the bones and you will find her.* He glanced down at the girl again. *She* was a "her." Maybe this girl was what he was here to find. Maybe she *wouldn't* turn out to be like the others here after all.

Except he doubted it would be as easy as that.

Besides, he hadn't seen a single bone in this whole messed-up place.

"I don't suppose you could tell me who or what it is I'm here to find, can you?" he tried.

She only stared up at him and remained silent.

"Yeah. I didn't think so."

As he watched, her gaze shifted to something on the other side of him.

He turned to see what she was looking at and found a man in a highway worker's orange vest standing against the glass wall. Unlike the other people who kept appearing, he didn't say anything to him, or even seem to notice him. He merely stood there, his mouth agape, staring off into space with wide and unsettlingly horrified-looking eyes.

His clothes were soaked with blood.

Eric considered him for a moment, then decided that this disturbing display was probably highly inappropriate for a child. He took the girl in the cupcake tee shirt and moved on.

"Is it always this crowded in here?" he asked, glancing down at her.

She stared up at him and continued saying nothing at all.

He nodded and turned his attention to his surroundings again.

The next area housed a large, silver sphere, about five feet in diameter. It was sitting in the middle of the floor, seemingly unattached to anything. Mounted on each of the four walls around it and on the ceiling directly above it were large, square blocks of that strange, translucent white material with the glittering crystals inside it. From each of these protruded a naked loop of that thick, gold cable. They looked almost like handles.

Eric paused and shined his light over the scene.

It was perplexing. He had no idea what to make of any of this. It all looked like some kind of futuristic technology to him. He felt as if he'd accidentally wandered onto an alien spacecraft.

But he didn't have time for his imagination to run very far with this new and potentially terrifying idea. At that moment, there was a loud bang from somewhere not far away.

The girl let out a frightened whimper and crowded closer to him, clutching his hand even tighter.

He glanced down at her. Was it only because she was already scared? Was she merely jumping at ordinary noises? Or was there something in here that she was rightfully afraid of?

Was it the thing that was banging on the glass before? Was it still wandering around, looking for him?

Or maybe it was that shrieking corpse-thing again…

He squeezed the girl's hand and hurried on.

A moment later, he stepped into a four-way intersection.

He looked left, then straight ahead, then right. Why was this place such a maze? And how big was this building, anyway? How long had he been wandering these queer, glass hallways? It couldn't have been that long, but it felt strangely as if several hours had passed. Was it something about this alien-looking technology, or just his overactive imagination? It was so hard to be sure when it came to the weird.

He looked left again and saw that something had shuffled silently into view while he was looking the other way.

He stood there, the girl clinging to his hand, staring at the thing not twenty feet away from him. It was the same vaguely-familiar and unsettling shape that he saw through the glass a few minutes ago, and in the forest before that. Suddenly, he understood why it had filled him with such dread. Without the unearthly mist of the forest or the warped glass to conceal it, he was finally able to see the shape for what it was.

And he knew that shape!

It wasn't human. It wasn't even the lingering spirit of a human. The thing was a corpse-like shade of pallid gray, hairless and wrinkled. Its arms and legs were a little too long. Its torso was a little too short. Its hands and feet were a little too big. It was shuffling along, its head drooping, its arms limp at its sides.

It was a wendigo.

The last time he encountered these things was two summers ago. It was the same day he met Tessa.

They didn't look like much, shuffling around in that slow, zombie-like state, but they were vicious creatures that instantly came alive the moment they spotted prey. They transformed in the blink of an eye. At once fully awake, they were much faster and much harder to avoid. And if you were unfortunate enough to be caught by one, you'd discover that they were also impossibly strong and nightmarishly violent.

This was bad. He was no match for something like that. And here in the middle of this glass labyrinth, there was nowhere to run. Unarmed, he wouldn't stand a chance against that thing.

The wendigo took another shuffling step, barely lifting its foot off the floor, and then paused.

It raised its head and turned its monstrous gray eyes toward him.

Chapter Ten

Eric stood motionless against the wall, his heart racing in his chest, clutching the frightened girl against him. He'd managed to duck into the passageway in front of him before the thing could spot him, but he didn't dare move another step. He didn't even dare to breathe.

The walls around him were all made of that warped glass. If the thing's eyesight was as advanced as its strength and speed, it might be able to see the slightest movement and perceive him as prey.

His past experience with wendigos had shown him that they weren't overly observant. Shuffling around with their heads hanging like that limited their field of vision, and they didn't seem to have the keenest sense of hearing or smell. One had once shuffled right past both him and Karen without ever realizing either of them were there.

And yet that time was different for one major reason. His gaze drifted down to his hand. The flashlight was still there, its light spilling out into the intersection where he'd just been standing, where the monster was now staring, giving away his position. It was probably painting a distinct silhouette of him through the glass he was leaning against.

But if he turned it off, he'd be utterly blind.

These things weren't very smart. Would it ignore the light? Or would it recognize it as a sign that prey was nearby? Even if it didn't register the light, it might react to the movement of shadows, and it was taking all his strength to hold the light still. His whole body was trembling.

Wendigos weren't from this world. They existed in the fringe spaces inside the boundaries *between* worlds. They were nasty things, far more dangerous than he could handle as they were. And rumor had it that if they managed to taste human blood, they'd transform into something even *more* horrifying. He wasn't sure that part was true, but he certainly had no desire to put it to the test.

The pale things that walk between worlds. Those were the words Tessa had used when she warned him of all the dangers lurking here in Evancurt. Yet these monsters hadn't crossed his mind until he was finally staring at one.

But *why* were there wendigos here? When they appeared in Creek Bend, it was because something was disrupting the fabric between the worlds. Specifically, it was that psycho woman he'd dubbed "Mistress Janet" and her insane science project with the titan.

His gaze shifted to the strange, glass walls, copper floors and gold cables all around him. Was this place doing the same sort of thing?

Of course it was. Now that he was thinking about it, Tessa had told him that, too. She said that something was eating through the boundaries in this place, letting things pass from one world to the next. That no doubt included the things that naturally lurked *between* those worlds. It was *exactly* like what was happening in Creek Bend that day.

The girl squeezed him tighter. A terrified whimper escaped her.

He squeezed her back. Gently. Just enough to remind her that he was there.

He didn't hear any footsteps approaching.

Carefully, he risked turning his head. He half-expected to see the thing staring back at him on the other side of the glass, just waiting for him to make eye contact...but nothing was there.

He leaned over, still holding his breath, and peered around the corner.

The wendigo was gone. It'd moved on.

He let go of his held breath as slowly and as quietly as possible.

Jesus, that was terrifying!

He looked down at the girl still cowering against him. "It's okay," he whispered. "It's moving away from us again."

She peered up at him, her eyes glistening. She seemed so real. He could even see the wet spots her tears had left on his jacket.

He studied her face, wondering. Why would a ghost have any reason to fear a wendigo? What could one of those things do to her? Again, he dared to wonder if it was possible that she wasn't a ghost at all. Had he actually stumbled on another living soul in this nightmare place?

But then, where did she come from? How did she get here? He remembered the way she appeared when he first saw her, backed into a corner, trembling with fear. As much as he didn't want to believe it, he was sure there wasn't anyone there the moment before his light fell on her. He would've seen her as soon as he stepped into that area.

The little girl turned her head and stared off through the surrounding glass.

Eric followed her gaze. He couldn't see anything from here, but that didn't mean there wasn't something over there. "Come on," he said, urging her to keep moving. "Let's get out of here."

Still clinging to his hand, she let herself be led onward.

He shined his light around and sighed. "Tessa, I sure wish you could tell me what it is I'm looking for."

"Who's Tessa?"

Eric turned his light down a narrow gap between two large, metal tanks. There was a young man standing there, staring back at him. He wasn't wearing a shirt, in spite of the building's lack of heat, and was covered in tattoos from his shaved head to his waist. The rest of his body was hidden under a pair of dingy, distressed blue jeans and well-worn sneakers. Almost everything he had was pierced at least once. His ears. His eyebrows. His nose and lip. He had studs sticking out of his cheeks and chin. Even his navel and nipples were pierced. It hurt Eric just to look at him.

But there was something else that he noticed about the man. He showed no reaction whatsoever to the blinding glare of the flashlight in the darkness, even when he shined it directly into his face. It was something he now realized that he shared with all the other spirits he'd encountered, including...

He glanced down at the little girl and bit his lip.

No. It didn't mean she was one of them. He pushed the thought from his mind and focused all of his attention on the pierced man.

"Actually, forget it," he said. "Don't matter." He had a slight slur to his voice that suggested he had more of those painful-looking decorations in his mouth, too. "Come over here. I wanna show you something." He turned and started walking away.

Eric hesitated, uncertain. He glanced down at the girl, but she only stared back up at him, as if waiting for him to decide what he was going to do.

He shrugged and set off after the pierced man. The spirits in this place were strange. Some of them didn't seem to realize that he was here. Others had gone as far as to speak to him, but didn't seem to be aware of anything he said back to them, as if they were lost in their own delusions. Still others seemed to think that he was someone else entirely. This was the first one that seemed able to communicate fully and with some semblance of sanity.

And he wasn't a wendigo. That was always a plus.

"Over here, dude," said the pierced man as he turned a corner ahead of them.

The way the man looked, Eric was surprised he didn't jingle like a keychain when he walked. He wondered if the guy ever had issues with metal detectors. He'd always wondered about that, but it always seemed rude to ask. Including now. Instead, he asked, "I don't suppose you have a phone on you, do you?"

"Naw, dude. No one brings their phones when they come here. Not real ones, anyways."

Eric wasn't sure what he meant by that, but he didn't press the matter. Instead, he changed the question: "Do you know where I can find one? It doesn't have to still work."

"Sorry, man. There ain't no phones in Evancurt."

"No phones?" This seemed peculiar. There was a time when he'd consider a place with no phones an absolute paradise. He'd always hated cell phones with a somewhat infamous passion, owing in no small part to the fact that he was a high school teacher. Cell phone-obsessed teenagers were his greatest pet peeve. But tonight he really needed to find a phone.

"I know," said the pierced man. "Weird, right?"

Why would there be no phones? It didn't make any sense.

Isabelle... How was he going to talk to her if there weren't any phones?

In the next passageway, there were more of those thick, gold cables encased in glass. They protruded from the walls and snaked their way to the ceiling, where they plugged into a long, rectangular box.

"It's just up ahead."

As he stepped through an odd, copper archway, the lights suddenly switched on, as if he'd walked into the path of a motion sensor. The very ceiling lit up above them, illuminating the entire building.

The pierced man paused and looked up. "Huh," he said. "That's never happened before. Weird, dude."

Eric looked up at the ceiling, curious. The lights appeared to be mounted above the translucent material. And they seemed to be in motion. There was a very strange and subtle *flowing* sensation about it. It gave the place an eerie sort of *trickling* glow.

More than ever, the place reminded him of some kind of alien spacecraft.

He switched off his flashlight, hoping that the whole building wasn't preparing to jettison itself into outer space with him aboard it, and turned his attention to the space in front of him. There was a sort of pedestal standing against the wall there, about chest-high. A box was sitting on top of it, made of the same, white material as the tunnels and those hot tub-sized pools filled with mystery liquids.

Something was growing in the box. It was some sort of plant, although he'd never seen anything like it before. It was mostly root. Black and moldy-looking, bulbous, with thin, slimy creepers that had slithered down the sides of the pedestal and spread across the floor like oily cobwebs. They'd also fanned out across the entire wall and most of the ceiling. What few branches it had were short and gnarled, covered in long, sharp thorns. It had only a few leaves and they were small and shiny, covered in prickly-looking spines. Instead of green, they were the color of fresh blood. Every surface of the thing was oozing a thick, muddy liquid that overfilled the box and dripped down the sides.

There was something very much off about it, and not just that it looked like it might've come from the sort of alien planet you wouldn't want to be caught wearing a red shirt on. It was utterly out of place. Everything else here was so clean.

"See?" said the pierced man, seemingly proud of himself. "Wild, right?" He shook his head, grinning. "Totally crazy!"

"What is that thing?" asked Eric.

"Dunno. But it grows without any light or water. And it gives off this crazy *vibe*, man. It's wicked *weird.*"

Eric didn't get any kind of "vibe" from the thing, but it *was* weird. He'd give the guy that much. "But why did—" The girl tugged at his hand and he looked down at her, distracted.

She pointed at something behind him.

He turned to find the angry blonde woman standing there. Like the last time she appeared, she slapped him hard across his face, then she turned and stomped away, disappearing again as she passed under the copper archway.

"Whoa…" said the pierced man.

Eric turned, his mouth still half-open, rubbing at his burning cheek. "What the hell is *her* problem?"

"Dunno, dude. Women, right?"

Eric, for one, didn't think it had anything to do with women in general. It was only that *particular* woman who seemed to have taken offense to him for some reason.

He looked down at the girl, who only offered him a shrug.

He shook his head and turned his attention back to the strange plant and the question he was trying to ask before being interrupted. "Why did you decide I needed to see this?"

The pierced man stared at him, surprised. "Isn't that why

you came here? To see this stuff?"

Eric squinted at him. "You know why I'm here?"

"Not many reasons you *would* be here," he reasoned. "I mean, you're not like the rest of us."

"Not...like *any* of you?" He glanced down at the girl. He still didn't want her to be a ghost. He was still clinging to some shred of hope that maybe she wasn't like the others. That maybe she was just lost and he could still save her and take her back to her family.

"You're not trapped here," explained the pierced man. "I don't know how, but you could leave if you want."

Eric looked up at him again. "You're trapped here?" This was the same thing Tessa told him. She said that something about this place lured them here, that it drew them from miles around, trapping them."

"We all are. Except you. I don't know why you're different."

Because he was still alive was his guess.

"And *everyone* here is trapped? No one else is..." he glanced down at the girl again, "...like *me*?"

"'Fraid not, dude. You're the first I've seen like you. 'Course, I ain't been around too long. None of us have. You don't ever leave Evancurt, but you don't stay here forever, either. You just...*disappear* after a while..."

Eric frowned. "Disappear?"

The pierced man took a step toward him. "Yeah. No one haunts Evancurt for more than a few years. Then they just vanish. They're never seen again. They say it *eats* us."

The little girl buried her head against his jacket again. He looked down at her, horrified. "Wait...*what*?"

"It's what they all say. Just before they disappear. Sometimes they scream. Sometimes they whimper. Sometimes they just mutter to themselves. But they all say the same thing. They talk about something coming. Something hungry. Something inescapable."

Eric stared at him, horrified. Suddenly, he felt as if he were back in Hedge Lake again, teetering on the edge of an apocalypse courtesy of the insatiable, gnashing teeth of a gargantuan conqueror worm.

"It comes for us all," said the pierced man. "There's nothing we can do." He turned and looked at the strange, alien plant. "And it's because of the people who did this stuff. I know it is. They did something. A long time ago."

"They broke the world," sighed Eric.

He turned back, surprised. "Yeah..." He nodded. "I think they probably did."

What happened here? What did these people create? What did they *do*?

Something struck the wall behind him and Eric turned to see another wendigo pounding on the glass. As he watched, a second appeared beside it.

The pierced man stared at the warped shapes of the monsters. "Looks like there're things in here that want to eat *you*, too."

Chapter Eleven

"You'd better get out of here, dude," said the pierced man. "I've never seen those things get so excited before. Usually they just ignore us."

Again, probably because he was the only one here who was actually *alive*, and therefore *edible*.

The pierced man pointed at a second copper archway in the corner of the room. "Go that way. There's a door just ahead. It should take you back outside."

But Eric hesitated a moment, his gaze drawn back to the alien plant. Tessa said he was supposed to destroy what the sinner's built. Did that include things like this? Should he pull the foul thing up by its roots and kill it?

"Whoa, dude," said the pierced man. "I see the gears turning. Break the things they made and fix the things they broke, right? Kind of makes sense, I know, but don't go getting any brilliant ideas. People who mess with things around here catch the attention of those funky shadow dudes."

He looked up, surprised. Funky shadow dudes? Did he mean the reapers?

"Trust me, you don't want to go drawing attention to yourself or you'll have worse problems than those things." He gestured at the monstrous shapes pounding on the glass again.

Eric nodded. So just smashing things at random wasn't a viable strategy. That was useful information to have. "Right. Thanks."

"No problem, dude. Be careful out there. And take my advice. Get off this property while you're still able to, before you end up like the rest of us."

Still clinging to the frightened girl's hand, he made his way down the narrow passageway and into an area containing a dozen of those bubbling, glass cylinders and a lot more of those heavy, gold cables rising up out of the floor. There was also another of those white tunnels here. It looked just like the one he passed through when he entered this funhouse maze of a building. And with the lights on, he could even see the outline of the door that awaited them through the glass walls.

He was almost free.

But before he could take another step, a wendigo shuffled into view in a passageway directly across from them.

He froze, his eyes locked on the monster as it dragged its feet across the floor and slowly turned toward them.

This was a third one, he realized, different from the two behind the glass in the last room. He knew because he could still hear those other two banging on the glass back there. How many of them were there?

It didn't seem to see them yet. Its head was hanging, its gray eyes fixed on the floor at its feet. But it could look up at any second. There was nowhere for them to hide and they couldn't go back. They'd only risk ending up caught between this monster and those other two. And he had very little confidence that he could survive a physical encounter with just *one* of these freaks. He knew from experience that they were much stronger than him. Twice he'd nearly had his face chewed off by these things and had only been saved both times because someone better armed than him stepped in and saved him.

He didn't like the idea of carrying a gun. Guns caused problems. Things often happened too quickly. It was far too easy to pull a trigger and impossible to take back a bullet. And other people who had guns were far less likely to use theirs when you didn't have one of your own. And then there was the fact that some of the monsters he'd encountered wouldn't be harmed by anything as simple as a gun. Trying to shoot a golem or an ogre or a shade would only waste time that could be spent running away. But he knew from experience that wendigos weren't bulletproof. This was one of those rare times when he actually wished he had a gun. But wishing he had one when he encountered something he could kill with it was as pointless as shooting at something he couldn't.

If they were going to escape this mess, the only option they had was the doorway on the other side of that tunnel. And the only way through there was to walk *toward* the wendigo as it stood facing them. The opening was right between it and them, about ten paces away.

It might look like a race they could easily win. The thing didn't exactly look like an Olympic runner, but as soon as it saw them, it was going to go from shuffling zombie to relentless killer *instantly*. He'd seen it happen, and there was absolutely no transition between the two.

He didn't make the decision consciously. He squeezed the girl's hand and his feet just sort of started moving on their own. One step… Two steps… Three…

His gaze remained fixed on the monster as it dragged its oversized feet across the copper floor one slow, tiny step at a time, its head still hanging. He'd forgotten how ugly the things were. It had a small, pointed nose and a mouth that took up too much of its face. Its eyes were especially freaky. He couldn't see them from here, but he knew they were the same, corpse-like gray as its body, like the eyes of a statue. But the worst part by far was its…uh…*lower* anatomy.

He wished these things wore pants. They were positively obscene. And there was a child present!

And yet, even with the awful, shuffling thing looming in front of them, the girl kept pace with him. She clung tightly to his hand, practically digging her nails into his palm. She kept her face pressed against his sleeve. He could feel her trembling with fright. But she moved each time he did without hesitation, trusting him far more than he would've been able to trust someone he'd only just met.

Elsewhere in the building, the banging on the glass stopped.

Had they given up? Or did they find their way around the glass walls? It was possible that the hideous things were making their way toward them right now, and probably *not* with those shuffling baby steps.

In the sudden silence, the one in front of them stopped and turned its head to one side, as if listening to the change.

Eric froze mid-step, his heart thundering in his chest.

Beside him, the girl froze, too. He felt her squeeze his hand.

Seconds passed in agonizing slow motion.

Were those footsteps he heard in the silence, or was it only his imagination? It was hard to be sure of hearing anything over the deafening pounding of his pulse in his ears. If it *was* footsteps he was hearing...were they getting closer?

After a moment, the monster lowered its head again and took another shuffling step forward.

Still clinging to the girl's hand, Eric took another step, then another.

Just a little farther.

He was almost there.

One more step.

He was close enough now to make a break for it. If it was just a matter of slipping into the tunnel and being free, he was confident he could make it. But that tunnel was twelve feet long, plus the length of the little room on the other side. There was no doubt in his mind that it would catch him before he reached the door. And even if he could make it outside, he wasn't confident it wouldn't be able to just break the door down and keep chasing him.

He needed to get all the way out of sight without it seeing him.

Mustering all his will, he stepped carefully around the exposed cables and slowly slid into the tunnel, never taking his eyes off the monster.

It dragged its foot across the floor again as he watched it. Then, with a sudden snort, he saw it snap its head up and finally look at the room in front of it.

For a fleeting second there, Eric thought his heart might've actually stopped. He backed into the tunnel at the very last second, out of sight, his eyes wide open, watching for the monster to rush in after them.

Again, it didn't seem to see them.

He squeezed the girl's hand and the two of them hurried through the tunnel, across the empty room and out into the snowy forest beyond.

He closed the door behind them and then leaned against it, his body trembling.

That was a horrible experience.

He glanced at the girl again. "Are you okay?"

She nodded. She didn't seem traumatized. Although he wasn't sure how she avoided it with that thing's god-awful junk dangling in plain view like that. He wasn't entirely sure *he* wasn't traumatized.

"That's good."

This appeared to be the rear of the building. They were standing in a small cone of soft light cast by a single lamp mounted above the door. Only a few feet away, the ominous darkness of the forest crowded in all around them, a grim reminder that although they'd escaped the monsters inside, they were now fully exposed to countless more.

He could hear more crows cawing in those dark branches. Were those things always so active this time of year, or were they just agitated because he was stirring up so much activity? He didn't feel like pondering it right now, so he pushed the thought from his mind and glanced back at the building behind him.

If there *was* something in there that Tessa wanted him to find, he very much hoped he'd found it, because he really didn't want to ever go back in there. Not for any reason.

Eager to leave this building far behind, he pulled his flashlight from his pocket and aimed it into the oppressive gloom of the forest. "Come on. Let's go back around to the front of the building and see where that road takes us." He rounded the corner, his eyes peeled for anything dangerous lurking in the trees. Ghosts were one thing, but knowing there were wendigos in these woods was an entirely different matter.

But after a few steps, he stopped and looked down at his hand, confused.

Where was the girl?

Wasn't she just holding his hand?

He looked back the way he came. He didn't remember her letting go. But he also had no recollection of her hand simply disappearing.

She was with him when he left the building. She'd nodded at him when he asked if she was okay. But after that…

He couldn't remember. He told her they were going back to the road…but was she still there when he said that? Or was he only talking to himself?

He returned to the back of the building and scanned the area, but she wasn't there, either. And he didn't expect her to be there. Not really. He knew what she was. The pierced man told him no one here was like him. And Tessa told him he was surrounded by spirits.

He looked down at his hand again. She'd felt so real. But so had the confused woman and the angry blonde.

He sighed and closed his eyes.

Why did it have to be a child?

They say it eats *us*, he thought, remembering the pierced man's eerie words. *They talk about something coming. Something hungry. Something inescapable.*

Another icy shiver crept up his back.

It comes for us all.

Even little girls in cupcake tee shirts…

He opened his eyes and stared out into the forest.

Whatever was happening here, he had to stop it.

Chapter Twelve

He scanned the forest, making sure there were no wendigos or giants rushing toward him, then he turned and walked back toward the road again.

He kept wondering if Tessa meant for him to find the girl. Now that he'd seen her, now that he'd looked into those big, blue eyes, now that he'd spent all that time holding her hand, protecting her, he couldn't let her be eaten.

He couldn't let that happen to *anyone*. Not if there was any way he could stop it.

Tessa told him that the people who built this place broke the world. They tore the boundaries that separated it from those nightmare places that lay beyond. They summoned monsters. They trapped spirits and doomed them to a terrible fate. He knew now that he had to stop it. But *how* did he go about stopping something like this? He couldn't even hope to understand how any of this stuff worked, much less how to put an end to it. That entire building was beyond his understanding. It was like something from some far-distant future world in a science fiction novel. Nothing he saw in there made any sense to him.

And if the pierced man was telling him the truth, he couldn't just go around breaking everything in sight without knowing what he was doing. That would only bring the reapers down on him.

He kept thinking about Hedge Lake. Was this the same thing? The pierced man said that something was *eating* the spirits trapped here. The conqueror worm that was shredding a hole in the fabric of reality beneath that lake was drawn by the immense, spiritual energy that was building up there. It fed on that energy. Was that what was happening here? Had Evancurt drawn the attention of another worm? Or even the same one?

But as far as he knew, the conqueror worm didn't feed on the spirits, themselves. On the contrary, it was the spirits that provided the spiritual energy. He was told that most of the ghosts in Hedge Lake had been there a long, *long* time. That was the whole point. The path to the spirit highways had been intentionally clogged, specifically to keep them from moving on in order to flood the area with the spiritual energy that attracted the worm.

If all the souls wandering Evancurt had only been here for a few years at most, then the amount of spiritual energy in this place couldn't be nearly as great as in Hedge Lake, where spirits had been gathering for hundreds of years.

There was so much going on here that was the same as Hedge Lake. But there was also much that was very different, right down to the spirits themselves. Of all the ghosts he encountered there, only one had been indistinguishable from the living. But almost all the spirits here were like that. In fact, he'd only encountered a few disembodied voices, unexplained, traveling lights and ghostly tugs on his jacket.

He needed more information.

And he needed to figure out where he was supposed to go next.

"Tessa?" he tried. "You here?"

Something moved across the ground in front of him, startling him, and he stopped to watch as a long, flattened shape with countless spider-like legs uncoiled itself from a shadowy pile and scurried off into the forest.

Right. He'd nearly forgotten about all those strange, alien creatures that were lurking in these woods.

As soon as it was gone, he continued walking, his eyes peeled for any more super-sized creepy-crawlies.

"Tessa?" he called out again.

But if Tessa was nearby, she wasn't talking. The forest remained silent. He was alone for the moment.

Or, he *thought* he was.

As he passed beneath the branches of an old oak, his

thoughts were scattered by a large, dark shape as it dropped to the ground right behind him and let out a startling cry. He twirled around and jumped back, uttering a scream that was *almost* manly enough to belong to a teenage girl who'd just seen a mouse run between her feet. He clutched at his pounding heart and stumbled backward, nearly tripping over his own feet. Then he turned and leaned against the wall of the building as he waited to see if he was going to be okay or if this was the scare that finally killed him.

"Damn you!" he gasped when he was still alive a moment later. "What the hell are *you* doing here?"

The cat stared up at him with those big, yellow eyes, its long tail swishing back and forth. It let out a strange, excited mewl and pawed at the ground between them.

He squinted at the little beast, confused. Why would Spooky be here? It didn't make any sense. He had no idea where he was, but he was fairly sure it was nowhere near home. How far would he have had to travel to get here?

But then again, the cat had never been normal, not since the day he first laid eyes on him. He had a tendency to turn up in strange places like this, but never so far from home before.

Isabelle had said on many occasions that there was something up with that cat.

Spooky cried up at him. The sound was loud and strangely impatient. Then he turned and hurried off into the woods, *away* from the road.

Eric stared after him for a moment, confused. He didn't want to go back into the woods. There were scary things out there. Of course, there were scary things *everywhere*...so he supposed it didn't matter. But at least he couldn't get too lost if he stayed on the road.

He groaned, frustrated, and then followed the little monster deeper into the forest.

Spooky was a Maine Coon, meaning that as far as cats went, he was *big*. But he was also fast, agile and well camouflaged against the shadows and winter foliage. It was all Eric could do to keep track of him as he pushed his way through the oppressive tangles of underbrush.

The mysterious creature led him down a gradual slope, weaving through the trees and the thickets. He did his best to keep up, but he was just too big and clumsy to navigate this terrain at such a speed. By the time he reached the bottom of the hill, he'd lost sight of the cat. He paused and scanned his surroundings.

Which way did he go?

Something moved in the corner of his eye and he turned to face it, expecting it to be the cat again. Instead, he was horrified to find a teenage girl hanging by her neck from a rope slung over a high branch. She was clutching at the noose, her face a dreadful shade of purple, her eyes bulging and her bare legs flailing.

With a terrified cry, he rushed toward her. Already, he recognized her long, black hair, short, pleated skirt and gray sweater. It was the same girl who threw herself from that high doorway in the locked-up building.

He seized her kicking legs and lifted her, straining to give the rope slack. Then, in an instant, the girl was gone, rope and all.

He stumbled backward, thrown off balance, and fell onto his butt, cursing.

He sat there on the damp ground for a moment, his heart still racing, gawking up into the naked branches above him. What the hell was that? Was that girl doing these things on purpose? What was wrong with her? Did she have some kind of death wish? The old saying "kicking a dead horse" came to mind...

He rubbed at his eyes, frustrated, and rose to his feet again.

Maybe it wasn't like that. Maybe she wasn't choosing to manifest herself in these ways. Maybe there were other forces at work here. A dangerous psychosis carried over from a tormented life, perhaps. What did he really know about anything? He barely understood any of the mysterious intricacies of life, if he were to be honest. He certainly knew nothing about the psychology of being *dead*.

He looked out into the snowy forest. Had he utterly lost Spooky's trail by now? He turned around, trying without much hope to hear the sound of an extra-large furball running across damp leaves through blowing wind and falling snow. Then his flashlight flickered and winked out again, plunging him back into eerie darkness.

He cursed under his breath and gave it a hard shake, which seemed to fix it. But the moment it snapped back on, he nearly screamed at the appearance of a man dressed in orange deer hunting gear standing right next to him.

"I ain't going home yet," he said. "I'm happy out here. I'll always be happy out here."

Eric clutched at his pounding heart and stared back at the hunter, confused. "Okay," was all he could think to say. He wasn't planning to stop him. He wasn't the boss of this man. "Knock yourself out."

"I could stay out here forever."

He nodded. "Sure." This guy really seemed to enjoy his hunting. He had no intention of pointing out that it wasn't deer season.

"I know what's going on at home," he said. "I ain't stupid. I know what she's doing. I know who she's with."

Eric wasn't sure what to say to that.

"But I don't have to think about that 'til I get home," said the hunter.

Was there always blood dripping down his chin? He didn't think there was. That seemed like the sort of thing he would've noticed sooner, no farther apart than they were standing.

"And I ain't going home yet." He cradled his gun in his arms, as if it were precious to him.

There was blood dripping down the barrel.

Eric took a step back as the awful realization struck him.

"I could stay out here forever," the hunter said again, his lips spread into a forced and bloody smile.

He didn't care which way Spooky went. He turned and fled, leaving the dead hunter where he was standing. But he couldn't run fast enough to flee the awful pictures his morbid imagination painted for him. It was far too easy to see that poor man sitting against a tree somewhere, the barrel of his rifle resting in his mouth…

He glanced back over his shoulder to make sure the hunter wasn't chasing after him, eager to tell him more about how happy he was out here and how he wasn't going home yet. But there was no sign of him.

When he looked forward, however, he found his path blocked by a plump woman with her tangled hair blowing about her face. Her eyes were red and swollen. She had tears streaming down her cheeks. She looked terrified. *"Have you seen my daughter?"* she cried.

Eric stumbled to a stop.

"I can't find my daughter!"

He opened his mouth, but he had no idea what to say to her.

"Please help me! She's only three! She's just a baby!"

He nodded. "Sure… Yeah. I…" He glanced around, uncertain, and ran his gloved fingers through his hair. "What…what does she look like?"

"I've looked everywhere!"

"Okay. Just tell me what she—"

"Please help me find my daughter!"

He stared at the woman. This was so confusing. She was looking right at him when he first saw her. She seemed to be talking to him. But now it was as if she couldn't understand anything he was saying. It was like trying to converse with a prerecorded message.

A lot of these people were doing that to him.

"Somebody, please!"

But he couldn't help her if she wouldn't tell him what he should look for.

Not that it mattered. A sick feeling deep in his belly told him that no matter how hard he looked, he wasn't going to find this poor woman's daughter.

"I'll go look for her," he told her. He turned and started up the side of the next hill. "You keep looking down here."

The woman continued to cry out for her daughter, as if he weren't there.

Eric felt awful running away. And he *would* remember her if he should happen across a lost-looking three-year-old girl. But he really didn't think there was anything he could do for her.

He couldn't help but wonder what happened to her daughter. Was she really lost somewhere? Could there really be another little girl wandering around this cursed property? A girl even smaller than the seven-year-old in the cupcake tee shirt?

He thought it more likely that the woman had died and left her three-year-old daughter behind. Now she was trapped here, confused and afraid.

The best he could do for her was to continue looking for a way to fix this broken world. Hopefully that would also set her and the rest of these desperate spirits free.

Maybe if they were able to move on, they'd all find peace.

As he crested the hill and started down the other side, he was startled by the sight of a large, hairy man leaning against the side of a tree, smoking a cigarette and wearing nothing but a pair of fishnet stockings and high heels.

"Hey," he said as if everything were perfectly normal. "How are ya?"

Eric hurried past him without slowing down. "Just fine, thank you."

"Glad to hear it."

That was weird, he thought. *That guy should really be wearing a scarf or something.*

In front of him, a much younger man wandered across his path wearing baggy shorts and a sleeveless tee shirt. He had a skateboard tucked under one arm and looked understandably lost. He didn't seem to have anything to say. He paid Eric no attention.

He watched the young man as he continued on, then glanced back, making sure nothing monstrous was following him in this darkness, but there was nothing there that he could see. When he turned his attention forward again, he caught a whiff of something foul and his gaze was drawn to a large, mossy-looking mound protruding from the surrounding brush. He had only a second or two to register that there was something unnatural about the shape before it lifted a great, shaggy head and snorted at him.

He jumped back, startled, and tripped himself. He fell onto his butt, then half-crawled, half-scooted across the forest floor.

The monster looked for all the world like a hippopotamus. It was about the same size and shape as those he'd seen at the zoo and on television, but it was covered in dense, shaggy fur.

It didn't attack him. It made no effort to get up. It didn't even make a sound. It merely lay there, staring at him with big, sleepy-looking black eyes.

Eric, on the other hand, got up as quickly as he could manage, ignoring the various pains in his battered body, and fled into the forest with a considerable amount of noise that he'd probably insist later were perfectly manly curses but were, in reality, little more than terrified, high-pitched whimpers.

He was starting to think that the only reason the universe kept choosing him for these jobs was because it enjoyed laughing at him.

He made his way over the next hill and down the other side, then stopped and leaned against the trunk of a towering pine tree as he scanned his surroundings for any more monsters, hidden or otherwise.

Instead of a monster, however, he found a man wearing a Green Bay Packers sock cap and a heavy sweater. "I'm so confused," he said. "Is there, like, an orientation or something? Like, what're we supposed to do?"

"Sorry," Eric told him.

The man turned and scanned the forest around him. "Is there at least, like…a *guidebook* or something? Like in *Beetlejuice?*"

"I don't…think that's how it…uh…works."

The man frowned and walked away.

Apparently death was a lot like life. There were no owners' manuals or tutorials. You were just shoved out the proverbial door and sent on your way. He hoped that all these experiences with the weird might at least prepare him a little better than the average person when it was his time to move on.

He watched the confounded man for a moment as he wandered off into the forest, then something above him drew his attention. A strange bird soared overhead, big, with a nearly three-foot wingspan. It was white and shimmering, with long feathers trailing from both its tail and the tips of its wings. He watched it glide off into the gloom until it was gone, then he looked back the way he came. "Spooky?" he called. "Where'd you go, you big hairball?" When he looked forward again, there was a scrawny, middle-aged man in an ugly, brown suit standing in front of him.

"Take the jewel!" he exclaimed. "Starve the lines! Close the streams!"

Eric stared at him for a moment, nodding. "Sure, buddy. Whatever you say."

"Worms!"

Again, he nodded. Where did these nutjobs keep coming from?

A loud cry drew his attention to the next hillside. He looked over to see Spooky sitting at the base of a fir tree, glaring back at him.

"Excuse me," he said. "I need to take this."

The scrawny, crazy man turned and watched him as he hurried away. "Break the machine!"

"Machine," confirmed Eric. "Got it. Thanks."

The cat lifted his head and let out a long series of loud and very irritable-sounding cries.

"Don't yell at *me*! You're the one who ran off. I can't see in the dark like you can!"

Spooky cried at him again. It was the sort of sound that Eric was sure probably translated to something obscene. Then he turned and hurried up the next hill.

"Slow down!" grumbled Eric. "How're you so *fast*? All you do is lay around the house and stuff your face!"

Of course, the cat wasn't *always* at home. He insisted on being let out and sometimes didn't come back for days at a stretch. Thinking about it now, he couldn't remember how long it'd been since he last saw him. At least four days, he thought. Had he set out for these woods as soon as Karen last opened the door for him? How long did it take him to get here?

And what other strange places did Spooky wander to?

He stopped and shined his light around. He'd lost sight of him again. But almost immediately, he heard a familiar cry from the darkness ahead of him. He continued on in that direction, and soon caught a glimpse of eyeshine staring back at him.

Then he caught sight of something moving off to his right. When he shined his flashlight over there, he saw a man walking. Or maybe he was more of a boy than a man. He was maybe nineteen or twenty at most, dressed in casual jeans and a white hoodie. He didn't seem to have anything to say. Like the lost skateboarder, he was minding his own business, just strolling around the dark woods in the snow with his hands stuffed in his pockets. But he was like the dancing girl. He was broken. His legs sort of glitched as he walked, bending in odd and unsettling ways. And although he wasn't moving his head, it seemed some-how disconnected, as if it were merely floating on his shoulders, unanchored to the rest of his body.

He turned his attention back to the path before him and re-alized that he'd lost sight of the cat again.

"Spooky?" He stopped and listened for an answer, but none came. He shined his light around, looking for that distinct eye-shine again, but the only thing his light touched besides the for-est was a young woman in baggy pajamas and fuzzy slippers.

She stood there a moment, staring back at him with a dazed, sleepy expression, and then turned and walked off without a word.

Maybe she just got up for a drink of water.

He dismissed her and shined his light the other way. "Spooky?"

When the cat finally answered, he was surprised to hear the sound of his cry from somewhere *above* him. He lifted his head and shined his light up into the branches above, expecting to see him staring down at him like Alice's Cheshire Cat. Instead, he found himself gaping at what appeared to be a tiny *house* hover-ing in the air above him.

For a moment, he couldn't seem to wrap his head around it.

Then he realized that he was looking at a *treehouse*.

It was very old, but it was well-made and he could tell that it was once an adorable little treehouse. It wasn't just a box with windows. It had a little porch with a railing, glass windows and a shingled, gable roof.

And yet, as he stared up at it, he felt an icy prickle wash over his skin.

Frightful memories came flooding back to him. Shadowy, floating corpses with empty, white eyes... Gory hands reaching out of puddles of blood... Sharp thorns piercing soft, fair skin...

Suddenly he was back inside that blood-soaked house in Haversby, cowering behind the couch after a deranged blood witch had tried to kill him.

That was where he heard the name Evancurt for the second time, screamed at him by the enraged spirit of the house's recently-murdered owner. But that wasn't the only message he was given during that encounter. Rupert Vashner's ghost had shrieked several things at him, none of which made any sense at the time.

But now five haunting words came back to him with fresh and eerie meaning...

Look for the floating house...

Chapter Thirteen

A floating house...

Eric stared up at it as the snow drifted down around him, the hair on the back of his neck standing on end.

It was like the broken girl, and the sign above the gate. This was clearly somewhere he was supposed to be. But...what was he here for?

From somewhere inside the treehouse came a loud and impatient mewl.

Eric stared up at it, shocked. "What?"

Again, Spooky cried at him.

"I'm not going up there! That thing's ancient!"

The cat jumped up onto the little porch railing and stared down at him with those big, shining eyes. He'd never heard such an angry-sounding "meow" as the one that came out of the little beast next.

"Do you think I'm stupid?"

Spooky stared down at him as if waiting for him to realize that he was, in fact, talking to a cat.

Eric ran his hand through his hair and glanced around. He knew the damned cat was right. This was obviously where he was supposed to go. This was how these things worked. And the longer he put it off, the more likely it was that something a lot worse than the pajama lady was going to show up and make things a lot harder than they needed to be.

He sighed and turned his light on the tree's trunk.

The treehouse was a fairly elaborate design, but the ladder was nothing more than lengths of two-by-fours nailed to the side of the tree.

He walked over and gave each one a firm tug. A few were

pretty rotten, but most of them still seemed fairly sturdy. Whether they'd actually hold his weight, though… He supposed he'd find out soon enough.

Trying his best to distribute his weight across multiple rungs and hopefully reduce his chances of plummeting back to the frozen ground, he slowly and carefully made his way up and into the opening in the treehouse floor.

Given his usual kind of luck, he was quite certain he was about to find some manner of supernatural horror or else a nest of angry raccoons and he couldn't decide which of the two options he'd prefer.

But the tiny little house seemed to be unoccupied. At least for the moment. The only signs of life were a collection of old wasp nests dangling from the low ceiling in a variety of sizes, from small to relatively horrifying, making him for the first time quite thankful that it was late January and not mid-summer.

Carefully, he climbed up the ladder and eased his weight onto the floor.

The entire structure creaked and groaned beneath him. He could almost feel it leaning to one side. It gave him a queasy sort of knot in his belly.

It'd be just his luck to survive all the insane things that'd tried to kill him since the weird started hijacking his life, just to end up being crushed in the falling ruins of a rotten treehouse.

The room wasn't quite tall enough for him to stand up in. He stood hunched over, careful to avoid the abandoned wasp nests (just because). He kept one hand on the topmost rung of the makeshift ladder, not quite daring to let go. With the other hand, he shined his flashlight around the room, taking in what little there was to be seen.

There was a small table with two equally small chairs pulled up to it. There was an old, stiff teddy bear with poseable limbs and dirty, somewhat mangy-looking fur sitting in one of the chairs and a dusty, miniature tea set on the table. There was also a small bookshelf mounted to one wall, with several moldy-looking books and a little ceramic pig. A simple dollhouse sat beneath one window with a handful of tiny furnishings. There was a ragged-looking doll and a limp, stuffed rabbit snoozing inside.

He looked out through the small doorway and onto the tiny little porch where a miniature, kid-sized rocking chair was slowly rotting away in the snow.

Spooky still sat on the porch railing, staring back at him with those big, yellow eyes.

"Okay, I'm here," he grumbled. "*Now* what?"

The cat didn't reply. He just sat there, looking at him as if he were stupid. And from his perspective, he probably was.

He glanced around again, taking it all in a second time. Why was he here? What was he supposed to get from this?

The tea set. The doll house. This treehouse belonged to a little girl. He couldn't help thinking of the desperate mother he encountered on his way here. But this was no place for a three-year-old. Did this belong to the little girl in the cupcake tee shirt?

That didn't seem right.

This treehouse wasn't built recently. These toys were hardly new. And didn't the pierced man tell him that none of the ghosts lost in this place had been here more than a few years. If the little girl who owned this stuff had lingered here...

He shuddered and pushed the horrid thought from his mind. He didn't want to think about little girls dying and haunting these woods. And he certainly didn't want to think about those same little girls being *devoured* by some awful thing from a broken world.

He looked at the rotting rocking chair. The moldy books. The abandoned toys.

This place was depressing. Why was he here? What was he supposed to find?

But a strange, shivery sensation began to creep through him then. Something in the air changed. The temperature seemed to drop even lower and a strange wind swirled around him, chilling him right through his clothes, making his teeth chatter.

The world, already dark, somehow dimmed around him. His head felt light. His knees trembled. He gripped the two-by-four rung of the ladder tighter to keep from toppling over.

Something was here.

A barely-heard voice whispered across the wind, but he couldn't make out the words it spoke.

He looked out onto the tiny porch. Spooky was just sitting there, watching him, utterly unfazed by whatever horror was crossing over inside the tiny house with him.

Again, the voice came. Louder this time. It was a woman's voice, shrill and desperate-sounding.

"*Perrine…*"

He shined his light around the room, expecting a ghostly shape to appear in the gloom. Instead, the doll fell out of the dollhouse on its own and thumped onto the floor.

He stared at it, his racing heart stuttering in his chest.

He wasn't particularly fond of dolls. They were high up on his list of things that creeped him out, right there with clowns and grown men who used the word "daddy." This particular doll appeared to be homemade, constructed with cloth and stuffing with a slightly crooked, hand-painted face and a little, yellow, hand-sewn dress.

He watched it for a moment, not trusting to take his eyes off it. When it didn't move, however, he became paranoid about the dark spaces that surrounded him. He shined his light around and froze when it fell on the bookshelf. Was the little, ceramic pig always looking at him? He couldn't be certain, but he thought it was facing the other way before.

Maybe he was just being paranoid.

"Perrine…"

He turned his light back onto the dollhouse, half-expecting the doll to be the one speaking, but the doll was gone.

He turned, sweeping the floor with the beam. Where did it go? What was happening? Why was he suddenly in a scene from *Poltergeist?*

He peered under the table and chairs, in the dark corners, even down at his own feet. Panic was welling up inside him. He didn't like this at all. Where'd the freaky thing go? He shined his light back at the dollhouse, only to find that the bunny was now missing, too.

Where had they gone? What were they up to?

"Perrine...is that you?"

"Who's there?" he asked. To his own ears, his voice sounded far too shrill.

The bookshelf fell off the wall, spilling its moldy books onto the floor and shattering the pig. The little teapot slid across the table and tumbled onto the floor as well. The chair with the bear tipped over onto its back. Outside, the rocking chair was rocking on its own.

This whole ordeal was one big horror movie cliché!

Spooky, meanwhile, never moved. He sat there, unfazed, staring back at him from the railing with an almost *bored* expression.

My cat's the devil, he thought.

Sweeping his light across the tiny room again, he finally found the doll and the bunny. They were sitting side-by-side on the windowsill, like best friends.

"Come home, Perrine..."

The voice seemed to be coming from behind him. He turned and shined his light at the wall.

Something was coming out of it. A dark, rippling shape passed over the old, splintered wood, as if something monstrous were trapped inside, struggling to break free.

Startled, he backed away from the wall and into the doorway leading onto the little porch. The treehouse creaked and groaned and leaned frightfully to one side.

The boards on the wall began to crack. A portion of it split open like a splintered mouth. It exhaled a plume of dust and moaned. "Perrine..."

He felt the treehouse moving beneath his feet. Was he falling? Was the whole thing sliding out of the tree?

No... It was the tree, itself, that was moving! It twisted and bent, cracking and splintering, making terrible groaning noises.

The treehouse tipped to one side. The dollhouse and the table and the clutter from the broken shelf slid across the floor. The doll and the bunny tumbled off the window sill. Then everything began to rotate as the trunk of the tree twisted around, tearing rusty nails out of aged lumber.

A portion of the roof tore upward with a terrible shriek of grinding nails and splintering wood, letting in a flurry of snow-flakes.

Somewhere beneath him, he heard a loud crack as some-thing gave way, then the floor beneath him seemed to drop a few inches. He had to grab the doorway to steady himself.

What the hell was happening?

Then a long, heavy sigh rolled through the space and he turned his light back on the shape that was writhing inside the wall. "You're not Perrine..." it said.

"Not Perrine..." echoed a second voice. He looked down to see the doll clinging to his foot, its freakish, lopsided face grinning up at him.

Startled, he kicked it, sending it flying into the wall.

"Not Perrine..." He looked behind him to see the bunny lying limp over the railing next to Spooky.

Spooky sniffed at it, curiously acknowledging the freaky thing's existence, but otherwise not reacting in the least.

He shook his head. "I'm *not* Perrine," he agreed. "I'm sor-ry?"

"Who are you?" asked the wall. The voice seemed to be sliding to the side, behind the trunk of the tree, toward the cor-ner of the room. Here and there, the wood split open and ex-haled a cold breath of dust and splinters.

Eric squeezed his eyes shut as the surreal absurdity of this situation sank in. A strangely knowing cat. A tiny house. And now a mysterious creature asking him who he was. Had he *literal-ly* wandered into Wonderland this time? He felt like Alice stand-ing before the caterpillar.

"I'm Eric," he replied, confused.

"Eric..." said the thing inside the wall.

"Eric..." repeated the bunny on the porch railing.

"Eric..." repeated the doll that he'd kicked across the room.

"Eric..." repeated a fourth voice that seemed to come from the vicinity of the fallen bookshelf. When he shined his light over there, he found the ceramic pig's broken head staring back at him, its small mouth slowly opening and closing, as if gasping for breath like a dying fish.

This was reaching unheard-of new levels of freaky.

"I've heard that name before..." said the wall.

"Heard it before..." echoed a new voice. He turned his light over to see the bear sitting upright on the floor next to the overturned chair, staring back at him.

"Well, it's not a very unusual name," he croaked.

"In my dreams..." said the wall, and the toys echoed the word.

"Dreams..."

"Dreams..."

"Dreams..."

"Dreams..."

A scratching noise caught his attention and he turned to find that a branch of the tree had curled downward and was grasping at the porch railing like a gnarled hand.

On the other side of the treehouse, the window broke and a second one reached through it and clawed at the wall.

"I get that a lot, actually," said Eric as he turned around, surveying his surroundings.

"Who are you?" asked the wall again.

"Who?"

"Who?"

"Who?"

"Who?"

He wasn't sure how to answer this question any better than he already had. He was Eric. That was pretty much all there was to it. Instead, he asked, "Who are *you*?"

He didn't expect an answer, but to his surprise, the wall said, "My name...?"

"Mine...?" asked the dolly.

"Name...?" asked the bear.

"My name...?" asked the broken pig.

"Who am I...?" asked the bunny.

Eric watched those reaching branches as they crept closer to him, seemingly searching for him. There were more, too. He could hear things scratching on the shingled roof above him.

"Bronwen…" sighed the wall.

Again, the other four voices echoed it.

"Bronwen," said Eric. "That's your name?"

A wave of vertigo passed through him, strong enough that he nearly fell over. He closed his eyes, his stomach lurching, and focused hard on not falling over.

When he opened his eyes again, everything was different. Gone were the cobwebs and the wasp nests. Gone was the age and the decay. The treehouse was new and clean. It was warm and bright. The sun was shining through the trees outside. And there was a young, blonde-haired girl sitting at the table with her back to him, having a tea party with a doll, a bear and a bunny that all looked decades newer than they'd looked a moment ago.

Then, just as quickly, the vertigo lifted. The warm sunlight vanished. Everything was old and rotten again.

He stood there, staring at the rotten table and the over-turned chair, trying to understand what he'd just seen. Did he just look into the past? Was it a fragment of someone's memory? What was happening to him?

And who was the little girl he just saw? Was that Bronwen? Was she the owner of this old treehouse? The voice didn't sound like that of a little girl, but perhaps that scene had been from sometime long before she became a voice in a treehouse wall. He looked back at the cracked and buckled boards and asked, "Did you die here, Bronwen?"

"No…" said the voice from the wall.

"No…" agreed the bunny.

"No…" said the bear.

"No…" said the shattered pig.

"No…" said the dolly.

Then the thing that called itself Bronwen was on the move again. It slid around the corner and across the wall, splintering the boards and opening up holes that now reminded him less of mouths than of empty, skeletal eye sockets.

"Did you die somewhere else on this property?" he pushed.

"Not…dead…" whispered the woman in the wall.

"Trapped…"

"You're trapped?"

"Changed…"

He turned and moved back toward the ladder as a third hand of branches crept in from above the doorway and felt its way across the ceiling. "What do you mean 'changed'? I don't understand."

"We're all trapped…" sighed Bronwen.

"All trapped…"

"All…"

"Everyone…"

"Trapped forever…"

Eric had no idea what the crazy woman trapped in the treehouse wall was talking about, but this was definitely one of the eeriest conversations he'd ever had.

"Please find her…" she begged.

"Please…"

"Please…"

"Please…"

"Please…"

"Find who?" he asked.

"Perrine…" said the bunny.

"Please…" begged the dolly.

"Find her…" said the bear.

"Find Perrine…" pleaded the pig.

"Please!" cried the woman in the wall. "Please help her!"

Out on the railing, Spooky cried out for the first time since this strangeness began. It was a troublingly alarming sound.

There was a loud crack beneath his feet and the treehouse suddenly lurched hard to one side.

It was time to go. He didn't think about it. He took hold of the ladder and began climbing back down to earth. But in his rush, one of the rungs broke in his hands and he fell the last few feet, landing hard on his back in the gathering snow.

Chapter Fourteen

He lay sprawled on the cold, hard ground, not moving, his body wracked with pain. He couldn't catch his breath. He managed only a long, agonized groan as he stared up at the treehouse that hovered in the gloom above him, wondering if it was about to break apart and come crashing down on top of him, burying him in falling debris.

But the seconds ticked by and the treehouse held to its branches. And even more impressively, no creeping tree hands or nightmare dollies or dismembered ceramic pigs followed him down.

Did any of that really just happen? It was so surreal that it already felt like a strange dream. Maybe the ladder broke on his way *up* and he'd been lying here this entire time, hallucinating all those strange and nightmarish things.

Spooky jumped up onto his chest and stared down into his face. "What're you doing just lying around?" his expression seemed to say. "Get off your lazy ass and do as the nice wall lady said!"

He groaned and rubbed at his eyes.

It wasn't a hallucination. Again, it wasn't just a serious head injury. He didn't have that sort of good luck. It was all real. The woman in the wall...Bronwen, she said her name was...she was looking for someone named Perrine. But who was Perrine?

He'd found no answers up there, only more questions. Why did everything always have to be such a riddle?

He opened his eyes and furrowed his brow at the cat. "Are you happy now?"

Spooky let out another angry and impatient-sounding cry.

"Just give me a minute," he snapped. He closed his eyes

again as he prepared himself for the unpleasant task of getting his feet back under him, and when he opened them, there was a woman bending over him, her face hovering directly above him.

"Are you okay?"

Eric let out a startled cry and sat up.

Spooky made an indignant sort of noise and jumped down off of him.

"I'm sorry," said the woman. "I didn't mean to scare you."

"It's okay," he grunted. "The cat *told* me to get up. That's what I get for not listening, I guess."

The woman appeared rightfully baffled. "Oh... Okay."

He stood up, grunting, and then turned and faced the woman. She looked to be in her early fifties and still quite pretty. She had a lovely face and kind eyes. His first impression was that she appeared far more sensible than the other residents of Evancurt, probably because she was the first person he'd seen since he arrived here who was actually dressed for the weather. She wore a fluffy, blue ski jacket, mittens, earmuffs and a warm sock hat with soft, blonde hair spilling out from under it. "Thanks, though," he said. It was nice of her to come check on him.

"You're welcome."

He rubbed at the back of his neck and looked up at the treehouse again. Had he found what he was supposed to find there? He wasn't sure what he was supposed to take away from that. A woman named Bronwen, who claimed to have been "trapped" and "changed," and who seemed to be desperately searching for someone...

Perrine...

She told him she wasn't dead, but how many of the spirits wandering these woods actually knew that they were ghosts? Maybe Bronwen was just confused. Maybe she couldn't handle the fact that she was dead and so she'd allowed herself to believe that she'd just been turned into something else.

The part about her searching for someone was perfectly familiar, after all. A lot of the ghosts here in Evancurt seemed to be desperately searching for something.

"You should probably stay away from places like that," said

the woman.

Eric glanced over at her, surprised. "Treehouses?" He *was* a bit old for them, he supposed.

The woman looked amused. "Well, yes. Probably. But I was talking about the twisted places."

"Twisted places?"

She lifted her face and looked up at the treehouse with a curiously superstitious expression. "There're lots of places like that around here. They're...*wrong*. It's like they're *alive*. The people trapped in those places aren't like the rest of us."

"Not like the rest of you?"

"They're not dead," she replied. "But they're not alive, either. They're...something else now. Something *awful*."

Eric felt a chill at these words. He turned and looked up at the treehouse again. He remembered the face in the wall. The living toys. The broken pig figurine. Was it possible that the thing that called itself Bronwen was telling the truth when it told him it wasn't dead? Was that encounter something far more than a ghostly manifestation?

He turned and looked at her. "Wait...so you know that you're..." He trailed off. He didn't want to say it aloud. He couldn't quite decide if it was rude. The last thing he wanted was to be insensitive.

"Dead?" she finished. "Of course."

He nodded. "Okay." That made things a little less awkward, he supposed.

"Not everybody accepts it, but I'm pretty sure everyone knows it." She leaned toward him, studying his face, her expression strangely sad. "If only somewhere deep inside them."

He didn't care for that look. It made him feel uncomfortable. He rubbed at the back of his aching neck and glanced up at the treehouse. He still expected something nightmarish to drop out of that hole and attack him again. "You said there were more places like this one?"

The woman nodded. "*Lots* of places," she said again.

"And they're the same as this one?"

"More or less."

Wonderful. He supposed Spooky would drag him to every one of them before the night was through.

But when he looked down at his feet, he found that the cat had vanished again. He turned and scanned the woods around him, but he was nowhere to be seen. "Where'd he go?"

The woman glanced around. "Who?"

"My cat. He ran off."

"Cat?"

"Yeah. The one that was just here? He was sitting on me when you first showed up?"

She tipped her head to one side, baffled. "You think that was a cat?"

He turned and frowned at her. "Didn't it...*look*...like a cat?"

She turned and looked out at the forest. "Not really..."

He ran his hand through his hair again. "I mean, I know it's not an *ordinary* cat, but..."

"There's nothing ordinary about that creature."

Spooky first came to him in Hedge Lake and did much like he was doing tonight. He led him through the forest, taking him places he needed to go. He was strangely knowing for a cat. And he even saved his life before that night was over. He came home with him and spent most of his time being a typical, lazy cat. Sometimes, however, when the weird called out to him, Spooky had a way of turning up in the most improbable of places and helping him out again.

"Can you tell me what it is?" he asked, hopeful.

But the woman shook her head. "I don't know what it is. But it's something very...*profound*."

"I see," he replied, although he didn't. Not even a little. "Okay." He stretched his still-aching back and looked out at the forest around him. "Well, *whatever* he was, he was the one showing me where to go, so...any idea how to get back to civilization from here?"

The woman pointed at the trees behind him. "There's a building just a little ways in that direction," she told him. "But I wouldn't go there. It's not safe."

He wondered if she was pointing to the same building he just came from, but didn't bother asking. If it was, at least he'd be able to find the road and continue on from there without getting lost. "I don't really have the luxury of sticking to safe places," he told her. "But thank you."

He turned and walked in the direction she'd indicated.

The woman walked with him. "My name's Peggy, by the way."

He glanced back at her, a little surprised. None of the other ghosts had introduced themselves. Unless you counted Bronwen, he supposed, which he wasn't sure about, since she apparently wasn't among the dead *or* the living. "I'm Eric," he replied.

"You're kind of profound, too, aren't you?"

He glanced at her. "I guess so. I mean, I don't really *feel* profound in any way. But I keep ending up in places like this." He gazed out at the dark, misty forest around him. "So *something's* going on, I guess."

"There's something special about you. You're different from the rest of us. You're not bound to this place."

He nodded. "Yeah that's what the last guy said." Once again, he was fairly sure it was because he was still alive. More and more, he had the feeling that these people thought he was one of them.

Something moved in the trees above him and he paused to shine his light up into the branches. But there was nothing there that he could see. A squirrel, perhaps?

But then a black shape took flight from a high branch. Another crow.

"They say crows are harbingers of death," said Peggy as she looked up at the disappearing bird.

Eric didn't reply. He never used to buy into that kind of superstition, but these days he hesitated to say that anything was impossible.

He pushed past some low-hanging branches and then paused and looked around. The trees in this area were covered in that slimy, black mold he found under the cabin, in the room with that monstrous eyeball. He could smell that metallic, sulfury stench. It hung heavy on the air here.

"The forest is sick," explained the woman. "All of the forest in this place is sick, but especially out here. It's rotting."

He shined his light deeper into the woods and saw that the mold quickly grew more dense in that direction. It covered almost every surface. It dripped from the trees.

"We shouldn't stay here. It's not safe. Not even for us."

Not at all eager to spend any more time than necessary in the "rotten" neck of the woods, he nodded and moved on, past the moldy trees and back into healthier parts of the forest. But here he paused again.

Someone somewhere was crying. And it wasn't a quiet sort of weeping, either. It was the sound of someone sobbing uncontrollably.

He pushed on, ignoring the sound. There didn't seem to be anything he could do for anyone anyway. But as he walked, he realized that he was getting closer to the sound, and soon he caught sight of her. She was young, a college girl, maybe, with long, curly black hair. She was wearing a short, black party dress and torn stockings with no shoes. She was sobbing into her hands and wandering blindly through the woods, almost staggering.

"She's *always* like that," said Peggy. "She wanders all over the place, wailing and crying and blubbering. She doesn't seem to see or hear anyone around her. The poor thing."

"I saw others like that," he said, remembering the weepy brute who was blubbering about someone pretty and the woman who was searching for her daughter.

But the woman shook her head. "The others come and go. But this one never rests. Not for a single moment. It never, *ever* ends."

What a sad thought. He stopped and watched her as she stumbled across their path, wondering what could've happened to make someone sob so long and so hard in death.

And now that he was watching her, it occurred to him that he'd heard that sobbing before. It was while he was making his way toward the property gate, before he saw the broken girl. He didn't see her then, but he heard someone crying in the woods around him. Remembering it now, he realized that this was the *same* sobbing.

If he could find whatever was wrong with this place, whatever broke the world, and fix it, would all these spirits be free? Would the poor, miserable girl be able to escape her intolerable sorrow? Could she find peace if she were only allowed to move on from this terrible place? He hated to think that the poor girl was doomed to sob like that for all eternity.

But there was nothing he could do for her now. Unhappy, he continued on.

But as he passed behind her, the girl suddenly gasped and turned. She stared at him through her splayed fingers, her eyes red and swollen, makeup running down her face.

"Oh..." said Peggy. "This is new."

The girl turned to face him, slowly lowering her hands. She never stopped crying. Tears streamed endlessly down her cheeks. Her mouth was drawn into a miserable grimace. Her nose was running. They weren't pretty tears. This was definitely what Karen called "ugly crying."

He stood there, frozen, unsure what he should say or do.

She took a step toward him, her breath hitching, a long, wailing sob escaping her. If there was something she wanted to say, she couldn't stop crying long enough to form the words.

He'd never heard such pitiful bawling in his entire life.

"Do you know her?" asked Peggy.

"No. Or...I don't *think* I do... I mean...?" He shook his head. Why would he know her? And yet, it did almost seem as if she recognized him... But then again, the woman standing beside him and the pierced man had both been capable of seeing that he was different. Maybe that was all this was. Maybe she sensed that he was alive and dared to hope that it meant he could help her somehow.

Although...he wasn't sure what he was supposed to do for her.

The girl took two more steps toward him, then stumbled and fell to her knees at his feet with a horrible, heartbreaking moan. Startled, he knelt beside her, taking hold of her shoulders.

She reached out and clutched at his torn jacket, wailing and sobbing.

"Hey, take it easy," he told her. The words felt utterly lame, but he wasn't sure what else to say. What an awkward situation… "It's okay. I'm…" He glanced up at Peggy, lost, but she offered him no advice. "I'm…here to fix everything," he decided. "So you won't have to cry anymore, okay?"

But the girl cried anyway.

Chapter Fifteen

She wouldn't stop crying. Several minutes passed as he knelt over the girl and her endless sobbing only went on and on. It was just as Peggy said, she seemed to be utterly inconsolable.

Eventually, she let go of his jacket, curled herself into a ball and lay wailing and blubbering on the snowy ground in front of him.

His heart ached for the poor girl, but he had no idea how to make her stop crying.

"There's nothing you can do," said Peggy as she stood over them. "She's lost in her own despair." She shook her head and again said, "Poor thing."

But he didn't want to just walk away. "I can't leave her here like this." It seemed *cruel*. Shouldn't he at least pick her up and carry her somewhere safe? It was so cold out here, and she wasn't even wearing shoes.

"She'll get up and wander off again. She always does."

He looked up at her, surprised by the lack of compassion in the woman's words. He was just supposed to leave her lying there in the snow, sobbing? She was in pain. She was *suffering*.

"She's dead. Like all of us. She doesn't feel the cold. Her pain is *inside*, and there's nowhere you can take her to escape that."

He looked down at the girl again. "Still..." Dead or not, she was still a human being. She deserved better than "just leave her." He couldn't bear to walk away like that.

"Did you mean what you said?" asked Peggy. "That you're here to fix everything?"

He didn't take his eyes off the girl. "I did."

She considered him for a moment, and then said, "It's a

nice thought. Making everything all better again. You *are* different from the rest of us. I can feel it. But I don't know how anyone can fix what's wrong with this place. I don't think it's something that *can* be fixed. It's like there's something wrong with the whole *world* out here."

"There is. It's broken."

She stared at him for a moment, as if trying to decide whether he was making a joke. When she saw that he was being serious, she said, "But you really think you can fix it?"

"It's why I'm here," he sighed. "It's *always* why."

"Huh," she said.

"It's complicated."

"I guess it is." She looked down at the girl as she pondered his words. "Okay then. I'll stay with her until she wanders off again. You go on ahead. Do whatever it is you do."

He looked up at her, unsure what to say.

She pointed. "That way. But be careful. I meant it when I said it's dangerous. There's something nasty inside that building."

He stared at her for a moment, then turned and looked in the direction she'd pointed. Was it his imagination, or could he already see something looming behind the trees over there? Finally, he nodded and rose to his feet. "Thank you."

"Just go on," she urged.

He glanced down at the girl once more, then he turned and continued on alone through the woods.

But the sounds of the miserable girl followed him for a long time, tearing at his heart. Was it just the fact that these poor people were trapped here, with no hope of moving on? Did such a thing leave them psychologically imprisoned, followed here by all the regrets of the lives they left behind? Or was there something more to it?

He remembered the weeping brute telling him how pretty someone was and how much he wanted to see her just one more time…the nicely-dressed man desperately searching the floor for something he'd dropped…the traveler forever seeking gate five…the desperate mother crying for her lost daughter… What made these ghosts so much different from those he encountered in Hedge Lake?

Slowly, the winter branches peeled back, revealing more and more of the ominous structure before him, and soon it became clear that it wasn't the same building from before. This one was much taller, more square, with narrow slits of windows circling its upper half and a huge door that looked like something that belonged on an airport hangar.

Movement to his left caught his attention and he turned to see a muscular man in workout apparel stretching, as if preparing for his nightly run.

Then he heard someone whimpering behind him. He turned around to find a flabby, middle-aged man stumbling along, his face pale, doughy and damp with sweat. He kept opening and closing his hands in front of him, as if he couldn't decide what to do with them. When he caught sight of Eric, he stopped walking and stared back at him. "There's something out there!" he gasped. "It keeps following me!" He turned and looked behind him. "I can hear it every time I stop…" His eyes grew wide with fear and he stumbled onward, exhausted but terrified. "It won't leave me alone!" he sobbed. "It's coming to get me!"

Eric watched as the man hurried off into the woods, horrified. *They say it* eats *us*, he thought, recalling the words of the pierced man. *It's what they all say. Just before they disappear.* The memory made him shudder.

His gaze drifted toward the sounds of the sobbing girl, whose miserable voice he could still hear between gusts of snowy wind.

Whatever was happening here, he had to stop it.

But could he really do it? He didn't understand what it was that was happening. He had no idea where to begin.

When he looked forward again, his path was suddenly blocked by an enormous man in old sweatpants, untied sneakers and a holey tee shirt with a Batman symbol emblazoned across the chest. He stopped, surprised, and stared up at him. The man's face was round and pudgy, with a large, lower lip that was pushed out as if he were pouting. His hair was blond and uncombed and sticking out in every direction.

For a moment, the two of them stood there like that. Then the giant reached out with one, pudgy arm and made a grab for his head.

Eric ducked and darted around him with a startled, "Whoa!"

What the hell was that?

He backed away from the handsy giant, expecting him to give chase, but he only turned slowly around and watched him as he moved away, with no indication of following.

There was something familiar about this guy. Was he the presence he felt in the woods when he first arrived? The large, shadowy, reaching figure that had appeared behind him while he was looking out into the forest and then vanished before he could get a real look at him? He couldn't say exactly why, but he felt certain that they were one and the same.

But as he backed away, he felt a hand close on his shoulder from behind. He twirled around, startled, but there was no one there. He turned to face the handsy giant again, but he, too, had vanished. He was alone again. Or so it seemed.

A voice drifted to him on the wind, soft, rasping, almost *hissing*: "Was it *you*?"

Eric turned around again. "Who's there?"

But there was no one. The woods were empty.

"It was, wasn't it?" came the phantom voice again.

Again, he turned, shining his light into the forest.

"It was *you*…"

"Okay…" said Eric. He took a step backward. He had a seriously bad feeling about this conversation.

"*You* did it…"

"I didn't do anything to anybody!" he said, and almost immediately remembered the foggy man. And then there was the cowboy and Pink Shirt. Jonah Fettarsetter in Hedge Lake… All those blood witches two summers ago…

Well, he'd never done anything to anyone who didn't *deserve* it.

Don't forget all the students you've failed over the years, offered his morbid imagination, quite unnecessarily.

"They earned those grades!" he muttered back at himself.

He took another step back, suddenly wondering if anyone he knew could've ended up here. It was scary enough dealing with the ghosts of strangers, he certainly didn't want to think about anyone here having a *personal* grudge against him.

"You…" growled the voice.

Something stirred in the shadows. A faint figure began to take shape in front of him. It was a man, he realized. But no ordinary man. He was extremely tall and thin, almost seven feet, he thought, like a towering skeleton dressed all in black. His black hair was long, thin and greasy. His eyebrows were great, bushy, scowling things creased over huge, bloodshot eyes. His lips were pressed so tightly together that he didn't appear to even have a mouth.

His expression was nothing short of scathing hatred.

Eric continued to back away from the man. "Nope. I definitely would've remembered you if it was me. Trust me."

"YOU!"

The furious man darted forward with impossible speed.

Eric never saw him move. But he felt it. It seemed to hit him everywhere at once, as if he'd been hit not by any kind of man, but by a *wall*, knocking him backward.

He landed hard on his back, several feet from where he was standing, the breath knocked out of him, his body wracked with pain. He lay there for several seconds, dazed and groaning, unable to make himself move. Then, slowly, he rolled onto his belly and pushed himself onto his hands and knees, grunting and blinking away the tears that had sprung to his eyes.

Was his nose bleeding? It felt like his nose was bleeding.

He sat up on his knees and looked up, only to find the man's enraged face hovering directly over him. Those great, bloodshot eyes were staring down at him.

He opened his mouth and found only a startled squeak where his voice should've been.

"You…" the ghost snarled, leaning closer. "You…"

Eric stared back at him.

"You're *not* him!"

And with that, the man vanished.

Eric blinked up at the empty space where that monstrous face was hovering only a second before. Then he turned and looked around at the silent forest. "*Yeah*," he croaked. "I *told* you it wasn't me." Slowly, he staggered to his feet and then turned and looked around. "Don't worry about it," he called out as he rubbed his sore nose and then shined his light onto his fingers. There *was* blood, but only a little. "No apology necessary. Honest mistake, I'm sure."

He turned and shined his light around, trying to remember which direction he was going when that handsy giant surprised him.

He was pretty sure it was this way…

Maybe…

He stumbled onward, his eyes peeled for any more creepy surprises, hoping that he hadn't gotten himself turned around and lost.

But after another few minutes, he finally stepped out of the woods and into an overgrown clearing surrounding a mysterious-looking building.

Here, he stopped, his gaze washing over the structure, wondering what manner of horrors he was going to find here. *There's something nasty inside that building*, he thought, remembering Peggy's words of warning.

He also wondered how he was going to get inside. He saw no way to open that enormous door from out here, and even if there *was* a handle, he wasn't sure he could lift such a thing. It looked quite heavy.

Movement in the corner of his eye drew his gaze to the far edge of the clearing where a small herd of very strange animals was gathered. They looked a little like very thin goats, but they had six-foot-long stilt-like legs covered with sharp-looking, bristling horns and equally long, flexible necks that allowed them to reach all the way to the ground. Their fur was various shades of gray in an odd pattern of overlaid stripes.

He stood there a moment, watching them as they slowly moved off into the deeper woods.

He felt like he should be used to this sort of thing by now, but it all still felt so surreal. It was as if he'd stepped into another world.

Then a rock flew out of the darkness and struck him on his shoulder. He looked over to see the boy in the black hoodie disappearing into the woods and shooting a hateful look over his shoulder.

"Don't think I won't kick your ass, kid!" he shouted after him.

He was still staring into the darkness of those woods, making sure the kid wasn't simply circling back to take another shot at him, when he felt a small hand close around his gloved fingers. He looked down, surprised to find the little girl in the cupcake tee shirt staring up at him again.

"Oh. There you are."

As before, she didn't say a word. She only stared at him with those big, blue eyes.

Asking her where she went would clearly be a waste of time, so he simply squeezed her hand and turned his attention back to the building in front of him.

It was such a strange design, with those windows circling only the upper half. They were very narrow, but very tall, spaced close together so that they almost looked like prison bars from down here. And yet the lower half of the building had no windows at all. Except for that enormous door, there was nothing but brick on the two sides he could see from this angle.

The clearing he was standing in looked like it used to be an open parking area. There was a dirt drive circling around to the right. He decided to follow it to see if there was another door. Surely there must be a normal, human-sized entrance somewhere.

But as he neared the corner of the building, he had to stop as a fat little creature hopped across the driveway in front of them. It moved like a very large toad, but was furry and made a strange, strangled sort of squeaking sound.

He watched as it hopped off into the forest, then glanced down at the girl, who simply stared back up at him, as if creatures like that happened by now and again and were nothing out of the ordinary.

He continued on. When he rounded the corner, he found no more doors, but there were several metal boxes mounted to the outside wall. They were square, about three feet across and about four feet off the ground. Three of those heavy lead pipes, like the ones he found sticking out of the ground when he first arrived, protruded from the sides of each box, curved ninety degrees straight down and then disappeared into the earth. Two arching lengths of that thick, gold cable connected the top of one box to the next.

He examined them as he walked past them, taking note that there didn't appear to be any panels to access whatever was inside them. Was this building like the last one? Was it filled with glass walls and cables and vats of mysterious liquids?

As he approached the corner of the building, he glanced up to see several heavy power lines stretched between the roof of the building and a utility post on the other side of the driveway.

A new thought crossed his mind as he stared up at them. Could this place be some sort of high-tech power plant? An experimental energy facility? It almost made sense. Wasn't that how scientists were always breaking the world in science fiction movies?

But as he pondered the idea, the girl tugged on his arm. He looked down, distracted, and she pointed out into the forest.

He looked up to see a wendigo standing in the gloom at the edge of the forest.

At the same time, the wendigo looked up and saw him, as well.

Chapter Sixteen

There were things Eric had done that he wasn't proud of, no matter how necessary it might've been. He wasn't proud of letting the foggy man open that jar in the room at the bottom of the cathedral. He wasn't proud of sacrificing the man in the pink shirt to the jinn that was trapped in the old, unseen schoolhouse. He definitely wasn't proud of his victory against Sissy Dodd in Illinois or the yellow-eyed witch in Chicago. He wasn't even proud of punching that annoying Owen kid in Hedge Lake (even though everyone agreed he had it coming). And now he'd just added to that list a particularly vulgar string of profanities that he'd just blurted out in front of an impressionable young girl.

Later, if he survived all this nonsense, he'd probably have to sit down and think hard about who the real monster was here, but right now he had other things to worry about.

The wendigo sprang to life in an instant, its limp body jolted awake as if someone had shocked it, its hideous head snapping up. No longer did it drag its feet along the ground. It was no Olympic track star—it had a strange, lopsided sort of lurching gait—but it was plenty fast enough to overtake him. All it needed was time.

Clinging to the girl's hand, Eric rushed around the corner to the front of the building. The main entrance was there, near the far corner, a normal-sized door for normal-sized people.

This was the front of the building, facing the overgrown road. He wasn't entirely sure how far he was from the last building, or if there were any other structures between here and there, but he was confident that he would've made his way here on his own sooner or later. Before Spooky showed up and led him into the woods to meet Bronwen-the-freaky-treehouse-wall-lady and her parroting toys, his intention was to simply follow the road and see where it took him.

He ran past another of those strange, outhouse-sized metal boxes and around what he thought at first glance was a large flagpole, until he noticed that there were a dozen or more heavy cables running between it and several metal boxes mounted to the wall of the building.

He dared a look over his shoulder just as the wendigo rounded the corner behind them. They didn't have much of a lead on the thing. If they reached the door and found it locked, he wasn't sure there was going to be time for them to find another escape route.

Looking forward again, he found a pasty-looking man in a stark-white dress shirt and a black tie standing there, clutching a bible to his chest.

"Excuse me, sir, but may I have a moment of your time?"

"You're kidding, right?" blurted Eric as he rushed past the man without pausing.

The man turned and called after him, "Heaven can't open its gates to you if you don't take time to accept the truth!"

"That's pretty much the idea, yeah!"

The door wasn't locked. In fact, as he approached it, he realized that it wasn't even closed all the way. It stood ajar, as if waiting for him. But he didn't have time to consider whether that was a good thing or a bad thing. He rushed inside and slammed and locked it behind him.

Almost immediately, the wendigo crashed against the other side. Apparently, *it* didn't want to stop and talk about Jesus right now, either.

He nudged the girl toward the back of the room, shielding her, half-expecting the door to fly off its hinges.

Why did it have to be wendigos? He *hated* wendigos. Why couldn't it be imps again? He'd handled imps before. They were a pain, but at least were small. He'd actually managed to kill a few of those with his bare hands.

But then he remembered that sometimes imps turned into bigger, stronger, *meaner* imps, and he changed his mind.

He glanced behind him to find a second door, leading deeper into the building. He didn't waste time wondering what might be waiting on the other side. Two doors between them and that monster were better than one. If the thing *did* break through, hopefully it'd be too stupid to figure out where they'd gone.

"Come on," he said, urging the girl through ahead of him. Then he slammed it behind them.

Only now did he take a moment to look around.

They were standing on a metal walkway overlooking a deep, gloomy darkness from which a *jungle* appeared to be growing.

At least, "jungle" was the first word that came to mind. It took only a single look to realize that this was like no jungle on earth. In fact, no part of it that he could see was *green*. But he wasn't sure what else he could call it. There were tall, brown, twisting stalks bristling with wicked, three-foot-long thorns rising up from the gloom and reaching for the faint light of those high windows. Large, grayish-black, furry-looking trees with swollen, drooping branches crowded among them, as did white, towering columns that looked less like plants than the giant, skeletal remains of strange, alien worms. And all of these things were entangled in the strangling embrace of an enormous web of gnarled vines covered in black, blister-like growths. And pink, fleshy tendrils dangled down from the highest branches, weighted by large, slimy-looking sacs that looked more like human *stomachs* than he cared to think too much about.

He grasped the railing and shined his light down at the space below them. Queer shapes loomed in the darkness there, a low canopy of dense branches concealed whatever was at the very bottom.

He glanced around, confused. How did this even work? This place wasn't a greenhouse. Even with all those tall, narrow windows circling the upper portion of the building, there shouldn't be enough sunlight to support this much plant growth. It also wasn't much warmer in here than it was outside, not nearly the sort of tropical temperature that should support a variety of flora this exotic.

Then he remembered the plant growing in the building with

all the glass and cables, the one the pierced man went out of his way to show him. He said it grew there without any light or water, like some kind of fungus.

Were all these plants like that? And did that one in the other building come from here? And if there was a whole building dedicated to these freaky things, then what was the point in keeping one over there?

And why did he keep insisting on trying to understand any of this nonsense?

The walkway circled around the office they passed through on their way here, to a set of metal stairs leading down into that dark, alien jungle.

He could think of at least ten things he'd rather do right now than go down and see what horrors were waiting in a place like this, but the only other option was to go back the way they came. And seeing as how he didn't want to have his face eaten by that wendigo or to talk about Jesus, he decided to head downstairs and get it over with.

As he walked toward the staircase, he glanced down at the girl still clutching his hand. "Do you know what's in this building?"

She looked up at him with those big eyes and nodded. It was a very small nod, barely more than a wobble.

"Any chance you could fill me in before we get there?"

She just stared at him and gave her shoulders a shy shrug.

"Didn't think so." He glanced over at those weird, towering plants. "Whatever it is…I'm not going to like it, am I?"

There was nothing shy or ambiguous about her reply this time. She shook her head. A definitive and unmistakable "no."

He reached the steps and paused there, shining his light down into that darkness. It went down farther than a single flight of stairs. He could see nothing down there but shadows and a few creeping vines and branches coiling around the steps and railing.

Again, he glanced at the girl. "Maybe you should stay up here," he suggested.

But the girl gave her head a hard shake, sending her long

hair whipping back and forth, and then crowded against him again, squeezing his arm as if she expected him to yank it free.

"Okay," he relented. "Just a thought." It didn't matter anyway. *She* didn't seem to be in any immediate danger. The pierced man told him that the wendigos ignored the ghosts. That was probably true of pretty much everything here.

He stood there, allowing himself just a few more seconds to enjoy this moment of temporary peace and safety, knowing damn well that something horrible was going to be waiting for him down there in that creepy, alien darkness.

Then, with the girl still clinging to his hand, he began to descend.

Chapter Seventeen

The floor was *much* farther down than it looked. The stairs descended the entire length of the building's front wall and then turned and continued down the next, sinking deeper and deeper into the shadows of the strange, alien forest.

And the deeper down he went, the more unnatural everything became. The strange plant life climbed the walls down here, enveloping more and more of the stairs as he approached the floor, until the walls didn't resemble smooth concrete anymore and he no longer seemed to be descending metal steps at all, but a steep, sloping tangle of vines and thorny branches that threatened to trip him and send him tumbling all the way to the bottom.

Soon, he began to feel that he wasn't inside a building at all, but descending deep into some strange and long-forgotten, prehistoric world. His unhelpful imagination had no trouble dredging up terrible images of gigantic, flesh-eating creatures stalking him as he made his way ever downward.

The air smelled funny here, too. There was a pungent, sour sort of odor in the air. In spite of all the plant life, it lacked any kind of freshness. And it felt *wrong* somehow. It was a little harder to breathe, as if he really were walking through the suffocating humidity of a sweltering jungle, but without any of the heat.

He glanced up, but by now he couldn't see the faint glow of those high windows through all the branches above him. Darkness had completely swallowed him. Only his flashlight pushed it back, and even that only a little.

He couldn't help being reminded of the cathedral he found at the end of his first journey in the weird. That, too, had been a long, spiraling descent into darkness. Except there he'd at least been able to see the sky the entire time, even if that distant sunlight didn't seem to reach all the way down to him.

This time, however, he wasn't surrounded by wide-open darkness. This darkness was claustrophobic. And there were strange things emerging from the gloom with every step he took.

From the branches above him dangled tufts of white, stringy stuff that looked eerily like human hair. And large, fleshy growths that looked like giant warts crowded the path at his feet, ranging in size from a few inches in diameter to almost two feet. And there were strange, shiny flowers sticking up from the dirt that looked eerily like slimy, impaled brains.

It was getting harder and harder to avoid touching anything. He had to duck under branches, step over creeping vines and squeeze past enormous, cactus-like growths with painful-looking clusters of sharp needles that his horrid imagination immediately convinced him were full of vile, flesh-melting toxins.

He was beginning to wonder if he was going to descend all the way into whatever hideous, alien world all these things came from when, at long last, his light finally reached the bottom, revealing a mostly-buried stone walkway separating the wall on the left from the earthen jungle floor on the right.

He was shining his light around, trying to seek out any immediate signs of danger, when the girl suddenly pulled at his hand, jolting him to a stop. He looked down at her, confused, then looked up to find a bristly, cone-shaped thing dangling in front of him, mostly hidden behind an ashy-colored, fern-like leaf. One more second, and he would've hit his head on it. And somehow, he didn't think the girl would've bothered pulling on him like that just to keep him from bumping his head. He glanced down at her again and pointed at it. "Don't touch?"

She nodded.

He looked up and considered it. Those spiny bristles sticking out of it… "Poison?" he wondered.

She shook her head.

"Worse than poison?"

She nodded.

"Okay then," he said in a slightly-too-high-pitched voice,

glancing around to make sure there weren't any more of the prickly things hiding in the surrounding branches. "Don't touch the scary death cones. Got it."

He ducked under it, careful to give it as much room as possible, and then crept down the last few steps and looked around.

There wasn't a lot of room down here. If those cone things turned out to be a common sight in this thicket, or if there were other dangerous things growing down here, then he was going to have to be extra careful about where he put his hands and really watch his head. And there were probably things down here he didn't want to step on, too, if he could avoid it.

Everything was *very* overgrown. He could tell that there'd once been open walkways snaking through the room. He could still see the shadows of them, like old footpaths that'd nearly become reclaimed by the forest.

How long had it been since anyone tended to this room? He remembered the calendar in the old office, the one turned to April of 1971. Had it really been that long? It didn't seem possible. After forty-seven years, wouldn't these buildings be much more deteriorated? It seemed far more likely that someone had simply stopped turning the pages on that particular calendar. The pierced man told him that he hadn't seen anyone like him set foot here in years, but also that he hadn't been here all that many years, himself. And for that matter, maybe he was lying. Or he could've simply been mistaken.

The fact was that he still knew almost nothing about this place.

From somewhere in the dense foliage came a long, low groan. He stopped and listened. His first thought was that sometimes trees made noises like that in the wind. But then he remembered that he was indoors and that there wasn't any wind.

The girl squeezed his hand and pressed herself against him again.

"Come on." He walked on, following the wall, taking advantage of the wider spaces, hoping to circle the probably-terrifying tangle of alien jungle, but it didn't take long until he found this path blocked by a thicket of thorny, tangled branches.

This was no good. He still couldn't risk going back. Even if the wendigo had given up and wandered off again, the stupid things moved so slowly when they weren't pursuing prey that it almost certainly couldn't have gone very far.

Besides, it probably wasn't an accident that he was here right now. Chances were good that he was supposed to find something inside this building.

He turned and shined his light into a narrow path leading into the shadowy depths of the jungle floor. Was it possible to navigate something like that? The building wasn't exactly enormous, but it was still quite large. It could be an impossible labyrinth in there. And it was no-doubt filled with dangers ranging from the mysterious bristly cone things to more wandering wendigos.

Then, as if just to prove that it could always be worse, his flashlight flickered, threatening to go out again. He gave it a shake which seemed to fix it again and then sighed. This wasn't going to be fun at all. He just knew it.

He looked down at his hand, suddenly realizing that it was empty. The girl in the cupcake tee shirt had gone again. He turned and swept his surroundings with his flashlight, but she was nowhere to be seen. And he didn't really expect to see her. She didn't let go of his hand. He would've felt it if she had. It was just like last time. She simply wasn't there anymore. She'd vanished into thin air, like the phantom that she was.

He stood there a moment, wondering how he should feel. On one hand, this was no place for a child, dead or otherwise. As frightened as she always seemed to be, there was no reason for her to be following him around. He was *always* finding himself in scary situations. There was no way she was going to be any less scared being at his side than off on her own. But on the other hand, he also wasn't all that thrilled about the idea of wandering around in this freaky, alien anti-greenhouse all by himself. The girl might be silent, but she did give him a little extra courage, if only because he felt like he should look out for her. Plus, if she hadn't been here, who knew what that freaky cone thing would've done to him. As much as he might pretend that he was protecting her, it was perfectly clear that it was *she* who'd been protecting *him* this whole time.

He stared down at his hand for a moment, then sighed again and turned his attention to the narrow path that lay before him.

Chapter Eighteen

He wasn't very far into Evancurt's alien jungle room, but he was already fairly certain that it wasn't going to rate very high on his list of places he'd like to return to someday. It was impossible to avoid touching all of the plants. He had to push past drooping vines and low-hanging branches. Clumps of those warty growths crowded the path in places. And the rest of the floor was littered with strange, sprawling things that seemed determined to snag his shoes and trip him.

He'd never in his life been so thankful to be wearing long sleeves and gloves.

Strange clumps of coiling, waxy-looking weeds that sort of looked like grass from a distance, but up close looked more like a crude mockery of it, were growing among a tangle of limp, greenish-black leaves that didn't seem so much to grow as simply lay upon the ground like the shriveled tentacles of some dead, deep-sea monstrosity, forcing him to tiptoe around them.

And every few steps he came across something new and even more alien-looking. There were fat, yellow fruits that oozed a thick, white substance from their tapered ends, blood-red flowers that looked eerily like long, bloody hands and spiky, open-ended pods that looked like gaping mouths filled with sharp, pointy teeth.

Up close, none of the plants looked like they belonged on this planet. In addition to the fact that there was very little green to be found, many of these things didn't look like plants at all. They were less like wood and bark than skin and bones.

Again, his flashlight flickered, this time going completely dark. He banged it against his hand again, but it didn't want to come back on. He cursed and gave it a hard shake, then slapped it harder against his gloved palm before it finally lit up again.

This was not an ideal situation. The last thing he wanted was to be caught in the dark. And the flashlight seemed to be gradually becoming less and less reliable. Maybe the batteries were sitting too long in the glovebox. So much for planning ahead, he supposed. But he could do nothing about it now, so he turned his attention back to his surroundings and hoped the stupid thing didn't die on him when he really needed it.

He had his doubts when he entered this nightmare that he'd actually be able to get anywhere on these overgrown paths. He'd assumed that these alien things had long ago crowded completely together and that he'd only end up killing time while he waited for the wendigo outside to wander off again. But he didn't have to go very far before he discovered a large, open area hidden within the jungle. Here, he found a strange landscape filled with what at first glance appeared to be bedsheets hung out to dry on clotheslines, but were, in fact, another part of the jungle. He wasn't entirely sure if these were giant leaves or gargantuan flower petals. They were a bluish-white color, fine and delicate, silky. He'd never seen such a thing before, or even imagined anything like it.

The ground, meanwhile, was spotted with more of those ugly, wart-like growths and huge, reddish disks, like great, sickly lily pads, except they didn't appear to be leaves and were growing right on the ground. Was this some manner of fungus? Or were the things in here some entirely new form of life never seen on this planet before?

They looked harmless enough, at least. They didn't try to grab his ankles as he walked past them, but he avoided stepping on any of them, regardless. His morbid imagination was still ever-eager to offer several horrific scenarios that might follow if he did, and he wasn't willing to risk any of them.

He shined his light up into the branches above him. There were more of those stringy clumps that looked far too much like human hair, as well as some of those bristly cones like the one he nearly bumped into on the stairs. There were also several long, purplish things that looked like giant bean pods, except for the fact that they seemed to be *pulsating.*

Another of those eerie groans rolled through the air. He turned around, listening, but he couldn't tell which direction it was coming from. Now that he was listening, however, he realized that he could hear something else, too, something far more subtle...and far more *creepy...*

He turned around again, scanning his surroundings. Somewhere, something was *breathing.*

It was soft, barely noticeable at first, but he could distinctly hear it. A raspy, wheezy sort of sound, almost sickly. And it was *close.*

The hairs on the back of his neck were standing up again. He wasn't alone.

Somewhere high above him, something rustled in the branches. He shined his light up into the canopy, already knowing he wasn't going to be able to see anything.

Again, his flashlight flickered, threatening to plunge him back into the vulnerable darkness.

He didn't like this. An unreliable flashlight and a hostile, alien jungle simply weren't a good mix. Anyone who'd ever watched a horror movie could tell you that.

That groaning noise came again. This time, however, it changed halfway through the groan into something more like a moan. It wasn't an improvement, as far as he was concerned. Then another unsettling sound—something between a hiss and a rattle—circled around him, like countless, unseen things rustling through every branch, twig and stem.

If these were spirits, they weren't behaving like the others he'd seen. And wendigos didn't have this sort of patience. This was something else.

That rustling sound above him was moving. It was getting closer. And it was drifting from one side of the room to the other, like something crawling through the branches, moving closer and closer with each pass.

He kept turning in a circle, searching his surroundings with the flashlight, trying to see what was there, but there was too much of the strange foliage. Anything could be hiding in there, watching him, waiting for the perfect moment to strike.

He couldn't just stand in one place. He needed to be moving. Then at least he wouldn't be a stationary target. He grabbed one of those huge, sheet-like things that were hanging in his way and shoved it aside. It turned out to be quite fragile for its size. It tore nearly in half. And the instant it happened, the others all sort of *shivered*. He froze mid-step, trying to decide if this was an "I shouldn't have done that" moment.

That eerie moaning sound came again. This time, it sounded like a voice. A murmur of words bubbled somewhere deep inside it, impossible to make out.

The thing above him was still moving. It was right above him, it seemed, but still his light couldn't find the source.

Then that hissing/rattling noise circled around him again. This time, it was more hiss than rattle, little more than a long, drawn out, "Ssssssss…"

He clenched his teeth, frustrated, and growled, "Come on, already," as if his heart weren't pounding and his legs weren't trembling. Scary or not, he wanted to get this awful night over with. "Quit screwing around."

"Ssssssssssummmm…"

Eric canted his head to one side, listening.

"Mmmmuuuuuuunnnn…"

The rustling above him now seemed to have spread all around him. Everywhere he shined his light, the strange, darkness-loving plants were trembling. It was as if the whole jungle were coming alive.

"Ssssssummmmmmwuuuuuu…"

Those huge leaves…or petals…or whatever the hell they were…shriveled and folded themselves up, like curtains drawing themselves open, revealing more of the clearing he was standing in. There were several large, bulbous flowers growing out of the sides of several of the trees. They were mostly white, with a strange, blood-red pattern that looked like veins.

"Ssssssomeone…there…?"

Eric took a step back, surprised.

"Who's…? There…?" The voice was the same as the

breathing he'd heard before: weak, wheezy, sickly.

He turned around to find that one of those odd flowers was slowly moving toward him, uncoiling on its twisted stem. As he watched, it peeled its petals back like fleshy lids and revealed a great, staring eyeball.

He backed away from it, startled.

"Why...? Are you...? Here...?"

All around him, freaky eyes were opening, staring back at him, measuring him.

Was the jungle, itself, speaking to him? This was now firmly ranking in the top thirty freaky experiences he'd had since he discovered the weird. Maybe even the top twenty.

"Who am I talking to?" he asked as he turned in slow circles, trying to keep all of those creepy eyeballs in sight. "Who are you?"

They weren't actual eyeballs, like the one in the slimy, black room under the forty-seven-year-old office. A closer inspection revealed that these were, in fact, flowers of some sort. They were a tightly packed ball of tiny, white petals, almost like a rosebud. But they seemed to function the same as eyeballs. When he shined his light on one, the petals closed, reducing the opening at its center to a fraction of its size, and when he turned the light away, the petals opened, allowing it to widen, exactly like the pupil of an eye.

"Who...?" said the jungle. "Who...? Am...?"

Eric raised an eyebrow. This seemed a little familiar.

"Who am...I...?"

It wasn't the same voice as the one in the treehouse. That voice, besides being distinctly feminine, didn't sound nearly so...*asthmatic*. This thing sounded like it could really use an inhaler. And yet, that wheezy, rasping quality did nothing to reduce the creepiness of this situation. On the contrary, for some reason it gave it a downright *sinister* quality.

"Who...? Am I...?"

Eric nodded. He didn't think it was going to be such a difficult question when he asked it.

This thing was like Bronwen. This room was like the treehouse. One of what Peggy had referred to as the "twisted plac-es."

The people trapped in those places aren't like the rest of us. The memory of her words made the hairs on the back of his neck bristle. *They're not dead. But they're not alive, either. They're...something else now. Something* awful.

He kept turning around, kept shining his light at one eyeball after another, making sure none of them were creeping closer to him.

Was it weird that he was most bothered by the fact that none of them blinked?

"I..." said the creepy, wheezy voice of the jungle. "I...am..."

Bronwen told him she wasn't dead, that she was only *changed*. And Peggy's words backed that up when she referred to them as "the people trapped in those places." That meant that, whatever they might be now, they *used* to be people, just like any-one else. "Did you work here?" he asked.

"Work...? Here...?"

Some of the creepy eyeballs began to turn in various direc-tions, as if only now realizing where they were.

"I...? Worked here...?"

"Did you?" he pressed.

"I was...? I...? Was...?"

Another strange shiver passed through the room. Suddenly, those creepy eyeballs all snapped back to him, making him jump. Each one was slowly opening, those creepy irises widening. All at once, the atmosphere had changed. Gone was the slow confu-sion in the thing's voice. Suddenly, it was *angry*.

"*Why are you here?*" it demanded again. "*What do you want?*"

He opened his mouth to reply, but couldn't decide on the correct answer. It was his turn to be indecisive, it seemed.

That rustling was back again. This time, however, it didn't sound like something moving through the branches. This time, it seemed to be everywhere at once, as if the entire jungle were coming alive.

And he supposed that was precisely what was happening. In

an all-too literal sense.

"*I've given you what you want!*" wheezed the voice of Evancurt's living jungle. "*The channels are built!*"

Eric blinked, confused. Did he miss something?

"*The streams are flowing, aren't they?*"

He glanced around, thinking that perhaps someone else had walked in on them.

Then, just as suddenly, the eyeballs seemed to relax. Those creepy, flower petal irises began to close. "Plant the seed... Cut open the peel..."

He was pretty sure that whoever this voice belonged to was a few perennials short of a hanging basket.

"The seeds are planted... Tell Voltner... Tell him... Seeds... Streams..." The voice trailed off and the creepy eyeball flowers closed and began to droop.

He looked around at them, confused. Did the batteries run down? He leaned closer to one of them. "Hello?" Then he frowned and scratched at the back of his head as he wondered why he was trying to talk into the thing's eyeballs...

That couldn't possibly be all there was, could it? He didn't understand anything he just heard. Something about building channels. And flowing streams. Planting seeds and cutting a peel...? Who the hell was Voltner?

But he wasn't going to get anything else.

Another of those strange shivers raced through the jungle around him, and something in the air changed. A cold wind suddenly began to blow. Something was coming. He could feel it. He turned and shined his light into the dense jungle branches.

Hungry, shining eyes stared back at him.

Chapter Nineteen

Eric had been very careful not to touch anything as he made his way down here. But it appeared that the time for being careful was over. This was the time for *priorities*. And at the very top of that list was *running*.

He bolted into the jungle and the monster with the shining eyes tore after him.

He shoved his way through the strange branches, ducking under low limbs and trying his best not to trip over all the tangled vines.

His second priority, he decided, was to watch for any of those bristly cones the little girl in the cupcake tee shirt warned him of. He still didn't know what those things were or what they'd do to him if he carelessly ran into one, but she'd made it clear that it was worse than poison. And he was sure there were plenty of other dangerous things growing in this mess, too, but he wasn't going to have time to avoid everything. He was going to have to rely on his strange luck.

He jumped over more of those ugly, warty growths, squeezed between two furry tree trunks and then dared a quick look back with his light.

The thing was right behind him. And it was huge. At least twice as big as a full-grown lion. But it was difficult to tell exactly *what* it was. His terrified mind couldn't seem to piece the thing together in the few fleeting glances he could afford to spare it.

Part of it was that the thing simply didn't make sense. How did something so big even fit through this dense vegetation? *He* was barely able to fit through it, and yet the thing behind him barely rustled the foliage as it pursued him.

Ahead of him was one of those skeletal-looking columns.

He still wasn't sure what these things were, but he was fairly sure they couldn't be classified as trees. They had no leaves or branches. They were about three feet in diameter, hollow, and comprised of what looked like a bunch of bleached-white bones fused together. But they *did* look like they'd be easy to climb. And right now that was just the sort of thing he needed.

Hoping desperately that it wouldn't turn out to be too fragile to hold his weight, he ran to it and hurriedly made his way up the side.

It was as strong as it looked, and easy enough to climb. But the surrounding plant life had invaded the hollow interior. Vines, thorny branches and slimy, dripping strands of some kind of foul, brown fungus slowed his ascent.

The good news, however, was that the monster wasn't climbing up behind him, snapping at his feet.

He looked down to find it pacing around the base of the column, those shining eyes staring up at him.

It wasn't just that he didn't get a good look at the thing as it was chasing him, he realized. Even now, as he shined his light down onto it, he couldn't make sense of what he was seeing.

It was covered in an ever-shifting armor of branches, leaves and vines that folded around it as it approached and enshrouded it, seemingly fusing with the beast until it had passed, changing its shape with every step it took.

Was there really a creature inside there? Something attached to those shining eyes? Or was it nothing more than an extension of this otherworldly jungle?

He squinted at it as it passed beneath him, glaring up at him. Was it only another manifestation of the person he spoke to in the clearing? Was this just another shape it could take, like those creepy, flower petal eyeballs? It wouldn't be any different, he realized, than the way the thing that used to be called Bronwen had animated the toys inside the treehouse and made the branches reach for him.

The monster grew impatient and rose up on its hind legs, its thorny claws scratching at the bone-like material beneath his feet.

He needed to keep moving.

There was a heavy, drooping branch from one of those huge, furry trees growing against the column just above him. He made his way up a little farther and crept onto it.

It didn't feel like wood at all. It was soft. *Fleshy.* It felt more like he was climbing onto the back of some enormous, hairy animal. But it was strong. It held his weight, allowing him to crawl toward the trunk and circle around the other side.

Once he was finally convinced that he was safely out of reach of the monster lurking on the ground, he shined his light down at it again, only to discover that it had vanished.

Where the hell did it go?

He turned around, shifting the flashlight to his other hand, and searched the ground on that side. But it was nowhere to be seen.

His heart racing, he turned it up, into the branches above him, convinced that it must've climbed up there. But it wasn't there, either.

It seemed to have simply disappeared.

Maybe it'd given up.

Or maybe whatever weird magic had summoned the thing had run out.

But as he shined his light farther out into the forest, he was startled by another eyeshine, this one much higher up. These eyes were different. They were bigger. Rounder. He stood there, squinting into those shadows, trying to figure out what he was seeing. It didn't look like the thing from before. It had a different kind of shape to it. And he could think of no easy way it could get to him from over there.

But then it moved, and he suddenly realized that the shape he was looking at was a *bird.* A great owl-like shape, with huge, shining eyes and a sharp, thorny beak. It spread its wings wide and shifted on its woody talons.

Like the hulking shape of the first monster as it prowled across the dense jungle floor, it shouldn't have been possible for this giant bird to spread its wings in such dense foliage, but instead of blocking them, the jungle fused with them. It was like something from a nightmare. It followed no kind of logic whatsoever. It was as if these alien plants were working together to create an army of *shadow puppets*. Except in terrifying 3D. Bristly leaves, coiling branches and snaking vines all bent and folded over themselves, forming the outline of the enormous bird as it launched itself and sailed straight toward him, those huge wings passing through every branch and vine in its path, constantly reforming itself into new shapes with new textures.

He turned and looked around, but now he was trapped in the tree that was supposed to save him. There was no way he could climb down before that thing reached him.

He turned his attention to another branch lower down. This wasn't the sort of thing a man his age and physical shape should be doing, but he was out of options and dangerously low on time. He braced himself for what he was sure was about to be a very painful ordeal, and threw himself from the tree.

The bird monster sailed over him, vanishing back into the jungle as he grabbed onto the lower branch, knocking the wind out of himself and dropping his flashlight in the process. It was strong enough that it didn't snap, which was a good thing, but it wasn't nearly as strong as the one he'd just left. It bowed under his weight, sinking lower and lower, bending almost ninety degrees, at which point he began to slip.

There was a moment when he thought he was going to hang on after all. His gloves offered a little extra grip. A glimmer of hope. But while the branch seemed capable of holding his weight, *he* wasn't. His fingers slipped. He fell. He crashed through a tangle of thorny branches and landed hard on his back.

He lay there, gasping for air, wincing at the pain and wondering if he'd finally managed to break something or if the thorns that had dug painfully into his exposed face had injected him with horrifying, alien toxins.

But the jungle wasn't going to give him time for a self-examination. As he lay there, looking up into the queer branches, he saw a new shape descending on him from the shadows.

A nightmare monkey was coming for him now.

He wasn't a fan of monkeys. The last time he met a monkey, it wasn't very nice. (Or were they apes?) Freshly invigorated, he rolled over and snatched up the flashlight. At the same time, he spotted a hole leading under a tangle of thorny brush right next to him. He didn't think about it. He wriggled into it and crawled under the thicket as something heavy crashed down onto the jungle floor behind him.

He wasn't going to have long. The foliage here was a major obstacle for him, but if the movements of that bird were any indication, it didn't slow these monsters down at all.

And sure enough, he felt something snatch at his foot as he scurried forward, ignoring the thorns that were biting into his cheeks and forehead.

He reached the far side of the thicket and scrambled to his feet. He didn't look back. He just *ran.*

But he was running out of stamina. His legs ached. He was gasping for breath. And he could hear the monkey chasing him.

Then his flashlight went dark. Like water from a burst pipe, blind panic flooded through him. He gave the light a hard shake, then banged it against the palm of his other hand, cursing at it as the thorny vegetation reached out of the darkness all around him, clawing at his face and snatching at his hair.

He tripped and stumbled.

His right shoulder collided with something that felt sort of like a tree, but also sort of like the muscular flank of a large farm animal.

"*Come on!*" he grunted, shaking the flashlight again. It flickered a few times, but kept going dark. "*Not-now not-now not-now!*"

What was wrong with the stupid thing? He was sure it hadn't been sitting in the glove box for *that* long.

Something reached out of the darkness behind him and snatched at the back of his jacket. Wooden claws tearing at the fabric.

Inside his head, where whatever mental disorder he had that kept getting him into situations like these was given a voice, he found himself wondering if Isabelle might be kind enough to tell everyone he was killed by something other than a monkey. It just seemed like a rather undignified way to go.

It was so strange, the way his brain worked. He should

probably be concerned about that.

Growling, he knocked the flashlight against his palm again and finally it came back to life, casting its glare over the alien foliage just in time for him to duck under another of those droopy, furry branches and very nearly collide with a concrete wall.

He was out of the jungle, which was good news...but now what?

He shined his light to the left, but there was nothing there. Then he looked right. There was a light over there. A window. He ran toward it as something tore through the brush behind him, drawing closer and closer. Had the monster changed again? It suddenly sounded far heavier than the monkey he saw descending through the canopy. Its footsteps practically thundered behind him.

Next to the window was a glass door, beyond which was an illuminated hallway.

That was his way out. If the plants were shaping these monsters, then it stood to reason that once he left the jungle, they couldn't attack him anymore. All he had to do was get out of this freaky room.

At least, that was what he told himself. It was the logic he used to force himself to run faster.

But he didn't have a moment to spare. The next few seconds were going to decide everything.

And by some miracle, the door wasn't locked.

He yanked it open and darted into the hallway on the other side, uttering a gasp of relief.

It seemed for a second that his luck might hold out. Now he only had to keep running until he was certain that the jungle monsters couldn't follow him anymore.

But he came to an abrupt halt as he locked eyes with another wendigo.

Chapter Twenty

So much for luck.

By the time he realized the hideous thing was there, it'd already spotted him and shifted into murder gear.

He backed away, cursing. This was bad. Wendigos weren't the fastest monsters he'd ever encountered, but it was already almost on top of him. There wasn't time to flee. And even if he *was* strong enough to fight one of these things off, he was exhausted from escaping those alien jungle beasts.

But as he crossed his arms in front of him to shield off those vicious, gnashing teeth, the glass door he'd just run through shattered and something with enormous, shining eyes and teeth like sharpened fence posts exploded into the hallway.

It was over in an instant.

Eric stood there, his arms still crossed in front of his face, his eyes wide with terror, his entire body trembling with shock.

That was definitely no monkey... He didn't know exactly what it was, but it was huge. He only saw the head and neck and crushing jaws of the monster.

All that remained of the wendigo was a splatter of gore and a trail of blood leading back into that nightmare jungle.

It took a few tries to make his feet start working again, but he managed to turn himself around and walk away from the broken window, putting distance between him and any other jungle monsters that might happen by.

There was a rough and frightful-looking old woman standing in the hallway in front of him, a smoldering cigarette clenched between two shriveled fingers, her painted-on eyebrows raised. "Holy shit!" she exclaimed in a gruff voice. "You didn't piss yourself, did you?"

He blinked at her, dazed.

It was a good question, actually. He didn't think he did, but he wasn't entirely sure just yet... His body was too numb to feel anything with any certainty.

That was *really* close.

Last time the weird called on him, he met a witch who told him that the universe loved good people and that it would sometimes go out of its way to protect those who were exceptionally good of heart. He still wasn't sure if he believed her or not. He wasn't sure he could be considered "exceptionally good of heart," for one thing. And then there was the fact that the same woman ended up betraying everyone pretty much because she believed that the universe had turned its back on her.

But he did have to admit that his luck wasn't by any definition *normal*.

The woman chuckled and puffed on her cigarette.

He walked past her, ignoring her, and peered around the corner to make sure there weren't any more wendigos shuffling around in the next hallway.

It was empty.

Now that the initial shock of his encounter with the wendigo had passed, he was aware of the strangeness of the light in here. It was an odd sort of glow that seemed less to radiate from a specific point of origin than to *flow* through the hallway. He glanced up at the ceiling, curious, and found that more of those strange, saucer-shaped light fixtures, like the one back in that first little building, were mounted at regular intervals overhead, each one shining brightly with a strange, swirling light that was like nothing he'd ever seen before. It looked almost *liquid*, as if those flattened orbs were filled with churning, molten metal instead of glowing gas.

He squeezed his eyes shut and looked away, the blazing afterimage of the lights seared into his vision, and decided to drop it. There were alien creatures and alien plants all around him, why *not* alien lighting?

Blinking, he turned his attention back to the hallway in front of him. There was an open door on the right, behind which there appeared to be some sort of lab. He didn't see any more wendigos, but as he stepped through the doorway, he caught sight of a man in a disheveled shirt and tie sitting on the floor, scribbling in a notebook. He looked frustrated. He kept making faces at the paper and pausing to scratch his head. His hair looked as if he'd been doing that for a while.

He left the man to his work and walked around the room, examining the various workstations. There were a number of plants growing in here. They were small ones, for the most part, nothing like the towering specimens in that strange, mini-jungle. But most of them looked like they'd long ago outgrown their pots. Roots and creepers had spread over almost every surface of the room. Knotted vines had slithered up to the ceiling. And there was a particularly messy mass of gray fungus in one corner that had encased the entire table.

On one wall, half-buried beneath a prickly-looking vine, he found another calendar. Like the one in that first office, it was turned to April of 1971. "That can't be right," he muttered. Could it? Wouldn't all these buildings be in a much greater state of decay if it'd really been forty-seven years since anyone was here? There weren't even any cobwebs in here. And yet, then again...why not? He knew from experience that time wasn't always a constant. Back in the fissure that led to the cathedral, he'd lost hours at a time. What made him think that those years would pass normally in a place where the entire *world* was supposedly broken?

That was two matching calendars in two different buildings agreeing on the same date. Whatever happened here, he was going to assume that it happened forty-seven years ago. Now he just had to figure out *what* happened here. What was it that prevented anyone from ever turning the pages on those calendars to May?

The people here found something they weren't supposed to find, he thought, remembering Tessa's haunting words. *They built something they weren't supposed to build.*

He turned and scanned the tables around him, but nothing stood out. There were occasional scraps of yellowed paper and open notepads, but he saw nothing written that he could make any sense of. He made his way to the back of the room, careful to keep well away from the things growing in here.

"Don't let me forget."

He turned around to find a chubby young man with great, pudgy cheeks standing there, staring at him. He glanced around, confused, then raised an eyebrow at him. "Don't let you forget what?"

But the chubby man scrunched up his face and frowned. "I...can't remember..."

Eric stared back at him for a moment, unsure how they were supposed to proceed from here. "Well... Let me know when you figure it out, I guess."

The man nodded and then turned and walked away, still wracking his brain over whatever it was he wasn't supposed to forget.

Eric turned to continue searching the mysterious jungle lab, and nearly collided with a very tall woman wearing a skimpy nighty and cradling a glass of wine in one bejeweled and manicured hand. He quickly backed up a step, surprised. "Sorry..."

She didn't look upset that he'd nearly bumped into her. In fact, she smiled. Her eyes swept down his body, then back up again. "Hi there."

He stared back at her. The hungry expression on her face was more startling than her sudden appearance. "Uh... Hi."

"Looking for someone?" she asked, lifting the wine glass and holding it near her lips.

"No. Just...the exit."

"Don't leave already," she purred. She didn't sip from the glass. Instead, she sort of licked the rim of it as those dark, haunting eyes swam over him. "I was just looking for someone to help me with a little chore."

"I'll keep an eye out for someone," he replied, then quickly stepped around the woman and hurried on across the room. He'd only taken a few steps, however, when he encountered a young woman with a pierced nose and short hair dyed a shocking shade of bright red.

"Have you seen my friend?" she asked. She was wringing her hands in front of her, looking desperately upset. "I can't find her anywhere."

"I'm sorry," he said, shaking his head as he walked past her.

"She was in the car next to me," she called after him. "But now I can't find her."

He cringed. A car? Was she talking about an accident?

"Please. I'm worried about her."

"I'll keep an eye out for her," he promised. But he didn't think he'd be bumping into the girl's friend. He had a bad feeling that the friend had survived the accident and the girl with the pierced nose and dyed hair never made it out of the car.

He hurried on, picking up his pace a little.

There was a door up ahead, an exit, perhaps, but there was an old man standing between him and it, his hands crossed behind his back, an irritated sort of expression on his face. He was turned to one side, facing a table that was ten or twelve feet in front of him. When he saw Eric approaching, he turned and scowled at him. "I've been standing in line *forever*," he complained.

He actually slowed down a little at this. "Um...?" He didn't see a line. There was no one standing in front of the old man. There didn't seem to be anything at or around the table that was worth queuing up for. "Sorry?"

"It's ridiculous," he growled.

Eric continued past him. "I'll, uh...let someone know about it."

He hurried past the old man and peered through the doorway, again scanning the room for wendigos, and discovered that it was a spacious office. Several freestanding chalkboards were occupying the floor, all of them covered in shorthand notes, diagrams and mathematical equations he had no way of understanding.

He stepped into the room, his eyes drawn to a large bulletin board on one wall, where there were several sketches of various, alien-looking plants, some of which he recognized from his unpleasant stroll through that freaky jungle room.

Why were the people here so interested in those plants, anyway? Was it just basic, scientific curiosity? Tessa told him that they'd damaged the border between worlds here, letting things pass back and forth. Did that include plant life as well as creatures? Did they open a rift and discover a new world filled with alien flora and simply decide they needed to study it? Or were they trying to use them for something else? His horrid imagination was quick to suggest that someone might be using these plants to develop horrific chemicals and hideous, deadly drugs.

And that *was* the sort of thing that always happened in books and movies, wasn't it? The moment someone discovered something new and amazing, there was always some warmongering villain that wanted to immediately weaponize it?

Before he could ponder the question any further, he was distracted by movement in the corner of the room. He turned to see two slender, sneaker-clad legs sticking out from behind a lab table. They were sliding back and forth on the cold concrete, flailing, *struggling*.

He rushed over to find the girl in the pleated skirt and the gray sweater lying there, a clear plastic bag pulled over her head and knotted tight around her neck. Her wide, bulging eyes were rolled back into her head, her mouth gaping open, gulping desperately for air, her body convulsing. Her whole face had flushed a dreadful shade of red.

Panicking, he straddled the girl's body and crouched down over her. He seized the plastic with both hands and tore it open.

The girl gasped. She coughed. She clutched at her chest.

Then she vanished.

Eric was left crouching there, his hands still clutching at the torn plastic bag that had vanished with her, staring at the dusty floor where a girl was dying only seconds before. His heart was still racing. "What the *hell?*" he shouted.

Chapter Twenty-One

He rose to his feet and ran his hand through his hair, then rubbed at the back of his neck.

That was upsetting. That was three times now he'd watched the girl nearly die. Which was weird, because judging by the way she kept vanishing, he was fairly sure she was already dead. What was the point?

And was she doing these things to herself? Was someone else doing these things to her? Or was she just caught in some strange, perpetual loop of impending death, the way the old traveler was eternally searching for gate five, the desperate mother was forever searching for her missing daughter and the old man in the previous room was doomed to spend all eternity standing in that endless line?

Any way he looked at it, it was messed up.

He turned away from the corner to find a short man with a receding hairline standing there. "The flower shop was closed," he said.

"Then come back later," Eric snapped, stalking past him.

"But…I was supposed to buy her flowers… I never got to buy her flowers…"

"Do I look like Dr. Phil to you?" he growled. "Go tell it to the wine lady out there. *She* seemed like she was looking for some company."

He rubbed at his eyes, exhausted. Now he felt bad. The poor guy was dead. He probably left this world suddenly. He'd left behind regrets. And now he'd never be able to buy those flowers.

He glanced back, but the little balding man was gone.

This whole ordeal was upsetting. He felt like this whole

place was waging emotional war on him.

He tried to push it all out of his mind and turned his attention to the wall in front of him, instead. Like the other wall, there were papers pinned up. But as he looked over it, he realized that it was more than just random yellow papers covered in indecipherable notes. There was something underneath it all.

He rushed over and began tearing them down, one by one, uncovering it. Then he stepped back and took it all in.

It was a map of the estate.

Evancurt.

There was the main gate and the road, near the bottom. There was the tightly-locked building with the banging machinery inside, labeled "vent house." There was the little cabin with the freaky eyeball room under it, labeled "coordination office" as if it were the most ordinary building in the world. And over there was the long building with all the glass walls and gold cables (plainly labeled "glass house" no less). Over here was *this* building, labeled "green lab" (which he supposed was probably a better name than "green*house*," given how dark and cold this place was, but still didn't seem like a particularly good name, given how little green there was in all those freaky plants). There were also six other large buildings on the map, scattered across the property, but all connected by the branching, overgrown road. They were labeled "little house," "barn," "workshop," "star house," "shed" and "main." The last two were right next to each other, and someone had added the words "reactor" and "core" beneath them.

He frowned at those words. "That...doesn't sound good..." His awful imagination was quick to go to work with this new information. He remembered staring up at those power lines as he circled this building, wondering if they were working on some kind of experimental energy facility.

The idea was horrifying. If he stumbled across a lethally radioactive nuclear reactor, would he even know what he was looking at until he dropped dead? Would he have any warning at all?

He scanned the rest of the map. There were dozens of much smaller things marked all over it, but none of them had labels, meaning they probably weren't all that important. They were probably things like those outhouse-sized boxes and that mysterious sewer-like pipe sticking out of the forest floor. If he was going to figure out how to put an end to whatever was happening here, he was probably going to find his answers in the big buildings.

He stepped up to the map again and took a closer look at the green lab. It appeared there was a lot more underground than above. And there appeared to be an underground passage leading between it and the workshop.

He turned and scanned the rest of the walls, if there was a detailed map of the *property* hanging here... He found what he was looking for behind the main desk. A much smaller map. The floor plan for the green lab.

There appeared to be a ramp circling down from that huge hangar door in back. That would take him back up to ground-level. But he doubted if he'd be able to get out that way. Instead, he found the tunnel entrance that would take him to the workshop.

Finally. Some decent luck for a change. All he needed was to snap a few pictures and he'd be all set.

But of course when he reached for his phone, it still wasn't in his pocket...

He cursed under his breath and glanced over the desk.

Why weren't there any phones here? It didn't make sense. A phone simply made an office more productive.

He sighed and scratched at the back of his neck. It was okay. He could still do this. He focused on the map again, on the tunnel. It should be down the hall from the lab, left, then right, past some stairs, near the loading area at the bottom of the ramp.

He went over the route in his mind several times, committing it to memory, then he turned away and nearly collided with a skinny woman with thick, oversized glasses.

He took a step backward, startled.

She was an attractive woman, in a cute and nerdy sort of way. She wore a long skirt and a large sweater with sleeves that went almost all the way to her fingertips. Her dark hair was pinned up in a sloppy bun. She was staring up at him, her brown eyes magnified by her glasses. "They're amazing, aren't they?"

"Uh…?"

"They actually brought them back from another *world!*" she exclaimed. "They're not even really *plants!* Technically, they're an *entirely new lifeform!*"

Eric stared at her, unsure what to say. He didn't find the freaky things nearly as interesting. He kind of wanted to torch the whole place on his way out, if he were to be completely honest. but he didn't want to be rude.

"Did you know there's something about the genetic makeup of these plants that anchors them to their world of origin?"

He opened his mouth, but wasn't sure how to answer. How, exactly, would he know something like that? How did *she* know something like that?

But an answer to her question apparently wasn't required, because she continued on without one: "That means that while they're growing in this world, they thin the boundaries *between* the two worlds!"

"Fascinating," said Eric, because he felt like that was the polite thing to say.

"And the way they *used* them is absolutely *ingenious!*" she babbled on. "Because of these thin areas, they can actually funnel energy *between the two worlds!* They basically created *conduits* that could connect machines in *multiple worlds*, potentially taking advantage of *different laws of physics*. And because working machines could be placed simultaneously in multiple realities, they could achieve actual *four-dimensional functionalities*. The scientists here created an entire network of powered lines using this. They called them 'channels' and used them to carry and manipulate streams of all sorts of *exotic energy* that haven't even been proven to exist yet! And they did all of it, like, *fifty or sixty years ago!*"

He frowned. Streams? Channels? Didn't that crazy voice back in the jungle room say something about streams and channels when it started shouting at him?

The channels are built! The streams are flowing, aren't they?

And for that matter, hadn't he heard some of this before

that, too?

One of the crazy people outside in the woods was shouting something at him about starving the lines and closing the streams… He hadn't paid much attention at the time because…well, because he was fairly sure all those people were crazy, to be blunt.

Break the machine!

He frowned.

They built something they were never meant to build.

A machine?

"Isn't that, like, the coolest thing *ever*?"

Eric thought it was the most *insane* thing ever, but he didn't say so. Instead, he asked, "How do you know all this?"

"I've been through all their files," she replied without a moment's hesitation. She gestured at the rows of filing cabinets lined up against the back wall. "It's fascinating. There're journals in there of *actual expeditions* to *other worlds!* And detailed research logs about *exotic energies* and *reality-manipulating organisms!* The lead scientist here was a man named Ira Lofleder. He was *insanely* ahead of its time!"

Eric had no doubt about the "insane" part. But he didn't waste time dwelling on the subject. *Exotic energy*, he thought, letting it sink in. Isabelle occasionally used that phrase to describe the various non-physical energies she sensed when he traveled to weird places. Psychic and spiritual energy were the most common, but they'd also become aware of a variety of different kinds of magical energies as well as a number of other, lesser understood types, including the energy given off by the unseen places, the dark energy she sometimes felt when he was in the presence of nameless agents, a theoretical *life energy* given off by all living things and even a possible *hell energy*. Were these the same sorts of energies? He *had* been suspecting all along that there was an abundance of spiritual energy flowing over this property.

"It seems like these energies are the primary power for what was going on here," she went on. "And apparently, they don't mix well with electricity, so most modern technology doesn't work for very long here. Electronics are useless. Anything that works on batteries. Vehicles stop running and won't start again, so a lot of the work here had to be done very low-tech. The lights here had to be engineered specifically to work off exotic energy. And phones won't work *at all* here."

He lowered his eyes and stared at her for a moment, surprised. *That* was why there were no phones? And why the lights were so strange? And why his flashlight kept giving him trouble?

The woman stared at him for a moment, and then an embarrassed look overcame her. "I'm sorry," she said. "I just started blurting all that at you and you don't even know me." She looked away, blushing a little, and started chewing on her fingernails. "I'm Dora," she said. "Sorry."

"It's fine," he assured her. And it was. He found that he liked her. She was cute. And she reminded him of Holly when she chewed her nails like that. He turned and looked up at the map again. "Actually, you've been very helpful." Thanks to her, he understood a little more about what they were doing here. There was a machine somewhere on this property. A machine that was wreaking havoc on the world around it. It utilized exotic energies which could flow back and forth between worlds thanks to the use of these bizarre plants. "Thank you."

But when he looked back at her, Dora was gone.

He stared at the spot where she'd been standing for a moment, distracted. Then, finally, he turned and walked back to the door, his eyes drifting to the larger map one last time.

If he had to guess where such a machine would be located, he'd put his money on the building someone had labeled "main." It and the neighboring "shed" were both at the farthest end of the longest road. Those were the ones that were ominously labeled "reactor" and "core."

Distracted by thoughts of nuclear energy and deadly radiation, he stepped through the doorway and directly into the path of another wendigo.

Chapter Twenty-Two

His heart nearly stopped in his chest.

The monster was right there, only inches away, shuffling toward him, its head hung low, its arms limp.

He quickly ducked around the corner and pressed his back against the wall, barely stifling a scream.

The wendigo grunted and lifted its head, its hideous, gray eyes fixed on the empty doorway.

That was entirely too close.

And it wasn't over yet. Seconds passed and the monster didn't move from the doorway. It was just standing there.

Please go away, thought Eric. He was holding his breath, afraid to make the slightest sound. *Just go. The hell. Away.*

Finally, those shuffling footsteps started again. But instead of moving away, they were moving *closer*. It was coming into the office!

His eyes wide with terror, he backed away from the door as silently as possible and moved toward the corner of the room, where he could be partially hidden behind one of the freestanding chalkboards.

Very slowly, the monster shuffled into view.

Wendigos weren't known for their keen observational skills. This was one monster that didn't exert a lot of energy *searching* for its prey. He might actually have a chance if he just stayed out of its direct line of sight until it wandered off again. He just had to make himself relax. But it was going to be hard to relax. As he backed himself into the corner, he bumped into something.

No… Some*one*.

A gigantic hand fell on his left shoulder.

Barely biting back a fresh scream, he snapped his head up

and found himself looking into the pudgy face of the handsy giant in the Batman tee shirt.

He stared up at that pouty lower lip and messy blond hair, forcing himself to remain calm. Any noise, any movement, might alert the wendigo to his presence. And then there'd be nothing to stop it from rushing over and devouring his face.

It was only a ghost, after all. He could handle a ghost.

The giant slowly lifted his right hand and brought it down on top of Eric's head. Then, as he stood there, choking back a scream, his heart thundering like a runaway train in his ribcage, the brute slowly and firmly dragged his hand backward and down, all the way to the collar of his shirt, pulling his head backward in the process. Then he lifted his hand, returned it to the top of his head, and repeated the motion. Then again. And again.

Each time, the giant pulled Eric's head backward, then let it go. Each time Eric wondered if this time he might snap his neck all the way back.

He stood there, his teeth clenched so tightly he could feel sparks of pain shooting through his jaw, his wide, horrified eyes staring at the shuffling, zombie-like wendigo, his stomach twisted into a burning knot, his heart feeling as if it might burst at any second, all while the blond giant in the gray sweatpants, untied shoes and Batman tee shirt stood there *petting* him…

As if this whole ordeal wasn't awful enough already…

"Shiny…" whispered the handsy giant.

Eric's eyes twitched toward him, but only for an instant. He didn't dare take them off the wendigo for longer than that. If the thing *did* notice him here, it wouldn't waste a second before charging him.

"Shiny…man…"

A small and pitiful sort of whiny sound escaped him. He couldn't help it. It just sort of slipped out.

The wendigo paused its slow, constant shuffling and tipped its ugly head to one side, as if listening.

He thought a very bad word.

He thought it over and over and over again while the bloodthirsty monster tried to decide if that was a potential meal or just a random mouse it heard squeak in the corner. And the whole time the large, overly-friendly Batman fan continued petting his head as if he were a stray puppy he'd found on the street.

Just for the record, this was *not* his idea of a good time.

The wendigo lowered its head again, seemingly deciding that it hadn't, in fact, heard the sound of a grown man squeaking with terror while being fondled by a giant ghost with no respect for other people's personal space.

"Shiny man…"

Safe in the silence of his head, Eric screamed, *Shut up!*

But somehow, although the monster only stood about ten feet away, it didn't seem to hear the giant's creepy whispers. Did these ghosts' voices only speak to him? Was everything else in Evancurt deaf to them? The pierced man told him that the wendigos ignored everyone else. Did they know somehow that they were only ghosts and therefore didn't possess tasty faces for them to feast upon? Or were they simply unable to see or hear the spirits that surrounded them?

He'd probably never know. Wendigos weren't known for their great conversational skills, after all.

"So shiny…"

Eric shuddered. Why did he keep saying that? What did it mean? *Who* was shiny? *He* wasn't shiny!

The giant continued petting his head, pulling it back, letting it go, pulling it back again, letting it go again…

The wendigo lowered its head, but it didn't continue walking. It was just standing there now, staring down at the floor, its oversized hands dangling at its sides.

Move, damn you!

"Shiny man…"

For the love of God, MOVE!

But the thing didn't move. It just stood there, utterly still, utterly silent, right there between him and the only exit from this insanely uncomfortable ordeal.

Then a terrible thought occurred to him: what if the stupid thing had fallen asleep like that? What if he was trapped here like this for the remainder of the night?

How long would he have to endure this absurd slice of hell?

Finally, the wendigo began to move. But instead of wandering farther into the office, allowing him a chance to sneak behind it and through the door, it turned *toward* him.

Now it stood facing him.

He stared back at it, his eyes wide, his heart pounding so hard it was making his entire body quake.

For one terrifying moment, the world began to spin around him. He was going to pass out. He'd slump to the floor right in front of the monster and then it would definitely notice him.

How did the idiotic thing not see him there, anyway? He was standing right in front of it. All it had to do was lift its gaze just a little bit… But those creepy gray eyes remained fixed on the floor.

Finally, and so *very* slowly, the monster turned away and shuffled back out the door again.

He had to force himself to remain still for a moment longer, to give the hideous thing time to move away from the door, the better to not be heard. Then, at his very limit, he lurched forward and tore himself free of the handsy giant's grip.

He turned to face him, arms raised to defend himself if the brute should try to snatch him back again.

But the giant was already gone.

Eric stood alone in the office, as if he'd only imagined the whole awful ordeal.

Chapter Twenty-Three

He stood in the doorway for a few minutes, watching around the corner while the wendigo shuffled across the floor of the lab, waiting until there was enough distance between him and it that he felt he could risk making a run for the door. Then he slipped out of the office and crept toward the door as quickly and as quietly as possible, keeping one eye on the gray freak.

He was almost to the door when his path was blocked by the abrupt appearance of a fat, red-faced man in a tight-fitting business shirt and crooked tie.

"Have you seen how it is out there?" blared the fat man, thrusting a stubby finger at the door he was blocking.

Eric winced and pressed a finger to his lips as he glanced back at the slowly retreating wendigo. To his horror, he saw that it had stopped its slow shuffling and was standing motionless, its hideous head turned to one side, listening.

These things didn't seem to react to ghostly voices the same as they did to the sight of a living person. He was fairly sure that if *he'd* just spoken that loudly, the thing would've immediately charged him. But it seemed to have at least *some* awareness of the presence of these spirits.

The fat man, meanwhile, didn't seem the least bit concerned about the presence of a vicious, naked monster in the room. "The whole world's gone crazy!" he huffed, his voice as bloated and swollen as his immense belly. "The people have gone mad!"

Eric leaned toward the man and shook the finger he was holding in front of his lips. He was fairly certain that the gesture wasn't ambiguous in the least. It was quite clearly the universal sign for "shut the hell up already!" And yet the huffy fatso was utterly unwilling to quiet down.

"Society is *crumbling* all around us!" he bellowed.

The wendigo turned its head a little more. Those gray eyes lifted from the floor at its feet and gazed out across the lab. To Eric, it looked like it could hear the fat man's voice, but not quite pinpoint it. But even from here, he could tell that those unearthly, gray eyes were sliding slowly in this direction.

"Common decency!" huffed the fat man. "Respect! Dignity! *Basic intelligence*! It's like there's a *cancer* eating away at all the things that separate people from beasts!"

He was definitely noticing a lack of all that stuff right now. He gave up trying to make the ranting fat man stop shouting and instead hurried around him before the wendigo's deadly gaze made it all the way across the room.

Unfazed, the fat man merely turned and continued shouting after him as he darted into the hallway and out of the monster's line of sight. "This is all *Obama's* fault, you know! He *poisoned* this country!"

Eric looked down the hallway, first one way, then the other, confirming that there weren't any *more* wendigos attracted by the fat man's rantings. When he was confident that he was finally no longer in imminent danger of having his face eaten, he leaned against the wall and tried to will his frantic heart to slow.

Stupid fat guy… It didn't matter what your political views were, this was neither the time nor the place!

He took a deep breath and looked back and forth again, paranoid.

At the end of the hallway to his left, something was moving.

He stood up straight, startled. It wasn't a wendigo. It was much too dark and much too small. It was another of those creeping shadows Tessa warned him about. He'd almost forgotten about those things. Reapers, he'd called them, because she said they could tear out his soul. The guardians of the machine, apparently.

He really didn't want to deal with one of those things. And he shouldn't have to. If he was following the layout of the building correctly, that way led back to the jungle room, which wasn't the direction he wanted to go. He turned and hurried the other way. According to the map back in that office, the tunnel out of here should be this way, somewhere near the loading ramp. He just needed to make his way there.

But before he could reach the end of the hallway, someone seized his arm and he let out a startled yelp.

"Found you!" exclaimed the confused woman from the glass house.

"You again?" whispered Eric. He turned and looked back the other way. The shadow was still at the far end of the hall, but now it had taken shape. It appeared to be just standing there, watching him, those long, scythe-like fingers hovering in the corridor.

"Where'd you run off to?"

"I told you I don't know you."

"If we're not careful, we're going to miss our flight!"

If they weren't careful, he was going to get his soul reaped by the guardians of Evancurt's doomsday machine! But he didn't bother telling her this. She was utterly oblivious to anything he said. She snuggled against his arm and sighed a dramatic sort of sigh. "Can you believe we're finally on our way?"

"Oddly enough, I can't," he grumbled. He tried to pull his arm free but the woman wouldn't let go of it.

The reaper's black silhouette was still standing there, watching them.

"It feels like I've been waiting so long."

"I'm telling you, lady, my wife'll take you down. You have no idea who you're dealing with."

She straightened up suddenly, her eyes flashing wide. "What're we doing?" she gasped. "We have to hurry!" Then she was pulling him along the dark hallway.

"Make up your mind!" What was up with this woman? Where was it she thought he was going to take her? Was it like those other ghosts he saw? Was she trapped in a delusion, unaware of, or perhaps *unable to* cope with the reality of her death?

Again, he glanced down at her hand, at the shiny wedding ring on her finger. Was she on her honeymoon, perhaps? She clearly thought he was her husband. Had she somehow died on her way to some long-awaited romantic destination? Was that why she was acting like this? Was she merely unwilling to accept the fact that she'd never make it there?

That was an immensely depressing thought. He decided he didn't want to think too much about it. He wasn't sure he'd want the truth, even if she was capable of sharing it with him.

Not that it mattered at the moment. His first concern was the reaper. He kept looking back, kept expecting to see the thing chasing after him. But it was still standing in the same place, still watching them as they hurried away.

At least the woman was pulling him in the right direction, he supposed. She could just as easily have dragged him *toward* the shadowy monster.

But then they turned the corner and the woman stopped. She frowned at the new hallway that lay before them. "Is this right? I don't remember this."

Eric barely heard her. The corridor in front of them was covered in that slimy black mold.

Back in the forest, when he'd wandered into an area where this stuff was growing, Peggy told him that it was sick and rotting. She warned him not to linger there.

It's not safe. Not even for us.

The mold covered the floor, walls and ceiling in front of them. Long, dripping tendrils dangled from the tiles overhead, like tattered curtains.

"Maybe we should go back," worried the woman.

Eric looked back to find that the blackish form of the reaper had begun creeping toward them on those long, spider-like fingers, its skeletal head twisting from side to side, as if it were struggling to decide whether he was something it should ignore or something it should kill. "Not an option," he croaked.

He'd studied the building's floor plan. He knew that the closest exits were in front of them, on the other side of the moldy hallway. Once across, they could either go up the loading ramp or through the tunnel. Going back, however, he'd either have to go back through that awful jungle room or past it, following the outer hallway all the way around.

And he already knew that there was at least one wendigo wandering around in that area.

He started forward. Back in that freaky eyeball room, he'd stepped out into some of this mold. He'd even smeared some of it on his clothes while climbing that filthy ladder. It didn't seem to have hurt him so far. If he was quick about it, he should be okay to walk through it. As long as he kept his face away from those dangling strands.

Right?

He didn't think the woman was going to let him go. She didn't seem to like the mold. At the very least, he thought she might let go of his arm and abandon him to complete this foolish task alone. But she moved forward with him, still clinging to his arm as if he should have some idea of who she was.

He could see bare concrete showing through the mold again on the far end of the hallway, only about fifty feet ahead of them. Another hallway continued on to the right from there. It'd be over in a matter of seconds.

Still, he made it a point to breathe as shallowly as possible. Besides the fact that the stuff reeked, his foul imagination was thrilled to suggest that if he breathed in too much of it, it would almost certainly begin growing inside his lungs and soon he'd find himself coughing up slimy globs of bloody, black goo.

(Seriously, what the hell was wrong with his brain?)

"Are you sure this is the right way?" worried the woman. She was glancing around at their surroundings, apprehensive.

"You don't have to come with me," he told her.

"This doesn't look right," she went on, ignoring him. "I think we might've made a wrong turn somewhere."

He glanced down at her. She seemed unwaveringly convinced that he was her husband. And she either wasn't able to hear him, or she simply refused to. He wondered if she was seeing the world around him as it was, or only as she imagined it should be.

Either way, she seemed to be aware that this moldy place wasn't safe.

He glanced back as the reaper stepped around the corner

and cast its creepy, blank gaze onto them again.

Go away, he thought at it. *Nothing to see here.*

He couldn't afford to give the monster his undivided attention. He needed to watch where he was going. Carefully, he ducked under one of the drooping curtains of mold, then circled around a squishy, black stalactite-shaped mass that nearly reached the floor.

He hated the squelching noises the stuff made beneath his feet.

And it seemed to be getting more slippery, too. He had to slow down just to ensure he didn't end up falling and sitting in this filth.

But when he risked a look back, he saw that the reaper wasn't following. It stopped short of where the mold started and seemed to be examining it.

Even the monstrous sentinels, it seemed, weren't fond of the mold.

Again, his despicable imagination spoke up, asking him if that wasn't all the proof he needed that he shouldn't be wading through the stuff, as if he'd had any real choice in the matter.

"I'm scared," whimpered the woman.

He glanced down at her again, frowning. He'd only really been worrying about himself thus far. He was alive, after all, and she wasn't. It only seemed natural that he'd be the only one in any actual danger here. But he again remembered Peggy telling him that it wasn't safe. "Not even for us," she'd stressed. Was it possible that these places were *more* dangerous to spirits than they were to the living? Was he putting this poor woman in extreme peril right now?

Not that it was his fault. He told her to go back. She was the one who wouldn't let go of his arm.

But he didn't want anything bad to happen to her, either. It wasn't her fault she was trapped here.

"We shouldn't be here," she said, pressing against him. "This is a bad place."

He looked back over his shoulder. They were halfway through the moldy hallway now and the reaper still didn't seem willing to set shadowy foot on the mold. "It won't be far now," he assured her.

But this was also where the mold hung thickest from the ceiling, requiring the most care in avoiding it. And between the added weight of the woman pulling on his arm and the increasing slipperiness of the slimy mold beneath his feet, it was getting harder and harder to maintain his balance.

It was dark here, too. The thick, black mold not only completely covered and blotted out those strangely swirling lights, it also absorbed most of the light from either end.

"I want to leave," she whined. "Take me away from here. *Please.*"

"We're going! Stop yanking on me already!"

His foot slipped. His heart stuttered. His breath caught. His bruised ribs sent a jolt of pain through his chest as he jerked his body stiff to counterbalance.

That was close.

"I don't want to be here anymore..." sniffled the woman.

"We're almost there!" he hissed. "Shut up already!"

He'd ordinarily feel bad about talking that way to a frightened woman, but he was fairly sure she couldn't hear anything he said anyway.

He didn't dare lift his feet this time. Instead, he kept them dug into the slime-covered floor and shuffled a few inches at a time, trudging forward like a little kid on ice skates for the first time.

The woman buried her face against his shoulder and said not another word as he crept over the last of the reeking mold.

He glanced down at her, concerned. Was it only his imagination, or did she not look well? Her complexion seemed to have paled. She looked sort of *green.* "We're almost there," he promised her. "Just hang in there, okay?"

He didn't think she could hear him, but she seemed to nod her head against his shoulder. Had that actually gotten through to her?

He focused on the slimy floor in front of him. Every second dragged on, but finally he reached the far end and looked back. The reaper seemed to have vanished.

Relieved, he began scraping the slimy soles of his shoes on the bare concrete, eager to rid himself of every foul speck of the stuff, his gaze shifted to the filthy floor and the wet tracks he'd left behind him.

He'd left two long, crooked streaks where he slid his shoes through the dank, black fuzz like skis. And beyond those there lay a neat row of wet footprints.

But those were the only tracks.

The woman hadn't left any.

As he let this odd detail sink in, he suddenly realized that he was alone again.

He turned and looked down the hallway ahead of him, but the confused woman had apparently fled the moment she was safely out of the mold.

"That's fine," he said to himself. It was best that way. She made it hard to walk, the way she was always hanging on his arm like that. Maybe after that scary "wrong turn" he took her on, she'd steer clear of him from now on.

He started walking again, still dragging his feet across the floor with each step, trying to wipe away as much of that foul mold as possible. If he remembered the map correctly, the loading ramp should be in a room just around the corner up ahead. And the entrance to the tunnel leading to the workshop would be just beyond that.

But he paused as he passed an open doorway revealing a deep and unsettling blackness. This room shared a wall with the moldy hallway and seemed to be the source of the slimy infection.

He peered inside, curious. He didn't see any openings in the hallway as he made his treacherous way through that slippery, reeking mess. Had the mold grown so thick that it'd completely concealed a doorway, or had the mold somehow grown right through the wall? The very thought of such a possibility made him want to throw his shoes away.

He had to remind himself that this otherworldly lab and all its alien contents had been sitting here for almost half a century.

It wasn't likely to eat through his shoes and infect his flesh in one night. He'd walk it all off long before it could become a danger, he was sure.

But he still wasn't going to walk through any more of that stuff if he could help it.

He left the black room as he found it and continued on to the end of the hallway. If the map behind the desk was accurate and he remembered it properly after his ordeal with that stupid wendigo, the handsy giant, the ranting fat man, the reaper *and* the moldy hallway, then he only had to turn that corner and walk past the loading area on the left. The tunnel entrance should be on the right.

But when he peered around the corner, he found his path blocked by a massive, swarming *hive*.

Chapter Twenty-Four

It was just one thing after another tonight.

The oozing, porous mass of grayish mud blocked most of the next hallway, its slimy surface crawling with bugs that were like nothing he'd ever seen before. Each one was almost as big as a rat, armored in a blood-red exoskeleton, but with a grotesque, white, grub-like growth on its back.

As soon as he stepped into sight of the foul things, they became agitated and swarmed toward him, scurrying over the floor and walls as he backed away, making strange, threatening clicking noises.

"Careful," said a familiar, gruff voice.

Still backing away, he glanced back to see the old woman who asked him if he'd pissed himself after that close call next to the jungle room doorway. She was just standing there, puffing on her cigarette, looking utterly unconcerned about the endless swarm of hideous bugs that were crawling toward her.

"They've got a nasty bite."

He backed away a little quicker at this, but he wasn't sure what he was supposed to do. It wasn't like he could just flee back the way he came. The mold in that last hallway made a hasty exit impossible.

The old woman turned and jutted the smoldering tip of her cigarette toward the doorway of the mold-filled room. "Cut through there. Things around here don't like going near those places."

Still backing away from the encroaching swarm, he once again recalled Peggy's words of warning about the rotting places and the confused woman's terrified reaction to passing through that infected hallway. "Is it safe for me?"

The old woman puffed on her cigarette again. "Well, I wouldn't hang around in there any longer than I had to."

He looked down at the floor again. The bugs were growing more agitated by the second. They were advancing faster now.

"But you've only got one alternative."

"Right." He turned and ran for the doorway. "Thank you!"

"Good luck not pissing yourself!" the old woman called after him, cackling.

She wasn't the most charming ghost he'd met here. But she'd proved to be more helpful than most of them. He stepped through the doorway and slammed the door closed behind him.

But the effort proved pointless. Almost immediately, those creepy bugs began squeezing through the gap beneath the door.

He backed away as they approached, wondering if maybe the old woman might've lied to him. After a few steps, he felt the squelch of black mold beneath his shoe.

This was looking less like an improvement over his previous situation.

But as he continued backing away, taking extra care now to keep from slipping, he saw that the bugs refused to crawl over the mold. In fact, as soon as they made contact with it, they immediately turned and fled back the way they came.

Relieved, he took one more step back and bumped into something. He turned to find himself standing outside what appeared to be a large, iron cage.

He forgot about the bugs at once, his eyes fixed on the strange, mold-covered shape that lay pulsing on the floor behind the bars.

He withdrew the flashlight and aimed it at the thing. It was about the size of a full-grown bull, but didn't seem to have any distinguishable limbs. In fact, coated as it was in that foul, black mold, it was difficult to tell if it had any features at all. But it was definitely *alive*. He could see it breathing.

He leaned forward, as fascinated as he was repulsed, and reached between the bars with the flashlight, trying to get a better look at the thing. But all he could make out was a fleshy, mold-covered mass.

It was like the eyeball under the cabin, he realized, although he wasn't yet sure what the existence of either thing meant.

Then the light flickered off. He gave it another shake, but it refused to come back on.

Dora warned him that electricity didn't mix with the exotic energies in this place. That included the flashlight's batteries and meant that it was only a matter of time before it died for good. And for all he knew, this room could be more disruptive than other areas.

He remembered the spare batteries in his pocket and fished them out. The light blinked on as soon as they were inside and he twisted the handle closed again. But even with the light, he couldn't peer through the darkness to see what was in the cage. It was too dark. The mold was too thick and featureless. And he wasn't entirely sure he *wanted* to know what was in there. So after another moment, he gave up, returned the flashlight to his pocket and stepped back from the bars, looking over the cage as a whole.

It was curious. Both the breathing thing and the eyeball had been concealed in dark rooms and both at the centers of large masses of this foul, black mold. Both seemed less like living things than living *parts* of much larger and even stranger things.

Were the two related?

He'd encountered the mold three times now. The second time was in the forest, where he followed Peggy's advice and didn't investigate it. Now he wondered what he would've found if he had. Was there another strange, living thing hidden in the woods somewhere? Maybe another cabin or some sort of stable hidden at the center of the rot?

He might never know, as he had no pressing desire to return there and snoop around.

He needed to keep moving. Another wendigo could show up at any time. Or another reaper. Or more bugs. Or some other random, monstrous creature from whatever neighboring dimensions were spilling over into this one.

But he found himself troubled by all these things he kept finding. Strange, living things half-consumed by foul, black mold.

Alien plants. Otherworldly creatures. Unrecognizable technology. Roaming spirits trapped and preyed upon by some unseen force. And then there were those twisted places that seemed imbued with queer life but were neither alive nor dead. What did it all mean?

More and more, this whole ordeal reminded him of some science fiction novel about a hostile, alien invasion.

Could it be possible?

After all, it wasn't the first time the weird had given him a glimpse of something from another world. Back in Hedge Lake, he'd nearly been fried by a strange, lightning-spewing aircraft that strangely never seemed to have anything to do with any of the other things he'd encountered there.

Was it weird that he was so reluctant to believe in visitors from another planet? He'd fully acknowledged the existence of ghosts, creatures from other dimensions, witches and magic, psychic powers, time anomalies and even fairies, nymphs and genies...

Thinking about it now, shouldn't the existence of beings from another planet be the *least* improbable thing on that list?

He stepped carefully through the slippery carpet of slimy, black mold and made his way to another door that opened onto a separate hallway.

To his right, the mold had again seeped through the wall and begun to cover the floor. To his left was another door. Eager to get away from the rot and its noxious stench, and calculating that the tunnel he was searching for should be somewhere to the left of where he was standing, he made his way to the closed door, still dragging the soles of his shoes along the concrete in hopes of ridding himself of every drop of slime.

He was reaching for the doorknob when he felt it.

An eerie presence.

He turned, the hairs on the back of his neck bristling.

She was standing at the far end of the hallway, staring back at him. A young girl, a little older than the girl in the cupcake tee shirt, perhaps nine, with thick, reddish-blonde hair. She was dressed casually in blue jeans and a light sweater, but there was something dreadfully wrong about her. She was filthy. Her clothes and hair were covered in dirt. And her sweater was all stretched out. It drooped over one shoulder and dangled past one hand. Her skin was grimy. And she was only wearing one shoe.

Eric took a step back, his hand moving toward the doorknob behind him. This was a bad kind of wrong. He could feel it. This girl wasn't like the sweet girl in the cupcake tee shirt. There was a dark energy coming from her that even he could feel.

He couldn't see her face. Her head was bowed and her hair hung over her eyes, partially obscuring them. And the shadows were too deep.

It was much darker where she was standing than it should've been.

The light was fading. Darkness was swallowing the doorless hallway.

"Uh-uh!" he gasped. "Nope. Not dealing with that." He turned and grabbed for the doorknob, only to find that it was gone.

In fact, the entire door was gone.

The hallway now ended in a blank wall.

"*The hell?*"

He turned back again, his heart pounding. The other doors were gone, too. There was no way out. And the girl was closer than she was before. She was just on the other side of the mold, barely twenty paces away.

And the empty hallway was growing darker with each passing second.

"Not cool, creepy girl," he groaned.

What was with this place, anyway? It was just one thing after another. It was like he was trapped inside the notebook where Stephen King jotted down all his ideas, surrounded by a chaotic jumble of monstrous thoughts and morbid daydreams.

The girl was walking toward him now. Slowly. Her arms dangling at her sides, her head bowed. It was eerily like the way the wendigos moved before they flipped their murder switch. Except she didn't move quite as slowly as they did. She took actual steps, limping as she switched between the one muddy sandal to the one grimy foot.

Eric shook his head. "Yeah, no. How about you just stay over there where you are?"

But the girl kept walking toward him.

The hallway grew darker and darker with each step she took. It wasn't the lights, he realized. Those strange, flowing lights never changed. Instead, it was as if this girl were absorbing the light, slowly plunging them into darkness as she drew closer and closer.

"Maybe turn the lights back up?" he tried. "Please?"

She seemed to be single-mindedly making her way toward him. But like the confused woman and the reaper, she didn't seem to like the mold that was seeping through the wall. She was careful to walk around it. He noticed this and for the first time wished there was more of the stuff. In fact, he rather wished he was still in that room with the moldy cage. It suddenly seemed like the best place in the world to be. If the door hadn't vanished, he would've happily sprinted straight back to the middle of that reeking carpet of slime.

He turned and scanned the wall behind him again.

The door was here. He knew it. This was just an illusion. A ghostly trick. There had to be a way to reach through it and find what was real.

And yet, he could feel nothing but cold concrete against his hands.

When he looked back, the girl was closer than she should've been. She was right in front of him. She was holding her arms out now, reaching for him. One sleeve dangled down from her outstretched hand. The other, he saw with mounting horror, was both filthy and *bloody*.

What manner of spook was this, anyway?

He stared at those muddy, battered fingers. At the clumps of dirt in her tangled hair. The mud stains on her clothes.

She looked as if she'd just clawed her way out of a *grave*.

His awful imagination went straight to work, convincing him that something terrible had happened to this little girl, that she'd fallen victim to some murderous monster who did terrible things to her and then left her small, lifeless body in some shallow hole somewhere.

He gave his head a hard shake and pushed the thought away. *No.* He didn't know that. It could just as easily have been an accident. Maybe she was playing on a big dirt pile and fell. That was a much better thought.

Well, maybe not *much* better… It was still tragic. It was still *awful.*

Again, he shook his head. Again, he scanned his surroundings. Again, he found no way out.

The dirty little girl was right in front of him. Those reaching fingers brushed the fabric of his tattered jacket.

He lifted his hands and balled his fists. "I'm serious now," he told her. "Don't make me have to…uh…" What? Don't make him have to get violent? Creepy, freshly-risen corpse or not, he wasn't really going to strike a little girl. He couldn't.

"Please?" he tried again, his voice squeaking.

But the muddy little girl wasn't going to stop. And there was nowhere for him to go. He was trapped.

As those filthy arms closed around him, he squeezed his eyes closed and turned his head, his jaw clenched against the anticipation of whatever unspeakable horror was coming next.

Except…

Seconds passed and nothing happened. There was no pain. There were no claws or teeth or monstrous jaws. He wasn't even being dragged to hell.

He was used to frightful things like this just disappearing at the last second, but the girl hadn't disappeared. He could still feel those cold arms encircling him. The smell of earth and rot surrounded him.

He opened one eye and dared a peak.

The girl had her face pressed against his jacket. She wasn't moving. She was just…*hugging* him…

"Uh… Okay." He glanced around at the dark, doorless hallway, confused. "You, um…" He nodded and ran his hand through his hair again. "Okay." He reached down, hesitated a moment, and then just, sort of…placed his hand on the girl's head. "It's, uh… It's okay."

The girl hugged him tighter.

He patted her dirty hair. "You're okay. I promise."

He closed his eyes again. His heart was still racing. When he opened them, the girl was gone, the lights were on and the doors had returned.

Apparently, that one really *did* just need a hug…

He was still holding his hand where the girl's head had been. He turned it and stared at it, dazed.

Somewhere in the silence, he heard the old woman chuckle again and a faint scent of cigarette smoke wafted past him. "Did you piss yourself *that* time?"

He ran his hand through his hair again and frowned.

"Not that I'd blame ya," she added. "Creepy little shit, that one."

Chapter Twenty-Five

He pushed the awful experience in the hallway from his mind, then cracked open the door and peered into the next room.

It was a maintenance room of some sort. Large workbenches took up most of the floor while the walls were covered from floor to ceiling in large, metal shelves still filled with boxes of all sizes and shapes.

There didn't appear to be any wendigos shuffling around the room. Nor were there any strange, alien plants, giant, otherworldly bug nests or creeping black mold.

And there were two other doors to choose from.

This seemed promising. He stepped into the room, daring to feel just a hint of cautious optimism, and eased the door closed behind him.

One of the two doors stood open. He made his way over there first and peered through it, making sure there was nothing lurking in there.

The room appeared to be a large storage space, filled with piled pallets of dirty white bags and stacks of steel barrels and five-gallon buckets. It was, he deduced, where they kept things used for tending strange gardens. It looked like fertilizers and soils and insecticides, but given the strange, alien characteristics of the things growing here, he imagined this stuff could just as easily be toxic waste and graveyard dirt.

The other door leading out of this storage room was facing the wrong direction, back toward the green lab's jungle room, so he pulled the door closed and turned his attention to the other exit.

He paused here, however, as it occurred to him that maybe

he should poke around for a weapon of some sort among the tools here.

But he'd barely turned his gaze back onto the room when he felt the hairs on the back of his neck stand up. A chill crept all the way through him.

It was the same feeling he had back in the treehouse, and then again on the floor of the jungle room.

He wasn't alone.

This was one of the twisted places.

A shiver seemed to pass through the room. Then something considerably greater than a shiver. The entire wall rippled and a sort of wave moved through it. It was like watching something large swim just beneath the surface of a calm lake, warping the water around it, painting a churning wake behind it. But whatever swam around the room did so not in water, but through solid concrete. It buckled and cracked. The metal shelves popped and twisted as it passed behind them, snapping screws and twisting the railings, sending boxes and crates crashing to the floor, spilling hardware and supplies onto the bare pavement.

Eric spun around, keeping his eyes on the strange, traveling shape as it rounded the corner and raced along the next wall.

Then it simply vanished.

An eerie, unsettling silence followed for a moment. Then a strangely weary sort of voice rolled across the still air.

"Voltner…"

He'd heard that name before. Back in the jungle room. The last time this sort of thing happened to him. *The seeds are planted…* he recalled. *Tell Voltner… Tell him… Seeds… Streams…* He had no idea what any of it meant at the time, of course. And he still didn't know. It seemed like nothing more than rambling nonsense. But slowly those insane sputterings were beginning to take an unsettling shape. "Who's Voltner?" he asked.

Instead of a reply, he was answered with a cold and sudden wind that whipped through the room, not unlike the one he felt back in the treehouse when the thing that called itself Bronwen first awakened.

The wind swirled around him, tossing his hair and giving

him a fierce and instant chill. Then it sped across the floor, picking up dust and debris and lifting it into the air, churning it in a sort of angry whirlwind. "You're not Voltner..." it sighed. Then it vanished and the dust rained back down to the floor and swirled into a pile.

"I'm not," said Eric.

That strange wind rippled across the floor in front of him, stirring the dust into a strange pattern that resembled a gaunt, bearded face. "Not Voltner..." it said again, and as the voice drifted across the dusty air, that strange face seemed to move with the wind, mouthing the syllables as they were spoken. "Not Lofleder..."

He stared at the face in the dust. Lofleder? Wasn't that the name Dora mentioned? The lead scientist? "No... My name is Eric."

"Eric..." said the man in the dust. The phantom wind made its lips ripple with the words. It even seemed to make it turn from one side to the other.

It was beyond strange. It was utterly surreal. But he'd already conversed with talking toys and a living jungle with ever-staring eyeball flowers, so...why not?

(He was going to end up in a straight jacket yet, he was sure of it.)

"Do I...know that name...?"

"I don't think we've met," replied Eric. But he recalled Bronwen telling him that she'd heard his name in her dreams. "Who are you?"

"Who...? Am I...?"

Oh good. They were doing this again. Last time this was the part where the jungle man became agitated, the eyeball flowers went limp and a bunch of terrifying animal puppets tried to kill him.

He wondered how the dust man was going to top that. Something with all the dangerous tools scattered around the room, he expected.

But the dust man didn't turn crazy. Instead, the face on the floor seemed to contemplate the question very carefully.

"I...am..." it replied. That dusty face scrunched up. Then another strange wind blew open its eyes and it seemed to look at him. "*I am Port.*"

"Port?" sad Eric. Was that a name? Short for Porter, perhaps?

"I am Port," the voice said again, as if contemplating the notion that it had a name. "I am Port..."

"Did you used to work in this building, Port?"

Again, that cold wind stirred the dust, wiping away the face and remaking it again a few feet to the left, facing the other way. "I-am-Port..." it said again, still seeming to think very carefully, "...worked in *all* the buildings... I-am-Port...fixed things...*built* things... I-am-Port...kept all the things working..."

So Port was a handyman. This was a much more productive conversation than the last one he'd had, in spite of that weird "I-am-Port" thing he kept saying. "Do you know what happened to you?" he asked.

The ghostly wind shifted the dust back to where it was before and reshaped that gaunt face into a deeply thoughtful expression. "No. I-am-Port...was inside...green lab... I-am-Port...was...going over checklists... It was almost time..."

Seriously, why was he talking like Groot from *Guardians of the Galaxy*? It was weird.

"Almost time...to turn it on."

"Turn what on?" pressed Eric.

That wind stirred the dust and the face seemed to lift and stare up at Eric. "*The machine.*"

"Machine?"

"The machine that changed I-am-Port."

This was still a very weird conversation, but things were continuing to fall into place. Bronwen, the woman in the treehouse wall, said something about having been changed, too. And cute, babbling Dora had said something about a machine, as had the crazy-sounding man in the woods.

But how did Port end up like this? It still didn't make any sense to him.

"I am Port..." sighed the dust man, frowning. Then, contemplatively, "*Port...*"

"Can you tell me about the machine?"

The dust rolled itself into a much darker expression.

"It was *evil...* Voltner never should've taken those plans... Nothing good could ever come from those monsters. Should've left them in the wreckage. Should've *burned it all...*"

Eric felt overwhelmed. An *evil* machine, built from plans taken from the *wreckage* of *monsters?*

His imagination was eager to fill his head with images of a crashed spaceship filled with awful, forbidden technology.

"Who's Voltner?"

"*Voltner!*" snarled the dust man. The wind creased his brow and gave him a furious scowl. "Walter Voltner! *He* did this to Port! It's *his* fault!"

"So this Voltner guy was the one in charge?" prodded Eric.

"It was *Voltner's* machine that changed Port... *He* caused all this... Him and the others..."

"Others?"

"Roden... Lofleder... Patelemo... Shinne... They were the ones... The *experts...*" He said the word with such scathing venom that Eric felt himself cringe. "They built the machine... They turned it on... They changed Port... They changed *everything.*"

"The men who broke the world," sighed Eric.

The dust man turned his face and stared at him. "Not men..." he said, speaking in the cold wind. "Monsters... Demons... *Devils...*"

A delicate subject, Eric realized. He had a feeling he should tread lightly here. "You mentioned Lofleder's name before..." It was the same name Dora mentioned. Ira Lofleder, the head scientist. "Can you tell me about him?"

"Lofleder..." The face shifted again. "The botanist... The devil who brought those awful trees..."

He nodded. Just as Dora said, Lofleder was in charge of the green lab. That was his office he found. But it sounded as if Voltner was the one in charge of everything.

The wind swirled. The face in the dust slid back and forth, as if Port were shaking his head in frustration. "Lofleder...built the channels...made the streams flow...made the impossible machine work...broke the very laws of nature..."

I've given you what you want! thought Eric, remembering the words of the thing back in the jungle. *The channels are built! The streams are flowing, aren't they?* That was *him*, he realized. Lofleder, himself. He was the man trapped in the jungle.

It didn't seem that the devil botanist had fared so well for his involvement with the machine. It sort of sounded like there was a considerable amount of tension between him and Voltner in those final days, too.

The phantom wind stirred through the room, cold and irritable.

"Lofleder..." growled the man in the dust.

Eric decided it was time to change the subject. "What about Bronwen?" he asked. "Did you know her?"

The wind at once died down. The face on the floor churned, the anger washing from its expression in an instant. "Bronwen...?"

"I think I spoke to her a little while ago."

"Bronwen... She's...still here...?"

"She says she was changed. She's...like you."

The wind swirled the dust man's face into an expression of anguish. "Still here..." he sighed. "Changed... Like...Port..."

"She was looking for someone. She kept asking for—"

"Perrine..."

"That's right."

"Perrine is...not like Port. Perrine is...gone..."

Eric stared at him. Gone?

But the strange wind stirred the dust man's face, making him shake his head back and forth, an expression of anguish overtaking him. "Bronwen was... She was..."

Another wave of intense vertigo swept through him, churning his stomach and nearly toppling him over.

Suddenly, he was standing in blinding sunlight, squinting out at a sprawling garden.

A tall man with a familiar beard was tending to the flowers while a lovely woman with long, auburn hair sat on a bench nearby, wearing a long dress and a sun hat. A familiar little girl in shorts and a sleeveless shirt was running around the flower beds.

Like the last time this happened, no one said anything. It only lasted a moment, just time enough to see the man Port once was turn and smile at the woman and the girl.

Then the vertigo washed over him again and he was standing back in the cold maintenance room as if he'd never left.

"Cared for her…" sighed the face in the dust. "Taught her… Raised her… *Loved* her…"

Eric stared at the ghostly face, a feeling of mounting horror rising inside him. The girl in that vision he had in the treehouse wasn't Bronwen. She was Perrine. Bronwen was a caregiver to Perrine. A legal guardian, perhaps. A mother figure… No wonder she'd been searching for her all these years.

"But Perrine is gone…" lamented the man in the dust, his face blowing into deeper and more agonizing expressions of sorrow. "Not changed… Not like Port… Not like Bronwen… Gone forever…"

Eric shook his head. Did he mean that the girl was dead? Had she been swallowed up with Evancurt's earliest haunters?

The wind picked up again. "The devils…" growled Port, his expression swirling into something darker. "*Monsters!*"

He took a step backward. This topic was apparently even more sensitive than Lofleder. He needed to be careful.

"Voltner… *Roden*…"

"Roden?" One of the five men he'd called "devils." Scientists, he was beginning to realize. The men who built whatever god-awful machine could break the world and reduce a man to a mere face in a scattering of dust.

The face on the floor turned furious. It trembled in the swirling wind, constantly shifting and churning. "Roden…gave her to it… *Used* her. Just another piece…of that damned machine. She was…the *spark*…that started it…that brought the machine to life…"

The wind whirled and the face in the dust was blown away. A storm suddenly raged around him, blowing things off the tables and remaining shelves, forcing him to shield his eyes from dust and splinters.

"*He was evil. A monster!*"

Eric couldn't remain here any longer. More than just dust was flying now. Heavier things had taken to the air. Broken boards. Nails. Screwdrivers.

He squinted through a gap between his upraised arms and saw a hammer fly past him, twirling end-over-end.

He turned and fled through the other door, slamming it behind him.

In an instant, the storm inside the room vanished. The howling of that unnatural wind suddenly stopped and there followed a brief clatter and clanging of raining wood and metal as everything dropped to the floor.

Then there was only silence.

As he stood there, his back pressed to the door, his heart racing, he heard the thing that used to be a handyman named Port whisper to him, the voice seemingly coming from the door, itself. And the words he said chilled him all the way to his bones: "He sacrificed his own daughter."

Chapter Twenty-Six

What was wrong with this place?

Devilish scientists. Plans for a terrible machine salvaged from the wreckage of monsters. Child sacrifices. Unknown scores of wandering souls waiting to be devoured by some mysterious force. Alien plants eating holes between dimensions. Monsters from in-between places. Rotting worlds. Changed people.

This is where they broke the world.

He shivered and stepped away from the maintenance room door.

To his left, the hallway turned back the way he came. If he remembered correctly, just around the corner he'd find the door to the loading ramp and that hideous hive he'd just escaped. And that would mean that the heavy, steel door just to his right was the tunnel entrance he'd been looking for.

He walked over to it and cracked it open. The tunnel looked like something from a movie. Made entirely of concrete and only dimly lit, it was about twenty feet wide, with an arched ceiling, twelve feet high at its center. A three-foot-wide walkway ran along each side, with a deep channel between them, like some large, metropolitan sewer line. A shallow, oily stream was flowing down the channel, carrying a subtle and sour stench. A half dozen gold cables, three times as thick as the ones back in the glass house, were mounted to the wall nearest him, one above the other, running as far as he could see. On the opposite wall of the tunnel were four large, lead pipes mounted in the same way. And a much larger pipe, at least three feet in diameter, ran along the center of the ceiling.

This was one end of the tunnel. The door opened directly

onto the very end of the rightmost walkway. To his left was a low, barred opening in the wall, allowing that foul-looking liquid to pass through, but not people. He could hear the echoing splashes as it spilled over some black ledge somewhere in the darkness beyond and into whatever unknown reservoirs were buried there. On the other side of the water, at the very end of the leftmost walkway, was another of those curious, outhouse-sized metal boxes. Like the others, it didn't seem to have a door. But those lead pipes all seemed to bend away from the wall and attach directly to the far side of it.

The much larger pipe overhead, and the fat, gold cables next to him, in contrast, continued straight on through the wall.

Everything here had a filthy sort of mildewy griminess about it. He was starting to really wish he had one of those respirator masks they used for cleaning up hazardous materials.

He stared into the gloomy emptiness ahead of him, wondering if this tunnel was going to take him to the machine he kept hearing so much about. The map back in Lofleder's office showed that this tunnel curved to the right some considerable distance ahead of him, eventually carrying him to the building marked "the workshop," which already sounded like a good title for a horror movie.

It was probably going to be a long walk, judging by the scale of the buildings on the map. He started walking, already convinced that he was going to have to deal with something deeply unpleasant down here. Going back wasn't really an option. He was going to have to get around anything that tried to block his path, and he seriously didn't want to have to step off the walkway into that awful-looking water.

But several minutes passed in silence without anything happening.

Then he realized that he wasn't alone. He glanced behind him to find a very small, middle-aged man following close on his heels, staring at him.

"Uh… Hey," he said.

The man said nothing, but only stared at him, his eyes wide with a strange sort of wonder.

Eric turned forward again, ignoring the man. Maybe he didn't speak English.

It was a little unsettling, being stared at that way, but like most of the ghosts he'd encountered here, the little man didn't seem to mean him any harm, so he focused on the path ahead of him and tried to ignore those wide, staring eyes.

A shadowy shape emerged from the gloom ahead of him, slowly materializing into the form of a very old man sitting on the cold walkway with his back to the wall, his knees drawn up to his chest and his face buried in his arms. He had a distinctly homeless look about him. His clothes were dirty and ragged and his hair was disheveled and sticking up in places.

Eric's gaze washed over him as he walked by. He felt bad for the old man, but if he was like all the other people he'd encountered here, there was nothing he could do.

As painful as it was to just walk past someone like that, the best thing he could do for any of Evancurt's wandering souls was continue forward until he found a way to fix what was broken and set them all free.

He continued on, pushing the miserable-looking old man from his thoughts and focusing on the walkway ahead of him.

A flurry of footsteps behind him startled him, but before he could turn and look, a small boy darted past him and ran on ahead.

A moment later, he caught sight of a young woman in a short skirt and heels stumbling around on the other walkway, giggling drunkenly to herself. When she saw him looking at her, she laughed and said, "Does anyone know where I parked? I'm *so* fucking lost right now!"

Eric couldn't seem to help thinking that finding her car while drunk off her ass might've been exactly why she was here, and the thought made him cringe.

"Can you see them?" said a frightfully thin and pale woman who was suddenly standing right in front of him. She was wearing a hospital gown and a scarf that hid what little hair she had left. Her eyes were sunken and shadowy.

He couldn't stop himself from taking a startled step backward, nearly bumping into the little man still following him with that gaping stare.

"They're white," she explained, "like the snow. So bright it almost hurts to look at them. But with all-black eyes. They don't walk on the floor like people. They crawl around on the walls and ceiling."

He opened his mouth to reply that he hadn't, in fact, seen anything of the sort, but found the words difficult to form. There was something immensely creepy about her description of these white beings.

"I told Mamma about them. I told her they were there. She said they were angels, come to get me. But they're not. I know they're not."

A lot of the spirits he'd encountered in Evancurt spouted crazed nonsense, but this seemed different. The words she spoke, her sickly pallor and the hospital gown all told an eerie story that ran far deeper than the anguished cries of regrets he'd heard from so many of the others. This was someone who was truly haunted.

He stood there, unsure what to say.

"She couldn't see them," said the woman. "She thought it was the fever. She thought there wasn't anything there. But you can see them, can't you?"

He glanced around, half-expecting to see brilliant white figures with empty black eyes crawling along the ceiling. But there was a blissful lack of any such creatures within sight at the moment. "Like…right now?" he asked.

He thought she'd ignore him, but she turned and looked around. "No… They've gone away for now… But when they finally come…" again, she turned those haunted eyes on him, "…you'll be able to see them, right?"

He wanted to tell her that her mamma was probably right. That it was probably whatever sickness that took her, giving her delirious and frightful hallucinations in her final, tragic hours, but something deep inside him made him hold his tongue. Instead, he said, "I *do* sometimes see things."

She nodded. Her expression was utterly serious. Grave,

even. "I could tell."

Something about this woman's words seemed strangely significant.

"Watch out for them," she warned him. "They're real. They're not angels. Don't let anyone tell you different."

"I won't," he promised.

Then the woman turned away and vanished. It happened just that quickly. It was as if she only existed as long as you were viewing her from the front. As soon as she turned away, she simply wasn't there anymore.

He stood there, staring at the space she was just occupying.

They're white like the snow. So bright it almost hurts to look at them. But with all-black eyes.

He shivered. What a horrific image.

Then he glanced over at the little staring man. He was crowded right next to him, peering up at him with those wide, fascinated eyes.

"Personal space, man. Come on."

Chapter Twenty-Seven

Eric continued his trek through the enormous tunnel and the ghosts of Evancurt continued to haunt him, though none were as eerily engaging as the woman in her hospital gown.

The staring man had eventually lost his fascination with him and moved on, but he passed a very confused-looking man in swim trunks, a nervous-looking woman in a bright-purple bridesmaid dress, an uncommonly cheerful old man in waist-high fishing waders, a weirdo wearing one of those stupid horse masks and a naked drunk man urinating on the wall and belting out a butchered version of Abba's *Take a Chance on Me*. A rude, stuck-up man in a stiff sweater complained that this was the most disorganized cruise he'd ever been on and intended to file a complaint as soon as he disembarked in Antigua. A woman with blue and purple hair asked him if he'd seen her cat. A young man in full military gear asked him for his orders. A fiercely intimidating, heavily tattooed man wanted to know when the next episode of *The Great British Baking Show* was going to be on. And a little girl in a glittery Cinderella dress informed him matter-of-factly that he was too fat to be a prince.

All told, it was considerably more crowded than he thought a reeking sewer tunnel in the middle of nowhere should've been.

And the spirits kept coming. As he rounded the first curve in the tunnel, he walked past a grouchy-looking man who was pacing back and forth, grumbling to himself, a boy in his early teens who appeared to be trying to teach himself to tie a necktie and a small, excitable-looking woman who was mumbling something to herself about a doorway on top of a burning mountain.

Then he caught sight of a tall, wild-eyed man standing on a narrow bridge connecting the two walkways and gawking at his surroundings. As he approached this man, he turned those wide eyes on him and exclaimed, "This is all wrong!"

Eric paid him little mind. It seemed like just more of the endless random nonsense that all the other ghosts had been spitting at him, after all. He probably thought he was in a bus station or something. But he stopped as the man pointed up at the large pipe running overhead and said, "Whatever's running through that…it isn't liquid or gas or even energy. It doesn't flow like anything I've ever seen before."

He stopped and stared up at the pipe, curious.

"This whole passage is wrong," said the man, gesturing at the alien space all around him. "It doesn't follow the laws of this world!"

Eric, being fairly sure that none of this technology came from this world in the first place, wasn't exactly floored. He considered telling this guy he should check out the stuff on the other side of the door at the far end of the tunnel behind him. That'd *really* irritate him.

He recalled Dora telling him that Lofleder's alien plants allowed the people here to access another world and take advantage of different laws of physics. Was this one of the places where that had happened?

Then the man pointed down at the channel beneath the bridge. "And what *is* this stuff? *It's not coming from anywhere!*"

This caught him off guard. He looked down to see that the man was right. When he first entered the tunnel, there was several inches of foul-smelling water flowing in the channel and through the barred opening in the wall. But although he hadn't seen any of the reeking liquid entering the tunnel at any point, it had shrunk to a mere trickle beneath the bridge. And farther up, the channel appeared to be completely dry. It was as if the water were collecting out of thin air.

"None of this should even exist!"

Eric looked back the way he came. Was this tunnel a part of the machine he was looking for? He turned back to the wild-eyed man on the bridge, curious to ask if he could tell which way the strange energies were flowing, if there was some central point to all these workings, but he'd already vanished.

Perhaps he'd used up all his energy being loud and excitable.

He continued on his way, still contemplating the wild-eyed man's exclamations that everything about this tunnel was wrong and didn't follow the rules of this world.

The passage curved to the right again. If he remembered the map correctly, the entrance to the lower levels of the workshop would be waiting at the end of the silent tunnel, directly in front of him.

But it was about now that two very troubling things occurred to him. First, although the tunnel had been crowded with ghosts a few moments ago, he hadn't seen a single soul since the wild-eyed man on the bridge vanished. The tunnel was eerily silent and unsettlingly deserted. Second, there was a strange sort of *vibration* flowing through the tunnel. He could feel it in the floor, rising up through the soles of his shoes and into his feet. He reached out and placed his hand on the wall next to him. It was there, too, a faint, but discernable sensation that didn't seem entirely physical, although he wasn't sure what else it could be.

As he stood there, pondering what all this could mean, he felt a strange *numbing* sensation in his thumb and he snatched his hand back, alarmed.

What was that? And did it come from that gold cable his hand was resting above? His thumb was the part that was closest to that.

Again he found himself itching to reach for his phone. He could almost hear Isabelle telling him that something in the energy had changed and to get out of there.

He looked around at the walls and ceiling of the empty tunnel around him. He didn't need Isabelle to tell him that something was happening. Something *bad*.

Get out of there, Eric.

It'd be nice if that voice in his head really was Isabelle, if their lack of a phone had finally triggered something in his brain, allowing her to speak to him in the easy way that he spoke to her. But he was certain that it wasn't her. It was only his own common sense, dredging up her voice to help spur his stupid ass into moving, because he apparently meant to just stand there and wait to see what horror was heading his way at this very moment.

And still he wasn't moving!

It was time to go. He started to turn and hurry onward, intending to pick up his pace. But then his gaze fell on the channel between the two walkways and he paused again.

The foul liquid had completely dried up well before he reached this point in the passage, but now it was suddenly flowing again. And it was flowing the *wrong way*.

He stood there, trying to piece together what it meant. Did the water in the tunnel ebb and flow like a tide? That didn't seem quite right.

But as he stood there, stupidly watching, he realized that it was getting deeper.

A few more seconds passed in what he couldn't deny was utter stupidity. He could almost imagine Karen and Holly and Paige all sitting around the phone, horrified, as Isabelle shouted something along the lines of, "Don't just stand there! *Run, you idiot!*"

Even then, he took only a single step backward as his numb brain processed the rising liquid, the heavy, steel door that brought him here, the sour, reeking breeze that pushed with increasing intensity at his back and that mildewy griminess that covered every surface, even the large pipe that ran along the highest part of the ceiling… What was about to happen, he realized, was a sort of *backflush*. In the next few seconds, he was going to get an up-close demonstration of one of this tunnel's jobs.

Somewhere, deep in his brain, whatever lazy synapses were in charge of pulling the big, important "Get the Fuck Out of There" lever finally woke up and he fled.

Chapter Twenty-Eight

He cursed as he ran, spitting the same foul word over and over again.

Already, the oily water was racing alongside him, lapping at the edges of the channel, splashing higher and higher. Very soon, it would spill over the edge and flood the walkways, drenching his shoes.

The idea of wandering these snowy woods in late January with wet feet was unpleasant enough, and that was the very least of his worries. He had no idea what horrible, sour-smelling liquid was rushing toward him, but he was confident it was nothing as pleasant as dirty runoff. And far from merely soaking his socks, if he didn't get through the door, he was likely to *drown* in the foul stuff.

Immediately, his hideous imagination went to work against him, wondering if he'd really only drown in it or if it would turn out to be some horrific chemical that would melt the flesh from his bones the moment it touched him.

That strange vibration had grown into a steady roar and that sour wind blew harder at his back.

He could feel an icy mist beginning to rain down around him.

The waves lapped higher at the sides of the channel, splashing onto the walkway around him. It was churning harder now, beginning to froth and foam.

He hoped the walkway didn't turn slick. If he slipped and fell, he was quite sure it'd be the end of him. And he could think of far more dignified ways to end his epically weird biography than to be taken out by a freak tidal wave in an alien *sewer*.

Was it only his imagination again, or were those golden cables running alongside him beginning to glow?

He recalled that strange numbing sensation he felt in his thumb when he placed his hand too near one of them and an entirely new category of horrible thoughts flooded his panicked mind.

Could whatever strange energy those cables carried actually kill him? If he found himself submerged with them, would it send that numbing shock through his entire body? Could it numb his lungs and heart? His brain?

How long was this damned tunnel?

More and more of that icy, sour mist was falling around him, slowly soaking his jacket. The walkway in front of him was increasingly wet. The waves were splashing higher and higher.

He could see the door up ahead, a beacon for him to focus on. Now he only had to hope it was unlocked. And as he raced toward it, he couldn't help but wonder why it *wouldn't* be locked. Why hadn't *all* the doors been locked? He could only hope that his strange luck continued to hold out.

The sour waters were raging at the bars at the end of the channel. He could hear the roar of an oily waterfall pouring into the black reservoirs beyond. Iridescent foam and slick, chaotic rain poured down around the doorway as he closed those last few steps between him and safety.

He could hear it coming. A great, rumbling thing bearing down on him from behind.

The door *wasn't* locked. He yanked it open and darted through it. And as he turned to pull it closed again, he saw the raging wall of water that was rushing toward him, only seconds away.

Never mind drowning. He slammed the door between him and impending, watery death and almost immediately felt it shudder against the terrible impact. If he'd waited any longer to start running, he realized, he would've been swept into that raging current and slammed against the wall with enough force to shatter his skull.

He turned and leaned against the wall, his aching legs suddenly shaking under the grim reality of how close that was.

"They've been getting more frequent lately."

He turned to find an older man in worn jeans, a flannel shirt and a baseball cap standing in the dark corridor, his eyes fixed on the door as it shuddered against the raging storm behind it. "What?"

"The flushing of the tunnels," the old man replied. "The venting of the streams. The depressurizing of the lines. They didn't used to happen so often."

The flushing of the tunnels? He turned and stared at the door. Venting of the streams? He remembered the building with the doors locked tight, with the unseen machinery banging away inside. The map in Lofleder's office revealed that the place was known as the "vent house." The last time he heard that machine's banging, the first group of ghosts that appeared to him suddenly vanished. Just like they did in the tunnel shortly before the tidal wave came. Did flushing and venting the system do something to the spiritual energy and disrupt the spirits' ability to manifest themselves? "What does it mean?"

The old man turned his weary eyes on him. "Whatever this place was built for," he said, "I got a real bad feeling it's almost done doing it."

Eric stared at him, letting the weight of those words sink in. It was like all the other times the weird involved him. The clock was running down. The enemy was at the gates. Destruction was nigh. This he had no problem understanding. But he still had no idea what it was he was supposed to do.

And it seemed that the old man had enlightened him as much as he was willing because he faded away into thin air and was gone.

Eric stood up straight, frustrated, and looked down the empty corridor that lay before him. It was little different from those in the lower levels of the green lab. Dusty, empty and silent. More of those strange, swirling light fixtures were mounted on the ceiling, making the space much brighter than the tunnel.

According to Lofleder's map, this was supposed to be the workshop.

But what sort of workshop needed a basement with a large

sewer tunnel entrance?

He wasn't eager to see what kind of new hell he'd undoubtedly wandered into, but he couldn't go back and just standing here wasn't an option, so he began walking.

The hallway wasn't very long. In less than a minute, he spied a metal staircase leading up to the next floor. There were no other doors or hallways. But things became more complicated when he ascended the steps into a complex labyrinth of machinery sunken into a cold, confounding darkness.

This new space was much more sparsely illuminated than the green lab had been. The lights here were fewer and spaced farther apart. They were also much higher and hung from long, metal poles that descended from an ominous darkness that loomed overhead like an empty and starless sky.

He stood at the top of the stairs, studying his surroundings. If it really was a machine he was searching for, this definitely seemed like a step in the right direction. But there were *countless* machines here. To his left stood a twisted conglomeration of coiled pipes of all sizes that were arranged in a way that reminded him a little of those anatomical models of the human digestive tract, as if he were looking at the rusting, metallic guts of some enormous and strangely-organic robot. To his right, on the other hand, was a much simpler, but equally confusing shape that looked like a bunch of giant balls stuffed into an enormous sock and then coiled into a sort of cone-shaped pile. And in front of him, dividing the path into two separate walkways, was a large, iron disk set into an enormous, cylindrical, concrete tube with several large pipes branching off it. The disk, itself, was fitted with several large, metal boxes with an assortment of meters and dials, suggesting some sort of pressurization of the space behind it. He had no guess as to what its purpose might be. It looked like some kind of unnecessarily complex bank vault, but he doubted there were any stacks of cash hidden inside.

The place had the distinct feel of an abandoned factory, except that "abandoned" wasn't the right word for it. This stuff looked old and rusty and was covered in dust and cobwebs, and he was confident that he was probably the first living soul to set foot inside this place in many years, maybe since that ominous April on those decades-old calendars, but he found himself convinced that this place was anything but abandoned.

The shadows were as silent as they were many. But the things in this building were still working. He could feel them. There was a distinct and ominous energy flowing through the cold air. He could feel it deep inside his brain. Forces he could neither see nor hear, nor even hope to vaguely understand, but which he could nonetheless feel, were still hard at work in this place, chugging along even after all these decades.

He turned his gaze up into the darkness above him. He couldn't see the ceiling. All those swirling lights could reach was a vast tangle of enormous pipes twisting and winding through the gloom like giant snakes.

It was strange. Searching his surroundings, he could see plenty of great, blocky shapes and lots of tubes and pipes of all sizes and even more of that strange, gold wiring. But he saw no moving parts. There were no exposed wheels. No visible gears. No pistons or levers or chains or belts.

His thoughts drifted back to the dust man, Port, and his ominous talk of monsters and wreckage and infernal technology and he couldn't help but wonder if all of this could really have been reverse-engineered from the remains of some crashed alien spacecraft. Could he really be looking at proof of life among the stars?

He was distracted from these thoughts by the appearance of a tall, potbellied man with messy hair wearing nothing but a pair of plaid pajama pants. He was circling a large, vertical pipe that ran up from the floor and into the gloom above, feeling his way around it with his hands.

As he watched, the man laid his head against the side of the pipe, as if listening to whatever was inside it. Then he turned, seemingly noticing Eric standing there. "I think…" he said, looking confused. "I think there're people in there."

Eric stared at him. People? Inside the pipe?

The man shook his head, as if he couldn't understand it himself. Then he put his ear to the side of the pipe again. "I can hear them," he explained. "Voices... Inside."

He wasn't sure what to say. There was something deeply horrific about the idea of people being trapped inside the machinery.

"They're calling out," said the man. "I think...they're in pain."

Eric turned and looked around at all the pipes. There were so many of them. Miles of them, it seemed.

When he looked back, the pajama pants man was gone, leaving him once more alone with his thoughts.

Again, he glanced up at those great, bulky shapes looming over him.

Break the machine, he thought, remembering the frantic words of the little man in the woods. Was this what he was talking about? Was this the thing Tessa was describing when she said that the people here built something they weren't supposed to build.

He could just start smashing things, he supposed. But something told him that wouldn't work. First of all, this stuff wasn't exactly fragile. Even if he had a crowbar and a sledgehammer, he wasn't likely to put more than a dent in any of this stuff. And even if he did, he had no idea what any of it was. What if he smashed a pipe and was rewarded with a face full of scalding steam or a lethal dose of radiation? With no idea what any of this stuff was, or how it worked, he could get himself killed and accomplish nothing for his troubles. At the very least, he'd probably draw the attention of those freaky reapers.

He needed more information before he did anything drastic.

Lofleder's office had provided a little bit of information. Besides those maps, he'd found Dora, who explained the purpose of the plants as conduits for the exotic energies they were utilizing here. And according to the helpful, dust-faced handyman, he knew that there were four other scientists involved in the creation of the Evancurt Machine. Maybe one of them had an office in this building. If he could just find his way to it...

But before he could formulate a plan to navigate the machines, something seized his arm, nearly knocking him over.

Chapter Twenty-Nine

"Got you!" cried the confused woman as she pressed her body against him, pushing him against one of the pipes. "Where did you go?"

"You again?" he growled. (Although he *was*, admittedly, glad to see that she was still okay after her frightful reaction to that moldy hallway.)

"I've been looking everywhere for you!"

"*You're* the one who disappeared!"

Still clinging to his arm, she stood up on her tiptoes and quickly kissed him again before he had time to turn away.

"Stop doing that!" he snapped, leaning away from her.

She didn't seem bothered in the least by his reaction to her kiss. She either wasn't able to see that he wasn't the person she thought he was through her delusions, or she was determined to ignore it. She tugged on his arm, pulling him toward the path on the left. "Come on!" she urged. "We're never going to make it if we don't hurry!"

"Why don't you go on ahead and I'll catch up?"

But the woman dragged him along. Again, he was surprised at how strong she was. It didn't seem like ghosts should be this strong. For that matter, he didn't think ghosts should feel this *real*. He was told more than once that everyone else here was different from him. This woman, in particular, had disappeared twice into thin air. She wasn't among the living. And yet the arms that held him were solid. They were strong, yet soft. They were warm. He could feel her body heat even through his jacket.

As far as he could perceive, she was every bit as real as he was. Why were the ghosts here so much more physical than the others he'd encountered? Did it have something to do with the machine he kept hearing about?

He recalled the man in the plaid pajama pants telling him that there were voices in the pipes. He looked around at them as he was pulled along, taking in the great, hulking shapes and the endless, winding plumbing. Again, he recalled babbling Dora, who spoke of "exotic energy streams." Were some of these pipes pumping spiritual energy through them? Was that what made her so solid?

"Do you even know where you're going?" he asked. Was there any reason why she picked left back there? Or was she just choosing directions at random?

They came upon a large, metal tank, about the size and shape of an average, above-ground, backyard swimming pool. It blocked the way forward, forcing them to choose between going left and right. Here the woman stopped. She seemed confused about which way to go, which seemed rather absurd since he was fairly sure she had no idea where she was going from the start.

Eric tried to wrench his arm free, but she wouldn't let go.

"Which way was it again?" she asked. She turned and looked at him. "You know the way, don't you?"

Clearly, she had no idea where she was. She was only wasting his time. "Why would *I* know the way?"

"I was sure we came this way before," she fussed, ignoring him again.

"Why do you keep asking me things? You're not even listening to me. I could tell you anything and it wouldn't matter."

She looked one way and then the other, puckering her face in a confused sort of way that made him think of Holly. She often made faces like that. On her, it was adorable. And utterly endearing. But he just wanted *this woman* to let go of his damn arm.

"If we don't hurry," she huffed, impatient, "we'll never make it in time."

"How about you go that way and I go this way?"

She looked up at the darkness overhead. "There should be a sign or something."

"Time is running out," said a familiar, warbling voice.

Eric turned to find Tessa standing next to him, staring at him with those creepy, bloody eyes. "Oh thank God!" he exclaimed. "Please be able to tell me something."

The confused woman pulled at his arm, crowding closer to him. She was looking at Tessa now, her gaze darting up and down her naked form. "Honey..." she said, "who is she?"

"I'm not your honey!" Eric snapped at her.

Strange... She couldn't seem to grasp that he wasn't who she thought he was, but she could see Tessa just fine?

Tessa's words flowed over him before her lips began to move and continued for a moment after they stopped. "The cells are nearly charged." The sound of her voice was nightmarish, even painful to listen to, but this was a minor thing compared to the relief he felt simply by having her here again. She and that damned cat were the only familiarity he was allowed in this ghost-infested madhouse, after all. "Before the morning light comes," she warned, "the second process will be complete."

He stared at her. Time was running out? The cells? Before the morning light... He remembered the old man who appeared to him in the basement, after his escape from the tunnel. *Whatever this place was built for, I got a real bad feeling it's almost done doing it.*

"Come on," said the confused woman, her voice icy. She tugged at his arm. "We need to go."

He ignored her. "What do you mean, second process? I don't understand."

"The three processes of the machine," explained Tessa. "The first stage took only seconds, and transformed this land, and all who were present."

"Transformed...?" As in *changed*. Bronwen and Port... Lofleder... Everyone who was present? As in anyone who was within range of the machine that day? All five scientists and all the help, too?

Everyone except young Perrine...

The words of the man in the dust drifted back to him, haunting him: *He sacrificed his own daughter.* He shivered at the memory.

"We're going to be late," huffed the confused woman. "It's

time to go."

"The second process requires a tremendous amount of energy," Tessa went on. "Energy it takes from the souls it lures and traps here. And soon the collectors will be at maximum capacity."

Eric stared at her. "Wait… You mean it's the *machine* that's eating the ghosts here? That's why the spirits disappear after a few years?"

She nodded.

"We have to go!" shouted the woman. She pulled on his arm, nearly overbalancing him. He stumbled a few steps after her.

"Knock it off!" Eric shouted back at her.

She glared at him. "I have been waiting *way* too long for this day for you to ruin it just so you can stop and chat with some…" she turned her glaring gaze on Tessa, her eyes sliding down her body, a shockingly hateful expression on her previously gentle face, "…cheap, naked *floozy!*"

Tessa hadn't paid any attention to the woman up until this point. But now her bloody gaze drifted to her. For a moment, the two merely stared at each other. Then Tessa pursed her lips and blew, as if to extinguish a candle. A great, phantom gust that Eric couldn't feel struck the woman, blowing back her brown hair. At the same instant, every stitch of clothing was blown off of her in the gale, leaving her as stark naked as Tessa.

There were a couple seconds of stunned silence, then the woman let out a piercing scream and let go of his arm to cover herself.

Then Tessa made a subtle, waving gesture with the fingers of one hand and the rest of the confused woman blew away like smoke in a breeze.

Eric stared at the space she'd been occupying only seconds before. Then he held up his liberated arm and stared at it. Apparently, it wasn't wise to make insinuations about Tessa's choice to spend her afterlife in the nude. Sometimes he forgot she was a witch as well as a ghost. "You…didn't hurt her, did you?"

Tessa shook her head.

He nodded. "Good. Then *thank you*. Maybe she'll leave me alone now."

She gave him a cheerful smile, apparently happy to have been of help.

"So the machine's just been sitting here for the last five decades, collecting spiritual energy?" he asked, getting back to what was important.

She nodded again.

"That's why Evancurt lures and traps ghosts?"

"It calls out to confused and vulnerable spirits, drawing them in. And once a spirit sets foot on this land, they can never leave. They're trapped here until the machine absorbs all their energy and they vanish forever."

He recalled what the pierced man told him about those who vanished. About how in their final hours they all told of something coming for them, something hungry and inescapable.

Those poor souls must've had some idea that the machine had nearly depleted their energy. They must've seen what was coming in some capacity. They obviously *knew* that they were about to be devoured, but they probably had no idea what it was or how it was happening. To them, it must have seemed that some mysterious and terrible force was bearing down on them, stalking them.

They must've been terrified. Every last one of them.

"And then what?" he asked. "What happens when the second process is finished? When the machine finally gathers all the energy it needs?"

"When the second process ends, the third process will automatically activate."

"And the third process is…?"

"No one knows for sure. No one knows what the ultimate function of the machine is or what it will mean for this world. No one knows how far the immediate effects will be felt. But it is certain that everything, living and dead that exists within Evancurt will cease to exist."

"Everything will just be *gone*?" He shook his head. "And that includes me, too, of course…"

She gave him a sad nod and smiled. "Unless you choose to leave now," she reminded him, "before the machine is finished."

There was always that option. Just as the pierced man told him back in the glass house. He wasn't like the ghosts. He wasn't trapped here. He could take himself out of range of whatever hell the Evancurt Machine was about to unleash on these woods. But if it was allowed to reach its third process, what would be the consequences for the world? What would he be escaping to?

Everyone kept pretending that he had this choice, but the truth was that he really didn't have any choice at all.

He shook his head. "I can't just..." He paused and looked down at his hand. Suddenly, there were small fingers closed around it. The girl in the cupcake tee shirt was back again and staring up at him with those big, blue eyes.

When he looked back at Tessa, she was staring down at the girl, her dark eyebrows raised. Recalling what she did to the confused woman, he suddenly leaned forward, shielding her with his body. "This one's okay!" he said quickly, not wanting her to send the poor girl to whatever far corner of the property she'd banished the confused woman to.

Tessa looked back up at him. Then she gave him another smile, as if to say, "Okay then."

He gave a sigh of relief and started to run his gloved hand through his hair again. But he stopped himself and glanced at the glove, remembering the black mold that had been smeared on them way back in the eyeball room.

Surely it'd been wiped clean by now...right?

But now he found himself trying to remember just how many times he'd run his hand through his hair since then. Suddenly, he felt the need for a shower, but that was about as likely as a hot cup of coffee and a donut.

He pushed the thought away and looked down at the girl, his weary mind swimming through the heavy things Tessa had told him. Slowly, a deep frown overtook his expression. "Wait..." He turned his gaze back to Tessa. "If every spirit who enters the borders of Evancurt are trapped here forever..."

She offered him another smile and nodded.

"No…"

"If you can't stop the machine," she confirmed, "then *I* can never leave this place, either."

"*Why?* Why would you come here, then? If you knew you'd be trapped…?"

"I came because you needed me. I'll always be there when you need me."

"But you'll…"

Tessa shook her head. "I'm not afraid. I don't have to be. Because I know you're going to save me." Again, she looked down at the girl. "You'll save us all."

Eric stared into those big, blue eyes. *No pressure or anything,* he thought. "Where is the machine?" he asked. "How do I break it?"

"I don't know that," replied Tessa, her warbling voice seeming to withdraw across the room.

He looked up to find that she'd gone again. "Tessa?"

"Follow the bones…" she whispered across the darkness at him.

"What bones? Where?"

But she was gone again.

He ran his probably-clean glove through his hair before he could stop himself and sighed once more. "Great…"

The girl tugged at his hand. When he looked down at her, she gestured for him to bend closer.

He knelt down beside her, curious. She'd never spoken before. He didn't think she could. But she leaned close to him and whispered in his ear, "Why was that lady naked?"

Chapter Thirty

The girl in the cupcake tee shirt didn't seem all that satisfied with his answer, which was basically that he didn't know, and that Tessa just seemed to like it that way. But she seemed to accept that it was the only answer he had to offer her and said not another word.

It wasn't like he *wanted* her to be naked. He had no perverted interest in seeing her like that. Quite the opposite, in fact. Like those bloody eyes and bruises, it was too much of a reminder that she was not only dead but had died *horribly*. It always made him a little sad when he looked at her.

"Did Mavis get the check?" asked a scruffy-looking old man who was suddenly standing beside him.

Eric blinked at him, distracted. "What? Who?"

"I hope she got it!" he moaned. He was wringing his hands, looking troubled. "I need to know she got the check in time! If she didn't get it in time..." He shook his head. "Oh, Mavis..."

"I'm sure she got it," decided Eric.

"I hope she got it in time," he said again.

"You know what," said Eric. "I remember now. She *did* say she got that check in time. Everything was fine."

But the man didn't seem able to hear him anymore. He was already wandering away, muttering, "Mavis... Oh, Mavis..."

Then he faded into the shadows and was gone.

"I really hate it when they do that..." he grumbled. It made him feel so helpless.

When he turned back, there was a skinny young man standing in his path with extremely thick glasses and an oversized, bright-yellow tee shirt with the words "Party in the Back" printed on the front. "They ran out of duck sauce," he said. Then, while

Eric stood there, wondering what in the world he was supposed to say to that, the young man turned around and walked away.

Eric shook his head and glanced down at the girl. "Is it always like this around here?"

She just gave him a bashful sort of shrug and continued staring up at him.

"Right. Well..." He peered into the shadowy nooks and crevices between the unidentifiable contraptions that crowded around them and towered over them as he walked. "I really wish one of them would tell me something *useful*."

Admittedly, a few of them *had* told him useful things, he supposed. But it was difficult to tell the helpful ones from the crazy ones.

He continued onward. Soon, an enormous concrete wall emerged from behind the tangle of pipes and machinery. Several massive holes were bored through it. They looked like subway tunnels. And there were no lights inside any of them. An unsettling blackness pooled inside each one.

He was getting a little tired of all this darkness. Why was the glass house so much brighter than the workshop? That whole place was brilliantly lit up once the lights came on.

But he was collecting a *great many* questions. Why did those lights in the glass house only come on after he'd made his way almost all the way to the rear of the building? And did the lights in the green lab and the workshop come on at the same time? Had the light in the coordination office above the freaky eyeball room come on?

Before he could decide on which terrifying black portal he wanted to venture into, the girl suddenly began pulling at his hand, urging him to the left. He'd resisted the confused woman's incessant pulling as much as possible. She didn't seem to know where she was going, after all. Except for her reactions to that moldy hallway and later to Tessa, she seemed mostly oblivious to what was going on around her. But the girl seemed much more aware of her real surroundings. So when she decided that they needed to get out of the open and duck into the shadows between two blocky machines connected by several lengths of welded-together pipe, he humored her and let her lead the way.

It wasn't as if he had a particular destination in mind, anyway. Was he supposed to find something in here? Or was he only trying to get back outside again? No one was telling him anything.

But as he stood in the darkness, peering out at those black tunnels, it became clear what had frightened the girl.

Something was moving in one of those inky holes. A great, hovering thing began to take shape in the darkness. Then an enormous and frightful *head* emerged, and Eric felt his heart stutter in his chest at the sight.

It wasn't a human head by any stretch of the imagination. If anything, it looked like some sort of dark fantasy realm *dragon*. It had a long, toothy, crocodile-like muzzle and huge, black, featureless eyes. Its skin didn't appear scaly, but rather glistened, as if wet, and was the blotchy, yellowish-black color of a very overripe banana.

He watched in mounting horror as the thing's neck followed it from the darkness, continuing to pour from the black tunnel until it became apparent that there was no body between the neck and tail. It was an enormous serpent-like shape, but with several rows of strange, undulating, feather-like fins running down the lower half of the sides of its body, giving it an eerie, deep-sea-creature appearance.

It shouldn't have surprised him. He knew there were creatures from other worlds wandering this land, including something enormous that bent back the tops of the trees and sent strong branches crashing to the ground. If that thing, whatever it was, could be wandering around these woods free, then why not a gargantuan snake...eel...sea serpent...*thing*?

He held the girl's hand and crowded deeper into the shadows of the unknown machinery as he watched the terrible shape slither higher and higher into the darkness above, winding and twisting its way through the huge tangle of pipes.

He wondered how the thing moved. It was such an enormous monstrosity that he couldn't see the whole thing at once and couldn't tell whether it was touching the ground. Did its body function like a snake's? Or was it somehow being propelled on those strange, delicate fins?

As the creature's prehistoric head disappeared into the darkness above them, he cautiously crept around the machine and watched as the final third of the beast slowly emerged from the black of the tunnel, revealing a strange, fin-like tail that made him decide that the creature belonged less to the snake family and more in the realm of mythical sea monsters.

As he stood there, watching the slithering horror vanish into the shadows above, still wondering if it was slithering or flying, the girl tugged at his hand, drawing his attention downward again. As soon as she had his gaze, she gestured impatiently at the dark holes from which the monster had just come.

"Right…" he said, distracted. "Go where the monster's not." He glanced up again at the monstrous tail disappearing among the shadowy pipes. "Good call."

Quickly, but quietly, he crossed the floor and slipped inside the nearest of the giant holes in the wall. Immediately, he could see that there was more light up ahead. And as a bonus, it was enough light to see that there wasn't another ocean trench-dwelling dragon's head floating toward him, a fact he was grateful to have, because he really didn't want to chance meeting one of those things head-on in the dark.

He wondered what the purpose of these tunnels were. There was a fairly large step up into it, making it impractical for any kind of vehicle. There was no machinery inside them. At least, not inside this one. There didn't seem to be any logical reason for them to exist, as far as he could tell.

He turned the corner and cautiously made his way to the end of the passage.

The space beyond was illuminated in the same way as the area behind him, with those strange, swirling fixtures casting circles of eerie flowing light down to the concrete floor below. But this was an entirely different gloom. This was a much more *empty* gloom. Gone were the oddly-shaped machines and the endless tangles of pipes. What he found, instead, was a large collection of identical, silver balls, each one about three feet in diameter, arranged in what appeared to be concentric, oblong rings. Each one had a single, gold cable protruding from the very top which snaked up into the darkness above the hanging, alien lights. There were dozens of them in all.

He scratched at the back of his neck as he walked out among the strange orbs. It reminded him of a pumpkin field. Or at least some strange, industrial *perversion* of a pumpkin field. It looked more like an art exhibition than a factory. "What *is* all this stuff?"

If the girl in the cupcake tee shirt had a guess, she kept it to herself. She held onto his hand and walked alongside him, looking around at the queer surroundings.

He stepped up to one of the orbs and examined it more closely, remaining careful not to touch either it or the golden cable rising out of it like a gilded stem. He'd seen something similar to this back in the glass house, he recalled. Except there'd been only one of these silver balls and it had been much larger. Also, there wasn't a cable rising out of its top. Instead, there'd been a number of white boxes mounted on each side of it and above it with a loop of that gold cable jutting out toward it.

Did that larger sphere in the glass house have the same purpose as the smaller ones in front of him now? He wondered if they performed some specific function. Could they be a part of the machine he was looking for?

Again, he wondered whether it would slow down the machine at all if he started smashing things. But each time he thought about it, his imagination promptly went to work offering up theories of what might happen. These things could be the equivalent of giant electrical transformers for all he knew.

He needed to find someone who could tell him exactly what he should do to stop the machine. He couldn't risk making a mistake. Tessa's very existence was at stake. The existence of *every* spirit trapped inside Evancurt was at stake, including the frightened little girl who was clinging to his hand right now. Not to mention his own existence. If he stayed here—and there was no way he could just leave Tessa and the others to such a grim fate—then he, too, would cease to exist when the machine finally finished its second process.

"Please..." gasped a cracked and wavery voice from behind him.

Eric turned, startled, to find a woman staggering toward him.

"Please help me..." Blood was running down her face from a gash in her forehead and from her nose. Her lip was swollen. She was clutching one arm with the other, holding it against her. She was limping. "Please... They took my children... They took them away from me..."

He stared at her, horrified. "Your...? What?" He squeezed the little girl's hand and stepped in front of her, doing his best to shield her from this awful sight. It was the only thing he could think to do. He couldn't even think of something to say to the poor woman.

"Please help me... Please..."

My god, he thought. He prayed this was nothing more than the delirious utterings of a confused spirit.

"I couldn't stop them..." The wounded woman stumbled closer to him, her eyes wide with desperation and anguish. "I tried... I tried so hard... But I couldn't stop it..."

The woman died in an accident, he decided. That was how she obtained those injuries. The trauma of her death confused her. She must've seen the paramedics take her children away to the hospital. That was all. That had to be it. Because the alternative was just too horrible to imagine.

"They were screaming... Crying... And I couldn't help them..."

Eric couldn't help taking a step backward. When he did, he bumped into the strange, silver ball he'd been examining. Somewhere, deep in the back of his mind where his sanity seemed to be numb to all the horrific things he kept seeing, he managed to take note of the fact that bumping into one hadn't electrocuted him. It neither exploded nor cracked open to unleash some new kind of hell upon him. Now he knew.

"Please..." begged the woman.

He shook his head and closed his eyes. There was nothing

he could do. Even if he thought there was any chance of helping the woman's children, even if he knew who to call and what to say, it wasn't as if he had his phone.

When he opened his eyes again, the awful woman had vanished.

The girl in the cupcake tee shirt gave his hand a gentle pat. "It's all right," the gesture said.

Again, he ran his gloved hand through his hair and glanced around.

There was a shirtless man with a very hairy chest and a long ponytail strolling between the orbs. When he caught Eric's eye, he nodded and said, "Hey, brother. This party blows. Where're all the chicks?"

Eric frowned at the man and then turned away without replying. When he did, he caught sight of another of those broken spirits. This one was an old woman. She was shuffling along, hunched over a cane. But each tiny step she took seemed to cause her body to break apart and stitch itself back together again.

Like the dancing girl and the strolling boy, she didn't say a word. She seemed to be minding her own business.

He wondered what the story was with those particular ghosts. Why did they look like that? None of the other ghosts looked like that. What made them different?

"Hey, mister?"

He turned to find a thin, shaky-looking young woman standing behind him. She had dark shadows under her eyes and a sickly sort of complexion. Her hands were stuffed into her pockets and she avoided looking at him. Her gaze remained fixed on the floor between them, instead.

"I'm…uh…" She licked her thin lips. She looked terribly nervous, but also desperate. "I kinda got myself into some trouble and…uh… Well…I really need some money. I…I can work for it." She already couldn't look at him, but now she turned her head, as if she couldn't bear to even look in his general direction. "I'll…do anything you want."

Eric stared at her, horrified.

A tear streaked down her face. "Whatever you want to...to do to me is...it's fine... Really."

It was *not* fine! He wanted to tell the woman to leave him alone, but he hesitated to say anything harsh. The woman looked so lost and desperate, so utterly terrified and fragile, that it made his heart ache. But on the other hand he was fairly sure she didn't need the money to pay for her entrance exams. She had all the telltale signs of a drug addict.

It didn't seem right. The dead shouldn't have to be slaves to the mistakes they made in life.

As it happened, he didn't have to find a nice way to tell the young woman he wasn't looking for rental romance tonight. As he glanced awkwardly around, he spied a puddle of shadows crawling toward him among the orbs.

Chapter Thirty-One

Another reaper. Eric was beginning to wish he'd never called the freakish things that. It only made them all the more horrifying. He should've called them something much less creepy. Like "puddle people" or "melty men."

When he looked back again, the desperate-looking woman had vanished. He was relieved. As bad as he felt for her, that was a new kind of awkward.

Why did all these encounters seem to be getting more and more disturbing? Wasn't it upsetting enough that all these people were dead?

He couldn't help these people. Evancurt's lost wanderers were not only trapped on this property, many of them were trapped inside themselves, as well. He hoped finding and breaking the machine would set them free and allow them all to find peace. But that wasn't going to happen if those reapers began to realize why he was here.

Still clinging to the girl's hand, he hurried away from the reaper and toward another concrete wall with more of those massive holes bore through it.

Please don't let there be any dragons in there, he thought as he hurried inside the nearest one and followed the black tunnel to the next illuminated room.

The two of them emerged from the tunnel into a much smaller space crowded with bulky machinery. Eric paused here and glanced around, distracted. There was something different about these machines. They weren't the same sort of blocky shapes that he'd seen in previous rooms. These looked more like some sort of bizarre modern art exhibit. They had strange, angular shapes jutting off of them and oddly-shaped openings exposing the mass of fine wiring hidden within. It almost looked as if some powerful force had torn these machines open, except that the metal wasn't jagged and sharp. In fact, every surface was perfectly smooth and rounded, less torn than *melted*, but with no visible damage to the exposed wiring.

He leaned closer to one of the machines, studying its inner workings. It wasn't actually wiring, he realized, but rather a complex collection of fine filaments, thin metallic ribbons and tiny glass tubes. Again, he was struck by the utter *alienness* of the technology. But before he could peer any deeper, the girl pulled urgently at his arm.

He glanced down at her, distracted. She had her feet planted firmly, tugging on him, urging him to back away. Those blue eyes were alarmingly wide.

Something in this room was upsetting her.

He wasn't always quick on the uptake, like when things started going south in the tunnel downstairs, but something about the look on her face made him turn back without question. Before he could step up into the tunnel, however, a weak and strangled voice called out from the silence in a strangely agonized stutter.

"I-i-is...? Is...ssssss...ssssome....?"

He paused, shocked at the desperate sound of the voice. It sounded like someone in terrible pain.

"Ssssomeone...? Someone th...th-there?"

A part of him wanted to speak up, to assure the suffering owner of the voice that he was, indeed, there, but the girl tugged harder at his hand and he bit his tongue, uncertain.

"Help me..." gasped the voice from inside the machine.

Something was moving in there, he realized. Something beneath all those tubes and ribbons and filaments, something that squirmed and writhed.

Was someone trapped inside?

"Puh...p-please..." stuttered the voice. "P-please...huh...huh...llll... Huh...elp..."

The girl tugged at him with greater urgency.

Something wasn't right. He was starting to feel it now. He

took another step back as the thing inside the machine twisted and churned.

Was this another twisted place? Like the jungle room and the treehouse and the maintenance room? Was this another of the machine's unfortunate victims?

"Help m...m-m-m...meeeeee...."

He couldn't tear his eyes away from those strange half-torn, half-melted openings where some unseen thing was squirming.

Blood began to drip from it.

"Huh...huh...elllllp... Help m-me..."

This *was* one of the twisted places. He could feel it now. But it wasn't like the other places. This one was strangely unstable. More and more, he understood that he didn't want to see what was writhing inside the machines. Whatever was in there wasn't human anymore, and wasn't meant to be seen by human eyes.

"Help meeeeeee!"

As he backed into the darkness of the tunnel, letting the girl guide him, he realized that it was more than one voice. More than one person was trapped in this place. But they were fused with each other as much as with their surroundings. They cried out as one, their voices blending into a new and hellish sound.

"Help meeeee!"

Something dreadful pushed its way out through those fibers and ribbons inside the machine, something small and gnarled and dripping with blood.

"Eeeeee! Eeeeeeeeeee! EEEEEEEEEEEEEEEEE!"

There was nothing to be learned in this place. He understood that now. There was nothing here but utter madness. It was no wonder the girl wanted him to leave as soon as she realized where they were.

He turned and fled back into the darkness of the tunnel as the hideous voices of the unthinkable things inside the machines swelled into a horrid cacophony of shrieking and screaming. It was a terrible noise, as if someone had thrown open a door to all the wailing damned of hell. It made him want to cover his ears, but that would require letting go of the girl's hand, and he didn't want to do that. She knew where all the bad things were.

She'd already saved him several times. He had no way of knowing what might've happened if she hadn't been there to stop him from bumping into that prickly, cone-shaped thing in the jungle room. She also warned him of that wendigo outside the green lab. If he'd spotted that thing any later, he might not have had time to reach the safety of that front office. *And* she'd pulled him out of sight before that dragon could find him just a few minutes ago. Without her, he was quite sure he wouldn't be faring nearly as well as he was. Wherever she was leading him, he was sure it would be foolish not to follow her.

He stumbled through the darkness, steered from one invisible passage to the next, surprised by the size and complexity of the tunnels. What was their purpose? Why were they so dark?

Twice they approached an illuminated opening, but both times the girl steered him away from it and back into the deeper darkness. He wondered if she was navigating around more of those horrifying people trapped in the machinery. Or perhaps there were more of those dragon monsters prowling around in some of these rooms. Or was she merely showing him the shortest way through the labyrinth to where he needed to be?

As that horrid wailing noise finally began to fade behind him, it suddenly occurred to him how unnatural this darkness was. The areas they opened onto weren't very brightly lit, but there should've been enough light to reach fairly far into the tunnels. Instead, the interior of these round passageways were practically *black*. It was as if the tunnel walls, themselves, were somehow absorbing the light as it entered.

He turned another invisible corner and found himself hurrying toward another circle of light. This time, he wasn't yanked down another unseen passage. He stumbled out of the strange darkness and into the glow of those swirling, alien lights of the next corridor.

He blinked up at these lights, then turned and looked back into the blackness of the tunnel he'd just emerged from.

He was alone again. Somewhere in that darkness, he'd lost the girl. He was quite sure this time that she never let go of his hand. He had a firm grip on her the entire time. It was instinctual. There were frightful things behind them and nothing but un-known ahead of them and he was ready for her to change direc-tion. Her hand was there as they fled the screaming machinery and simply gone when he came out, with nothing in-between.

It was a little disorienting. And it felt kind of *wrong* losing a child like that, even if she *was* a ghost. But he didn't bother look-ing for her. She wasn't going to be standing around in the dark. For better or worse, he was simply on his own again.

Sighing, he turned his attention to the strange room he'd now found himself in.

Chapter Thirty-Two

Before him stood a great, gloomy space with a massive, concrete dome at its center.

All the pipes in the building seemed to converge here. They emerged from every wall, at every possible height, and angled straight toward the dome, where they then curved sharply upward and hugged the concrete surface all the way to the top, where they again made a sharp turn, each one angling straight upward and into the oppressive darkness above the swirling glow of those strange, hanging lights.

He stood there a moment, taking in the alien spectacle of the scene. He felt as if he'd stepped into some sort of vast, industrial dystopia. The darkness that perpetually swallowed the ceiling was particularly surreal. It was far too easy to imagine that there *was* no ceiling, that the only thing above him was the cold, black emptiness of space.

It was strangely different from the clean, otherworldly feel of the glass house. That had felt as if he'd somehow stumbled aboard an alien vessel and was adrift in endless space. But this was more steampunk than science fiction. And neither of these places seemed to fit the eerily primitive green lab and its monstrous jungle room.

He felt as if he were not only wandering through these woods, but through time, itself, wildly roaming from the distant future to the distant past and back again.

"Who are you?"

He turned, distracted, to find a young boy standing a short distance away, staring back at him with a distrustful look on his face.

"I don't know you," said the boy.

"I don't know you, either," replied Eric.

"You're not my dad!"

"You're not my kid."

"Stay away from me!" the boy shouted. Then he turned and ran away.

"*You* talked to *me*, kid!" Eric shouted after him. He shook his head and then turned away, only to find a heavyset, rough-looking man in a business shirt and tie stalking toward him with dark bags under his eyes.

"I'm not talking to anyone until I've had my coffee!" he growled, waving a pudgy hand at him as he passed.

Eric turned and watched him go, too. If these people were so antisocial, why did they keep approaching him like that?

When he turned to continue on, there was a teenage boy in a school jacket standing in his way. "There's some kind of monster!" he whispered. "It crawls around like a spider on long, hairy legs, but it has a man's face!"

Eric nodded and walked on. "Yeah, you've got to watch out for those."

"I'm serious, man!" He reached out and grabbed his shoulder, stopping him. Then he pointed toward the dome. "It's right there!"

He looked where the boy was pointing and saw that there was, indeed, a strange form crawling over the pipes on the surface of the dome like a giant, hairy spider. It was white as snow, sharply contrasted against the gloom, and moved around on four strange, spindly legs. "Oh…" was all he could think to say.

It clearly wasn't a wendigo or a reaper. It was probably one of the things that crossed over from other worlds, like the dragon and those freaky bugs. And he had a feeling it wouldn't turn out to be friendly.

But when he turned to hurry on his way, he saw an enormous dragon head emerging from another of the black tunnels and moving straight toward him. (Was it the same one again, he wondered, or was there more than one?)

He was quickly running out of places to go.

Scanning his surroundings, he caught sight of a door at the

base of the dome, too small for the dragon to follow him and hopefully strong enough to keep out an abominable spider-man.

He ran for it, clambering over several pipes and ducking under others. He didn't dare look up to see if the monsters had noticed him. He didn't stop until he was through the door and it was tightly closed behind him.

Now he suddenly found himself swallowed in darkness. And as he removed his flashlight and switched it on, it finally occurred to him that he should've probably shined it around *before* locking himself in with whatever was here.

This was how scantily-dressed campers ended up dead in old horror movies, he realized.

But by some absurdly miraculous stroke of luck, he didn't find himself immediately set upon by flesh-eating ghouls or a swarm of blood-sucking predators from another world.

The inside of the dome was utterly black. The interior surface appeared to have been painted with tar and the floor looked like it'd been covered with coal dust.

His first thought, of course, was *why?* What was the purpose of it? What was kept in here?

The black surfaces absorbed the light, making it impossible to see more than a few feet in front of him. His twisted imagination, of course, took full advantage and gleefully began assembling one terrifying scenario after another for him, ranging from man-eating bats to oozing zombies to darkness-dwelling, sanity-shattering Lovecraftian horrors.

Numb with fright, he pushed forward, expecting something awful to emerge from the darkness at any moment. But step after step, nothing appeared.

Was he really alone in here? He didn't dare assume he was so lucky.

Then, finally, he saw something. It was dangling down from above. A strange, coiled thing.

Then another. And another.

Eventually, it occurred to him that what he was looking at were strange, twisted *branches*. He was walking under an enormous tree of some sort.

Then the trunk of the tree came into view. It was as black as everything else in here, but shiny and smooth, less like bark than flesh, with a curious, veiny sort of pattern. And it was *huge*, at least five feet across at its base.

He stepped up to it, shining his light higher and higher into the branches.

This was odd...

Did they plant the tree inside the dome? Or did they build the dome around the tree?

Dora said that the plants were anchored to the world of their origin and that their presence in *this* world thinned the boundaries between the two, letting exotic energy streams flow back and forth.

"Channels..." he whispered. For directing and controlling the energy.

He recalled the way the pipes outside all converged on the dome and then followed the curvature to the top, where they all turned sharply upward. He thought he could almost grasp how it all worked. If those pipes were carrying exotic energy, then this dome, with the tree inside, was tearing away the boundaries between worlds and letting the energy flow from one world to the other.

"This dome is a part of the machine," he realized.

"Actually, the dome's only purpose is to keep the night tree in utter darkness at all times."

Eric turned to find a stiff-looking old man standing in the beam of his flashlight, gazing up at the tree with interest, his hands shoved into the pockets of his vest. "Night tree?"

The old man didn't look away from the tree. "You shouldn't be in here. That flashlight you're carrying..."

He looked down at it.

"You're waking it up."

Waking it up? He lifted it and aimed it up into those branches. Some of them were beginning to move, he realized. The smallest of the branches were beginning to sway back and forth, as if by a gentle breeze. Except the air in here was stagnant.

Finally, the man lowered his head and looked at him. "I know it's hard to take in such strange and wonderful things, but you need to leave *now*. The unusual energy in this place is making this one wake up much quicker than it should."

Above him, a long, snaking tendril began to uncoil itself and reach down toward the flashlight.

The sight finally shook him out of it and he turned and bolted for the door.

Except...which way was it again?

It was so dark in here he couldn't see so much as a crack in the door frame.

But the place was a dome. How hard could it be to find his way out? All he had to do was run in a straight line until he hit the wall and then follow it all the way around until he found a door.

He almost ran into the wall. It was so utterly black and featureless that it was little more than an extension of the darkness itself. If he'd so much as blinked at the wrong time, he would've run face-first into it. And knowing his luck, he would've broken his nose and knocked himself unconscious in the process.

He shined his light in both directions, wondering which way might be the shorter route. He was fairly sure he was somewhere near the exit. If he chose wrong, he'd circle the entire room before he found it.

He took a few steps to the left, hoping to catch sight of it, then turned and made a decision to go the other way.

Just when he thought he'd gone the wrong way again, he saw it. A subtle recess in the wall. A heavy rectangle in the darkness.

He sighed, relieved, and reached for the handle.

But it moved before he could touch it and the door cracked open. A dingy stream of oddly flowing light poured into the dome around him.

He took a step back, surprised, as unnaturally long fingers closed around the edge of the door and a face peered in at him through a tangled mass of long, snow-white hair.

It was the thing that crawled like a spider but had a man's face.

Chapter Thirty-Three

Eric backed away. What the hell was he supposed to do now?

The thing opened the door wider and crowded into the darkness with him. Its arms and legs were twice as long as an average man's, with an extra pair of elbows and knees leading out from its hairy, bloated body to its freakishly long, monkey-like hands. Its body was hunched and its head was mounted low on its shoulders, almost protruding from its chest. And up close, he saw that its face wasn't that of a man at all. It was a *nightmare*. Big, black eyes and a strange, fleshy nose. Its mouth was mostly hidden behind its shaggy beard, but even so he could tell there was something terribly wrong about it.

This wasn't good. According to that old man, who seemed to actually know a thing or two about that tree, he was in terrible danger just by being here. But this monstrous thing was blocking the only way out.

It must have seen him run in here and followed him. Was it just lurking out there the whole time he was inside, working out how to operate the latch?

Again, he was starting to wish he had a gun. This seemed like another one of those occasions where it'd solve more problems than it'd cause.

The monster crossed the black threshold and stalked toward him, those eerie, black eyes fixed on him. It moved so strangely on those abnormal legs. Everything about it looked *wrong*. He couldn't quite explain it, but its movements weren't like anything from this world *or* from any special effects he'd ever seen. It was as though the creature's joints worked on an entirely *alien* biology.

And then there was that awful mouth… As he backed away, its jaws began to open, revealing an impossibly large, gaping maw that split the thing's entire, horrid face apart, both from ear to ear and from forehead to chin.

Something caught at the hood of his jacket and he froze. Something was behind him, yet he didn't dare take his eyes off the thing in front of him. Instead, he changed direction and took a step to the side.

The monster snorted, its huge, freakish mouth opening and closing. He could see thick strands of saliva spraying outward in the beam of the flashlight. He could even smell its foul breath.

He took another step. From the corner of his eye he could see one of the night tree's tentacle-like branches twitching in the gloom, pulling at his hood.

It was just like the old man warned. The tree was waking up. And it was dangerous.

He'd seen something like that before, he realized. Back in the depths of Hedge Lake. There were trees down there with those same kinds of coiling branches. The lost spirit of a fat man with an unhealthy obsession for one of his female coworkers had briefly possessed him in order to warn him about them. These trees snatched people up with those tendrils and strangled them.

But those trees had looked nothing like this. They were much smaller. They were red instead of black. Bristly, rather than fleshy, almost scaly. And they were covered in strange, grayish buds that looked less like leaves than mossy growths.

He turned his gaze back to the monster in front of him and took another step to the side, tearing himself free of the night tree's grip. From somewhere deep in the back of his mind surfaced that deathless creep, Fettarsetter, the man responsible for the crisis that was taking place in that strange, Michigan lake. He'd said something about those trees, he recalled. Something about them being a hybrid of some sort, related to a much larger variety of tree. At the time, he hadn't been interested in talking about alien flora. He didn't listen. He probably should have. He didn't know it'd be on the test.

The monster snorted again. This time, it lurched a step toward him.

He kept his eyes locked on the monster, but he couldn't stop himself from taking an equal step back. As soon as he did so, he felt something snatch at the sleeve of his jacket.

This was bad. He was fairly certain he'd be no match for the monster in a wrestling match, and it wasn't likely to let him get around it. But those coiling branches were getting livelier with each passing second. And if those small, blood-colored versions in Hedge Lake were deadly, then this giant, obsidian version was going to be way more than he could handle.

He had no idea what to do now.

The good news, if he was going to be ridiculously optimistic, was that he didn't have to decide what to do next. The monster decided for him. It opened its awful mouth and uttered an enraged howl, then lunged forward and snatched at him with both of its freakishly long hands.

He jumped backward, out of the way, and felt something grab his arm.

A black, twisting tendril had wrapped around him, squeezing him. And as he tried to back away, he felt another one grab his hood. A third seized a lock of his hair.

Not good! he thought. *Not good! Not good!*

He tried to twist away, but the monster's foul, monkey-like hands closed around his neck. He thrust his arms out and pushed at its shoulders, trying to pry it away, but it was much stronger than he was. That ever-widening, cavernous maw drew closer and closer to his face.

He could see its teeth, now that it was close. They were way back inside the mouth, and there were rows and rows of them, circling the thing's widening throat. With mounting horror, he realized that he was going to be well inside this monster's mouth before it even began to eat him.

Would it use those teeth to tear his face off, he wondered. Or was it going to bite his entire head off in one chomp? Or was it simply going to swallow him whole, using those teeth to drag him kicking and writhing into its black belly?

Whatever it meant to do, he didn't think it would end with

the two of them laughing about it over a beer at any point in the future.

He was losing his footing. The monster was pushing him down toward the filthy ground. The only thing holding him up was the limb coiled around his right arm. No, *two* limbs now. One above his elbow and one around his wrist. And there was another clutching at his shoulder, slithering toward his left armpit.

The one in his hair was twisting tighter, tearing at his scalp.

He was helpless against it. It required all his strength to push back that horrific, gaping mouth and he could already feel his head beginning to swim as those freakish monkey hands slowly strangled him.

This seriously sucked. And he was having a really hard time imagining it getting any better.

Yet, as he found himself being pushed closer and closer to the ground, he suddenly realized that it was getting easier and easier to push the monster away. It seemed to be losing strength.

Then he saw it in the dull glow of the flashlight he was still clutching in his closed fist against the monster's furry shoulder: thin, black tendrils snaking their way around the monster's neck and arms.

He actually managed a grunt of a laugh. "Screwed up, didn't you?" he gasped. But on the heels of that, he thought, *Not that I'm doing much better...*

The two of them were going to make a particularly macabre display when they were both dangling from the tree, still frozen in this death grip and wrapped up in the night tree's serpent-like limbs.

Those big, black eyes had been pushed apart by the thing's monstrous mouth. Now they were beginning to bulge as the night tree tightened its grip around its throat. At the same time, Eric felt the grip around his own throat loosening.

He glanced down, blinking back the stars that were blossoming in the dark, and saw that the tendrils were pulling back its wrists. Ironically, it seemed that the monster's hands around his neck might've ended up protecting him from being strangled by the much more effective night tree.

But it was too early to celebrate. Because the monster's body was above him, it was shielding him from most of those coiling branches, but it was still gripping his arms and hair.

The monster let go of his neck and began thrashing, trying to free itself. This, too, seemed to work to Eric's advantage. Those creeping branches were drawn to the monster's thrashing instead of to him.

He was only going to have this one chance. He unzipped his jacket and wriggled out of it, dropping the flashlight in the process. His left hand came out easily enough, sliding through the smooth fabric, but the tree's alien tendrils were tangled around his right glove pretty tightly. He had to dig his heels into the black earth and pull with all his strength to tear himself free. And when his hand finally slipped out of the glove and he fell backward onto his butt, there was an agonizing flash of pain as the motion reawakened the injury from the accident.

For one, terrible second, he thought for some reason that the tree had ripped off several of his fingers. It was a fairly ridiculous thought. The pain had been exquisite, but not really the sort of pain he'd expect from having his fingers torn off. But there was a terribly vivid image in his mind of his hand coming back soaked with blood and half the size it was when he entered this room.

But that was only his awful imagination again. The worst part of the whole ordeal was the limb that had tangled up in his hair. He had to tear himself away, cursing at the pain, but then he was free. (Although possibly at the cost of a sizeable bald spot.)

He snatched up the flashlight and rolled away from the thrashing monster. Then he scrambled to his feet and sprinted toward the dull, rectangle of light that was the only exit. Just once, he thought he felt something swipe at the back of his head, but he reached the door without being entangled again.

He looked back just once as he grabbed the door. The monster's white fur made it light enough to see against the darkness. It was a wretched, writhing shape rising up into the gloom, slowly swallowed up by the monstrous tentacles of the night tree.

And he saw something else, as well. Those awful, coiling, twisting branches were reaching for him, like an unthinkable, tentacled hand with countless squirming fingers. Again, he thought of Lovecraft's dark gods of the deep and shivered as he slammed the door.

Chapter Thirty-Four

He ducked into that black nightmare in the first place to avoid that freaky dragon and he was relieved to find that it had moved on while he was preoccupied with the alien spider yeti. That was one bit of luck, at least. Of course, now he'd lost his jacket and one of his gloves. At the moment, his heart was still pounding and his blood was still pumping and he wasn't exactly missing them—the jacket was torn anyway, thanks to the moody, soaking-wet, half-naked woman—but when the adrenaline wore off, he was going to be reminded of how cold it was in these buildings. And going back outside in the snow was going to be even more unpleasant.

He removed the one remaining glove and tossed it aside as he approached another of those huge, concrete holes in the wall. He decided to just be thankful for now that he hadn't lost his flashlight as he shined it into the looming blackness, wary of any more dragons.

"Nasty thing, a night tree."

Eric let out a startled grunt and turned to face the old man, his free hand pressed over his heart. "Don't do that!" he gasped.

"In total darkness, it can turn completely dormant," the old man went on, seemingly oblivious, "and it can literally live forever like that. It just stands there, waiting for the light to come back. That particular one could sit there for centuries, until this whole building falls apart around it."

Eric glanced back at the dome, wondering what would happen when it finally caught the sun's rays again. It was a nasty thing to encounter while powered by a mere *flashlight*.

"Sorry," said the old man. "I get carried away. I'm Otto Lancanter." Then he frowned and looked down at the ground.

"Or...I suppose I used to be. I'm not entirely sure if I still belong to that name or not...being dead and all."

Eric looked the man over. "You seem different from most of the...uh...*other people* I've met here."

"I suppose I do. From what I've seen, most of those who've come here are either too afraid to move on or harbor too much regret."

Eric nodded. He'd noticed that, too.

"It's fascinating, really. From a scientific standpoint, I mean. I died a peaceful death. And I've come to believe that those who went like I did and were ready to move on weren't distracted by the pull of this place. They went where they were supposed to go instead. They followed the light, you might say."

That made sense, Eric thought. He'd begun to wonder why there weren't more elderly ghosts wandering around if Evancurt was sucking in any spirits that happened by. People who'd grown old and lived a full life should've been much more common than those who'd died young and tragic, but they also would've been more at peace with their passing. "But not you?"

Otto smiled. "No. And it's my own fault I'm here." He nodded at the dome. "And that thing in there, I suppose. Thing is, I happen to be..." The smile disappeared, replaced with a thoughtful frown, "...or, to have been, I guess...one of the few scientists in the world who were privileged with knowledge of those night trees. At least, as far as I know, anyway. We found one, you see. Deep inside a cave in Mexico. I won't bore you with details, but when I sensed that there was one here on this property...well, I couldn't resist having a look."

"And now you're trapped with the others."

"I am. Ironic, isn't it? I accepted my mortality and passed on with dignity and courage, only to end up here, where the dead never move on, but just...wink out, like candles in the dark."

Eric shivered. What a way to put it. He looked down at his hand. He could almost feel the little girl's fingers clinging to it. He thought of the poor, desperate woman who promised she'd let him do anything he wanted to her if he'd only give her the money she needed. And the terrified woman whose children were taken... And all the other haunted, desperate and regretful souls he'd encountered. It was so depressing. How many of them had "winked out of existence," as Otto had so eloquently put it? How many had suffered in this forest, searching for what they'd left behind, only to disappear, forever unable to find solace?

He couldn't let that happen to anyone else.

"The people who built this place," he said, looking up to meet Otto's kind gaze. "They built something. A machine. Do you know anything about it?"

The old man scratched at his chin and considered the matter for a moment. "Let's see... There're lots of machines in this place. I couldn't tell you anything about any specific one. I only really know the purpose of that dome, and only because I know a thing or two about night trees. But I can tell that they're using the plants to funnel energy in and out of this physical plane."

Eric raised an eyebrow at him. "You understand how this place works?"

"No. Not really. But after I arrived here, I found that I could feel the energy flow. Something about being dead, I suppose."

Eric was surprised at the casualness with which he said that last bit. He was taking being dead much better than many of the ghosts he'd met tonight.

"It moves very purposefully," he went on, "as if carried by some sort of *current*."

"By using the plants to create channels," said Eric, remembering what Dora told him..

"Exactly. Naturally, I investigated. Scientific curiosity and all. I discovered how the plants they cultivate here affect that energy flow." Then he gestured at the dome. "All except *that* one. The night tree isn't like the other plants. It's not related. It doesn't work the same way. I couldn't begin to tell you how they've utilized it. It's always possible they brought it here without knowing what they had and simply sealed it up in there so it wouldn't wreck the place."

Eric was growing restless. This was all very interesting, but it wasn't helping him find Voltner's monstrous machine.

"I *have* noticed since I've been here, however, that there are a handful of places that have a particular kind of energy about them." He looked up at the tunnel in front of them. "If you keep going straight from here, you'll find one of them. Maybe those're the key to finding what you're looking for."

Eric shined his light into that darkness again. "What kind of energy?" But when he glanced back, Otto Lancanter had disappeared. Instead, he was staring at a small, naked woman with huge, startled eyes. She was trying to cover herself, but doing a poor job of it, and her entire face was flushed bright red.

"*Don't look at me!*" she shrieked.

Eric twirled back the other way, his own eyes wide and startled, his own cheeks burning. "*Sorry!*" he stammered. Although he wasn't entirely sure what *he* did wrong. He wasn't *trying* to look at her. He didn't even know she was there. He was talking to Otto.

And why was she naked if she was so sensitive about it? She was a ghost, wasn't she? Just manifest some stupid clothes!

He didn't try to look back again. The woman was probably already gone, but he wasn't going to risk it. Besides, he needed to keep moving. Before he vanished, Otto told him there was something on the other side of this hole. Some kind of strange energy. Maybe it'd be something that finally shed some light on what it was he was looking for.

Still watching out for that dragon, he walked toward the dull light at the end of the tunnel, wondering what horrors were waiting there for him.

The flashlight flickered in his hand, threatening to go dark again. He'd almost forgotten about that. He was lucky it hadn't gone dark inside the dome, trapping him in there. He gave it a gentle shake and it stopped flickering. But he had a bad feeling that it was only a temporary solution, and he wasn't sure what he was going to do when it finally died for good.

When he stepped out of the darkness again, he was in a vastly different kind of room than any he'd encountered before. Gone were the wide-open spaces with the ominous darkness looming high overhead. Gone were the cumbersome pipes.

Gone were the lumbering, blocky contraptions that stood like bulky sentinels. Instead, he was standing in a claustrophobic labyrinth of small, churning machinery where every surface was covered in whirring, grinding, sliding parts that immediately reminded him of the fine, inner workings of some overly complicated clock.

It was darker in here than it was in other areas of the workshop. Although there was less space to light, those strange, hanging lamps weren't any closer to the ground than they were elsewhere, and these crowding walls of churning clockwork reflected less light than they blocked, casting shadows across every surface that crawled and churned atop the moving parts, adding to the already creepy atmosphere.

He shined his light across these tiny workings, revealing countless, delicate cables sliding back and forth among turning gears and pumping pistons, all of it operating a strange conglomeration of twisting and folding parts that made the entire wall seem to flex and relax in an eerily organic sort of motion. It was like the breathing sounds the jungle made, except it was visual instead of auditory. The only sound in this room was a soft, uncomfortable sort of humming noise, the collected music of subtle friction in the tiny workings all around him.

Was he *inside* some giant machine?

He stood there for a moment, staring at it all, wondering again if he could really be looking at actual alien technology.

None of these parts were dull or rusted. In fact, everything looked shiny and new. Looking closer, he saw that the moving parts were covered in a thick, clear oil of some sort. It dripped down through the workings, oozing over every surface, lubricating and protecting the parts of the machine and adding to that queer, organic quality.

The floor beneath him was a thick, steel grating that let the slime drain away and added much-appreciated traction for the soles of his shoes. He shined his light down into it, noting that the space below was covered in a pool of indeterminant depth. Did the stuff collect down there to be recirculated back through the machinery?

Again, his flashlight flickered. This time, he decided to switch it off and save the battery. He could see well enough. But he kept it in his hand, ready in case he needed it as he wandered deeper into the gloom of the clockwork labyrinth.

As the light around him faded, he found himself immersed in a strange, writhing landscape of heaving and undulating machinery. Strange, twisting forms rose to the surfaces and monstrous, mechanical shapes seemed to reach out for him as he passed. Wriggling, snaking things turned to follow him, snapping at him, snagging at his pants legs. A long, coiling shape on the ceiling bristled as he ducked beneath it, extending rows of gleaming pins and fine wires. And all of it dripped and oozed that strange, clear slime.

This was getting weirder and weirder. More and more, the place seemed less like a machine and more like some monstrous, clockwork *organism*.

With no way of knowing where to go, he chose directions at random. Predictably, he soon turned a corner and found himself at a dead end. Or, more specifically, he found himself at a point where it was impossible to continue. The narrow path he was following turned not left or right, but straight *up*.

It was here, as he stood peering into the writhing shaft above him, marveling at how far this mechanical madness ascended into the darkness, that he realized he wasn't alone.

Chapter Thirty-Five

The peculiar energy Otto Lancanter spoke of was one of the twisted places.

Eric turned around, scanning his strange, clockwork surroundings. The first time he went through this, Bronwen essentially became the treehouse, moving through its walls and animating the toys inside it. She even made the *tree* move. Lofleder, likewise, became the very jungle. And Port manifested himself as the very dust on the floor. He didn't need his master's degree to tell him that whoever was in this room had fused with this strange machinery. It was probably why everything in here had that unearthly, organic quality about it.

And indeed, now that he was looking for it, he could already see several mechanical eyes staring back at him from the walls. Or maybe they were just random circles his frustrating imagination was trying to convince him were eyes. He kept being startled by eyeballs, after all. It seemed like it was becoming a theme.

Those first three had spoken to him as if they were struggling to wake up. They seemed confused and slow-witted, unaware of who or what they were, but this time, the voice spoke up clearly right from the start, but in a voice that was altogether alien: "You don't belong here."

He turned around again. This voice didn't seem to have a single point of origin. It came from many different directions and across many different distances. And the words, like the pulsating clockwork monstrosity that surrounded him, contained no hint of anything organic. Instead, the voice seemed to be the sounds of various grinding and shrieking parts from somewhere deep within the churning machinery, pieced together into an unsettling perversion of human speech. "I'm sorry?"

"I can't be bothered now. Go away."

He turned back and tried a different passage. This one led him to another intersection where a strange, metal abomination about the size of a wine barrel was suspended from the ceiling by dozens of heavy cables and thick hoses. It appeared to be made entirely of slowly rotating pieces that folded and unfolded themselves repeatedly, making the entire thing slowly swell to nearly twice its original size, then quickly shrink again. The effect was that it pulsated like a giant, mechanical heart.

He ducked under the horrid thing and hurried on his way. The more he saw of this place, the less he cared for it.

"I have work to do. Leave me alone." The voice was loud, but even. It wasn't shouting at him, exactly. Yet it still possessed a distinctly angry quality.

"Who am I talking to?" he asked, hoping to confuse this voice as he had the other three, buying him some extra time to navigate the clockwork labyrinth. He wanted to find the exit before something monstrous had a chance to begin chasing him. But the owner of this voice didn't have to ponder the question the way the others did. "I am Doctor Cecil Patelemo," it replied without hesitation. "State your business and stop wasting my time."

Patelemo... That was one of the names Port mentioned. One of the "devil" scientists who ran the project under Voltner, like Lofleder.

"What is this place?" he asked, not really expecting the grouchy voice to answer him.

"This is my workshop. Don't touch anything."

"Wasn't planning to," he replied as he passed under several clear, slimy hoses pumping strange, bile-colored fluid.

"Go away," said the voice again.

"I'm trying to," grunted Eric as he turned a corner and found another dead-end. "Kind of lost here."

"Leave me to my work."

He wasn't sure how a *disembodied voice* could be so busy. Busy doing what? Celebrity impersonations? Beatboxing? The guy was just being rude, if you asked him.

He turned another corner and squeezed through a narrow gap. Ahead of him there was another of those large, silver orbs, this one half-swallowed by the creepy, moving clockwork parts. There were two passages to choose from, one on either side of the orb. When he looked to the right, he saw the path opening like a great, mechanical throat lined with rings of sharp, wriggling, teeth-like spikes and immediately chose left.

"I dislike being disturbed," growled Patelemo in his creepy, mechanical voice.

Eric stopped as several long, gleaming spikes began to slide into the path around him, threatening to skewer him.

"And you're disturbing me."

This wasn't looking good. He stepped over one of the spikes and then ducked under another. He had to keep moving. He had to find the exit. But there were a lot more spikes sliding into his path, closing in on him. He wasn't going to make it.

"Voltner's machine!" he blurted.

The spikes stopped moving. He had Patelemo's attention now, for better or worse.

Eric didn't dare stop moving. He made his way through one gap after another, hoping he was getting closer to the exit.

"Voltner's machine?" said Patelemo.

"You helped him build it, right?"

"Voltner's...?"

Like in the treehouse and in the maintenance room of the Green Lab, a fierce wave of vertigo washed over him, this time strong enough that he had to crouch down and brace himself against the floor with his hand to keep from stumbling into the churning machinery.

Except the clockwork machinery was gone. He was standing at the top of a staircase, peering through an open doorway into a spacious office.

A short, stocky man with a bristling mustache was sitting at a desk, studying a stack of blueprints. "The other components have to be set up *perfectly*," he grumbled.

"Don't worry about the other components," replied a much

taller man with graying hair and a strangely imposing presence.

"I *will* worry about it," snapped the short, mustachioed man. "If there's a failure in the system, it won't be my fault. My work is flawless."

"It'd better be," growled the taller man.

The short man looked up from his blueprints, his eyes blazing. "Don't you threaten me," he growled back. "You wouldn't be anywhere without me to translate those plans you found *and* build these machines. Don't forget, half the concepts these things work off of are purely theoretical and the other half are entirely unheard of in this world."

"Just make sure it works," said the tall man.

Then everything was back the way it was before. He was crouching in a narrow passageway, surrounded by heaving and churning clockwork.

He frowned. Purely theoretical? And concepts unheard of in this world? What sort of alien horrors had these people stumbled across? And what were they trying to do with it?

"Voltner's machine?" sneered Patelemo. "Really? Don't make me laugh. *I* built the machine. No one else in this world could have done it. Only *I* possess the genius involved in such a construction."

Eric stood up and continued forward while those spikes were still stopped. "My mistake," he gasped.

The tall man he'd just seen... Was that Voltner?

"That old fool only provided the blueprints and the power source."

"Power source?" asked Eric.

"Some kind of crystal, he claimed" replied Patelemo, sounding dismissive. "The arrogant bastard refused to show it to us until the machine was completed. An energy generator unlike anything in this world, powerful enough to kickstart the machine and start the first process."

"That sounds pretty impressive," said Eric. Again, his imagination flooded his head with thoughts of advanced, alien technology.

"It was nothing more than a glorified sparkplug," snapped

the clockwork man. "*I* was the one who figured out that the blueprints were written across an extra dimension. *I* was the only one who could understand that the exotic energies had to be diffused through parallel space. Lofleder only provided the channels. Roden only provided the various energies. Shinne provided only the means to break through the constraints of our current laws of nature. *My* work pieced them all together. Without me, all of them were nothing."

Eric nodded. "*Your* machine. Got it." He turned left, then right, then right again, searching for a way out of this monstrous mechanization. "Out of curiosity, where did you build *your* machine?"

"Where?" said Patelemo. "It's right here."

"Here?" He looked around at the strange, clockwork abomination that surrounded him.

"It had to be here. This property was one of the few places in the world where such a thing could be built."

"Oh…" So not *here* here. Of course.

"The placement of the machine was critical. It had to be placed exactly over specific dimensional crossroads. That's why it took Voltner more than ten years to locate and obtain the Evancurt estate."

"Okay," said Eric. That sounded familiar. Didn't someone tell him once that his own hometown of Creek Bend sat on such a place? Were these places common? As he dodged a strange cluster of clockwork tentacles that was reaching out from a twisting mass of needles and gears, he decided to ponder the thought later, when he wasn't lost in a deathtrap labyrinth. "More specifically, then," he said, "where would someone go if they wanted to shut it off?"

"Shut it…off?"

"You know, in case things went sideways? An emergency?"

This seemed to baffle Patelemo. "The machine doesn't have any such means. The process can't be halted."

"You can't turn it off?"

Then something changed in the room. Eric could feel it. "Wait…" growled Patelemo's strange, emotionless voice. "Why are you here?"

"Oh shit," groaned Eric. He knew he was pushing his luck with this conversation. He hurried around a corner and found his path blocked by a wall of churning clockwork that writhed and twisted in ways that metal shouldn't be able to move. It looked less like a machine than a pile of wriggling worms, an illusion that was only furthered by that strange, slimy oil that oozed and dripped throughout the workings. He took a step back and watched as the thing changed shape before his eyes, turning into something new. For a moment, he wasn't sure what was happening, but then he let out a startled yelp as a great, scowling face turned to look at him, its wide, whirling eyes glaring at him.

"Who are you?" it demanded, its clockwork lips forming each word, a familiar mustache rippling. That clear slime oozed down its chin as it spoke and dripped onto the grated floor beneath it.

"Safety inspector?" he tried.

The monstrous, clockwork face of Patelemo turned sinister, its whirling eyes narrowing. "Intruder," it snarled.

Chapter Thirty-Six

Not good.

Eric turned and fled as a fresh wave of panic rushed through him.

All around him, the clockwork machinery whirled and churned faster, reshaping itself into long, skeletal arms and snake-like things that snatched at him as he passed.

"You don't belong here," growled Patelemo, his voice drifting from deep inside the machinery.

He needed to get out of here, but he had no idea which way to go. In fact, as he weaved through the strange, reaching machinery, it occurred to him that there might not be a way out. Patelemo's clockwork monstrosity might have covered the only exit out of this place.

Then, as he passed a narrow opening to his left, something yanked hard on his shirt tail.

"This way," said a whispered voice in his ear.

He didn't think about all the reasons he shouldn't trust a mysterious, disembodied voice in a living, building-sized transformer robot imbued with the soul of a deranged scientist. He turned and ducked through the opening.

Something slashed at his elbow. Something else tore at his pants. Another something lashed out at his face, narrowly missing him as he ducked.

At the end of the narrow passage, he encountered three more possible options.

"Hurry," said a voice from the right.

Again, he followed it.

"You can't stop it," said Patelemo. "The machine is the future. It is progress."

"Progress?" gasped Eric. "You're a goddamn face in a giant clock!" He reached the end of the next passage and paused to consider between left and right. A hand against his back shoved him to the right. "Okay!" he yelped.

"Ignorant, closed-minded fools like you can never understand the importance of my work."

"Face!" he shouted back at it. "In a clock!"

"Here," said the mysterious voice from his left.

He stumbled to a stop and turned to find a doorway and a set of cobweb-filled stairs leading up. He didn't hesitate. He fled the clockwork labyrinth, shouting, "Thank you!"

Patelemo's voice followed him up the steps as he plowed through nearly half a century of accumulated spiderwebs: "My work will change the world."

"That's pretty much the problem," grumbled Eric.

The stairs led him to an office that was covered in a ghostly sheet of settled dust and hoary cobwebs, but otherwise was identical the one he'd just seen in that strange flashback.

As he wiped at his face and arms, he wondered again why the spiders only seemed to make their homes in certain areas. He could sort of understand the clockwork labyrinth. Almost every surface down there was constantly in motion and dripping that slime. But the rest of Patelemo's workshop was relatively spider-free as well, even though he was fairly certain that no one had been there in almost five decades. The room with all those orbs. The dome room. The machine room. Even those strange, subway-sized tunnels were clear.

Or maybe those massive, dragon-like things kept those areas swept clean. Was that it? Or were there other reasons why the spiders avoided Evancurt's strange technology? Perhaps they preferred to avoid the exotic energies that supposedly flowed through the machinery.

He glanced around the office, taking in the ancient-looking surroundings. There was the usual furnishings. A desk and chair. Lamps. Filing cabinets. An old couch and an armchair. But there was nothing here that wasn't practical, he realized. There were no decorations. No paintings or photographs. There were blackboards mounted to two of the walls, both of them covered in markings that were either the alien workings of a mad scientist's crazed imagination or, more likely, perfectly normal formulas and diagrams that were simply indecipherable to a high school English teacher who never was very good with mechanical stuff.

There was, however, another of those old calendars on one wall, frozen like all the others on April of 1971.

"Closet," whispered the mysterious voice.

He turned and searched the room around him, but he was still alone.

There were two doorways leading out of the office. A closet and an exit, he presumed. He opened the closet first and found several light lab coats and a heavier jacket. "Oh," he said as he took the jacket and shook the cobwebs off it. "That's helpful. Thank you." It was a little dated. And a little small on him. But it was better than going out into the snow in just his shirt. As he slipped his arms into it, his eyes washed over the desk, still hopeful that he might find a phone.

"They're coming," whispered the voice.

He stood up straight, startled, and looked back the way he came. "What?"

"Get out."

Then he saw them. They were on the stairs. Two of them, black and creeping, those long, scythe-like fingers probing at the doorway ahead of them.

Reapers.

He didn't hang around to see what they wanted. He opened the second door, fled down a short hallway, past a bathroom and a second, smaller office, and then burst through the door and out into the cold, snowy night.

He paused for a moment, trying to get his bearings. He was standing in what he was fairly sure used to be a gravel parking lot. It was difficult to be sure through the overgrown brush and the gathering snow, but the road was just beyond it, running from left to right only a short distance away. If he still remembered Lofleder's map correctly, going right should take him back toward the green lab.

Already he missed his gloves and hood. The temperature had dropped noticeably since he was last outside. The wind had picked up, too. It whistled at his ears and stung his eyes.

And all around him the forest seemed to be alive with the cawing of those unseen crows.

He pulled out his light and shined it around, quickly catching sight of another reaper creeping around the corner of the building.

He ran out into the road, but stopped again when he saw another shadowy shape making its way toward him from the right, ambling down the middle of the road. He turned the other way, but there was another stepping out of the forest on that side of him.

He cursed and turned, shining his light from one to the next as the two that he saw climbing the stairs scuttled through the doorway.

They were quickly surrounding him.

That pompous Patelemo must've given him away. He wondered how many there were and if every one of them was even now making its way here.

His flashlight winked out again. He cursed and gave it a hard shake. It came back on immediately, and he let out a shrill yelp as he found an old man with wide, staring eyes standing right in front of him. He took a step backward, then shined the light around again, surprised to find that the old man wasn't alone.

Dozens of spirits were standing around him now, all of them staring at him. There was a woman with long, lovely red hair in a torn dress, a middle-aged man in a policeman's uniform, a teenage boy in a hunting vest, a tall, prim-looking woman in a gaudy sweater and a chubby man wearing nothing but a pair of dingy briefs. *And so many more.* They were everywhere. And they were all staring at him.

The reapers had all stopped, their shadowy faces twitching back and forth, looking from one ghostly form to the next.

They seemed confused, and he didn't blame them.

"Run," said the voice in his ear. And just like that, the spirits all turned and ran in different directions.

The reapers didn't appear to know what to do about this unexpected change of events. They seemed utterly unable to process so many souls in one place. They stumbled around, snatching at the passing spirits, but each one vanished before those wicked fingers could touch them. Although they were supposedly able to pierce a person's soul, he couldn't help but notice that they didn't seem to be able to catch a soul that had already departed its body. The spirits appeared to be too fast for them.

He didn't wait around to see how it turned out. The mystery voice told him to run and he didn't intend to stop listening to it now. He turned and fled into the forest, leaving the clockwork workshop behind.

Chapter Thirty-Seven

The reapers didn't seem to notice his departure. Nothing shadowy and sinister followed him into those dark woods. In spite of this, Eric continued to run long after Patelemo's nightmare workshop was out of sight. He weaved through the trees, scrambling over low hills and stumbling through tangled brush and down rocky slopes, until his legs and sides ached and he could no longer catch his breath.

Finally, he stumbled to a stop and leaned against a tree, gasping, and coughing, wishing, as always, that he'd kept that promise he was always making to himself that he'd get in better shape. He was going to have no one to blame but himself when his poor health habits finally did him in.

He spent a moment trying to ease his pounding heart, then stood up and stumbled forward, wondering how lost he was now.

When he shined his light forward, there was a man standing in front of him. He was facing left, his head tipped back, staring with wide, almost horrified eyes at the night sky.

Still gasping for breath, Eric walked toward him, squinting through the falling snow, until he was standing right next to the man. Then he turned and looked up at the sky, too. But there was nothing there. Nothing he could see, anyway. He looked at the man again. He waved his hand in front of his face. He even nudged the man's shoulder. Then he turned and looked around to see if there was anyone else around who was preoccupied with the snow clouds. But they were alone.

He gave up and continued on, leaving the man to his endless, creepy staring.

A moment later, he caught sight of an attractive woman in a

long, flowing dress. For a moment, she, too, was just standing there, gazing off into the forest. Then she turned and looked at him. For a second or two, she seemed surprised to see him there. Then she gave him a sweet smile and waved.

When he glanced forward again, the angry blonde woman was standing in front of him. Once again, she slapped him across his face.

The woman in the flowing dress gasped and covered her mouth.

"*Seriously*, lady?"

But like the last two times, the angry woman turned and stomped off without a word, vanishing into thin air as she took her third step.

"I don't even know her!" He said to the woman in the flowing dress.

She said nothing. She merely stood there, watching him, her hands still pressed to her lips, probably not believing him.

He rubbed at his cheek and continued walking. For a moment, the forest was blissfully quiet. Even those damned crows seemed to have taken a momentary break from their incessant cawing. Then something small and dark burst from its hiding place in the brush and darted away through the trees. He stumbled backward, clutching at his chest. It happened so quickly, he couldn't be sure whether it was a creature from this world or something that crossed over from some nearby hell.

"Not good," grumbled a voice behind him. He turned to find a shaggy-looking man wearing shorts, flip-flops and a variety of beaded necklaces draped over his bare chest. He was stumbling around, mumbling to himself. "Not good. Not good." He looked up to see Eric staring at him and said, "Broken. All of it. The tools. The cycle. The *rules*. What're we going to do?"

Eric didn't have an answer for him.

The man turned and continued on his way. "Wasn't supposed to happen that way... Hands... All gone... What'll we do?"

Overhead, several crows cried out and took flight.

Eric looked up at them, distracted, and watched them fly

away. Then he heard a branch snap somewhere behind him and high above. He turned, startled, to see a flurry of snow falling and treetops bending.

He stumbled backward and bumped against a tree, his eyes wide as he stared up at a great, towering shape parting the forest canopy above him.

He'd forgotten about the giant.

His flashlight illuminated only fleeting glimpses of its towering, trunk-like legs. The rest was a black, looming shadow, fifty feet high, roughly man-shaped. It stepped toward him, its great, hoof-like foot crunching into the gathering snow only a few paces in front of him.

Then it stopped.

It bent over, its shaggy head descending from the sky. Its eyes reflected his flashlight beam and shined like huge headlights as they gazed down on him from the center of a huge face that was so furry he could discern no other details. It remained that way for a moment, staring at him, seemingly measuring him, its long, shaggy beard blowing about in the wind. Then it made a strange gurgling noise at him and straightened itself again. As he watched, his heart racing in his chest, the towering monster turned and wandered off the other way, vanishing back into the forest from which it came.

Well... That was different.

Feeling more than a little numb, he turned and continued on his way. Vaguely, he realized that he had no idea where he was going. He wasn't even entirely sure at this point which way he came from. He could be circling right back to those reapers for all he knew. And even if he *did* know which way was back, he had no clue where he was supposed to go.

He thought back to Lofleder's map. Which of the labeled buildings had he not been to yet? He'd visited the glass house, the green lab and the workshop, as well as the coordination office with its freaky eyeball basement. There wasn't a way into the vent house. That left the buildings marked "barn," "little house," "star house," "shed" and "main." And somewhere among those places he was sure to find the rest of the twisted scientists, too.

The "devils" Port spoke of. He'd already had the pleasure of meeting Lofleder and Patelemo. That left Roden, Shinne and Voltner. And no telling how many others who might've been caught in whatever horror was unleashed here forty-seven years ago.

As he walked past a fallen tree, he was startled by something rustling in the tangle of branches. He paused and shined his light down on it. A pair of shining eyes stared back at him. The creature cowering there was reddish brown, about the size of a small dog and roughly the shape of a teddy bear. He stood there a moment, staring at the creature. It whimpered up at him, apparently frightened.

"You're not from around here," he said, daring to lean in for a closer look. So far, with the obvious exception of the wendigos, very few of the things he'd found here that weren't from this world had been hostile. There were those dragon things that the little girl in the cupcake tee shirt warned him to avoid, and the freakish white monster that attacked him inside the night tree dome, but most of the creatures had fled like mere frightened animals.

The creature sniffed at him, still whimpering. Its curiosity seemed to be outweighing its fear. It was adorable. Eric wished he had his phone so he could take a picture. Karen would love this thing.

Cautiously, the little creature crept toward him, still sniffing at the air.

"Don't tell me you're friendly."

It wasn't. Its adorable, teddy bear face split open to reveal a monstrous mouth full of bristling fangs and the horrible beast launched itself at him.

Eric jumped back and fled into the forest, cursing in a voice that he knew would never make the cut in a macho action flick.

I know! he thought, responding to what he was sure Isabelle was probably yelling at him. *That was stupid! Don't tell Karen!*

He wasn't sure how far the hellspawn teddy chased him through the woods, or if it had even given chase at all. He saw exposed fangs and he ran, like anybody with half a functioning brain cell. The thing might never have fully left the cover of its fallen tree. All he knew was that when he finally dared a look back, it wasn't snapping at his heels.

He stopped running and shined his light back the way he came. He saw no animal eyeshine staring back at him. And he heard nothing moving through the snow.

He was just going to assume from now on that everything in this forest wanted to eat him. Which, of course, was what he should've been assuming all along.

He turned and continued walking, but stopped, distracted, as a skinny man in a Star Wars tee shirt wandered across his path. He was gawking around at his surroundings, a strangely awestruck expression on his face. When he caught sight of Eric, he froze. "Dude…" he whispered. "I'm *so* tripping right now…"

Eric continued on his way, ignoring him.

A moment later, a pudgy woman dressed in gothic black clothes and makeup stumbled toward him. "I don't want to do this anymore," she wept, her mascara streaking down her face. "I don't like playing dead anymore. I'm scared."

"Where the hell did I park my truck?" growled a man dressed from head to toe in western apparel.

"*Man* I could go for a beer right about now," groaned a fat man in a stained and baggy tee shirt.

Eric stopped walking and rubbed his eyes. These woods were getting entirely too crowded. Where the hell were they all coming from? Did someone put a sign on him or something?

Then, with a gasp, he opened his eyes wide.

He was alone again. The spirits had vanished. And the forest had gone utterly silent around him. The snow and wind had stopped. Every branch and twig had gone still. And inside, some deeply-buried, primal terror welled up, rapidly overwhelming him.

It was the same awful feeling that drove him from the scene of the accident that brought him here. And just like the first time, he fled. He couldn't control himself. Every instinct told him that he was in danger, that something awful was coming. He had to run. As fast and as far as his legs would carry him. *Right now.* He tore through the forest in a blind and overwhelming terror, ignoring the aching in his legs, unconcerned with any trivial thoughts of getting lost. Getting lost was far better than whatever unspeakable horror was coming for him.

His flashlight winked out as he ran, but he didn't stop. He kept running, his arms raised in front of him to shield his face from unseen branches, using the stark contrast between the white snow and the black trunks to navigate the trees.

He could hear that dreadful buzzing noise again, but he couldn't tell which direction it was coming from. Was he running away from it or straight toward it?

He crested a small hill, pushed his way through a tangle of naked underbrush and rushed down the other side, where his foot caught on a rock and he fell hard, sliding the rest of the way down the slope.

It was too late. The horror was already on top of him. There was nowhere left to run.

He curled himself into a ball, squeezed his eyes closed and covered his ears as that terrible buzzing sound closed around him.

Chapter Thirty-Eight

Covering his ears did nothing. The hellish sound was inside his head. It grew louder and louder, until it felt as if his very brain were shaking apart inside his skull. The pain was like nothing he'd ever felt before. His ears and eyeballs throbbed. It felt like turrets of water were rushing through his sinuses. Even his *teeth* ached. He tried to scream, but the sound never reached his own ears. Was the agony of the buzzing choking it before it could escape his throat, or was it simply drowned out in the noise that filled his head like a thunderous swarm of stinging hornets?

The world seemed to come apart around him. Darkness poured over him like rushing water through a breaking dam. The pain, the cold and the awful, screaming agony of the hellish buzzing began to bleed away and he drifted into a deeper darkness where strange, alien voices washed over him, speaking languages he was quite sure, even in this murky, barely-conscious, floating state, that he'd never heard before.

"The dead have business with you, Eric."

He blinked. Confused. He was in Mexico. The air was heavy and sweltering. Hundreds of filthy, rotting dolls were staring at him. The beautiful toll collector was standing before him, stark naked, staring at him with her sleepy eyes, just the way she appeared to him that frightful night, more than a year ago.

He was sleepy, too. His eyes were heavy. They drooped. Darkness closed around him again, even as he realized that something about the scene was wrong.

Why did the toll collector speak with Tessa's voice?

He groaned and tried to open his eyes. Why did he hurt so much? And where was he? For a moment, the world swam into view. He was lying on the cold ground, looking out at the forest. It was dark and hazy. He tried to lift his head, but it was so heavy. It hurt to move.

Was he...back were this all began? Back in the woods by the ruined PT Cruiser? Face down in the damp earth again?

That didn't make any sense.

Had he only dreamed it all?

But he was too tired to think about it. His eyes fell closed again. Darkness enveloped him.

Wait... Maybe *this* was the dream...

Voices washed over him in the cold, black void. Two of them. One was rough and strangely musical. The other was soft, feminine and oddly breezy. Neither of them sounded entirely human. They were speaking in strange, alien languages. They seemed to be arguing, but he couldn't understand any of the words.

Then everything floated away from him again.

"She's called for you," said Tessa. "It's time."

Who had called for him? Time for what? He was so confused.

What was happening to him?

Suddenly, he was underwater, sinking into dark and murky depths. His lungs ached for air and his heart was pounding from some terrible fright that he suddenly couldn't remember.

Someone was here with him. Someone was floating with him in this darkness. A dark, yet softly glowing shape loomed over him. Long, black, flowing hair. Dark and haunting eyes.

She was beautiful.

And she was familiar. He'd seen her before somewhere. If only his head would stop hurting, if only his thoughts would stop spinning, then maybe he could recall properly.

She was speaking to him. Her voice was as lovely as the rest of her, but her words were in a language he couldn't understand.

Then that strange, radiant glow faded.

Darkness swallowed him again.

"Find what was lost," said a familiar, ghostly voice.

He opened his eyes.

He was lying face-down in the snow, his skin numb from the cold, his head pounding.

The horrible buzzing noise was gone.

He was alone.

"That was weird," he grunted. He tried to move his arms and felt a sharp, jarring pain in his left shoulder. It was an extremely familiar pain, exactly the same pain he'd felt when he first tried to sit up after the accident. And as he pushed himself up onto his hands and knees, he realized that his left knee was throbbing again and his ribs were freshly sore. It hurt to breathe. Apparently, taking a short nap face-down in the snow had allowed his muscles to stiffen back up and freshly awakened the injuries from his crash. It was as if he were waking up from that ordeal all over again.

No wonder he'd dreamed that he was back there on the ground near the PT Cruiser.

How long had he been lying here?

His flashlight was on the ground next to him. He picked it up and gave it a shake, but it only gave a weak flicker and then fell dark again.

Slowly, he rose to his feet and stumbled forward. Already the dream was beginning to slip away. He remembered seeing the toll collector. (Mambo Dee, who'd created her as a gatekeeper to her mysterious, hidden home, had named her Ari, he recalled now that he was thinking about her again.) He remembered Ari telling him that the dead had business with him, but in Tessa's voice...

He rubbed his eyes, weary. That was probably just his dreams messing things up. He'd never seen either of the two wearing clothes, after all. His brain probably just made that comparison and then mixed up their voices.

He almost never recalled his dreams anymore. Not since the events at the cathedral three and a half years ago. Something about this place was obviously messing with his mind if he was able to remember them now. It made sense that his dreams would be especially vivid and weird, he supposed.

He dismissed the entire ordeal and bumped the flashlight

against his thigh. It flickered briefly for a moment, stubborn, but then it came on and stayed on and he was finally able to look around. He was standing in a long, flat valley stretched between several low, rolling hills. There was a very small, mostly frozen stream running down the middle of it, cutting it in half. At least a hundred of those strange, silver orbs had been placed here, each one with several dingy, golden cables protruding from one side and disappearing into short pipes rising from the earth. A great many trees had sprung up among the orbs in the years that they'd been here, crowding the spaces between them, some of them quite large and casting deep shadows, even without their leaves.

What he saw next was much stranger. He stopped and stood there, rubbing the back of his head as he tried to process it. He even closed his eyes hard and opened them again, in case that helped. But it didn't change.

It was the snow. It was falling *up*.

How hard did he hit his head when he fell down that hill?

He walked into the field of orbs, watching the rising snow-flakes all around him, mesmerized. He reached out with his hand and tried to catch them, expecting them to collect in his down-turned palm, but frowned when nothing touched his skin. He moved his hand around, but no matter where he placed his hand, the snow simply didn't touch him. It was as if it were intentionally avoiding him.

Then he noticed something. He brought his hand closer to his face and shined his light at it. As he watched, tiny beads of water were forming on the fine hairs on the back of his hand and freezing into delicate crystals. Then each one took flight and floated up into the air.

Backward, he reminded himself. Snow in reverse didn't rise from the ground to the sky, it rose from wherever it would've landed if it were falling *forward*. He moved his hand around, trying to catch the snow as it rose, trying to change its past by interrupting its movements in the future...or something like that...but it proved impossible.

"Trippy," he breathed.

There was a strange cry from above him and he looked up

to see a crow flying overhead. Except…it was flying in *reverse?*

As he watched it glide backward through the sky, he caught sight of a clump of snow rising from the ground and settling itself into the crook of a high branch.

He *really* wished he still had his phone with him. No one was going to believe this.

"Time is just another broken thing in this place," said a familiar, warbling voice from behind him.

He turned to face her. "Tessa…"

She stood there, her face turned up, watching the snow vanish into the gloomy sky. "And yet, it's still running out," she said.

Eric shivered and shoved his hands into the pockets of the jacket he found in Patelemo's closet. "I really wish you'd put some clothes on," he told her. "Just looking at you like that's going to give me pneumonia."

But if Tessa heard him, she showed no sign. She stood there, her naked body proudly exposed, without so much as a goosebump to indicate that she was the slightest bit cold. "Can you hear them?"

He squinted at her, confused. "Hear what?"

She lowered her head and turned her bloody eyes on the orb closest to them. "The devoured," she replied.

He looked down at the orb, confused. Devoured…?

"These are the spirit cells," she explained. "Where the energy that's stolen from us is stored."

Eric's eyes grew wider. "Wait… That's what these are? They're…ghostly *batteries?*" Again, he recalled the man in the plaid pajama pants with his ear pressed to that large pipe. *I think there're people in there.* The very memory made him shudder again. *I think…they're in pain.*

And now that he was staring at the orb, he couldn't help but think that he *could*, in fact, hear them. Countless, distant voices, all of them crying out.

Or was that part only his stupidly overactive imagination? It was hard to tell for certain. He was already processing a lot of weird information tonight. (And he still wasn't giving up on the possibility of a head injury.)

He looked up at the rising snow again. Even for the weird, this was...well...*weird*. What kind of sick mind could come up with something like this? This place was essentially harvesting *human souls* to power some kind of doomsday device. It was beyond depraved.

Port was right. The men who built this thing really must have been devils.

The wind was picking up. The rising snow became lost in a whirlwind of ice and mist, forcing him to close his eyes and shield his face.

He was really missing the hood and gloves he lost to that night tree.

"The sentinels have noticed you," warned Tessa. "They know you don't belong here."

He nodded. Thanks to that pompous jerk, Patelemo, he was sure. And he hadn't even learned anything useful for his troubles.

"They'll be looking for you now."

He squinted through the blowing snow. "What if there isn't a way to shut down the machine?" he asked, remembering the clockwork man's discouraging words. "What if there's no off switch?"

"There *will* be a way to stop it," she assured him. "You wouldn't be here if there wasn't."

"Is that fact or faith?" he asked.

"Both."

Another hard gust blew past him, forcing him to cover his face again.

Was that a real answer to his question? He hated that no one could ever just tell him anything. It always had to be some sort of riddle. He was sick of all this dramatic nonsense.

"But you have to find her soon."

"Find who?"

But if Tessa had an answer for him—which he doubted—he never heard it. A hard gust of wind hit him, nearly knocking him over. He stumbled to one side and steadied himself against the strange, silver orb.

Then the wind vanished.

He stood there a moment, peering out between his upraised hands, confused.

He was standing in the same place, but it was suddenly daytime. The sun was shining. The snow was gone, both the queer, floating snowflakes and the thin carpet that had blanketed the ground. The temperature had risen at least ten degrees. Birds were singing in the surrounding woods. A pair of squirrels were frolicking in the branches.

"What just happened?" He turned and looked around, squinting in the bright sunshine. But there was no one to answer him. Tessa had vanished with the snow and the wind. He was alone.

She said something about time being broken. Had he just jumped forward to morning? It couldn't be the previous day. It hadn't been this sunny in at least a week. It'd been nothing but dreary and damp and cold.

And most of the trees had vanished along with Tessa, he realized. He and the monstrous spirit cell balls were now standing in an utterly open field.

Before he had time to consider *when* he might be, there was a great, earth-shaking boom.

A vast ball of fire and smoke blossomed on the horizon, rising high up into the air like the hellish form of an ancient god rising to devour the souls of the wicked.

(And for the record, that wasn't just a creative simile he thought up on the spot. He'd actually *seen* an ancient god rise from its sleep to devour wicked souls. And that great, devilish shape that once took form in the churning clouds over a perverse, nightmarish hellscape version of Chicago had very much resembled what he was looking at now. In fact, for a moment there, his heart had skipped in his chest with the not-entirely-irrational thought that the ancient deity had actually returned to claim *his* soul as payment for its services that terrible morning.)

But this wasn't the diety they summoned in Chicago last year. His second impression was the slightly more rational but equally terrifying image of a great cloud of volcanic ash and gas expanding high into the sky.

Before his awful imagination had time to tell him all the awful, agonizing ways in which he might soon expect to die, he was struck by a bone-jarring shockwave and knocked onto his back. And for that brief instant, as he was falling, his head was filled with the terrible sounds of people screaming.

He cried out in horror as he lay there.

It was no ancient god. And it was no volcanic eruption. It was the machine.

He rolled over, wincing at the pain in his ribs and shoulder, and struggled to his feet. He had to get out of here.

The sky was turning dark. Debris from the explosion began to rain down around him, trailing flames and smoke behind them.

He ran.

Following the stream, he cut through the center of the field of orbs.

He was sure he could hear them now. Not so much individual voices as a distant roar of desperate screaming that probably sounded a lot like the tortured howls of the damned in hell. He clasped his hands over his ears as he fled.

The temperature changed around him. It turned hot. Then cold again. Then *very* cold. The light cycled between bright and dark, sunny and dreary, clear and foggy. It rained and it snowed. The wind whipped across his face. And all the while, flames continued to streak down from the sky above him.

He shoved his way through the trees, shielding his face from the weather and the foliage alike so that he never saw the low bluff.

The ground disappeared beneath him.

He fell. He hit the ground. Hard.

He lay there a moment, groaning, the wind knocked out of him. He'd landed partially in a pile of soft gravel, which had softened his landing a little, but not much. He could already feel that he'd skinned both his palms and banged his elbow. His left knee was screaming with freshly awakened pain, as was his right hand. And his ribs and shoulder weren't about to let him forget about them, either.

His right shoe was wet and cold.

The flashlight lay next to him. Somehow it was still shining. He snatched it up, rolled onto his back with a grunt and stared up at the dark sky above him.

Everything looked to be back the way it was before. It was nighttime. Snow was lightly falling. There didn't seem to be a volcanic devil cloud looming in the sky, but there were still burning bits of debris raining down around him.

"You saw it, didn't you?" said Tessa. She was standing at the top of the bluff, staring up into the hellish, smoldering drizzle. "The moment it all began? The day they broke the world?"

He turned and looked up at her. The day they broke the world? That was what he'd just witnessed? That was the *past*?

"Like everything else, time is broken here," she said again. "It turns back on itself sometimes. Back to that day."

He stared at her for a moment, watching her as the last of the fire drizzled down around her.

Then his gaze slid down to her feet, to the rocks she was standing on. The stream tricked over the bluff there, creating a small, gurgling waterfall. But right now it wasn't gurgling. It was barely trickling. It was mostly frozen.

He stared at the ice as the flames and snow drizzled down from the sky.

When it rains fire and ice over the frozen waterfall, he thought. The pain became numb as he recalled the words. They were spoken to him several months prior by Ari, the mysterious and beautiful toll collector, the same one who told him the dead had business with him.

As the last of the flames fell around them and winked out in the darkness, Tessa lowered her head and looked down at him. "Do you know what to do next?" she asked him.

He turned his eyes up to the sky again. There were power lines running over him, crowded by decades of untended trees and visible in the gloom only thanks to the snow that was gathering on them. "'When it rains fire and ice over the frozen waterfall,'" he recalled, "'follow the power to the house with no bottom.'"

"Find her," said Tessa. "She's waiting."

"Who's waiting?" He turned to look at her again, but she was gone.

He was alone again.

Chapter Thirty-Nine

Eric stumbled from the ditch, limping a little on his sore knee. He was also now aware of a pain in his ankle that he hadn't noticed over all the other pains until he put his weight on it.

And then there was the pain in his hand again. He rubbed at it, wondering if he might've broken something in the accident. When this was finally over, he should probably take himself to the emergency room and get some x-rays, but chances were good he wouldn't. By the time he was done here, he'd only want to go home, take a hot shower and go to bed.

Assuming, of course, that he ever made it home.

He looked around, taking note of the lack of boiling black clouds and raining flames. Was he back in his own time again? Had he *lost* any time? He hated to think of the possibility. Or maybe he'd *gained* an hour or two. That'd be a nice change of luck.

Follow the power…

He shined his light up into the sky. Two fat crows were perched on the lines, cawing at him. From the sound of it, there were dozens more in the surrounding trees that he couldn't see. He wished the feathery beasts would go away. Their incessant noise was becoming unsettling. Especially after what Peggy told him about them being harbingers of death.

Crows weren't even night birds. They shouldn't be active at all this late. There was definitely something unusual about them.

He pushed aside the thought and focused on the task before him. Ari's instructions didn't tell him *which way* to follow the power. He was picking a direction at random and hoping for the best.

And speaking of power…why were there power lines here

in Evancurt if there was no electricity? Were they merely dead lines from a time before Voltner and the others began pumping exotic energy around the forest? Or were those lines carrying something other than electricity?

He had to remind himself once again to not waste his time trying to understand the twisted mechanizations of madmen and monsters.

His flashlight went dark again and he gave it a hard shake. Dora warned him that electric technology didn't work long in Evancurt and he was starting to think that the flashlight was quickly approaching the end of its time in this world, which was a dreadful thought as he stood there in the sprawling blackness of Evancurt's haunted forest. Without a light, he had no way of knowing what might be lurking nearby, just waiting for an opportunity to rip him apart.

And indeed, when it finally flickered back to life a moment later, he was startled to find himself looking at a set of strange tracks in the snow. Something had passed through here recently, something with seven long, widely-spread toes and a club-shaped pad as big as his face.

Those definitely weren't the feet of a wendigo, but he quickly decided that he didn't want to meet whatever it was that was attached to them. He shined his light out over the tracks, first one way and then the other—because on other worlds, giant, seven-toed monsters' feet might not necessarily point forward when they walked—then he hurried on, his eyes peeled for any sign of hostile, alien lifeforms, wendigos or reapers.

He glanced back the way he came, half-convinced that something in these woods must be stalking him by now, and his gaze drifted up to the churning sky. That enormous explosion he witnessed... If the machine did that when they first turned it on, how was it still working today? How had it not destroyed itself in that blast?

He kept thinking of all those screaming voices he heard when that shockwave hit him. His awful imagination was quick to insist that it was the voices of all those who were here that day, the five scientists, Port and Bronwen, those unfortunate, screaming souls trapped in Patelemo's machines and anyone else who might've been present, their voices carried with the blast as they were changed forever into those horrid mockeries of their former selves. But his imagination was only that. Perhaps it was merely the voices of the many dead he'd been running into all night. Perhaps they'd experienced the strange hiccup in time, too, and were crying out in surprise.

But those voices hadn't sounded surprised. They sounded terrified. They sounded like people in unspeakable pain.

He pushed the thoughts from his head and carried on beneath the power lines, trying not to think of it anymore.

Distracted by the sound of a girlish giggle, he turned to find two young women stumbling toward him through the woods. One had long, shiny black curls, the other had shorter, frizzier hair. Both of them were dressed less for a snowy, late-night walk in the woods than for a night of drinking and dancing.

"Hey, *you!*" called the long-haired girl. "You wanna play with us?"

The other girl couldn't seem to stop giggling. She was hiding her face, embarrassed. And rightfully so, in Eric's opinion.

"Come on!" whined the long-haired girl. "Let's go get some drinks! We're fun! I promise!"

He walked on, ignoring them. Being invited to spend time with attractive young women wasn't the worst thing that could happen in a haunted forest, he supposed, but he wasn't interested in socializing. He just wanted to make it home to Karen when this was all over.

And if he'd learned nothing from the horror movie industry, it was that when two ghost girls ask you to "play with us," you *keep fucking walking.*

"Aw, you're no fun!" pouted the long-haired girl.

He squinted into the darkness ahead of him. Something was there, but he couldn't quite make it out in the gloom.

An excitable-looking man was suddenly crowding next to him, staring intensely at him and scratching at his cheek as if he had a rash. "Was it a dream?" he asked. "Or wasn't it?"

Eric leaned away from him. "What?"

"It's driving me crazy!" he gasped, still scratching at his face. He was slowly moving down his cheek, toward his chin.

"It shows," he informed the man.

The thing in front of him was a large pipe running through the woods. About three feet in diameter, it snaked its way across the forest floor, over hills and across shallow gullies. It was raised off the ground, but only by a few inches. It was resting on concrete blocks that allowed no room to slip under it. He was going to have to climb over the top of it to continue following the power lines.

He didn't waste time thinking about it. He brushed away the snow and heaved himself over the top of the pipe with his usual level of grace, which was far less Olympic gymnast than clumsy rodeo clown.

"Are you supposed to be doing that?" asked a new and much smaller voice.

He paused in the middle of straddling the pipe and looked back at the spot where the itchy man had been standing. There was now a small girl standing there, her little fists propped on her hips, staring up at him with an incredibly severe look on her face.

"I don't think you're supposed to be doing that," she decided. "You're going to get in trouble."

He swung his other leg over and slid down the other side without responding, landing neatly on his feet and fortunately only wrenching a little pain from his twisted ankle.

Then he shined his light up at the power lines overhead again.

"Are you even listening to me?" snapped the little girl.

He continued on, ignoring the hateful eyes that were watching him from under the pipe.

"What's your name? Don't walk away from me while I'm talking to you!"

A fat, middle-aged man with a big, bushy beard ran across his path, gasping, "Shit! Shit! Shit! Shit! Shit! Shit! Shit!"

A little farther along the path, he found a miserable-looking man in a disheveled suit sitting with his back against a tree, a bottle of gin resting in his lap. He looked up at him as he walked by, regarding him with a weary expression, his face downcast with such emotional weight that it was difficult to meet those watery eyes. "I never did get around to reading that last *Harry Potter* book..." he lamented.

Eric moved on.

The forest fell silent around him and he walked undisturbed for a while.

Now and then he caught sight of more of those lead pipes sticking up out of the ground. He spotted two more of those round grates sticking up, too. There was also another of those strange, outhouse-sized boxes standing in the middle of the forest with no apparent use.

Several times, his flashlight stopped working and he had to stop and bang on it until it came back on, which probably, wasn't helping to slow its imminent demise, he realized, but he didn't know what else to do.

After a while, the overhead lines led him to a tall pole, where they abruptly stopped. At first, he was confused. There didn't appear to be anything there. But as he drew closer, he realized that there was a concrete slab protruding from the ground next to the pole. And looking closer, still, he found that it was an old cellar, with a rotten, wooden door that had collapsed over a set of dank concrete steps.

Lifting the door wasn't really an option. What little there was left of it was covered in decades of accumulated dirt and had rotted to the consistency of wet cardboard. He shined his light through the opening, checking for dangerous, hibernating monsters, and then carefully made his way over the debris and down into the darkness below.

Before his experiences with the weird, he would've had considerable doubts about descending into such a place. And he still *did* have considerable doubts, because *duh*. But these days he didn't bother standing around worrying about all the reasons why such a thing was stupid. The weird told him to go down there. In a way, at least. It'd sent him to lots of scary places, including the voodoo land of the dead, Guinee, where he met Ari, who in turn told him that when it rained fire and ice over the frozen waterfall, he should follow the power to the house with no bottom. This concrete slab sticking out of the ground was hardly a house, but even from outside, he could see that it was quite deep. His light had yet to reveal any floor at the bottom of the steps. All he could see was darkness, cobwebs and aching discomfort. This was where he was supposed to be and no good would come of standing around wasting time.

He descended into the silent gloom, raking the endless cobwebs from his path with his flashlight as he went, listening to his stupid imagination recite an endless list of unspeakable horrors that were probably waiting for him at the bottom of the steps.

But there was nothing waiting for him but more darkness, more cobwebs and more discomfort.

It was deep for a cellar. About two stories deep. And it was bigger on the inside. When he finally reached the floor, he found himself in a room that was three times larger than the slab above.

There was an ancient desk sitting to his right. To his left were three uncomfortable-looking chairs. Directly in front of him was a door. One of those strange light fixtures hung from the center of the ceiling, but it wasn't glowing with any light, swirling or otherwise.

It looked like some sort of waiting room.

He didn't bother wondering what sort of cellar had a waiting room. What sort of cellar was two stories deep? What sort of cellar was hidden way out in the woods, without so much as a road leading to it?

There was another calendar on the wall. Like the others, it was turned to April of 1971. He stared at it for a moment, recalling that strange explosion he'd witnessed. He remembered the cold wind and warm sunshine that washed over him for that brief moment.

Was he really there? Had he really visited the spring of 1971? Had he actually traveled back in time to eleven years before he was born?

He frowned as he rolled the thought around in his head. Or had April, 1971 come to him? There was a difference, he supposed. On one hand, he'd actually traveled through time. On the other, he'd simply remained still and the past had come to him. That latter option seemed a lot more disappointing somehow.

Was that weird?

Thinking too much about it made his head hurt. He pushed the thought away and turned his attention to the door in front of him. Unlike the one at the top of the steps, this door was solidly built. Heavy. Imposing. It was the sort of door that hid dangerous secrets.

Or so his insufferable imagination insisted on telling him.

He didn't stand around wondering if he should open it. Of course he should open it. Why would he come all the way down here and not open it?

He didn't hesitate. There was no point. He opened the door and stepped into a second room about the same size as the first.

He stood there, shining his flashlight around. This room was a little more to take in. It was crammed full of stuff. There was another desk in here. A much smaller one. A writing desk. There was an old gas stove in the corner, next to a small sink. There was a small refrigerator in the next corner, a table with a single chair in a third corner and a tiny, walled-off bathroom wedged into the fourth. There was also a sofa that unfolded into a bed and a tall, metal cabinet. A large chalkboard took up most of one wall and was filled up with a massive chart of various numbers that made no sense to him. There was a dust-covered bible resting on the table and an old crucifix hanging on the wall over the desk. The rest of the walls were decorated with various paintings of the sea.

There was another of those strange, swirling light fixtures— or perhaps it was actually a *bulb*, now that he was thinking about it—but again, it wasn't working. He wondered why these were dark when everywhere he'd been since the lights came on at the back of the glass house had been lit. Had this building blown a fuse or something?

There still wasn't a phone, of course. He understood that they didn't work here, but he kept hoping he'd at least find one lying around somewhere.

Whatever this place was, it was a lot more cramped, but far homier than the offices of Patelemo and Lofleder, who didn't have so much as a motivational poster to brighten up the space. This room looked like someone had once lived here.

Another door waited to take him even deeper into the subterranean weirdness. But as he brushed aside the curtains of cobwebs and started walking toward it, he caught sight of something lying on the floor. It was an old photograph. He knelt down and picked it up, shining his flashlight at it.

It was a battered picture of a young soldier.

Eric stared at it. Once again, voices from his past were bubbling up through his memories.

Vashner again. The old, hateful, dead man who told him to look for the floating house.

Well, not so much *told* him as drove the words directly into his brain like rusty nails. The ordeal was as painful as it was horrifying. It was like the unsettling way that Tessa spoke, but magnified to an excruciating degree.

Still kneeling over the photograph, he closed his eyes and tried to recall the mysterious, broken words the old man shrieked at him.

Look for... The floating house... he recalled. That much he'd already done. He'd visited the treehouse. He'd spoken to Bronwen. Then: *Find the... Abandoned... Soldier... The secret... In the... Prophet's... Tomb...* And after that, three numbers. Twelve, thirty and twenty.

He opened his eyes and stared at the photograph.

The abandoned soldier.

Then his eyes drifted to the crucifix and Jesus' tortured form hanging on the wall. In this cold, underground place, where no light had been cast in almost forty-seven years, it really was like a tomb...

He stood up and looked around. He'd found the frozen waterfall. He'd followed the power and found the house with no bottom. He'd found the abandoned soldier in the prophet's tomb...

But what was the secret that was hidden here?

What did Vashner want him to find?

He walked over to the next door, brushing aside cobwebs as he went, and opened it.

The next room was much smaller than the previous two, and was occupied entirely with a strange conglomeration of silver tanks, glass tubes, gold cables and clear, rubber hoses.

He stood in the doorway, looking over the machine.

Did this count as a secret, he wondered. Because he had no idea what it was he was looking at.

Then an icy shiver raced up his spine and a cold wind blew through his hair.

He wasn't alone here.

Chapter Forty

He turned around, the hairs on the back of his neck standing at full attention.

It was another twisted place. And this time he was cornered. Standing there in the doorway, he realized that the only way back out of here was the way he came, which meant walking through the twisted room, which was already waking up.

Something was moving in the concrete. It slid up the wall, across the ceiling and down again. It was the same way Bronwen and Port had moved through the walls, except the wooden walls of the treehouse had splintered and snapped. And the walls of the maintenance room had cracked and crumbled, violently knocking over shelves. This time, it was as if the concrete were *melting*. It swelled and blistered, oozing its way around the room.

Concrete wasn't supposed to melt. But treehouse walls weren't supposed to talk, flowers weren't supposed to have eyeballs and piles of dust weren't supposed to blow into the shape of a bearded face and complain about their bosses, but here he was.

His heart was pounding again. What was it going to be this time? He'd already dealt with creepy, living toys, killer plant puppets, a dust man and a clockwork jerk. His eyes drifted to the crucifix on the wall. Jesus wasn't going to talk to him, was he? That didn't seem like it'd be in very good taste. Rather disrespectful, he thought.

But the only thing that seemed to be alive in this room was the creeping bubble that was moving through the concrete. As he watched, a ghastly face pushed out from the bulging mass. A huge, yawning mouth opened wide and a low, mournful voice called out, "*Jacky!*"

Eric took a step backward, his eyes fixed on that oozing face.

"Jacky? Is that you? Are you finally home?"

"I'm sorry," said Eric. "I'm not...uh...Jacky."

The face...or the oozing, slightly-face-shaped thing...sagged back into a shapeless glob and slowly oozed down the wall. "Not...Jacky..."

"I'm sorry," Eric said again. The voice sounded so pitifully disappointed that he couldn't help but feel bad about not being Jacky.

"...Jacky..." moaned the wall.

Eric turned and looked around. Nothing else seemed to be happening. The paintings of the sea hadn't come alive. Jesus didn't turn to look at him. The furniture didn't come to life and try to eat him. "Was Jacky someone close to you?"

The oozing, melted face was slowly disappearing behind the sofa, as if hiding. "...Jacky..." it sighed as it sank out of sight. "...brother..."

"Jacky was your brother?"

"...said he'd come back...promised he would...but it's been so long..."

"Where did he go?"

From behind the sofa came a single word: "...war..."

"He went to war?" Eric looked down at the photograph in his hand. "I found a picture on the floor. Is this him?"

He looked up to see a great glob of oozing concrete drooping down almost right on top of him. Gaps opened in grainy goo, forming the shapes of empty sockets and a gaping mouth. A long, dripping hand reached out for the photograph, pushing through the hanging cobwebs.

"...Jacky..." sighed the oozing concrete man.

Eric resisted the urge to back away. Instead, he let those strange, melted fingers pluck the photograph from his hand. "I'm sorry about your brother," he said.

The melty man held the picture close to its face, staring at it.

"I'm sort of waiting on *my* brother, too," tried Eric.

"...brother..." sighed the melty man. But the voice didn't

come from the face that was studying the photograph. It came from under the couch. There were *two* faces.

"Yeah. Except *my* brother didn't go off to war. Nothing like that. It's just that he should be coming to pick me up. He's taking his time getting here." He ran his hand through his hair and frowned. "I think he's still a little mad about me leaving him stranded in Canada this one time…"

At the far side of the room, a third face was bubbling from the wall above the doorway.

"What's your name?" he asked.

"My name?" said the face above the door.

The first face oozed out from under the couch and began to rise upward, revealing shoulders and a scrawny torso. "Name?" it echoed.

Eric waited.

"Charles," said the face hanging in front of him.

"Charlie…" said the face over the door.

"Charlie," agreed the face rising from the floor.

"Charlie," said Eric, nodding. There were three faces, but only one person. Or what *used to be* one person, he supposed. It was just like the treehouse. There was a voice in the wall, a teddy bear, a dolly, a stuffed bunny and a broken pig, but they were all only one voice. They were all Bronwen. "What did you do here, Charlie?"

"…I…do…?" asked the Charlie that was rising from the floor in front of the couch. It wasn't just a face anymore. It was almost an *entire* Charlie. Thin as a skeleton, with long, dangling arms and a too-big, oozing face, it looked to him like something Tim Burton might've dreamed up, only scarier.

"…monitor…" said the Charlie that had been above the door but was now sliding down the wall, plowing through the cobwebs.

"…record…data…" said the upside-down Charlie that was still staring at the photograph he gave it.

"…measure…" said a fourth voice as a new face bubbled up from the corner behind the stove. "…the streams…"

"…critical…" said the voice of the Charlie that was now an

entire, human-shaped thing as it walked toward the upside-down Charlie with the photograph. It lifted its foot and took actual steps, and yet it never parted from the floor. The concrete simply stretched beneath its oozing feet as it moved.

"...must maintain balance..." sighed the Charlie that was oozing over the top of the stove.

"...my job..." said the Charlie that was settling into a puddle beside the door.

Eric turned and looked at the bizarre machine behind him. Then his gaze shifted to the chalkboard on the wall. "So...you guys were in charge of monitoring this thing?"

"...measuring..." said the Charlie that was now bubbling around the side the stove. "...streams..."

"Monitoring and measuring *streams*," amended Eric. *My mistake*, he thought.

"...critical..." insisted the human-shaped Charlie as it bent toward the upside-down Charlie, as if it wished to look at the photograph, too. As he watched, the two merged into a single, oozing shape that stretched from the floor to the ceiling. "...very important..."

"I'm sure it was," Eric assured them. No...assured *him*. The twisted place might've pulled him apart, but Charlie was just one man. Or...he *used to* be a man... Now he was several globs of scary-looking, oozing concrete.

He just kept finding new kinds of weird.

"...Jacky..." sighed the thing that used to be two Charlies and was now... Well, Eric wasn't entirely sure at this point. The thing seemed to have two legs, three hands and one and a half faces.

"I'm sorry," he said again.

"...Jacky..." sighed the Charlie that was growing a body of its own in front of the door.

Eric watched it, concerned about the fact that it was blocking his escape route. If Charlie suddenly turned violent—and not one of these encounters yet had ended without a scare—he wasn't going to be able to make a quick exit.

He took another step backward, away from the merged

Charlie and into the room containing the machine. Then he glanced back at it. "So this must be a pretty important machine," he reasoned. It wasn't doing anything that he could see, but the machines in Evancurt didn't operate under the strict laws of nature as he understood them, so maybe it ran silent.

Again, he wished he could talk to Isabelle. She'd be able to tell him if that thing was giving off any exotic energies.

"...critical..." replied the fused Charlie. "...collect the data..."

"...monitor the streams..." added the Charlie that was oozing across the floor in front of the stove.

Eric nodded. Streams. That was one of the words Lofleder used. And the crazy guy out in the woods, too. Could it be that he'd found it? Was *this* the Evancurt machine? Was this what broke the world?

"...not anymore, though..." sighed the Charlie that was blocking the door.

"...broken now..." sighed a new Charlie that was oozing out from under the refrigerator.

He looked at all the oozy Charlies, surprised. It was broken?

"...no more data..." lamented the fused Charlie.

"...burned up in the first process..." added the Charlie that had moved from the stove to the table. "...all done..."

"...nothing left to measure..." groaned the Charlie by the fridge.

"...but I'm still here..." sighed the fused Charlie. It was shrinking, he realized, withdrawing back into a blob of melted concrete on the ceiling. He watched the thing's feet slowly peel away from the floor as it drew upward, his mind racing.

"...still here..." agreed the Charlie under the table.

If this machine no longer worked, then it wasn't what he was looking for. Smashing it would probably do no good and might bring the reapers to him again.

But if not for the machine, then why was he here?

The question had barely passed through his mind when the Charlie under the table oozed up the wall and knocked it over, spilling the bible onto the dirty floor.

A yellowed envelope that had been tucked inside it slid free and landed at his feet. He bent and picked it up.

The Charlies didn't seem to notice. Or else they didn't care.

There was no name on the envelope indicating who it was for. He tore it open and found a brief, handwritten letter inside. It was addressed to Charles (way back when he was just Charles and not all these Charlies) and the handwriting was very feminine.

I pray that you read this in time, he read. *I've discovered a dreadful secret and you're in terrible danger!* He frowned. A secret? As in "the secret in the prophet's tomb" that Vashner's ghost was bellowing about that night? *There's no time to explain, but you must leave Evancurt before sundown. Please meet me in the woods across from the main gate as soon as possible. We'll leave this place together. Please hurry!*

The letter was signed simply, "M."

He frowned. That wasn't a secret. It was just a *mention* of a secret. Was this really what Vashner meant for him to find here?

He folded the note back up and slipped it into his pocket as he looked around at all the Charlies. There were twice as many as there were before. They were oozing from the concrete on every surface. Clearly, Charles never got this letter. It hadn't been opened. And he never escaped Evancurt. It was a fair bet that the machine's activation was the danger that someone was trying to warn him about. This "M" must've figured out somehow that something bad was going to happen. He wondered what prevented him from reading it and escaping this awful fate?

He hesitated to ask the question that needed asked. So far, Charlie had been the calmest of all the changed people he'd met. He hadn't grown agitated or angry once. He only seemed to be missing his brother. Asking the question that needed asked would probably trigger a much stronger reaction, and he was already surrounded by Charlies.

He definitely didn't want to risk seeing an *angry* mob of Charlies.

But the Charlie that was blocking the door had stepped forward and was reaching for the picture, opening an exit.

Careful not to step on any of the melty Charlie faces that

were emerging from the floor, Eric made his way through the door and into that odd little waiting room. Then, with his back to the cold that was blowing down the concrete steps, he asked, "Do you know someone who's name starts with the letter M?"

On the other side of that first doorway, all of the Charlies turned their oozing faces toward him.

A dreadful silence fell over the room.

Then, one by one, they began to speak.

"...Millie..."

"...Millie..."

"...Millicent..."

"...Millie..."

"...Millicent..."

Eric took a step backward.

The Charlies began to swell, their eerie, oozing faces bubbling. The chair and desk overturned. The paintings fell off the walls and clattered to the floor. And those eerie voices kept saying the names Millicent and Millie over and over again, overlapping in a maddening din.

"Yep," he said, backing away. "Knew that wasn't going to go over well..."

At least he knew that "M." was for Millicent. That was one more thing than he knew a moment ago. Even if he didn't know who Millicent was...

The doorway in front of him was filling with oozing, melted concrete and hideous, bubbling faces. But the way out was clear. He backed through the door behind him, his gaze fixed on those oozing, agitated shapes.

All things considered, this was going far better than usual.

But when he turned around to flee back up the steps, there was a reaper hovering over him.

He barely had time to utter a startled yelp before a long, scythe-like finger plunged through his chest.

Chapter Forty-One

This was it. This was how it was going to end.

Eric stared up at the reaper's face as it leaned over him. Its flesh was like glistening tar, wet and oozing. Unlike the gritty, gloopy faces of Charlie in the next room, this thing was smooth and firm, almost rubbery. A brilliant blossom of crimson red bloomed above one, empty eye and streaked down its face as if it'd been pierced by some unseen weapon, spilling streams of bright blood that coursed through its half-liquid skin, briefly painting the contours of its shadowy face.

And it *did* have a face. Now that he was close up, he could see it. It even looked familiar. He'd seen that face before somewhere. But he couldn't remember where.

It was too difficult to think.

There was a great, searing pain deep inside him.

Slowly, he looked down at himself, at that long, glistening black blade that was protruding from his chest. Where it entered his body, it sputtered like a hot iron in a downpour. Was that his blood sizzling against it? His bodily fluids burning away inside his own chest?

The pain was greater than anything he'd ever felt before. He didn't know it was possible to feel this much pain. It coursed through him in rapid, agonizing waves. His vision blurred. There was a loud ringing in his ears. He could feel his pulse pounding in his veins and every heartbeat felt like an explosion inside his body.

He felt his legs going weak beneath him, but he didn't fall. He couldn't. The reaper's blade was holding him up. He could feel it pushing upward as his weight settled onto it. It felt like it was tearing him in two.

He thought of Karen, waiting for him at home.

Holly and Paige.

Paul.

Isabelle.

Was she watching right now? Had she seen? Did she feel this awful pain he felt?

For the first time tonight, he found himself hoping that she *wasn't* there. That she could be spared this torturous hell.

But if she *was* there…

I'm sorry, he thought as his hand slowly fell slack and the flashlight fell to the dirt-covered floor at his feet.

The reaper yanked its bladed finger from his chest. The motion was accompanied by an agonizing sensation that he couldn't describe even if he could think clearly enough to try. The closest his imagination could come was a sensation like molten metal filling the hole it left behind, burning its way through him.

He cried out and dropped to his knees.

He saw no blood. It must've burned away before it could leave his body. Instead, a black plume of smoke and ash seemed to be spewing from the hole in his jacket.

He recalled Tessa telling him that the reapers had the power to pierce one's soul.

I'm sorry…

He lifted his head and looked up at the reaper. His head was spinning. The world was churning. The shadows all swirled together.

The monster was leaning over him, all of its gleaming, black fingers rising into the air like spiders' legs, preparing to finish him off.

He supposed he'd always known it'd be something like this.

Tell them, he thought to Isabelle. *Tell them all…I'm sorry…*

And as he felt the icy waves of a vast darkness begin to crash down onto him, he saw something else. There was a strange glow at the top of the steps.

The reaper turned to face it.

There was a shout. Or perhaps it was a howl. Or even a scream. It was hard to tell for sure.

His eyes fell closed.

There was a flash of warmth. And a splash of something cold. And there were voices. Both distant and near. But he couldn't understand what they were saying.

He was falling forward, onto the ground.

The smell of dank earth and rotten leaves rushed up to meet him.

And as the world swam away, he felt himself floating into an icy wind.

Chapter Forty-Two

Again, Eric found himself adrift in the churning waves of that strange and endless black ocean, helpless against those icy, ethereal currents.

Was this death?

He'd been dead before, hadn't he? Sort of? He seemed to remember that he met Ari in the land of the dead. The "after place," she'd called it.

But he couldn't remember it very clearly. It was too hard to think.

Should he be able to feel this much pain if he was dead? There was a terrible burning deep inside his chest and an awful aching in his hand. And his head began to ache each time he tried to remember what had happened to him.

She's called for you.

Was that a voice from the gloom? Or a voice from his past?

It's time.

"Time for what?" he asked. "*Who* called?"

Or *did* he ask these things? Was that a memory? Or just a dream?

He tried to open his eyes, tried to peer through the endless murk. And for just a few brief seconds, the void thinned. He could smell the earth. He could smell the crisp, winter air.

And he could smell *blood*.

Snow was falling around him. His face was pressed against the bare earth. The burning in his chest seemed to ease. The pain in his hand dulled, too, but fresh pain flared in his shoulder and knee in its place. His head hurt. His ribs ached.

This was where he started again, wasn't it? Back in the woods where he first woke up? Near the wreckage of the PT

Cruiser.

Why was he back here?

Was it *all* only a dream?

He tried to lift his head, but he couldn't move. The effort did nothing more than drain what little energy he had left.

Somewhere in the trees above him, a crow called out. And then the void closed around him again. His thoughts melted away. The pain disappeared. And he sank back into that icy ocean of pain and nothingness.

Chapter Forty-Three

"Don't give up."

Eric's thoughts were scattered through the void, tossed like doomed boats caught in the giant waves of a deadly storm. Only slowly did they begin to knock together and collect into something capable of realizing that someone was speaking to him across these murky depths.

"Come back."

Who was there? He couldn't see anything. There didn't seem to *be* anything. He couldn't even be sure that *he* existed.

"Please, Eric."

Gradually, he felt himself drifting back to the surface, slowly moving toward the voice that was calling out to him.

But as awareness began to dawn on him through the darkness, it picked up speed. He became aware of several things. There was cold. And there was searing pain. And a terrible noise. And he wasn't lying face-down on the forest floor, he realized. He was lying on his back, his head propped on something. There were hands on him. They felt warm and gentle.

Slowly, he managed to pry his eyes open.

"He's coming back!"

The void melted into shadows and falling snow. He was outside, beneath the branches of the forest. It was dark and cold. There were people bending over him. It took a great deal of effort to make his eyes focus enough that he recognized the face that was floating there.

She said her name was Peggy. The warmly-dressed woman he met after he fell out of the treehouse. The one who told him about the twisted places and warned him to steer clear of the rot.

"Thank goodness," she breathed.

"That was a close one," sighed a man's voice. It was the man from the workshop's tunnel entrance, the one in the flannel shirt and cap who warned him that things were happening more frequently and that time was running out. The white snow lightened everything up just bright enough to make him out. He was standing a few steps to his left, his arms crossed over his chest.

"Totally," agreed the pierced man, who was sitting cross-legged on the ground next to him, unfazed by the cold and snow in spite of being bare-chested and bald.

"He's not safe yet," whispered a voice that didn't seem to have an origin, but instead merely drifted to him through the falling snow.

He looked around. Dora, the overly-excited young woman from Lofleder's office, was bending over him, a worried look on her soft face. The severe-looking old woman he saw when he first arrived in Evancurt was standing behind her, staring at him with the same, judging look she was giving him that first time.

And then there was Tessa, whose naked thighs his head was resting on, smiling down at him with those bloody eyes.

This was an odd collection of dead people. He wondered what they were all doing here.

But it was hard to think clearly with all the noise. The trees were filled with cawing crows.

A noisy murder, he thought to himself. And if he hadn't been so confused and weary and in so much pain, he might've chuckled at himself.

He groaned and looked down at his chest. Someone had removed his shirt and jacket and he was lying on the icy ground, shivering. The snow was falling onto his bare belly and chest. But the cold wasn't at the top of his list of concerns at the moment. His gaze was drawn to the strange, sticky glob of gray, spiderweb-like stuff plastered over the injury the reaper left there like a crude bandage. Tiny wisps of strange, black smoke and ashy flecks were rising from it, just like what he saw when the monster first withdrew its deadly finger, but reduced from a gushing plume to a mere sputter. That searing pain he felt started there and seemed to pass all the way through him, exactly where that reaper's shadowy blade pierced him. "What happened to me?"

"You nearly bit it, dude," said the pierced man.

"Don't be insensitive," scolded Peggy.

"How do you feel?" asked Tessa, her broken, warbling words spilling over him like a bucket of rocks. He'd grown accustomed to the jarring sound of her voice, but in this condition, each syllable seemed to pass through his injured chest like a jolt of electricity.

"Like I should be dead," he grunted.

Tessa smiled, as if he'd said something amusing, but he wasn't joking. Seriously, why *wasn't* he dead right now?

He tried to move, but the pain in his shoulder and ribs flared up again, second only to the endless burning in his chest. It was like the worst heartburn he'd ever felt in his life.

"Take it easy," urged Peggy.

"You'll need to ease into it," agreed Dora.

Tessa laid her hands on his bare shoulders, urging him to remain still. How cold was his body that her once icy hands felt warm against his skin? How long had he been lying here?

But he didn't want to be still. This was awkward. And he had so many questions. "What did that thing do to me?" he asked first as he probed at the strange patch with his cold fingertips.

"Don't go picking at it," snapped the voice that carried on the wind. He glanced around and realized that it was the unfriendly-looking old woman. "You open that wound up and you're done," she growled without moving her lips.

"What is this stuff?" he asked. It was sticky and strangely warm.

"The only thing holding you together," replied the man in the flannel shirt. "So like Mrs. Avery said, don't touch it."

"It's some kinda *ectoplasm*, I think," explained the pierced man as he leaned over him, studying it.

Eric glanced over at him. "What, like that slime from *Ghostbusters*?"

He shrugged. "More like the stuff psychics and mediums

used to barf up at seances in old black and white pictures."

Eric grimaced. "Well *that* sounds gross."

"Nobody…uh…*barfed* anything on you," Dora assured him, wrinkling her nose at the unsavory word.

"Well *we* didn't, anyway," the pierced man clarified. "Somebody might've. That stuff was there when we got here."

When they got here? He wondered who it was, then, that pulled him out of that stairwell. But another and more troubling thought crossed his mind as he recalled that awful encounter with the reaper. It hadn't merely grazed him with that blade. It'd pierced him all the way through. He twisted himself to one side and tried to reach under his back, but the pain in his shoulder stopped him before he could get very far.

"*Easy!*" Peggy said again. "That's right. There's another one of those on your back. Now be still!"

"How am I not dead?" he grunted. Even if he were lucky enough for it to have missed his heart, it should've at least pierced his lung.

"Dude," chuckled the pierced man. "That's not how it works."

"Shush," said Peggy.

"He's not like us," said Dora. "He doesn't understand."

Eric reached over and rubbed at his aching shoulder, but he found that his hand ached even worse and he stopped and flexed it a few times.

Maybe he was just getting too old for this kind of thing. He was seriously beginning to consider an early retirement.

"Yeah, I still don't really get that," said the pierced man. "I mean, *why* is he different?"

"He's still tethered to the living world," replied Tessa in her painful, warbling voice.

In other words, he was still alive, reasoned Eric. He lifted his head and propped himself on his elbows, wincing at his various pains as he did. "So then what happened back there?"

Tessa helped him to sit up. "I told you, the sinners' sentinels have the ability to pierce your soul."

He looked down at the wisps of black smoke and flecks of

ash that trickled through the patch. "Huh?"

"That ain't a physical wound," the pierced man explained. "It has nothing to do with your *body*."

Wait... The reaper stabbed him in his *soul?*

This was a lot to take in. And those damned crows weren't making it any easier to think straight. What had them so worked up, anyway? He squinted up at them, but he couldn't even see them in this gloom. He could barely see the faces of those crowded around him.

When he looked down again, he saw that Dora was holding his shirt out for him so that he could slip his arms into it. Feeling embarrassed to be fussed over, he started to simply take it from her, but the motion sent a twinge of pain through his shoulder and ribs and he decided it wouldn't hurt anything to just let the sweet girl help him. Just this once.

He did, however, insist on buttoning it himself. He wasn't a toddler.

"Will he be able to continue?" asked the ever-unfriendly-looking Mrs. Avery.

"He has a *hole* in his soul," snapped Peggy. "He's lucky to even be—" she stifled herself and glanced down at him.

He stared back at her, surprised.

"I mean, we can't rush him," she finished.

"But can he complete his *job?*" said Mrs. Avery.

"He can," replied Tessa.

"Are you sure?" she pressed.

It was a strange conversation to listen to, one voice a warped record and the other a haunted wind.

Tessa turned her bloody gaze on her. "He can do it," she insisted. "I know him."

"Good," said Mrs. Avery. Then she turned away and vanished into thin air.

"Always a pleasure to see her again," grumbled the man in the flannel shirt.

Slowly, carefully, Eric rose to his feet.

"Careful," pleaded Dora.

"I'm okay," he said. Getting up was difficult, but more because of the pain in his shoulder and hand than the unpleasant burning sensation deep inside his chest. That seemed to be getting better. Or maybe he was just getting used to it. He wasn't entirely sure.

"No, you're really *not*," said Peggy. "Haven't you been listening? Your *soul* is damaged."

"I'm a fast healer," he said as he took the jacket from Dora and slipped it on. It was the truth. Something about what he found on that first journey into the weird helped him to heal more quickly than most. And for reasons he still couldn't fathom, he healed *much* more quickly when there were witches around. (He was well aware of how crazy that sounded, but it was true. Just last year he'd survived being stabbed by a blood witch.)

"That's got nothing to do with it," said the man in the flannel shirt. He reached up and awkwardly adjusted his cap. "We're talking about your *soul*, son. Don't you understand?"

The pierced man rubbed at the back of his neck. "Souls don't heal, dude. Like, *ever*."

He stared at the pierced man for a moment longer, then turned and looked around at the others. "What does that mean, exactly?"

"The damage those monsters inflict..." said Dora, wringing her hands, "...is *permanent*."

"And you can never regain what you've already lost," added Peggy.

What he'd already lost? He looked down at his chest. He could still see those black wisps of smoke and ash escaping through the fabric of his shirt.

"You can see it coming out, right?" said the pierced man. "That black stuff? That's your soul, dude. Or *used* to be, anyway."

Eric stared at the blackness that was bleeding through his shirt. He recalled the vast plume of smoke and ash that poured out of him after the reaper withdrew its deadly finger. He thought that was caused by the shadowy blade burning him. Was he really looking at his own *soul*? Was that really possible?

"That's why you have to be careful," explained Peggy. "It's

like Mrs. Avery said, if you open up that wound again…"

"Break either of those patches open," warned the pierced man, "or let one of those shadow dudes stab you again, and it'll all come spilling out."

He felt dizzy. He turned to face Tessa. "Are you…saying I'm going to *die*?"

"Death?" scoffed the man in the flannel shirt. "We're talking about your *soul*, not your *body*. Your body is just a shell you leave behind when it's your time to go. But your soul is everything you are. It's *you*. If it all bleeds away, if there's nothing left of it, then there's nothing left of *you*. You'll be gone. Not even dead. Just…" He sighed. "Just *gone*."

"Even if your wounds don't open back up," said Peggy, her gaze returning to his shirt, "I can't say for sure how long you have."

He stared at her, confused. "Wait…"

"Nothing can fully contain it once it's damaged," lamented the man in the flannel shirt. "Those patches are only slowing the flow. Eventually…"

"Don't say it," begged Dora. She looked miserable.

"I'm so sorry," said Peggy.

A terrible numbness had begun to spread through his body. If what he was hearing were true… How did you go about processing something like that? He looked down at those black flecks and wisps of smoke.

No. This was absurd. You couldn't *see* your own soul. It couldn't just *bleed out* and disappear forever. It was a mistake. It had to be. Otherwise, what in the world could he tell Karen? Dying was one thing. She'd at least have the comfort of knowing that he'd be waiting for her on the other side. But to just…be *erased* from existence? Forever?

Such a thing shouldn't happen.

He refused to believe it.

"I wish it wasn't true," said Tessa. She didn't even have a sad smile for him this time. "With all my heart."

He stared at her, his thoughts racing as a dreadful, icy feeling began to fill him.

Not even dead, he thought. *Just gone.*

Chapter Forty-Four

"Are you okay?" asked Dora. Her voice seemed so small. He hated to hear someone speak to him like that, like he was some traumatized child.

"Of course he's not okay," said Peggy.

But Eric shook his head. "No. I am. I'm fine. I'm just..." He took a breath and turned to face Tessa. "One thing at a time," he decided. He made a mental note to take extra care not to let anything happen to those ectoplasm bandages—or whatever the hell those sticky, web-looking things were—but he couldn't be distracted by some silly notion of disappearing. That wasn't going to happen. He'd been in dire situations before. These things always worked themselves out.

(*Not even dead. Just* gone.)

He pushed the ridiculous thought from his mind and turned his attention to his surroundings for the first time. There was nothing but dark, snowy forest in every direction. There was no sign of the squat, concrete slab where he was attacked. "How did I get here, anyway?"

"*She* brought you here," said the pierced man.

Eric turned and looked at him. "'She'?"

"The Lady of the Murk," said Dora. And as if reacting to the name, the crows above them began to caw louder.

"She snatched you away from that monster," explained the man in the flannel shirt, raising his voice to be heard over the din of the unseen birds. "Brought you here."

"And patched you up," said the pierced man.

"And called all of us here," added Peggy.

Eric looked around at them. The Lady of the Murk? Was he supposed to know what that meant?

Although...now that he'd heard it...it *did* sound strangely familiar.

A memory teased at him from somewhere deep in his mind. (She's called for you.) Then it vanished back into the murky depths again.

"He doesn't know her?" asked Dora, speaking louder. The crows seemed to respond by increasing their volume again, forcing her to speak even louder. "I thought she was the one who brought him here. *Oh my god!*" she shouted, lifting her face and glaring up at the darkness above. "*Shut up!*"

Surprisingly, some of the crows *did* shut up. The cacophony diminished to about half its volume, which, though better, was still louder than they were when he first awoke.

"I hate those stupid birds," she groaned.

"Harbingers of the dead," said Peggy. It was what she called them the first time he met her. "They're always present here. Especially in places *she's* been."

"This 'Lady of the Murk,'" said Eric.

Again, the crows grew louder as if in response.

"She watches over us," explained Tessa. "The protector of the dead. A guardian angel, of sorts. It was she who sent the messages that brought you here."

The messages that brought him here? Those things she and Vashner and Ari said to him? About broken girls and fire and ice and floating houses and prophets' tombs?

"She knew that only you could stop the evil that was taking place here."

Eric shook his head. "Why *me*? I mean, I know I've kind of done this sort of thing before, but..." He glanced down at his chest, at those faint wisps of blackened soul bleeding into the air. "I feel like she might've overestimated me on this one..."

Seriously, it was a really big world out there. Surely *someone* had to be better qualified for this job than he was.

Tessa gave him that sad smile again. "Don't you remember what you learned at Bellylaugh Playland?"

Bellylaugh Playland? He frowned. The place where he faced that freaky clown and the rat demon? What did that have to do with any of this?

"Hey, I've been there before," said Dora. Then she blushed a little as everyone turned and looked at her. "But that's...not important. Sorry..."

"The ones you met there," Tessa reminded him. "They told you that you straddle the worlds of the living and dead."

"Right..." He frowned deeper as the memory came back to him. It seemed like such a long time ago now. She was talking about the *fairies*. Or, at least, that was the name they'd chosen for themselves. They claimed to have gone by many. They were the ones who revealed to him that he had a deeper connection to the spiritual world than most people. And it was supposedly because of what happened on his *first* journey into the weird, way down at the bottom of that cavernous cathedral.

He'd set off on that first journey with nothing but a pressing urge to drive and an unremembered dream that had woken him up the previous three nights. But as he made his way along the fissure, the dream came back to him in vivid details, revealing that it wasn't merely a dream, but in fact a vision of the future. It became a map, showing him the way to the cathedral.

Except the dream hadn't revealed the journey as it was *that* day, after he'd awakened from it for the third time. Rather, it showed him how the journey would've gone if he'd set off the *first* day he awoke. As a result of those extra two days, things had changed. The Eric in his dream faced different obstacles...and in the end, Dream Eric had lost half of his right hand to a monstrous beast and then died a terrible, agonizing death in the depths of the cathedral.

Judith, the deceptively childlike elder of the fairies who'd taken up residence in a fairy circle hidden deep inside Bellylaugh Playland's playground equipment explained to him that the dream that sent him to the cathedral was much more than a vivid vision of a possible future. It was, in fact, a glimpse of an alternate timeline. And because he'd died in an alternate timeline, he possessed a strong connection to the spirit realm.

(As Paul had once said, *everything* was a thing. Nothing was impossible in this weird world, it seemed.)

"It's because of your connection to the world of the dead that lost spirits like us are drawn to you," explained Tessa. "And why *she* chose you to for this task."

"Is *that* why this guy's so special?" wondered the pierced man.

"No," said Tessa. "Just *one* of the reasons." She stepped in front of Eric as he buttoned up the jacket and placed her slender hands on his shoulders. Her bloody eyes locked onto his. "Listen to me, Eric," she said, her voice still warbling through the air, unsynchronized with the movements of her lips. He could still feel every syllable in the reaper's wound like the thudding of a pounding bass beat. "I know that we've asked a lot of you. We've asked *everything* of you. More than we have any right to."

"You asked me for my help," said Eric. "And I promised you I would. That's all that matters."

The smile she gave him was beyond sad. He almost couldn't bear to meet her bloody gaze.

"We'll deal with what comes next after. Right?"

She nodded. "Right."

"So, just tell me what I should do."

"*She* can only do so much," explained Tessa. "She gave me two messages to pass on to you. First: beware the Spirit of the Forest."

"Spirit of the Forest?"

"You've encountered it twice now," she explained. "It manifests as pure, primal terror."

"Oh, *that*," said Eric, recalling the two strange experiences he'd had now. Once when he first awoke in this place and then again shortly after he fled Patelemo's clockwork workshop. "Wait…that was a *ghost?*"

"Not a ghost," explained the man in the flannel shirt. "*Spirit*. Not all spirits were once human."

He nodded. "That's right," he recalled. The fairies and the nymph at Bellylaugh Playland had referred to themselves as spiritual beings. It was why Isabelle felt so much spiritual energy in spite of the fact that there turned out to be only two actual ghosts on the premises.

"The Spirit of the Forest is more like a god, really," said Tessa. "It's ancient beyond words. And very, very powerful."

"And it's *pissed*," said the pierced man. "It *really* doesn't like what's going on here."

"Can you blame it?" asked Peggy.

"It's taking all she has to keep it from killing you," said Tessa.

"Oh…" was all he could think to say. This "Lady of the Murk" was protecting him from the Spirit of the Forest's wrath? He thought back to the second encounter, when that freaky buzzing sensation overwhelmed him and he was plunged into those weird dreams. Hadn't he thought for a moment that he could hear voices arguing in strange languages?

Was one of them her? Was that the Lady of the Murk defending him from the Spirit of the Forest?

Why was his life turning into a fantasy novel?

And why did that name seem so familiar? Where had he heard the name "Lady of the Murk" before?

"And second," Tessa went on, "she says you'll be shown the way."

"'Shown the way,'" repeated Eric. "How so?"

There was a familiar cry from the forest behind him. He turned to find Spooky standing in the snow, staring back at him and holding the flashlight he'd dropped at the bottom of the stairs in its mouth.

"Oh," said Tessa. "There you go. Like that."

Eric nodded.

"Such an odd creature," said Peggy.

"What is it?" asked the pierced man.

The man in the flannel shirt shook his head. He had no answer.

Eric had almost forgotten about that part of his first conversation with Peggy beneath the old treehouse. According to her, Spooky wasn't a cat at all. He was something else. Which wasn't all that much of a surprise, really. He always knew there was something odd about the cat.

Eric frowned. "What about you guys? You said this 'Lady of

the Murk' called all of you here after she saved me." Again, the mere mention of her name seemed to stir the noisy crows into a louder state of agitation, forcing him to raise his voice as he continued speaking. "I mean I get Tessa. She came here with me. But what about the rest of you?"

Peggy shrugged. "We just do as *she* tells us," she replied. "Like when she told me to go to the treehouse, where I found you."

"Or when she told me to show you that freaky plant," agreed the pierced man.

"Or to tell you about the research I found," added Dora.

"She can't help us escape this place," said the man in the flannel shirt. "But we can feel her watching over us. She lends us comfort. Those of us who can hear her voice and move around freely can't help but answer her call."

"Most of the spirits of Evancurt are lost," explained Tessa. "They're confused or confined by their emotions or weighted down by their grief or regrets."

Eric nodded. That much he'd already figured out. It made sense that they wouldn't be able to come to his aid. "So you guys are, like, the sanest of all the ghosts here or something?"

"Something like that," chuckled the man in the flannel shirt.

"We're the most *whole*," said Peggy. "The most like what we were before we died."

Eric looked around at each of them. He wondered how it was they all died. They all looked too young to be here. But he couldn't help feeling that it might be an insensitive thing to ask. Instead, he looked up into the noisy branches above him, into those looming, snow-drizzled shadows.

The Lady of the Murk.

He wished he could remember why that sounded familiar.

"Time is still running out," said Tessa. "You should go."

"But be careful," begged Peggy. "Don't forget to protect those injuries."

"Don't take any unnecessary risks," agreed Dora.

He glanced down at his chest, at those eerie wisps of black smoke and tiny, ashen specks that sputtered through his stolen jacket. "Right," he said. Then he turned back to the group. His gaze immediately fell upon a short, pudgy man in cargo shorts, flip-flops and a baggy tank top. He was standing between Peggy and the man in the flannel shirt, an open can of beer in one hand.

Everyone else turned and looked at him, too.

The man glanced around at them, a pair of bushy eyebrows raised in an expression of curiosity. He lifted his beer to his lips and said, "What's goin' on over here?"

Chapter Forty-Five

He collected the flashlight from where Spooky dropped it. He was a cat, after all, or at least something that resembled a cat to mortal eyes. He wasn't about to degrade himself further by actually letting a mere human take it from his mouth. It was amazing the little beast brought it as far as he did. And by the time he'd confirmed that it hadn't broken when he dropped it and that the batteries still worked, Tessa, Peggy, Dora, the pierced man and the man in the flannel shirt had all vanished. Only the nosy man in the cargo shorts remained. He seemed perfectly content to simply stand there, drinking his beer and watching the not-dead guy with the hole in his soul take direction from a cat.

(Where did the ghosts keep finding alcohol, anyway? Did the afterlife come with open bar privileges?)

At least the pain had dulled. Getting to his feet and loosening up his muscles seemed to ease the pains in his shoulder and knee. And the searing pain in his chest, though unbearable at first, had almost dissipated completely. Was that normal for an injury to the soul, he wondered, or was this more supernatural help?

He supposed it didn't matter. And he didn't have time to ponder it. Apparently deciding that Eric had wasted quite enough of his valuable time, Spooky abruptly turned and took off into the forest.

Eric hurried after him as fast as he dared to move with his soul apparently held in by nothing more than a pair of less-than-adequate, ectoplasmic Band-Aids. Fortunately, it wasn't as hard to follow him this time, owing to the snow that had been gathering all night. All he had to do was follow the tracks.

But he almost wished he didn't have this particular luxury. Without worry of losing track of the little beast, his mind was free to wander. And he couldn't help looking down at his chest, at those creepy wisps of black smoke and those little, ashy flecks.

Was it true? Did that reaper actually pierce his mortal soul? And was he really doomed to not only die, but to utterly *disappear*?

That seemed grotesquely unfair. Karen had suggested on numerous occasions that there must be some higher power looking out for him. It was the only explanation, she'd theorized, for how he kept getting out of tight spots. There always seemed to be some way out, no matter how dire the situation seemed, going all the way back to that first golem he encountered. That thing would've killed him for sure if an old man named Grant hadn't plowed a tractor into the porch, breaking the monster's focus.

Without Isabelle, he never would've escaped the insane Altrusk House. Without Father Billy, he would've been a meal for that pack of corn creeps. And his strange luck had followed him long after he returned from the insane depths of the cathedral. He'd survived an angry jinn, murderous witches, an immortal madman, an evil clown and a rat demon. He'd faced terrifying, nameless agents and dangerous monsters from alternate dimensions. He'd lost count now of how many guns had been pointed at him. There was always *something* to get him out of trouble when things were most dire.

Why should this time be any different?

After all, if this "Lady of the Murk" had really brought him here to put a stop to the machine that broke the world, shouldn't she have foreseen this? Surely she didn't mean for him to perish here.

Right?

And wasn't there still so much left for him to do? What about the curse that had been forced upon everyone during that blood witch ordeal? He had to live long enough to find a way to save them from that looming reckoning, didn't he? And what about Isabelle? He couldn't disappear before he'd figured out a way to save her from her queer, timeless prison. It seemed like the universe had some sort of plan for him. Surely this couldn't be it.

And yet, no matter how he tried to rationalize against it, he couldn't seem to lose that sick lump deep in his gut.

There was something about this whole situation that troubled him. Something was deeply *off*. He'd felt it from the very start, but he simply couldn't seem to put his finger on it.

What if it *was* true? He couldn't help but wonder. What did he do? What would happen?

Would he get a chance to see Karen again? Would he get to say goodbye? And how did he go about telling her such a thing? Death was one thing, but how did you say goodbye *forever*?

He shook the thought away. He couldn't deal with that right now. He just couldn't.

But as soon as Karen was out of his mind, he found himself thinking about Isabelle.

Isabelle wasn't just a friend, after all. She was inside his head. She could read his mind. She could feel his emotions. He'd often wondered what it would be like for her if he died. It was hard to imagine it being anything short of traumatizing to be inside someone's head at a time like that, to feel their pain and their fear and their anguish, to hear their voice fall silent forever.

But death was only death. Death was something that was supposed to come for everyone eventually. Having your very *soul* extinguished…

He clenched his jaw and forced the thoughts away. It did no good to dwell on such horrors. He had a job to do. If he just pushed on, he was sure the problem would solve itself. Just like it always did.

But his hand crept toward his pocket. He really wished he had his phone. If he could just get a response from Isabelle… Just a simple acknowledgement so that he could know that she was there…

He just wanted to feel a little less alone. Just for a little while.

But the thought had barely crossed his mind when a small hand closed around his reaching fingers.

The girl in the cupcake tee shirt was walking beside him again.

He smiled down at her.

Right. He still had a job to do. Hole in his soul or not, if he didn't find Voltner's hideous machine and put a stop to it, this girl, Tessa, and every other spirit wandering these strange acres was going to be wiped from existence. He couldn't live with himself if he let that happen. It didn't matter if it cost him his very being.

He had to stop the machine.

Whatever came next, he'd deal with it *then*.

He ignored that hot lump in his belly and turned his attention to the tracks in front of him. Spooky would show him the way. Tessa said so. The *Lady of the Murk* said so. Whoever she was…

For now, all he could do was trust that everything would work itself out. The universe looked out for him, after all. It always had. It wouldn't let him down now.

The first thing the universe offered him, however, was an immensely overweight and copiously tattooed woman spilling out of a way-too-skimpy halter top and an obscenely small pair of short shorts.

She strolled past him, heading the opposite direction, and actually turned her nose up at him, as if he'd shown any indication whatsoever that he'd liked what she was showing off.

He dismissed the snobby woman and her seasonally inappropriate—and arguably just plain *inappropriate*—wardrobe and continued following the tracks in the snow. (The woman, in spite of her less-than-dainty size, left not a single snowflake disturbed in her wake.) And after another minute or so, he passed a lost man in dress pants and a polo shirt who was looking back and forth from a piece of paper in his hand to the forest around him.

Eric shined his flashlight at the paper as he passed by and immediately noted that the man's apparent confusion might have had something to do with the fact that the paper was a Chinese food menu and he seemed to be trying to follow the street map on the back.

He didn't think the poor guy was going to be finding his way to the Lucky Dragon tonight. Or ever again.

He moved on, leaving the lost man to his useless map.

He couldn't help but wonder if sudden and unexpected deaths could have been what left so many of these people trapped in their odd delusions. Had the man with the Chinese takeout menu, for example, been hit by a car on his way to pick up dinner? He remembered the old man back in the green lab who told him he'd been standing in his invisible line forever and it was far too easy to imagine that the poor fellow had dropped dead of a heart attack while waiting his turn at the DMV. Had the nicely dressed gentleman in the glass house who was searching for gate five passed away while waiting for his flight at an airport?

"The sawdust man!" shrieked a pale and wispy woman, startling him from his thoughts. She wore a handmade dress of light, flowing fabric and was draped in countless pieces of gawdy jewelry. Her hair was long and thin and blew about her face in the wind. As soon as he turned to look at her, she thrust a jangling arm out and pointed toward an old and knotted tree. "In there! That's where they sealed him! Ages and ages ago, when the world was still new and terrible and forgotten things wandered the land!"

Eric stared at her for a moment, confused. Then he glanced over at the tree where, apparently, an ancient sawdust man had been locked away since some ancient time when he was fairly sure there weren't any trees like that.

"He was a monster!" hissed the woman. "A *devil!* An evil curse on this world!"

Eric nodded. "Okay," was all he could think to say. He'd be careful not to release any ancient, tree-dwelling sawdust men while he was here, he guessed.

"He has a message for you," the woman whispered.

He stared at her. A message from the evil sawdust man in the tree? Sure. Why not? "Okay," he said again. "What's the message?"

The woman squinted and tilted her head to one side as if

listening very hard.

Eric waited.

"What?" she said to some voice that only she seemed to be able to hear. She listened a moment longer, her thin face scrunched into a baffled expression.

He glanced down at the girl beside him. She looked back up at him and shrugged her shoulders. Apparently, she couldn't hear a voice coming from the tree, either.

Then the woman gasped. Her eyes flashed wide with shock. She twirled to face the tree, the patterned fabric of her dress blooming around her like a great, gawdy flower. "*I'm not saying that!*" she shrieked at the tree. "You're disgusting! Find someone else to deliver your filthy messages!" Then she gasped again. "I do *not!*" she shrieked. "That's none of your business, you *prehistoric pervert!*" She twirled around again and stomped away, growling, her thin face, so pale before, was flushed bright red. "*Men!*" she shouted.

Eric watched her go, not entirely sure what *he'd* done to be lumped in with the obscene, tree-dwelling sawdust man. "Huh," he said once she was gone.

"Bad tree," said the girl in the cupcake tee shirt.

"I guess so."

Chapter Forty-Six

Eric left the obscene sawdust man's tree and continued following the tracks in the snow. The girl walked along with him, still clinging to his hand, and he found himself unconsciously glancing down at her as he went. He kept expecting to find her gone again. And after a while of this, it occurred to him that he simply didn't want to be alone. That business with the reaper had unsettled him more than he cared to admit and there was something particularly comforting about the girl's presence.

"I'd sure like to know your name," he tried. "It'd be nice to know what to call you."

She looked up at him with those big, blue eyes and said nothing.

"Okay then," he relented, and continued on without pushing the matter.

The forest had been quiet for the past few minutes, but now it began to grow more crowded again. They passed a very distraught-looking priest who looked as if he couldn't understand why he was here in these woods instead of somewhere else, a very angry-looking old man who kept checking his watch and looking around as if he'd been waiting on someone for far too long, a very miserable-looking young woman who was sitting in the snow with tear streaks running down her face and a very lost-looking woman wandering around in oversized sunglasses in spite of the fact that it was the middle of the night and her arms laden with shopping bags.

He hadn't seen a trace of the cat since he began following the tracks. Nor had he heard any of the odd little beast's familiar cries. It seemed Spooky trusted that even an idiot like Eric could follow a clear trail of animal tracks in the snow on his own.

He stopped walking, distracted, and tipped his head to one side, listening. For just a moment, he thought he heard a familiar wailing carried on the wind, the heartbreaking voice of the endlessly sobbing girl. Peggy promised him she'd stay with the girl until she wandered off again. Given that she was back there with the others when he woke up, he'd assumed the girl had returned to her miserable wanderings. She could be anywhere on the property by now, and it was perfectly likely that her voice had carried to him for a moment. But if it was her, then she was somewhere far off.

He returned his attention to the tracks, only to be distracted by another phantom light. Like before, it looked like an ordinary flashlight carried by someone moving through the forest. But unlike the others he'd seen, this one was high up in the air, well above the tree tops.

He craned his neck and looked up at it, a puzzled look passing over his features. *Could* ghosts fly, he wondered. He'd never really thought about it before. Ghosts always flew in cartoons. And some of the ghosts he'd encountered, like judgy-looking old Mrs. Avery, didn't ever seem to actually touch the ground. They'd moved more by *gliding* than by walking. Not one of them left footprints, but he'd never seen one just take off soaring through the sky, he didn't think.

Then he remembered the ghastly spirit of cranky old Rupert Vashner hovering over him as he shouted about floating houses, forgotten soldiers and prophets' tombs, just before screaming the name "Evancurt" into his face and then vanishing through the wall.

So he supposed he *had* seen a ghost fly before, now that he was thinking about it.

He looked back down at the tracks he was following and stopped. There was a second and much larger set of tracks crossing Spooky's prints here.

Startled, he quickly turned and shined his light first one way and then the other, expecting to find something charging toward him out of the gloom. But there was nothing within sight.

These were different from the tracks of the seven-toed

monstrosity he encountered earlier in the night, much more human-shaped. A wendigo, perhaps? The tracks were big enough to belong to one, considerably larger than his own footprints, and made by something that sort of resembled bare, human feet, no less. But unless a wendigo was actively pursuing prey, it barely moved. Whatever this was, it had a long stride. And there was no way one of those ugly things shuffled that distance between when Spooky had passed through here and now.

A closer look revealed that these tracks definitely crossed *over* Spooky's. Whatever had passed through here, it wasn't a wendigo and it wasn't a ghost, meaning it was probably from another world. Remembering the spider-yeti thing in the workshop's dome room and that monstrous teddy bear, he decided not to take any unnecessary chances and moved on, picking up his pace.

About the time the tracks were disappearing back into the gloom behind him, an extremely hairy man wearing nothing but muddy cowboy boots, dark sunglasses and a Stetson strolled across their path.

A startled groan of disgust escaped Eric and he quickly covered the girl's eyes and hurried on.

Why were there so many dead naked people? Seriously, it was the middle of winter out here! What the hell?

A little farther along, he found another man, this one fully-dressed, thankfully. He was standing with his face turned toward the sky.

Eric stopped and looked him over, curious. It wasn't the same man he saw after he left Patelemo's workshop, but he had the same strangely horrified expression on his face as he stared up into the falling snow.

Again, he squinted up at the gloomy sky, wondering what might be up there.

"Strange sky," said a voice from behind him.

Eric turned to find another man looking up at the same sky. He was older than the first, dressed in a neatly pressed, blue dress shirt, with a bushy mustache and thin, slicked-back hair.

"Even when it's clear," said the man, "it always feels like

something's up there. Even when you can see all the way to the stars."

Again, he squinted up at the sky. Was it just because of the man's mysterious words, or did there seem to be something moving in those clouds?

Before he could consider the matter further, however, something rustled in the trees behind him. He turned and shined his light around again, but found nothing staring back at him with that creepy eyeshine.

Probably those crows. They'd settled down considerably since he'd awakened with his head propped on Tessa's thighs, but their presence had remained constant as he followed Spooky's tracks through the snow.

The little girl tugged at his arm, urging him forward, and when he looked back, he saw that the two men had vanished.

He continued walking. How far was the cat leading him, anyway? It felt as if he'd been following these tracks for miles.

"There's a world beyond this one," croaked the hoarse voice of a woman.

Eric turned and shined his light onto a face that was too young to look so haggard. Her eyes were sunken and bloodshot, her skin pallid. Her blonde hair hung about her face in greasy tangles. She was trembling.

"A world of *eternity*," she breathed. "Eternal space... Eternal time... Eternal darkness... Eternal *suffering!*"

He nodded and took a step back, instinctively placing himself between her and the girl, even though he was quite sure no spirit here could harm her. "Sounds like a terrible vacation spot," he said.

The woman took a step toward him. "An endless forest... A *graveyard* for *dead worlds*."

Again, he nodded. "That's...uh...*neat?*"

She took another step toward him, her sunken eyes widening. "It'll swallow us all eventually. Everything that dies ends up there."

Eric wasn't sure what happened next. The woman didn't take another step. It was as if someone had skipped ahead on him. Suddenly, her body was pressed against him. Her cold lips brushing his ear.

"*But the living should never go there.*"

He cried out and tried to push the woman away, but she was already gone.

There was no one there but the little girl at his side.

He looked down at her, his heart racing. "You saw that, right? That woman?"

She nodded.

"It wasn't just me?"

She shook her head.

"Good." He shined his flashlight at the surrounding trees, half-expecting the haggard woman to be peering back at him, ready to freak him out again. "That's good." He couldn't have gone crazy and just started imagining freaky women appearing out of thin air and spouting terrible nonsense at him if the little ghost girl who was holding his hand could see her, too.

He continued on, still feeling a little rattled, his eyes open for any more ghostly messengers. For the next few minutes, things were mercifully quiet. No ghosts appeared to him. No otherworldly monsters charged him. No reapers came to finish tearing out his soul.

Then he stepped into a large clearing and found himself standing before a strange structure. It was about the size of his house back in Creek Bend, but was dome-shaped and sat upon a two-story-tall, concrete pillar at the center of a huge, slick, bowl-like depression. Three iron bridges spanned the gap between the rim of the depression and the narrow walkway that circled the foundation of the building. Several large satellite dishes stood surrounding the depression and several much smaller dishes were mounted around the lower portion of the domed roof of the structure, itself. Strange, concave disks made from that curious, translucent-white material he found in the glass house were set into the upper portion of the dome, each one with dozens of heavy, gold cables protruding from its edges and snaking up toward the apex.

He stood for a moment, staring at it. It looked like some

sort of observatory. It was quite clearly the "star house" that had been labeled on Lofleder's map.

Once again, his imagination ran wild with the thought of crashed alien spacecraft and unthinkable advanced technology. He remembered the light in the sky. The ghosts who stood with horrified gazes fixed on the clouds.

He looked up at the sky directly over the structure and realized that the clouds there were swirling in an unnatural fashion, almost as if some invisible current were passing through there, disturbing the atmosphere.

Curious, he started to take a step toward the building, but the girl at his side tugged on his hand, pulling him back. He glanced down at her, surprised, and watched as she pointed to Spooky's tracks. They didn't lead across any of the iron bridges. They continued on, past the star house and down a length of snow-covered gravel.

"Right," he said, nodding. "Stay on task. Got it."

The girl had saved him from that "worse than poison" cone-shaped thing in the jungle room and that leviathan monster and the machine people in Patelemo's workshop. If she said he wasn't supposed to go into the star house, then he wasn't supposed to go into the star house.

But he couldn't help shining his light back toward it as he continued following the cat's tracks, wondering what strange and probably terrible things were hidden inside.

Chapter Forty-Seven

Almost as soon as the star house had faded back into the snowy gloom, Eric became aware of a light shining through the trees ahead of him. And after a few more minutes of following the fading cat tracks, he saw that the source of the light was a large picture window in a small, run-down house pushed back into the woods at the end of a long, overgrown driveway.

Strangely enough, he found the light somewhat unsettling. It seemed strangely unnatural compared to the other buildings he'd seen. The alien interiors of those places had seemed utterly separate from these woods so that he barely connected one with the other, as if they were entirely different worlds. (And for all he knew, they might have been just that.) This light was so out-of-place in the otherwise constant darkness of the forest that he couldn't help feeling anxious about what he might find here.

It almost felt as if he were about to walk into a trap.

As he made his way down what could no longer even properly be described as a driveway, he looked the place over. He was going to go out on a limb and say that this was probably the "little house" marked on Lofleder's map. It was a single-story building, with a large front porch.

The place was rundown, but like all the buildings on this property, it didn't seem nearly as decrepit as it should have been after being left to rot for forty-seven years. Again, he recalled Tessa telling him that time was also broken in this place, and wondered if it passed differently here than in the outside world.

And now another, far more unsettling thought crossed his mind: how long had *he* really been here? Was it possible that time was traveling far slower for him than for the rest of the world? What if he emerged from this nightmare forest only to find that months or even years had passed?

But he shook the thought away as soon as it entered his mind. He knew better than that. One thing at a time. Just like with this hole in his soul nonsense. Whatever happened after, he'd deal with it after.

He followed the tracks right up to the front porch, where he found Spooky curled up on the porch railing, fast asleep.

He stood there a moment, observing the snoozing creature that apparently wasn't a cat at all, not even a very strange cat. "I guess that's all the help we're getting from him," he sighed. Then he looked down to find that he was only talking to himself.

The girl in the cupcake tee shirt was gone again.

He spent a moment trying pointlessly to recall precisely when she left him, then turned his attention to the front door.

It was unlocked. He pushed it open and peered into the front room of the little house, scanning the space for anything unpleasant. The first thing he saw was that no one had opened this door in a very long time, judging by the crypt-like curtains of hoary cobwebs and undisturbed layers of dust. The second thing he noticed was that the house was not only illuminated, but *warm*.

Heat? But surely it hadn't been running all this time, even accounting for time anomalies.

He remembered the lights flickering on in the glass house as he was entering the space where the pierced man showed him that first alien plant and wondered if that was also when power was restored to this building and the workshop. Had he triggered some sort of main power switch?

No... More likely, it was something else. He remembered the man in the flannel shirt telling him that the systems were flushing and venting more frequently than ever before, that time was running out and whatever was going to happen was going to happen *soon*.

Looking around now at all the cobwebs and the dust-covered overhead fixtures, he was sure that there was some sort of automated system at work. Power had been restored to portions of the property for the same reason the tunnel was flushing more frequently and the vent house was banging away every few minutes.

The machine was warming up.

The countdown had begun.

He had to hurry.

But he still had no idea where the machine was and how he was supposed to stop it.

He pushed the door all the way open and stepped inside, quickly scanning the room in search of any hidden horrors, and was immediately struck by a surprising familiarity.

It wasn't the house, itself, that was familiar. He'd definitely never been here before. It was the *purpose* of the house that was familiar. Beneath the decades of settled dust and accumulated cobwebs was none of the usual furnishings of an ordinary house. Instead, every wall had been fitted with sturdy shelves and small tables of various sizes had been placed in seemingly random places. And on each of these carefully arranged surfaces sat one or more heavy, hollow rocks broken open to reveal a colorful interior of glittering crystals.

Geodes. Just like the ones in Rupert Vashner's house. The same Rupert Vashner who's angry spirit had shouted cryptic hints about this place more than a year before.

Vashner, he recalled, was a master of crystal magic and a very reluctant mentor to the crystal witches. His house wasn't merely decorated with these pretty stones. He'd devised an ingenious way of using them to collect, channel and magnify magical energy with them. Essentially, he'd turned his entire house into a sort of magical *machine*.

Eric stood there a moment, surprised.

Another machine.

His hand itched to reach for the phone, but he didn't need it. He found that he was certain what Isabelle would tell him if she could speak to him. This house was flooded with magic energy. He wondered if it was the same energy that filled Vashner's house. Was it the same machine? Even without Isabelle to tell him, he felt that this one was much more complex and powerful than the one he encountered that night.

Was there a relationship between Vashner and Evancurt,

then? Could the old and cranky crystal mentor have had a hand in this monstrosity? He'd likely never know. Vashner's life was a mystery, even to those who knew him best. He'd spent his youth searching for some mythical wellspring of magical power and then one day gave it all up and withdrew into his house of crystals, never to set foot outside again.

Eric was no witch, but he was certain this was a crystal machine, which meant that one of the exotic energies Evancurt utilized was magic.

Not that knowing this made one bit of difference, he supposed. He didn't know what to do with this knowledge now that he had it. Back in Vashner's house, he'd wrecked the machine and defeated the blood witch who murdered him, but wrecking *this* machine might only bring the reapers down on him again.

He pocketed the flashlight again, relieved for a chance to save the batteries, and pushed his way through the spiderwebs and into the next room, marveling at the size of some of the geodes. Some were nearly as big as he was.

The place looked like a museum. Or maybe it more resembled an art gallery with its unusual arrangements of stones. Several were mounted on shelves way up near the ceiling. Others just a foot or two off the ground. One particularly odd-shaped one was sitting on a shelf that was actually suspended from the ceiling by welded metal rods.

There was a small hallway to his left with three doors. He walked over here and opened the one on his left. Once upon a time, it had probably been a bedroom. Now it was merely an extension of the crystal displays in the previous two rooms.

He turned and opened the one in the middle. This used to be a bathroom at one point. There was a sink, an old tub and a toilet. But water didn't flow here anymore. Instead, all three fixtures had been filled with slimy black soil and planted with queer, alien plants.

Recalling what happened in the night tree dome in Patelemo's workshop, he closed the door and decided not to study any of them further.

He then opened the third and final door, only to find the

old, drunk woman from the glass house standing there amid the oddly-displayed geodes. She was still holding her vodka bottle, but for some reason she'd misplaced her shirt and was staggering toward him in a sagging, dingy-white bra.

"I *tol'* ya y'd be back!" she cackled.

Eric slammed the door shut again and quickly retreated back the way he came, a shudder of revulsion racing through him. "Wrong door!" he gasped.

Toward the rear of the house was what used to be the kitchen. He stepped through the doorway, brushing aside the cobwebs, his eyes peeled for any more drunk and/or horny old women he might need to flee from. The appliances had all been removed ages ago, as had all the cabinet doors. Some of the shelves, too, had been removed to make room for larger geodes.

"You can feel it, can't you?"

He turned around to find a young woman standing there. She had a shaved head, except for her long and shockingly purple bangs that covered one eye. She had almost as many piercings in her face as the pierced man. (The rest of her, thankfully, was covered up by her tank top and tattered jeans, so he didn't have to ever know any more than that.) She had tattoos down both arms, around her neck and on her chest and shoulders. Plus a few were peeking out through those holes in her jeans. It was the kind of look that screamed, "Don't screw with me or I'll mess you up!" and yet she had such pretty, delicate features and such a look of childlike wonder on her face that he wasn't entirely sure how to react to her.

"That power?"

He glanced around. Was she talking about the crystal energy?

"It's *magic*, isn't it?"

He nodded. "It is," he replied. "Or...I'm pretty sure it is."

Her expression became even more elated. Her one, visible eye gleamed with emotion. "I knew it!"

"Wait, were you a..." He shook his head. He didn't like speaking of the people here in the past tense if he could help it. "You're a witch?"

She nodded. The gesture wasn't unlike the response of the young birthday girl who'd just been asked if she wanted to open her presents. It was eerily endearing. "I am now," she sighed. "I finally did it. I finally found her…"

He cocked his head to one side, confused. "'Her'?"

"The goddess! She's here! I know it!" She turned around, her wide, wondering eyes scanning the room around her. "I prayed to her! I begged her to take me! I offered her my *life*!"

Eric frowned. "You did what now?"

When she turned back to face him, there was blood running down her hands and dripping from her fingers.

"She accepted me!" gasped the girl, a look of maddening glee on her face. "She took me in! She called me here!"

He took a step backward.

He knew a lot of witches, and that wasn't how you became one.

She turned and looked around the room again. "All that's left is this final test. I know it."

He nodded. "Okay then. Good luck with that."

"*Goddess, cast upon me your blessing!*" she cried out, lifting her face to the ceiling.

Eric turned and walked away. The poor girl wasn't even close.

There was another doorway in the kitchen, leading out onto a closed-in porch. He headed straight for it, eager to get away from the tragic, wannabe sorceress.

"Has today's paper come?" asked a tall, pretentious-looking man who was standing in front of the window.

"Not yet," Eric replied without hesitating.

The man frowned and stroked his neatly-trimmed beard. "It's late today," he remarked.

He stepped through the doorway, brushing through the cobwebs as he went, and was immediately startled by a great commotion from the back door. Turning to look, he found the suicidal, black-haired girl convulsing on the floor. Startled, he rushed over and rolled her onto her back. Her eyes were bulging. There was a foul-smelling foam spilling from her mouth and nose and an old bottle clutched in her hand. "No-no-no-no-no!" he gasped, snatching the bottle and tossing it into the corner for all the good it was going to do at this point.

There was no label on the bottle. Whatever was in there was probably fifty years old. And given the strange things that went on in this place, it could've contained literally *anything*.

What was he supposed to do? He tried to remember his first aid training, but with no phone and no transportation, he had no way to get her to a hospital.

He scooped the girl up into his arms and hurried back to the kitchen, praying that the water still ran.

Somewhere inside, he knew this was pointless. The girl hadn't really poisoned herself because the girl was already dead. And yet he made it all the way back into the kitchen before he stumbled to a stop, looking down at his empty arms, feeling stupid and confused.

He ran his hand through his hair and took a shaky breath.

"Somethin' wrong with that one," said a chubby man wearing nothing but skimpy bondage gear and a leather mask. He was leaning against the counter and shaking his head as if he found the girl's behavior utterly shameful.

"Hey," said a concerned-looking young woman in a short skirt, "does anyone know if six ecstasies could be fatal?" Then she bit her lip and added, "Totally asking for a friend."

"*Goddess take me!*" cried the wannabe witch in the next room. "*Take my body!*"

Eric turned and walked back out of the kitchen, shaking his head.

Chapter Forty-Eight

There was one last door he hadn't tried. It was to the right as he stepped back onto the closed-in porch. He didn't hesitate. Ready to get this nightmare over with, he opened it, revealing grimy, concrete steps. The cold, dank scent of musty underground places belched out at him.

Of course he'd have to explore the basement. Why *wouldn't* he have to descend into the scariest realms of this nightmare house? He should've been looking for this the whole time.

"I don't like it."

He turned to see a handsome man in a pair of long cargo shorts and sandals sitting on the corner of a sturdy table, one muscular arm draped over a large geode, the other resting in his lap. It was a cool pose, and he looked like he had the body for a lucrative career in modeling, but he wasn't sure who the man was trying to impress. "What?"

The man pointed at the door he'd just opened and made a gesture that was both a sort of nod and something that was the exact opposite of a nod. He thrust his chin upward and pursed his lips into a sort of frown. "Whatever's behind that door," he explained. "I don't like it. Not one bit."

Eric turned and looked down the steps. Even through the densely draped cobwebs, he could see that the floor at the bottom was covered in shallow water. As far as basements went, it was high on the creepy scale, but it didn't just *look* creepy. He could already tell why the cool, handsome ghost didn't care for it. He felt a knowing shiver creep down his back. "It's twisted down there," he said. Another of Evancurt's unfortunate residents was waiting for him.

"Whatever you wanna call it," said the handsome ghost.

"All I know is I don't like it."

"That's okay," said Eric. "I'm the only one who has to go down there." And with that, he made his way down the dark and cobweb-choked steps.

"Good luck," called the ghost. And then, in a much softer voice that may or may not have been meant to reach him: "Better you than me."

The basement of the little house was a cold, dank and grimy mess. The floor was crumbled, uneven concrete, half-submerged in mud and water. Almost every surface was covered in cobwebs. And the raw floor joists overhead were crumbling and worm-eaten. Yet the crystal machine extended even down into this cramped, gloomy chamber. Geodes of all sizes and colors had been mounted on makeshift shelves anchored to the bricks or hanging from the rough-hewn beams. Others were sitting on small tables and stools or just resting right on the muddy floor so that he had to navigate around them in the gloom.

As he turned the corner and looked back across the room, his gaze fell upon the largest geode he'd ever seen. It was easily big enough for a grown man to sit inside it. (Although it didn't look very comfy.) Its exterior was a dull, gray stone while its interior was a glittering carpet of shining purple and white crystals.

Eric stood there a moment, staring at the stone, pondering just how in the world they'd gotten such a thing down here. Only after a moment did he notice the bracings in the beams above the stone and realize that someone had actually gone to the trouble of cutting a hole in the floor in order to lower it down.

It seemed like a lot of extra trouble to him. Surely there had to have been an easier way, one that would've allowed the giant crystal to rest on the ground-level of the house. But he supposed he was hardly an expert on magic crystal machines.

"Who's…there…?" came a hoarse whisper that resonated strangely through the stale air. The origin of the voice seemed to slide around him, almost oozing from one side of the room to the other.

He turned around, scanning the space all around him. Like the rest of the house, there wasn't anything here except those crystals and the various surfaces on which they sat. "My name's Eric," he replied. His last experience with the twisted places had left him jumpy. He was ready to bolt the second this voice grew even a little hostile.

"Eric..." sighed the voice. It spoke very, very slowly, as if each syllable were a great and terrible labor.

Something moved in the corner of his eye and he turned to face it, but he only found himself staring into the dusty, pink interior of a tall geode.

"Yes..." said the voice after a long pause. "Eric... That was the name..."

He turned to follow some perceived motion to his right this time, but again found nothing but another geode.

"She said you'd come."

Eric raised an eyebrow at this. "She?" She who? The same "she" the odd assembly of ghosts back in the woods had spoken of? The "Lady of the Murk"?

"I've been..."

He stood there, listening to the stretching silence.

"...waiting... ...for you," the voice finished at last.

"You have?"

"You're here..." There was another agonizingly long pause. Then: "...to stop... ...Voltner's madness."

He nodded. "I am. Yes." Again, he saw movement in the corner of his eye, again he turned to find himself looking at a geode, but this time, there was something else there, too. Something was moving through the yellowish crystals. A shadowy shape, like a reflection on those tiny, angular surfaces. Except he was fairly sure it wasn't *his* reflection. He wasn't moving.

The basement sighed. "I've been waiting so long..."

"Can I ask who I'm speaking to?"

"My name... Everette..."

"Everette. Okay." So far this seemed to be going well. Not *fast* by any means, but definitely better than his conversation with Lofleder. But he still had no intention of letting his guard down. "Does that mean you can help me, Everette?"

"As much... ...as is possible... ...for me."

331

He nodded again. This was going better than his other encounters *by far*. If only the Everette thing could speed it up a little... "Can you tell me where the machine is?" He turned to see the strange shadow pass through the bluish interior of another geode. An almost-perceptible shape slipped through it.

Was it a shadow or a reflection? He leaned closer to a white one that was mounted on a shelf at eye-level.

"Everywhere..." gasped the breathless voice.

He frowned. "Everywhere?"

"All... ...around you..."

He stared at the crystals in front of him. Did he mean these? The geodes? The crystal machine?

"Every machine... Every structure... Everything...visible. And everything...not."

Eric stood up straighter. "All of it..." he sighed, finally understanding. "The entire property. *All of Evancurt...*"

"Yes."

It made a certain sort of sense, he realized. No wonder he couldn't just go around smashing things. It'd be like trying to sink a battleship by blindly throwing around a hammer.

The *whole estate* was *one big machine.*

"Okay," he said, shaking off the sudden enormity of the task before him. "But what *is* the machine? What does it do?"

"No one..." breathed the Everette thing, "...knows."

Eric frowned. "They built a machine the size of a small town and no one knows what it does?"

"Everyone... ...had theories. Guesses."

He ran his hand through his hair, exhausted. Well as long as they had *guesses*...

"Most thought it would be... ...something *profound*. Something that would change... ...the world. Propel us into... ...a glorious future. Scientific advancement... *Enlightenment.* Voltner... ...compared it to the discovery... ...of fire. Of the wheel. Penicillin. Nuclear energy."

Eric shuddered at the comparison of the Evancurt Machine to nuclear energy. He had a sick feeling that the two might have the same devastating potential. "Where did they find it?"

"It was... ...at the end... ...of the war. Voltner and I... ...recovered it... ...from a Nazi bunker."

"Nazis?" He frowned. Those were the "monsters" Port was referring to? He had to admit, it actually made more sense than aliens. Although it seemed a bit cliché, if he were to be honest.

"They found it... ...among archaeological artifacts... ...pilfered from an unknown site... ...originating from some-where... ...in the Sahara Desert."

"Wait... The plans for a giant *machine* were found in ancient, desert ruins?"

"No one knows... ...where they came from. Or who drew them. The writing on the pages... ...like no language known to man."

Eric nodded as if any of this made any sense. So...basically they were back to aliens again?

"Voltner figured it out," breathed the Everette thing. "I don't know how. He'd always had a morbid fascination with the occult. Almost an obsession. He found... ...the power source. Gathered the only scientists... ...capable of such a task. Brought everyone here. Built it all. Then..." Inside the crystals, the half-reflected shape seemed to wither, as if weary.

"Then *the rest* happened," finished Eric. "Yeah." Voltner somehow translated the plans, in spite of it being in an utterly unknown language. Back in the workshop, Patelemo claimed to have helped with that, figuring out that the plans were drawn across extra dimensions and that the machine had to be placed exactly over specific crossroads that took more than ten years to find and claim. Using Lofleder's plants, they were able to build the machine across those other dimensions, taking advantage of otherworldly laws of nature.

Why did it have to be so damn complicated?

"Okay," he sighed. "So, how do I break it?"

"Can't," sighed the Everette thing.

He blinked, surprised. "What?"

"It cannot... ...be broken."

"Oh." So much for helpful, he supposed.

"Too many... ...redundancies... ...backups... Even if you

destroyed... ...every machine you could find... Wouldn't stop... ...once started."

Eric rubbed at his eyes. This conversation was requiring a lot more patience than most. He practically itched to tell the mysterious Everette thing to spit it out. But he didn't dare risk angering another twisted place. And this one was at least giving him some much-needed answers.

"You'd have to find... ...components... ...that have been buried... ...in places that cannot be traveled to... An impossible task."

"I see." He turned to face the enormous geode. The shadow was there. A shape swam through it. He stepped closer, trying to make out what he was seeing there. In these larger crystals, he began to see that it was neither a shadow nor a reflection, but merely subtle changes in the tint of those crystals. "So what am I supposed to do?"

"There is... ...only one way."

He leaned closer to the geode, squinting into the twinkling interior at the strange, shadowy shape. "Yes?"

"You must... ...remove the jewel... ...from the machine's core."

"Remove the jewel?" He frowned. Hadn't he heard something like that somewhere before?

"The jewel... ...is the *key*... ...to the entire system."

"The power source," Eric realized. The one Patelemo told him about, the one he kept secret until the machine was finished. *An energy generator unlike anything in this world, powerful enough to kick-start the machine and start the first process.* He'd described it as a crystal of some sort.

A jewel...

"Remove it..." gasped Everette, "...and the streams will dry up. The lines... ...will starve."

Take the jewel! he recalled at last. *Starve the lines! Close the streams!* These were the words of that scrawny little man who confronted him in the woods when Spooky was leading him to the treehouse. At the time, he'd barely begun to unravel what was happening in Evancurt, had not yet realized that what he was looking for was a machine, and had dismissed the words as nothing more than crazed, ghostly nonsense, no different from other ghostly cries of sounds turning black and sailing endless seas of the stars. But he was the first one who actually had *real* information for him. He'd even shouted after him as he hurried off to, "Break the machine!" Thinking about it now, he realized that he was the first to use the word "machine."

"The core," he said, recalling Lofleder's map. "That's in the main house, right?"

"It is," replied Everette.

Suddenly, he realized that the shadowy reflection he kept seeing in the crystals was human-shaped. There was a face reflected back at him. An older man, with a balding head and a clean-shaven face.

"But you won't... ...be able... ...to access it," Everette went on. "That house... Broken now. Impossible to navigate. The core... Sealed up inside. Protected... ...by what remains of Voltner."

In other words, it was another twisted place. Probably the most twisted place of all. "So how do I reach the jewel?"

"By breaking..."

Eric waited, his eyebrows raised, as the reflected face in the giant geode twitched and strained with the words it was trying to speak.

"...breaking the rules..."

"Breaking the rules?"

"...the laws... ...that govern this world... The laws... ...that define... ...reality."

He nodded. "Right. Sounds simple enough..."

"Shinne..."

He perked up at this. "Shinne? That was one of the scientists here, right?" One of the five "devils" Port warned him about.

"Shinne's work... The abominations... ...he brought here. They were one of the keys... ...to building it. But also... ...the key to *destroying* it."

Eric took a step forward. "Okay. *Now* you're talking."

"The fauna he found... ...when brought to this world... ...alters the state of the universe around them... Makes it possible... ...to bend reality. Makes possible... ...what never was before."

He nodded again. He thought he could understand that. For one thing, the idea of altering reality wasn't new to him. He'd experienced reality manipulation first hand last year on the roof of the bokor's creepy apartment building in Chicago. It'd transformed the surrounding city skyline into a nightmarish hellscape.

If Shinne could change the laws of nature and make impossible things possible, and Lofleder, with his plants, could create channels into other worlds, where certain laws of nature varied, then it was no wonder they'd been able to build such a terrible machine. There was little they *couldn't* achieve with such power at their fingertips.

"But the abominations... ...don't mix well... ...with our world. They spread decay."

"The rot," Eric realized. "That black mold." For a moment, he thought the Everette thing was talking about those creatures that were wandering around the property, but he was referring to the even stranger monstrosities responsible for the rot. The eyeball under the coordination office. The great, heaving lump in the cage in the green lab. And whatever horror he would've found at the center of that black patch of forest he glimpsed between the treehouse and the green lab.

"The abominations... ...still allow the machine to function... ...but they are too decayed now... ...to allow you... ...to access the core."

This was quite the rollercoaster ride. Everette could help him. But the machine couldn't be broken. But he could stop it by removing the jewel from the core. But it was impossible to reach the core. But Shinne's research could let him in. But Shinne's research was rotten. "Okay," he said, rubbing at the back of his neck. This was starting to make his head hurt.

"You'll need... Fresh sample."

"So you're saying I have to go all the way to whatever nightmare world he brought those godawful things from?"

"There are... ...*preserved*... ...specimens. In Shinne's barn."

The barn. Of course he was going to have to go in there.

But he supposed it was better than traveling to whatever living hell those hideous things came from.

"Shinne's consciousness... Still alive. Like mine. Try to stop you."

"Not exactly a surprise at this point." He ran his hand through his hair once more and began to pace back and forth.

"Find the specimens."

Eric frowned. Why did that word sound so strangely *icky?*

"Take them... ...main house. Beware Shinne. Beware Voltner. Beware Voltner's stalkers."

The reapers.

"Find the core. Remove the jewel."

"Okay. Got it."

Then a different voice whispered into his ear, making him jump: "They're coming."

"The stalkers are here," said the thing that used to be named Everette. "Go."

Eric cursed and looked back toward the stairs.

"Follow the pipelines..." said Everette as the face faded from the crystals. "Hurry..."

Eric didn't waste another second. He hurried back to the foot of the stairs, but froze as he saw the inky shadow that was oozing through the crack beneath the door at the top.

Chapter Forty-Nine

He wasn't going to get out the way he came.

Eric turned and looked around. Spotting a high window, he rushed over and examined it. It'd been sealed shut decades ago, but didn't look too sturdy. He snatched a basketball-sized geode off a convenient shelf and hurled it through the glass. Then he used a second, smaller stone to break away any sharp glass. Vaguely, he wondered if touching the stones counted as sabotaging the machine, but it wasn't as if it mattered. The reapers were already here looking for him.

With a painful grunt, he heaved himself up and wriggled through the broken window and out into the snow.

"Hurry!" whispered the mysterious, helpful voice.

"I *am* hurrying," he hissed back at it as he rolled onto his hands and knees, wincing at all his various aches and pains. He wondered who the mysterious voice belonged to. He was fairly sure it was the same voice that helped him escape Patelemo's clockwork nightmare and told him to "find what was lost" when he first began exploring the forest, but he couldn't tell if the voice belonged to someone he knew. He couldn't even tell for sure if the voice belonged to a man or a woman. He didn't think it was Mrs. Avery. And it certainly wasn't Tessa.

But now wasn't the time to stop and ponder such things.

As soon as he was on his feet again, he saw the pipeline Everette had spoken of. It was the same kind of huge, three-foot-diameter pipe he'd crawled over on his way from the orb field to the prophet's tomb, the one the bossy little girl yelled at him for climbing over. It was connected directly to the side of the house by a ring of that translucent-white material and more of those fat, golden cables.

He didn't wait around to see how the reapers reacted to the broken window and the disturbed rocks. He pulled out his flashlight and followed the pipeline into the forest.

But the light didn't want to cooperate. It flickered and fell dark again. He gave it a hard shake. He banged it against the palm of his hand. He even knocked it against the trunk of a tree as he passed it. With each impact, the light flared on, but then quickly died away again.

He cursed under his breath and twisted the handle, opening it up so that he could rattle the batteries. Was this it? Had the weird energy of Evancurt finally killed his flashlight?

He never stopped moving. He could see well enough in the snow to follow the pipe, but navigation wasn't the issue. He needed to be able to see beyond his immediate surroundings. The reapers were after him. And even if he escaped them, there were plenty of other dangers in these woods.

Something big in the nearby brush burst from its hiding place and fled into the forest, startling a much-too-high-pitched yelp from him.

Animals. It could've been a perfectly ordinary deer. More likely it was something from one of those other worlds that was just as harmless. He'd seen plenty of them. But he didn't have the luxury of assuming that something didn't want to eat him at any given moment.

He gave the flashlight another good shake, letting the batteries rattle back and forth, then tightened the cap and tried the switch again. This time, it came on and stayed on.

"Finally!" He breathed as he turned it on the surrounding forest, assuring himself that he wasn't about to be mauled by something horrible and alien.

As he started down a rocky slope, he glanced back to see if there were any reapers following him, but he seemed to have slipped away from the little house without being spotted. When he looked forward again, however, there was an enraged wendigo charging straight into his flashlight beam.

With a startled curse, he changed direction and launched himself over the top of the pipe and fell sprawling into the snow on the other side, startling a number of loud crows into flight from the branches above him.

He jumped up again and backed away as he shined his light back at the pipe. The gamble seemed to have paid off. Wendigos, as it happened, didn't seem to be very good climbers. This one was jumping and clawing at the pipe, its hideous face glaring at him over the top of it.

He turned and fled, now following the pipeline on the other side and hoping the naked monstrosity didn't find a foothold.

He only made it about twenty yards, however, when movement to his right drew his attention to a great, bounding form approaching from the trees.

A terrified squeak of a cry escaped him as this new thing came rushing at him. For a split second, he thought it was something he'd seen before. It looked like a large cat, but with long, shaggy fur and droopy ears, just like the one he found in the fissure on that first journey into the weird, the monster that tore off half his hand in that other timeline, and the memory of that terrifyingly vivid dream encounter was so real that he almost forgot that the event had never actually come to pass.

He realized almost immediately that it wasn't the same creature. This thing wasn't feline in the least. Instead, it looked like a monstrous combination of a bear and a gorilla with strange, flopping appendages hanging like matted hair from its head and a great, fanged face like something from the shadowy realms of deep-sea trenches.

Terrified beyond rational thought in spite of the fact that it wasn't the same monster, he swerved and again launched himself over the pipeline and onto the other side, where he again fell sprawling into the snow.

It wasn't until he scrambled back to his feet that he remembered why he'd crossed to the other side in the first place. He spun around, shining his light back toward the little house with its crystal machine, and saw the wendigo rushing toward him again.

He stumbled backward, cursing, and lifted his arms to defend himself.

Then the larger and hairier of the two monstrosities bounded over the top of the pipe and, apparently not being particularly choosy about its next meal, came down atop the wendigo and drove it into the ground.

The wendigo let out a terrible, wailing shriek as those wicked fangs tore into it. Dark blood sprayed onto the side of the pipe and spattered the snow all around the two.

Eric stood there a moment, too stunned to move, then his senses returned and he fled before the monstrous gorilla-bear thing could decide that it didn't care for the taste of nasty wendigo meat and would much more prefer a heaping helping of plump English teacher.

Ahead of him, the mysterious star-house came into view. The pipeline he was following connected to the back of the building by one translucent-white coupler while a second pipeline exited the building from a second one and continued deeper into the forest on the other side of the clearing. Since Everette told him to follow the pipeline, it stood to reason that if he continued following it, it should eventually lead him to the barn.

It was as he was circling around the star house that he scratched absently at his chest and remembered the ectoplasmic patch Tessa and the other ghosts warned him to be careful with, back before he'd climbed through a broken window and twice jumped over that big pipe and rolled around on the hard, rocky ground like a hyperactive kid on a playground.

That wasn't being careful by anyone's definition. Indeed, as he looked down at it, he imagined that he could see those black wisps of smoke and little flecks of ash sputtering through the fabric of his jacket just a little faster than they were before and the thought gave him a hard shiver.

That was stupid. He was lucky he hadn't torn it completely open and spilled his apparently-not-as-immortal-as-he'd-been-led-to-believe soul to dissipate forever into nothingness.

He glanced over his shoulder, but he couldn't see what the one on his back might be doing. He'd just have to trust that if he'd torn it open, he'd already have ceased to exist.

He shook the thought away and focused on following the

second length of pipeline. He couldn't think about that awful stuff Tessa and the others said about his damaged soul. That would work itself out like everything always did. He'd find Shinne's undecayed specimens, retrieve the jewel from the core and save all the spirits trapped in these awful woods. And then this mysterious "Lady of the Murk" everyone was talking about would probably patch him up good as new for his trouble.

Or maybe the mysterious little gas station attendant or his daughters would appear and fix him up.

That's how these things tended to work, after all.

He *would* have to be more careful, but he refused to give any more thought to the ridiculous notion that he was simply *doomed* to ultimately *disappear*. Instead, he focused his attention on the pipeline itself. What was its purpose? Was it to carry magical energy from the crystal machine to the star house and the other buildings? Or was it carrying some sort of *cosmic* energy collected from that star house to other points? Or maybe it was Shinne's barn that was using the pipeline to export some other, far more unimaginable form of exotic energy.

It was pointless to speculate. He knew nothing about this sort of thing. It could just be here because someone in 1971 thought it'd look cool. But anything that kept him from thinking too much about even the remotest possibility that he might have an unrepairable hole in his soul was welcome.

He gave the star house one last, curious look, then turned and followed the second stretch of pipeline into the forest.

Chapter Fifty

The star house was barely out of his sight when someone seized his arm and pressed up against him, nearly knocking him over.

"Found you!" cried the confused woman.

Eric frowned down at her. "You again?" He thought for sure she'd stay well away from him after that last encounter.

"You've got to stop wandering off!" she told him.

"You're not my mother," he grumbled at her. "I can go where I want." But of course, she didn't seem to hear him.

She nuzzled his shoulder and sighed dramatically. "Is it almost time to go yet?"

"I wish you would." He eyed her up as he walked. "I see you found your clothes." She was wearing the same outfit she'd had on since she first took hold of his arm and refused to let him go way back in the glass house, which was good. This was awkward enough with her fully dressed.

She didn't respond to the comment. She didn't even acknowledge that he'd spoken. But he thought he detected the slightest, momentary tightening of her features, a subtle, repressed grimace crossing her fair features, and a barely-noticeable flushing in her fair cheeks.

Again, he wondered if her curious mental state was an illusion she was trapped in or a merely a stubborn refusal to accept the fate that had befallen her.

"We should really be on our way," she said. "We don't want to be late."

"Lady, I still have no idea where it is you're trying to go."

She didn't respond, of course. She only sighed and continued nuzzling his shoulder.

"Don't even think about following me home after this," he growled. "My wife will go full-on *exorcist* on your skinny ass. And *I'm* not going to stop her."

He turned and shined his light around, making sure there weren't any more fish-faced gorilla-bear hybrids stalking him, and found an old woman watching him with an absurd smile on her shriveled face.

"What an adorable couple," she gushed.

"Don't encourage her!" snapped Eric.

The woman's smile vanished in an instant. "Oh my!" she gasped and vanished back into the darkness from which she came.

He didn't like this. There were dangerous things prowling these woods and this clueless woman was hanging on him like a literal ball and chain. If something attacked him now, there was no way he'd be able to just throw himself over the pipeline again, or even to properly run away.

Looking around, he noticed that the forest was getting busy again. There was a skinny, soft-voiced, bald man off to his left who seemed to be calling for his lost dog. (He was going to go ahead and assume that "Snoofles" was a dog's name, anyway.) To his right, there was a burly man in a leather Harley jacket sitting with his back against the pipeline and sobbing like a frightened child. Ahead of him, a tall, prim-looking man with graying, but perfectly trimmed hair and beard was whistling cheerfully as he strolled past without an apparent care in the world. And as he pushed past some low hanging branches, he encountered a young, pretty woman with a distant, almost horrified expression muttering, "Messed up... Messed up *so* bad this time... So, so bad..."

A crow settled onto the top of the pipe ahead of him and cawed at him as he approached. "Shoo," he growled at it, but the bird just turned and watched him as he walked by.

Harbingers of the dead, he thought again.

Somewhere in the darkness, he heard a familiar sobbing, separate from that of the burly biker behind him. It was the endlessly wailing voice of the miserable girl he last saw on the other side of Lofleder's hideous green lab. But though he tried to trace the origin of the sound, he couldn't quite determine where it was coming from. It seemed to move about with the wind, coming sometimes from his left, sometimes from behind him and sometimes from the other side of the pipe.

Turning his attention forward again, he saw that the snow had given way to an unsettling darkness that spread as far as he could see ahead and in either direction.

The black mold, he realized.

The forest here was rotten.

According to Everette, the rot was a result of Shinne's hideous work with those monstrous creatures. Apparently, they decayed in this world, giving rise to the mold. If true, then this much rot in one place was sure to mean that he'd find Shinne's barn, the source of all those unnatural things, at the center of the sludge.

Although how far he might have to trudge through it, he wasn't sure. It stretched as far as he could see in this darkness, swallowing both his flashlight beam and the falling snow.

Should he be concerned about the fact that the snow didn't gather on the mold? Was that normal? Because it didn't seem natural to him. It seemed ominous.

As he approached that fetid blackness, the woman clinging to him suddenly gasped and yanked him to a stop.

"Will you let go of me already!" he snarled at her, rubbing worriedly at the patch on his chest that he felt pull at his skin when she tugged his arm back.

But as usual, the woman didn't seem to hear him. Or perhaps she simply didn't care. It was hard to be sure. The only certainty was that she didn't like the mold. "Not this way," she whimpered.

"Nobody invited you," he told her. He tried to pull his arm free, but still she refused to let go.

"We have to go around," she said, turning and looking first one way and then the other.

"*We* don't have to do anything. Let go of me."

Still ignoring him, she turned and looked back the way they

came.

Eric was rapidly losing his patience with this woman, but even so, he couldn't miss the look of desperate fear on her face. She'd allowed herself to be led down the moldy hallway, but it was clear she wouldn't set foot in *this* rotten place. And he had no desire to make her. He just wanted her to let go of his arm so he could get this unpleasant business over with.

He was beginning to wonder if he'd have to forcibly remove the stubborn woman from his arm before he could move on. He had no desire to harm her, but if he couldn't reach the barn, then he wouldn't be able to save everyone from Voltner's repulsive machine. Including *her*.

But before he could decide how to proceed, the wailing of the miserable girl suddenly drew close. He turned, surprised, and found her stumbling toward him, her hands still plastered to her face, tears still streaming down her cheeks.

Like last time he saw her, she staggered straight toward him. She reached out for him with one wet hand as she drew near.

The confused woman seemed to see her, too. She even let go of his arm as he turned to face her, just in time for him to catch the girl as she collapsed, sobbing, into his arms.

"Honey…?" said the woman, just as she'd said when Tessa dared to take his attention from her, except there was no jealousy in her voice this time. She seemed to be genuinely concerned about the girl.

"I'm not your honey," he told her again. "I don't even know your name." He knelt down, lowering the poor girl onto the ground. "Take it easy. I've got you."

He wondered why she seemed so drawn to him. Was it just because he was the only living person here?

Then a new voice drifted to him, seeming to float upon the wind: "Bones."

He looked up to find the scowling face of unfriendly-looking Mrs. Avery standing over him again.

"Follow the bones," she told him.

"Who are these people, honey?" asked the confused woman. Already, she was clutching at the sleeve of his jacket, trying to seize him in her clutches again.

Mrs. Avery turned her frightful expression on her next. "Shut your mouth, stupid girl!" she snapped. Her lips never moved. The wind alone carried her voice. But the expression on her face drove the severity of the words just fine on its own. "He has important work to do!"

The woman took an involuntary step backward and crossed her arms over her chest, a pouting, almost teary-eyed look crossing over her face like that of a scolded child.

"Bones," said Eric nodding. "That's what you said when I first got here. And what Tessa said to me way back when I first met her."

Follow the bones and you will find her.

"Time is running out," said Mrs. Avery, turning her judgy gaze back to him. "Mr. Nicholas is monitoring the systems. He says the tunnels are flushing nonstop. And new overflows are opening."

Eric nodded as if that made perfect sense. The flushing of the tunnels... Mr. Nicholas must be the man in the flannel shirt, then. "Final countdown," he muttered.

"He thinks we may only have a couple hours at most. If you're going to do something, I'd say you'd better do it now."

Eric slipped his arms around the sobbing girl and stood up, lifting her to her feet. Then he turned and passed her to the confused woman. "Keep an eye on this," he told her.

He wasn't sure she'd do it, but the confused woman—looking more confused than ever—took hold of the girl and gently sat down with her.

"Take care of her until she can wander off on her own again."

Showing more clarity than he'd yet seen from her, she nodded.

He turned and faced Mrs. Avery. "When I find the machine and pull out the jewel, everyone will be free to leave, right? You? Them? All the souls trapped in this place?"

"Presumably," she replied on the wind. "It'll be up to each of us, I think, what we'll be capable of. But there shouldn't be

347

anything holding us here if you can do it before the third process begins."

"And what about the people trapped in the twisted places?" he asked. "Everette and Charlie. Port. Bronwen."

The old woman stared at him for a moment. "Those souls are no longer what they once were. They're a part of the machine now. I can't say for sure that escape will ever be possible for them."

Eric nodded. It wasn't an entirely unexpected response, but certainly not the one he was hoping for.

"But none of us will ever leave here if you stand around asking pointless questions."

He turned and shined his light out into the blackness. "Right," he said. He glanced one last time at the sobbing girl and the confused woman. Then he stepped into the sea of black mold and set off for the nightmare that Shinne's barn was bound to be.

Chapter Fifty-One

Unsurprisingly, the forest here was dead. Everything the mold touched had been drained of life. And the farther he traveled into the rot, the longer it had all been dead, the more skeletal and sickly the forest became, until the trees were little more than black, jagged spikes stabbing at the churning clouds above.

Even the pipeline had been utterly coated in black slime. It now resembled a great, shadowy serpent winding its way through the black nightmare ruins of the forest.

The stench was worse than he'd imagined. He could actually taste the foul, sulfurous reek on the air. It seemed to coat his tongue whenever he tried to breathe through his mouth.

In fact, everything about this place was an assault on his senses. Every surface was covered in a slimy, diseased film that squelched beneath his shoes. The ground, hard and frozen before, was soft and spongy here, as if there were nothing holding up the earth in this place.

And then there was the silence. Nothing lived here. Even the ever-present crows had stopped their endless cawing. And although he could still feel the wind, it didn't have the same voice in this place of oozing, black death. Where it had gusted and howled with angry vigor in those healthy acres, it only crept and whispered here, as if the very air had been poisoned over these many years.

He found himself regretting the loss of his gloves and hood again as he pushed forward, not so much for the cold, though it *had* grown cold, especially after his shoe became wet, but simply as a covering for his naked skin.

As the diseased trunks grew thinner and thinner where the most ancient of the forest's remains had fallen away over time, he finally glimpsed the looming monstrosity of Shinne's great, black barn emerging from the gloom.

It probably wasn't black back when Shinne was still conducting his research, but now, like everything else in this hideous wasteland, every inch was covered in oozing, black mold. It drooped from the high eaves like dripping obsidian icicles.

He spotted the enormous front doors, barely visible through the slimy coating, and adjusted his course accordingly. He had no intention of spending any more time here than was absolutely necessary. But he'd barely set his sights on that imposing door when a long, rumbling groan rolled through the silent air, as if something inside had heard the squelching of his approaching soles and had begun to stir in anticipation of a meal.

That was probably a good sign that only an idiot would willingly venture inside, but it didn't seem that he had any kind of choice in the matter, so he did his best to ignore the screaming of those more sensible parts of his brain.

He couldn't help recalling his first journey into the weird and that other ominous barn. It was there that his world took its first turn into the truly bizarre. Until he stepped through those aging doors, he'd been telling himself that there must be logical explanations for everything. His peculiar dream and urgent obsession with getting somewhere were purely psychological in nature. His curious conversation with sweet, but creepy old Annette was mere coincidence and more than a mere touch of senility on her part. Even when he first saw the barn and realized that it had been a part of his dream, he kept insisting to himself that there was a perfectly logical explanation and if he pushed forward, he'd surely find it. But upon entering that barn all those months ago, he'd found strange and wondrous and *horrible* creatures. Sickly-looking, limp-necked chickens with frail legs and gnarled feet. Grotesquely bloated, alien livestock oozing foul, yellowish fluids and crawling with flies. And an unseen bleating horror that someone had gone to concerning amounts of trouble to box in and hide from sight.

As nightmarish as that barn had been, he was quite certain that this was going to be far worse than that ever was.

In fact, it already was, for as he walked up to the door, it occurred to him that he was going to have to open it somehow. And that was going to require him to touch the foul mold that had encased the handle.

He stopped at the door and spent a moment pondering how to proceed. The best scenario would have been to find a handkerchief or tissue or something in one of the pockets of his stolen jacket, but of course the pockets were empty. Instead, he thought to use the tail of the jacket to grasp the latch.

But out of the silence came a grotesque sound that startled him from his thoughts, a sickly sort of wet snort from around the corner behind the building. And as he turned his light toward the awful sound, a wendigo shuffled across the slimy ground and into view.

Frozen in terror, not daring to make any sudden movements, lest he draw the murderous beast's attention unnecessarily, he stood and observed the monster.

It didn't look well. Its foul, naked body was half-covered in that slimy, black mold. It sort of wobbled on its oversized feet. And it kept making that awful snorting sound, as if it were suffering a nasty cold.

Or, Eric quickly realized, as if it had been *poisoned*.

He was doubly squeamish about touching the slimy handle now, but also far more motivated to get inside before the diseased wendigo spotted him.

It was on the other side of the pipeline, which the other wendigo had had trouble climbing over, but the pipeline was higher off the ground here, connected to the wall about eight feet high, so that it would be no hindrance at all for the sickly monster.

Cringing, he grasped the handle with his free hand, wincing as the cold, viscous mold squelched between his fingers, and pushed. The noise was tremendous in the looming silence. The door sagged with age and the rotting wood ground against the slimy concrete. And the slick mold made it difficult to get a solid grip on the handle, retarding the process even more.

The wendigo didn't react immediately, but merely lifted its

dripping face in a stupid daze and snorted again. Its senses seemed to be dulled by the rot that was slowly engulfing it. It was a lucky break, to be sure, but at the same time ominous. How quickly did the rot take root in a living creature? How long did he have before he suffered the same fate? Wendigos weren't supposed to linger long in this world. They could wander here a few hours at most before they were sucked back to their home between dimensions. At least that's what he'd been told. It was always possible that he'd been misinformed. Or that something about the broken physics of this place prevented them from returning. This was the barn, after all, where Everette told him Shinne's abominations made things possible that weren't before.

Either way, he didn't have the luxury of standing around, wondering what might be waiting inside that eternal blackness behind the barn door. His gaze fixed on the sickly monster as it slowly turned toward the light in his hand, he heaved the sagging door open inch by inch, until he could finally squeeze through the gap and out of sight.

Even now, the thing only stared into the blinding light, unable, apparently, to understand what it was looking at. And it was no wonder, since half its face had been infected by that foul, black mold. It seemed to be eating away at one of the monster's eyes and oozing from its gaping mouth.

It was only as he ground the door closed again that it seemed to take real notice of him, and even then it only staggered a few steps before it slipped and fell into an angry, slimy heap of pale, flopping flesh.

Safe at last from the monster's reach, he stood there a moment, listening through the slime-coated door, waiting to see if the thing was going to try to force its way in after him. Several things were now quite apparent to him. Firstly, he wasn't going back out the way he came any time soon. Secondly, his suspicion that the black mold was hazardous to living creatures was horrifyingly confirmed. And thirdly, the interior of the barn was easily the most foul-smelling place he'd ever been. But the most unsettling of all the things he now realized was the fact that while he couldn't hear the wendigo on the other side of the door, he could hear things *behind him.*

He turned his back to the door, his heart racing, and started to cover his mouth and nose against that awful stench with his free hand. Just in time, however, he remembered that it was covered in that hideous mold. Revolted on *many* levels, he wiped it furiously on the stolen jacket and shined his light around, trying to get some feel of his new surroundings. But the darkness in this place was unyielding. The mold covered every surface, its blackness absorbing his flashlight beam almost as quickly as it poured out. If there were any lights installed in this place, they'd either stopped working or were completely covered in the all-encompassing rot. His only glimpse of his surroundings was the subtle gleam of his flashlight beam reflected on the mold's slimy, oozing surface as it clung to the contours of the building's structure.

He walked toward the glistening shapes in front of him, squinting through the darkness, until finally he was able to piece together that he was standing before an animal stall. The oozing mold dripped between the slats that made up the stall walls, turning it into a foul, mossy *cage.*

Those awful noises continued. Subtle, quiet snorts. Sickly, raspy breathing. Awful, wet scraping sounds. And of course the persistent dripping of the foul mold as it oozed down from the black emptiness overhead.

He followed the boards of the stall around the corner. Here, he realized that there were more stalls. *Many* more stalls. And each one, he realized, held something unthinkable.

He knelt down, cautious but curious, and shined his light through the gate.

There was definitely something in there. A great, black, mossy lump, like the thing in the cage in the green lab. He could see the subtle rise and fall of something breathing, but no other detail.

He turned around and peered through the slats in the gate behind him.

There was something here, too. Something much closer. But even with his flashlight almost touching the thing, he couldn't quite make out what the shape was that he was looking at through that all-encompassing, black slime.

Then it moved.

It didn't jump out at him in any way. It didn't do anything that he could consider, after the fact, to be hostile. It just sort of *flexed*. An opening appeared. And something long, moldy and flaccid uncoiled itself and flopped onto the slimy floor of the stall. But it might as well have lashed out at him with venomous fangs and a murderous shriek, because he jumped back with such a fright that he slipped and fell against the gate behind him.

The noise he made, both by slamming into the gate and by the embarrassingly girlish yelp that escaped him, startled whatever was inside—as well as several other nearby things—resulting in a series of grotesque snorts and wet convulsions that very nearly made him let out an even less manly scream.

His heart pounding, he turned and shined his flashlight all around him, convinced that at least one of these unthinkable things must have broken free of its bindings in all these years and would be wandering freely about, happy to devour anyone stupid enough to come fumbling around in this hellish darkness.

But in spite of his efforts, nothing ate him.

He took as deep and calming a breath as the putrid fetor would allow, steeling his nerves against whatever horrors awaited him, and then made his way deeper into Shinne's monstrous darkness.

Chapter Fifty-Two

Another of those long, rumbling groans rolled through the building. It was considerably louder and countless times more horrifying now that he was inside with the source of the terrible noise. He could practically feel it rumbling through the concrete beneath his feet.

The mold was both a blessing and a curse, it seemed, for while it kept him from clearly seeing what horrors now surrounded him, *it kept him from clearly seeing what horrors surrounded him.* A blessing *and* a curse. The mystery of those awful things was maddening, his curiosity gnawed at him, but seeing these abominations with any clarity might madden him even more.

The unnaturalness of this place was overwhelming. For forty-seven years the things in this barn had been languishing without food or water or any manner of tending whatsoever. Even the many wandering spirits of Evancurt didn't come here. The mold kept everything away. And yet in spite of that, the things here *lived.* He could hear them. He could *smell* them.

On a positive note, however, there weren't any spiderwebs in this place to stick to his face and hands. Although truth be told, he'd much sooner swim through an entire *sea* of spider-infested cobwebs than have to tiptoe through this sickening, slippery filth.

As he walked, he swung his flashlight back and forth between the hideous, whimpering-gurgling sounds on his left and the long, wheezing, snorting sounds on his right, careful to catch the unknown emptiness that loomed always in front of him in those brief seconds in between. And every few steps he was careful to also shine it back the way he'd come and even up into the dripping darkness overhead, because if *he* were an unspeakable, undying, moldy horror from some unimaginably hellish alternate universe, those were the places *he'd* attack from.

The all-encompassing mold turned everything the same, greasy, light-devouring shade of black, making it impossible to tell wood and concrete from flesh and hair. Most of the stalls were reduced to nothing more than those grotesque grunts and snorts and wheezes and whimpers, but some yielded strange, immobile lumps of undiscernible shapes that sometimes subtly moved with the heaving of labored breathing or occasional, sickly convulsions. Once, as he shined his light through the oozing curtains of mold, he was rewarded—or perhaps that was the wrong word for it—with a glimpse of blackness peeling apart to reveal a strangely deep orifice of oozing, glistening folds of bright-red flesh and grotesque wriggling things.

He decided immediately that he had no interest in observing *this* thing any further and quickly continued on his way.

Most of the stalls were the same, but every now and then he discovered one that had a different shape beneath the mold than the others. A closer inspection revealed that these stalls had been further enclosed with chicken wire, suggesting something within that was small enough to escape the other enclosures.

It was strange, he realized, just how numb he was to the horrors of this strange new world he'd discovered these past few years. As a child, and indeed well into his teenage years, he never considered himself all that brave. It was true that he was fond of horror movies in his youth, but that was only because his big brother was so fond of horror movies and that was the sort of mimicry that little brothers simply did. But he never bothered feigning any real bravado while watching them. Nor was he ever fond of Halloween haunted houses or other such attractions. He didn't care for the heart-racing thrill of breaking rules and sneaking around places he wasn't supposed to go. And he could think of *lots* of things he'd much rather be doing right now. Making love to his wife, relaxing on a tropical beach and soaking in a hot bath with a good book were all pretty high on that list. Or gorging himself on Karen's incredible cooking. (He'd missed dinner, after all, although in all the fright and excitement, he hadn't once felt even a little bit hungry.) Hell, a good, long *root canal* would be better than this. It was *terrifying*. And yet he kept pushing on.

It wasn't just that he was scared. It was that he *should be* scared. There were things here that could rend him to pieces. There were *real* monsters. His life was in terrible danger. At any second, something terrible beyond imagining could emerge from the darkness, something so horrifying that it could plunge him into irreversible madness before spilling his blood and entrails into the creeping black mold. And worse still, for hadn't Tessa and the others warned him that his very *soul* was damaged? Not just death but utter *termination*. A complete *cessation of existence!*

He kept feeling as if he should be too afraid to make his legs move. And yet on and on he went, plowing through the darkness, listening to the awful sounds of hideous things living and rotting at the same time, without food or water or light, trying to breathe as shallow as possible to keep his exposure to the barn's noxious air to a minimum.

But his thoughts on the subject were instantly washed away when something in the stall next to him let out an explosive sneeze and expelled a foul geyser of slimy, blackish, reeking filth all over him.

Repulsed beyond imagination, but somehow managing not to retch, he pushed forward with greater urgency.

At the end of the aisle, he turned the corner and discovered that the stalls here were built with iron bars rather than lumber and he immediately took care not to get to close, lest he discover all-too well exactly why these specimens required such greater means of restraint.

But he soon found that he didn't need to get too close.

Something was protruding from one of the stalls. A long, limp shape, like a great, rolled-up rug, was slung over one of the railings and lay stretched across the floor in front of him.

He stopped here and shined his light over the thing, trying to decide what, exactly, he was looking at. It wasn't moving, as far as he could tell. Was it just some *object* left lying there since the machine came online? Or was it part of a creature? And if so, *which* part? It kind of looked like a great, flaccid tail, but it ended rather bluntly for a tail. And there wasn't anything at the end resembling a head. An elephant-like trunk, maybe?

He hoped to God it wasn't some kind of gargantuan *penis*...

But of course, he was trying to apply "earth" logic to the situation. He'd seen a lot of things from other universes in his weird travels, and a lot of it wasn't so different from this world's fauna. Those coyote-deer-hybrid-like creatures called cakyiks and that grouchy ape he'd dubbed Furious George from his first adventure came immediately to mind. But in Hedge Lake, he'd encountered otherworldly creatures whose physiology was such that their bellies contained incinerating infernos instead of digestive tracts. He'd also encountered in his journeys strange shadow creatures, monstrous projections, creatures of myth and *actual freaking fairy tale beings*. At this point he wouldn't be surprised to find that this thing was a giant, sentient jellyroll named Squibbly.

The problem, of course, was what to do about the thing lying across his path. He seemed to have three options. He could go around it, being as careful as possible to give it a wide berth, but that would require him to get uncomfortably close to the stall across from this one and his awful imagination was quick to provide a great many examples of why that would be a bad idea. He could also simply step over the motionless thing, and his imagination was even quicker to provide a great many *more* examples of why that would be an even worse idea. Or he could go back the way he came and see if he could circle all the way around, which meant passing by all the stalls he'd already walked by and at least as many more that he hadn't, thereby vastly increasing his chances of a very unpleasant encounter, which his psychotic imagination, of course, had a field day with.

He turned and shined his flashlight at his immediate surroundings, making sure once more that he wasn't about to be devoured by some stealthy and hideous predator, then sighed and opted for the first choice.

Nothing in this place had so far proved hostile. He was going to have to wager that whatever was in that other cage was the same. And indeed, as he slipped between the giant, flaccid jellyroll thing and the silent stall, nothing stirred. But as he backed away, he was unfortunate enough to see the thing on the floor flex weakly and then spurt a foul, black stream of steaming sludge onto the mold-covered floor.

Definitely not a rug.

He turned, grimacing at the freshly intensified stench that rose from the putrid excretion, and continued on into the nightmare blackness.

As he passed the next stall, something inside bucked and kicked at the bars, sending a loud, echoing peal through the unsettling darkness and stirring up more of those hideous, half-imagined sounds from the other creatures in the building.

(He was pleased to note that his cry at the sudden noise was only half as girly as his last one.)

A moment later, he discovered another sliding door, this one already open, leading deeper into Shinne's menagerie of horrors. He paused here, reaching through the doorway with his flashlight first, taking in the greater open space beyond and listening to the subtle, monstrous sounds that greeted him.

There was a wall of some sort directly in front of him, just at the end of his light's feeble reach. His eyes peeled for danger, he crept forward to see what awaited him, and soon realized that he was approaching a massive cage of moldy iron bars sunk deep into the concrete floor and rising high up into the darkness.

His nerves wound tight, ready to spring away at the slightest movement in the dark, he peered through the bars and saw that the floor inside the cage dropped off drastically, so that he was peering into a black and terrible pit.

He could see disturbingly little of those things in the last room, but the sizes of the stalls seemed to suggest that they were creatures roughly the size of hogs or, at most, cramped cows. They didn't seem to him quite big enough to contain something as large as a sizable horse. But this enclosure could hold *much* larger horrors. Even one of those massive sea-monster dragon things from Patelemo's lab might comfortably fit in here, although he wasn't able to see just how far it reached from where he stood.

He kept thinking of that other barn, the one from his first

journey, the one that had somehow allowed him to travel the fifty miles between the field behind Annette's house and the old farmhouse where he met Grant in only a few minutes. He'd explored that barn in broad daylight and the monsters there weren't covered in foul, black mold. But there remained certain similarities that he kept finding himself thinking about. Those things, too, had been large and grotesque-smelling and moved very little in their confines, most of them too bloated and malformed to so much as roll themselves over. He kept wondering if the things in here would resemble the mutant livestock of that other barn if he could somehow wash away the mold.

But logic, as useless as it often was these days, suggested that they must come from different worlds or else those other creatures would've been covered in this black mold as well, and therefore their physiology would probably be nothing alike.

Unable to see anything in the depths of the monstrous pit, he began to follow the moldy bars, working his way along the side of the cage and around the corner, where he found a huge, iron-barred door allowing access to the pit via a very treacherous-looking, slime-covered ladder.

Here he stood, his light fixed on the door, a hideous dread welling up inside him.

The door was open.

Chapter Fifty-Three

Why did it have to be the big cage? There were dozens of smaller stalls in the previous room, filled with horrible things that he probably didn't want to have roaming free while he was locked in a dark barn with it, but at least they didn't need a *caged pit the size of a basketball court to contain them.*

His heart pounding with fright, he turned his flashlight onto the floor. There weren't any monstrous tracks in the mold. Nor did he see any sign of something crawling over the bars of the cage around the doorway or on the slimy ladder leading up from the blackness. He reminded himself that the monsters in the previous room hadn't exactly been restless. Those ancient, diseased things had all appeared half-dead. They didn't look like they could wander far even if their stall doors *were* open. With only a little luck, the things in this pit were the same. Open door or not, they were probably still down there, nothing more than great, unthinkable lumps of flesh and mold and unspeakable, alien limbs, just lying there, excreting grotesque fluids and foul gasses and the occasional sickening noises of endless, undying decay. But he was also quite aware that this door probably hadn't opened any time *recently*. The things inside had probably had *decades* to make their way out of that pit and any tracks they'd left behind swallowed by the ever-spreading rot.

If anything, Shinne's monsters would be patient.

Another of those awful, rumbling groans rolled through the barn, louder than ever, and paranoia washed over him like a cold shower. He turned and shined his light behind him. Then he turned and looked ahead of him. Then up into that dreadful darkness overhead.

Something in the previous room let out a long series of

yelping whimpers and somewhere in the darkness a gate rattled against its lock. At the same time, he imagined that something deep down in that black pit behind him gave a low, gurgling growl.

At least, he *hoped* he'd only imagined it.

Looking around again, he saw that there was a door nearby. A normal one, designed for people and therefore too small for anything gargantuan to follow him through, so he hurried toward it, forgetting for a moment the perilous slime beneath his feet and very nearly sending himself sprawling face-down into it when his foot slipped out from under him.

Fortunately, he managed somehow to keep his balance and made it to the door without falling or being devoured or even getting sneezed on again.

The knob was slippery and didn't at first want to turn, but he was more persistent than it was and managed to let himself in and close it behind him.

He now found himself in some sort of storage room, evident by several narrow aisles separated by walls of black shapes that could only be mold-covered shelves.

Nothing seemed to be moving here. But it didn't look like the sort of place where someone would keep highly-sensitive specimens. Shinne would've kept something like that somewhere important.

He told himself as he wandered around the room that he was being thorough. He wouldn't want to miss anything, after all. But the truth was that he was stalling. He didn't want to go back out into that room with that gaping, iron door and mysterious, monster-infested pit. Time may have been short, but he needed a moment to gather his wits before he risked a run-in with some moldy titan in utter darkness.

He examined the slime-covered shapes on the shelves, but without physically wiping away the mold, there was no way to know what sorts of things were here, and he'd already touched considerably more of that stuff than he was strictly comfortable with. He *did* use the outer rim of the flashlight to scrape away a few slimy streaks, but it was a pointless endeavor. The boxes and containers were so deteriorated and stained that there was little left to see. He'd have to settle for what basic deduction and his wild imagination told him was there—the former suggesting that it was obviously veterinary and livestock supplies, though admittedly probably with certain otherworldly allowances for alien physiology, and the latter insisting that it could be nothing less than vast stores of radioactive kibble, dormant monster eggs and hideous mutagens that would either turn him into a giant, exploding tumor or possibly some kind of sewer-dwelling turtle.

He moved on, intending to circle the shelves once to make sure there wasn't anything of pressing interest before moving on, and had almost walked by the door on the far side of the right-hand wall before he noticed it.

He turned the slimy handle and pushed the door open, then peered through it with his flashlight as he wiped his hand on the stolen coat (making a mental note as he did to burn it when this was all over).

This room was much larger than the storeroom, but not nearly as large as the other two spaces. There were three very large, mold-covered tables, each one surrounded by odd, blocky, fungus-covered lumps from which strands of slime-curtained cables stretched, connecting them to even more blocky, mossy shapes protruding from the walls.

More of Patelemo's twisted machinery, intricately woven throughout the entire estate, connecting all the elements, bringing the entire, hellish abomination to life.

As he walked out into the open space before him, still trying to take in all the disturbing details, he was once again struck by an intense wave of vertigo that made him clutch at the nearest of the three tables to keep from falling over. A brilliant light flickered before his eyes, blinding in the darkness. Then, without warning, the mold was gone and the room around him was warm and brightly lit.

Blinking at the sudden change, he turned and looked around. He was standing in exactly the same place, but time had turned back again. The floor was smooth, clean concrete. There was a ceiling of brightly glowing, translucent white above him, just like in the glass house, with the same queer, flowing quality about it. The machines were shiny and new. The cables, tubes and pipes running overhead no longer dripped with rot. The entire room was as immaculate and sterile as a hospital operating room.

In fact, an operating room was precisely what this place reminded him of. The table his hand was resting on was a cold, stainless-steel slab. There were carts and trays containing sinister-looking tools, some of which appeared to be surgical while others looked more like something that belonged in his father's tool shed. Standing against the walls, unseen beneath the spreading mold in the diseased future he'd just traveled from, were a great many shelves holding an even greater number of glass jars in which soaked a nightmarish variety of horrific things. But worst of all was the monstrosity lying on the farthest of the three tables.

It was a great, bloated thing with too many legs and no discernable head, skinned and hollowed out and surrounded by various plastic tubs containing piles of unspeakable stuff that he was quite sure had, until very recently, been *inside* the thing on the table.

This was a dissection lab.

And as he stared at the gruesome display before him, the most horrible details of all began to sink in. The thing on that table, though skinned and disemboweled, was *still alive!* Those many legs were still squirming, ever-so subtly, but definitely. He could see the strange appendages—hideous things that were indescribably and simultaneously hooves, talons and pincers—slowly flexing and unflexing. Even those vile piles of viscera lying in the plastic tubs were still squirming. As he watched, something slithered out of one and seemed to probe at the slimy tools on the filthy tray.

He turned away, cringing at the horror of it all, and realized that even the things in the jars weren't all dead. He could see things pulsing and twitching and writhing in their foul, aquatic prisons.

"Tell Voltner he can proceed without me," growled a gruff,

British-sounding voice from the far corner of the room. "And if he doesn't like it he can just piss off! He has my schedule. He can see that I'm busy!"

A short, fat man with an extravagant mustache strolled into the room then, dressed in a great, filthy gray raincoat that dragged the floor behind him as he walked. He was putting on a pair of awkward-looking rubber gloves and making his way toward the dismembered thing on the slab.

Then the little man caught sight of him and stopped. "You again!" he huffed. "I already told you to get out!"

Eric looked behind him, confused. Was he talking to *him*?

When he looked forward again, however, everything was once more black and moldy.

He closed his eyes tight, then opened them again, trying to shake off the disorientation of switching so rapidly between such different surroundings.

That man... He had the pompous authority of a man in charge. It was almost certainly Shinne. But what was that odd exchange?

He turned and looked around. He could still see the shadows of that unmolded time lying beneath the foul decades of slimy rot. He glanced up at the blackness above him and wondered if that translucent-white ceiling was still giving off that strange, flowing light, merely unseen beneath the pervasive mold.

Then he glanced down to find that he was still clutching the edge of the table, his bare fingers sunk into the reeking slime. Grimacing, he wiped his hand on the jacket again and looked out over the dissection lab at the table where the horrible skinned and gutted thing had lain in that brightly illuminated glimpse of the past. But there was no sign of anything on the table now. The moldy surface was as flat as the other two. Although he supposed it was possible that the thing had simply gotten up and squirmed away since then... But the equipment surrounding that table was different, too. There were fewer carts, with no sign of those tubs filled with awful, squirming things. He wasn't sure when it was he'd just glimpsed, but some amount of time had passed between the dissection of that disgusting creature and the breaking of the world in Evancurt. At the very least, someone had had time to clean up.

He turned his attention to the shelves where he'd seen those hideous jars filled with ghoulish things. Now that he'd seen the room without mold, he could discern the outlines of those creepy vessels and he could tell that most of it was exactly as it was in the flashback. And if very little had changed between then and now, then what he glimpsed, it stood to reason, was a moment not long before the machine came online.

And if those grotesque things had been preserved in jars all this time...

He walked over and used the flashlight to scrape away the filth, but the liquid inside had long ago turned as black as the exterior of the jar.

So much for preserved specimens... He very much hoped that these weren't the ones Everette was counting on him finding.

He took a step backward and shined his light over the rest of the festering shelves. He didn't like the way the rot seemed able to pass through solid barriers, entering glass jars and spreading through concrete walls. He wiped his hand on his jacket again as he turned and scanned the rest of the room.

It was mostly hidden now, but he recalled seeing a door on the other side of the room, not far from the one he'd entered through. He walked over, careful not to slip, and opened it. For a moment, he wasn't sure what he was looking at. The mold took away all the color and texture of the things it touched, and this was something bizarre. He spent nearly a full minute staring at the strange shapes that seemed to descend from the ceiling of the room in great, slime-dripping clumps that nearly reached the ground. Then, finally, it occurred to him—though he wasn't entirely sure how—that he was looking at another of Lofleder's alien plants.

These plants had been in the glass house, Patelemo's workshop and even in the crystal-littered little house. Likewise, Shinne's monsters had been found beneath the coordination office and in the green lab's basement. Had he explored more of it, he probably would've found one rotting away in the workshop, too. And Patelemo's machines were *everywhere*.

This was what Everette was talking about. All of these monstrous components were woven together across the estate, connected through incomprehensible networks of fat, gold cables, pipelines, tunnels and parallel universes in order to pervert the very laws of nature and bring to life a monstrous thing that should never have existed, not even on paper.

He kept wondering why anyone would want to build such a thing. It baffled the mind.

He closed the door on the moldy, upside-down garden and continued on across the dissection lab. There was a short hallway on his right. He stepped into it and opened the first door he came to. Here, he found a great, moldy mass of twisting, coiling things that spilled and flopped across the filthy floor. He stumbled backward, startled, as the hideous thing on the other side splashed its squelching form against the door and slammed it shut in his face.

He stood there a moment, blinking at the mold-covered door and listening to the foul, slithering sounds from the other side. "Okay then…" he croaked, and then turned and continued on his way. Hopefully that wasn't the room he was looking for.

The next door down stood open already, and a quick glance inside revealed it to be nothing more than a cramped and blessedly unoccupied bathroom.

On the other side of the hallway was a third and final door. Recalling the slimy thing that didn't appreciate being disturbed, he opened this one very slowly and peered inside. Even through the featureless layers of mold, he recognized those strange, orb-like spirit batteries.

Seeing no doors or other mold-covered shapes worth investigating, he closed the door and withdrew from the hallway, his gaze cautiously fixed on that first door until it was well out of sight, just in case the thing inside change its mind about not wanting company.

There was another door in the far corner of Shinne's monstrous dissection lab. He stepped through it an found himself again standing before the enormous and ominously-open cage.

It was here, as he swept his light around, expecting something awful to be waiting in the darkness to ambush him, that he found a strange pattern of mold-covered shapes protruding from the floor and stretching off into the darkness around the perimeter of the cage. For a moment, he couldn't quite decide what it was he was looking at. Then it struck him and he bent over and scraped away the mold with the rim of his flashlight, revealing the dingy, yellowish-gray surface beneath.

It was a great, mold-covered skeleton, as if from the long-decomposed carcass of a colossal serpent.

He stood up and shined his light along the outstretched remains, the hairs on the back of his neck tingling at the realization of what he was looking at.

"Follow the bones..." he whispered.

Chapter Fifty-Four

At last.

It seemed like days ago that the word first drifted to him on Evancurt's otherworldly wind.

These were the bones Mrs. Avery and Tessa had foreseen. These were the bones he was meant to follow. He felt a distinct thrill at making it one step closer to the end of this awful nightmare.

And yet there was something singularly awful about these particular bones. First, of course, was the vast size of the thing. He shouldn't have been surprised, given the measurements of the cage that was left open, but it was still utterly shocking to perceive with his own eyes. Second, and far more troubling, was the simple fact that the thing was dead. After all, *why* was it dead when so many other things in this awful place still lingered after being abandoned and untended for forty-seven years? Why was it dead when the thing on Shinne's unholy dissection table hadn't even given up its final breath?

Perhaps the thing had merely reached the end of its strange lifespan, but somehow he doubted it. He found himself glancing into the darkness that loomed ahead of, beside and above him, wondering if something even more vast and terrible had killed this thing and was now watching him with predatory eyes.

Alert for movement in the endless black hell, he followed the monstrous remains as his equally monstrous imagination offered up one suggestion after another for what it might've once been.

He couldn't help being reminded of the monstrous dragon-like thing that roamed the vast spaces of Patelemo's workshop, but that monster (if it was, indeed, only the one and not two or more) showed no sign of the mold that invaded this place. Everette said that the things Shinne brought over from the other world were the source of the rot, that they began to decay almost as soon as they appeared. That suggested that the other creatures roaming the property, the dragon, the giant, the killer teddy bear thing, the flying centipede monsters, and all the rest, were from a different world, maybe more than one, having crossed over through the rifts left by Lofleder's boundary-rending plants.

But of course that didn't necessarily mean that Lofleder only experimented on the mold-spreading abominations. Judging by the scene he glimpsed of the mad scientist's gruesome lab, he didn't doubt that the fat little man was the kind of psychopath who might cheerfully cut open anything that made the mistake of passing too close.

Or perhaps this was merely some otherworldly monstrosity that had the misfortune of wandering into this building and succumbing to the rot.

He was still pondering the possibilities when another wave of vertigo turned the world sideways again and he stumbled and fell against the iron bars of the massive cage. He cursed and rubbed at his shoulder, but the pain there was forgotten almost immediately as he realized that the lights were on again.

He was surrounded by a clean and well-illuminated space, utterly devoid of the foul, black mold and with no sign of the thing whose bones he was following.

As he stared stupidly down at the floor where there should've been a skeletonized corpse of an enormous monster, a man emerged from a nearby doorway. It was the fat little scientist in his raincoat. Except his raincoat wasn't filthy this time. And he wasn't wearing those huge gloves, either. He was carrying a box of empty jars.

"Who the fuck are you?" he demanded without deviating from his course. "You can't be in here! This is a restricted area and I'm busy!"

Eric watched him walk by, confused. What was happening? It seemed as if this were the first time the man had seen him. Was this *before* the incident in the dissection lab? He glanced over at the door he'd just walked through, wondering if the monster on the slab was different than before.

"And get away from those bars, you fucking idiot!"

With a start, he realized that he was still leaning against the giant cage and he turned to see what was there.

All he saw was a great, black mass of bulging, insect-like eyeballs staring back at him. He cried out, terrified, and jumped back, but the world had already reverted to blackness. His foot slipped. He fell backward and landed on top of the monstrous skeleton, his hands, thrown back to catch his fall, sank deep into something cold and slimy, wrenching a second, far wimpier cry from him.

He scrambled to his feet, revolted, and wiped his hands and his flashlight on the filthy jacket.

Forget the monsters and the twisted places and the reapers, it was going to be this foul mold that killed him.

He was still trying to wipe away the filth on his hands when he realized that something was moving in the darkness ahead of him. He froze and shined his light toward the doorway the fat little man came out of in the flashback.

A massive shape seemed to be there, something that twisted and churned over the space in front of that door, like an impatient predator waiting for prey to pass beneath it.

He could see so little in this all-encompassing blackness, but he was fairly sure that there was nothing on the floor. Whatever it was, it was either clinging to the upper wall or suspended from the barn's moldy rafters.

Fortunately, the bones didn't lead through that door. They were stretched around the back of the great cage. So with his light trained on that unsettling shape in the darkness, he carefully crept around the corner and away from it.

It didn't pursue him. No long, slimy tongue or tentacle shot out and snagged him by his leg. He wasn't sucked down into a great, gaping maw to be swallowed whole, for which he was exceptionally grateful, because he *really* didn't want to experience something like that a *third* time.

The skeleton stretched on and on, eventually leading

through a doorway near the far end of the cage. Had he gone right instead of left when he first entered this room, he realized, he would've found the bones without having to witness Shinne's grotesque dissection lab or risk being eaten by whatever lurked over that other doorway.

But he didn't have time to dwell on the matter of his luck. As soon as he stepped through the bone-crowded doorway, he felt a shivery sensation deep in his own bones.

Everette warned him that Shinne's consciousness was still lingering here and that it would try to stop him. It only made sense, then, that where he found Shinne, he'd find the specimens he came for. But as he stood there in that darkness, trying to make out the shapes of the surfaces beneath the ever-present mold, nothing moved or spoke. An unsettling silence was all he found.

Seconds passed like this, and the longer he waited, the more his own heartbeat seemed to fill the room. It could be nothing more than simple and well-founded paranoia, but it felt like someone was watching him.

Nothing moved.

Even the monsters had gone quiet again.

Finally, he crept on, still following the bones as they curved left, toward another open doorway.

This appeared to be some sort of lab, considerably smaller than the dissection lab on the other side of the building. It was divided into three aisles by two rows of tables and surrounded by black shapes that had once no-doubt been either lab equipment or more of Patelemo's mad machinery.

Follow the bones, he thought. He was only here for one thing. It didn't matter what else might be hidden here. If he was supposed to follow the bones, then they must, logically, lead to the preserved specimens. And the sooner he found those, the sooner he could get out of this diseased barn, finish this hideous business and finally go home.

And yet, he couldn't help but think that there was no way it could be as easy as just walking in and walking out.

He shined his light through the next doorway. Even under

all the mold, he could tell he'd found an office. And what better place for Shinne to keep something as precious as preserved specimens than right under his own extravagant mustache?

Something moved in the corner of his eye. He turned and shined his light back into the lab, but whatever it was, it had gone still again.

His heart fully racing now, he stepped through the doorway and looked around the office.

The monstrous skeleton ended here and he was puzzled by the fact that there didn't appear to be a skull. Then he recalled the lack of a head on the skinned and gutted abomination on the dissecting table and decided that maybe expecting a wholly alien lifeform to have a head might be something of a silly notion.

Looking closer, he saw that there was, instead, the subtle shape of several strange, trunk-like appendages stretching away from the point where the skeleton ended.

He was still trying to piece together a picture in his mind of a great, serpent-like creature with freakish tentacle-like things where its head should've been when his flashlight failed again. He switched it off, cursing, and gave it a hard shake. When he turned it on again, there was a great, moldy face turning to look at him from the wall.

Chapter Fifty-Five

Eric yelped and nearly slipped again. But as he steadied himself, he realized that he knew the face. It was the same pudgy features and elaborate mustache that he'd seen on the fat little rude scientist.

"I know you," said the moldy face in a repulsive, gurgling mockery of human speech. The man from the flashbacks wasn't just a shape beneath the mold, Eric realized. He'd become the mold, itself, much as Patelemo had become one of his many, precious machines and Lofleder had become his own, beloved plants. "You were here that morning. Poking around my lab."

He glanced around the room. There was a spacious desk at one end, now little more than a great, rectangular lump of black slime. The walls were floor-to-ceiling bookshelves and even through the blanket of dripping mold, he could see that there were more of those foul jars in here. "You remember that?" He wasn't sure if he should be horrified or flattered.

"I see now…" gurgled the black and slimy face. "You were cast back by the fractured space-time. Dropped through a crack and then pulled back again. I'd theorized such things might happen. I should've known that was it. But I was in the middle of research and I had no idea yet that Voltner intended to turn the thing on ahead of schedule."

If Eric were a deranged, genius scientist, where would he keep grotesque, alien samples so that they wouldn't rot?

"That explains what you were doing here that day," the thing burbled, "but what could you be doing here *now*?"

Eric didn't care for how this conversation was progressing. This guy wasn't as irrational or as confused as the other twisted remnants of Evancurt's past. He seemed more in-control of himself than the others had. There was something sinister in the way the moldy face was staring at him, as if he were another of the madman's grotesque specimens to be dissected and stuffed piece-by-piece into fat, slimy jars. And this time, he didn't have the luxury of simply fleeing. He needed those untainted specimens. Cautiously, he said, "You're name is Shinne, right? You were one of the...uh...*geniuses* who worked on this project. Is that right?"

The moldy mockery of Shinne's head turned a little. It seemed to squint at him, suspicious. "I *am* Rutherford Shinne," the thing gurgled, rather pretentiously, Eric thought. "And I did not merely 'work on' the project." The thing spat the two words back at him, spraying that foul, filthy mold in the process. "Without my work, the machine wouldn't even be *theoretical*. It would be nothing but science fiction and fantasy."

He seemed to have touched a nerve, but the fat little man was talking. And as long as he was talking, he wasn't trying to kill him. "How do they work?" he asked as he turned and scanned the room around him. "How can these things break the laws of nature?"

The face didn't just change its expression. It abruptly melted and reformed again, closer to him, with a more intense arrangement of its features, as if *this* Shinne were merely a more excited version of the one here previously. "It's a simple matter of origin," the mold man replied. "Life is always defined by and contained within its source. When you take a lifeform from the environment that spawned it and expose it to drastically different environments, the lifeform usually ceases to live. But if that lifeform comes from a nature where death as we know it is not a concept, then it is the new environment, rather than the lifeform, that must inevitably change. And when the laws of an entirely different reality are applied within the confines of our own world, amazing things can be accomplished. With my work, I can convert and create *energy*, perform entirely unrelated functions *simultaneously* and even manipulate space-time in such a way as to eliminate such basic inconveniences as time, distance and physical barriers."

Eric was carefully inching closer to the mold-covered desk, still scanning the room for some clue as to the whereabouts of the specimens he came here for, but at this he paused. He hadn't actually cared about the madman's hideous creatures or how they worked, he'd only wanted to keep the moldy old fart talking, but this was actually useful information. If these creatures could do the things Shinne said they could, then that explained how he could hope to use the specimens to gain entry to the machine's core. "These...uh...*creatures*... They can really do all that?"

"It's not all that different from Lofleder's silly plants," bubbled Shinne. "But they only allow things to pass to and from their world of origin. My creatures bring the very physics of their universe right into ours, allowing us to use *both* sets of laws simultaneously."

"Is that what allows the machine to utilize exotic energy?"

The mold man seemed to huff at that. "Exotic energy is *Roden's* area of expertise. I provide the necessary *means* by which he manipulated those energies. The rest is up to him and Patelemo's crude inventions."

Eric nodded. Roden. The fifth scientist. The one who sacrificed his own daughter to start the terrible machine. He wasn't looking forward to meeting *him* in whatever dark corner of Evancurt he'd been doomed to haunt.

He glanced around at his colorless surroundings. "What about the mold?"

The face melted away again and reformed itself, again moving a little closer, slowly following him as he made his way across the room. "What?"

"The rot," he explained. "These things...these *creatures*...they begin to decay almost as soon as they cross into this world, don't they? How do you account for that?"

The face seemed to study him for a long moment. Then it melted again and returned a little closer and with an expression of dismissive superiority. "That's an issue of little consequence. The deterioration is a very slow process."

"But it *does* weaken their effects in this world, doesn't it?" pushed Eric. "Over time? There must be some way to preserve them in their pristine state, right?"

The reeking, moldy thing that once called itself Rutherford Shinne didn't reply. That great, oozing face stared at him, its moldy eyebrows creeping closer and closer together.

He had to force himself not to turn and flee the menacing expression before him. "Did you find a way to do that?" he pressed.

"I see," gurgled Shinne. "So that's what you're after."

Eric took a step backward. "What?" he feigned. "No. Me?" But he'd never been a very good liar.

The face melted away. This time it didn't reappear an instant later with a new expression. This time something stirred in the doorway. And as Eric turned his light in that direction, he felt his stomach sink.

The skeleton he'd followed here was moving.

The mold rippled and swelled, lifting the bones and knitting them together into a great, slimy mockery of the thing it used to be.

"Aw crap…" he sighed as a great mass of slithering tentacles unfolded from the thing's moldy neck. Then several rows of grotesque, wriggling things sprouted from its back and belly, giving it an appearance like something that might have slithered through the black depths of some prehistoric, alien sea.

Perhaps it was related to the dragon back in Patelemo's workshop.

He backed away, cursing under his breath.

Then the thing lurched forward, those awful, swaying tentacles wriggling toward him.

He lifted his arms to shield himself. At the same time, he backed into the desk, unable to retreat any farther.

Then he was in the past again.

He stood there, blinking at the blinding, alien lights of the unmolded office, his brain struggling to keep up with everything that was going on.

Shinne's voice, his *human* voice, drifted through the doorway from the lab on the other side of the wall. He was cursing. And not in that classy sort of way that Eric found himself ex-

pecting from someone with an uppity British accent. The real
Rutherford Shinne had the kind of colorful vocabulary that
turned a singular statement into a host of vile accusations about
the recipient's intelligence, upbringing, hobbies, sexuality and
drinking preferences. "He can't just go changing the fucking
schedule!" the fat little man was shouting. "It's supposed to happen at fucking *dusk*! That's what we all agreed on! I have important work to do this morning!" He followed this with a message to be given to whoever "he" was, which Eric didn't think he
would've been able to deliver word for word without turning red
in the face. "I'll fucking get there when I fucking get there! And
not a goddamn second sooner!"

Geniuses sure were a moody bunch.

His head was still reeling and his heart still pounding from
his encounter with Future Freakshow Shinne, but he thought the
1971 Shinne might have been shouting about Voltner. What was
it he said in the present? Something about not knowing yet that
Voltner was going to "turn the thing on ahead of schedule"?

Then his hand crept to his pocket and the unopened letter
from Millicent to Charles, a warning that he had to leave this
place before sunset.

He recalled the flashback he had in the orb field, when he
was dragged back to the day of the explosion. It wasn't dusk
when that fireball rose into the sky. It'd felt more like late morning.

Was that why the letter was never opened? Had Voltner
moved the activation up so that there was no time for anyone to
escape?

He pushed the thought aside. It made little difference at the
moment. And he could snap back to the present any second. He
needed to figure out what to do about that giant worm thing and
find out where Shinne hid the preserved specimens.

Turning to take in his yet-untainted surroundings, his eyes
were immediately drawn to a large, black safe set into the wall
beside him, bigger than an average door and impossible to miss,
but utterly unseen beneath the black layer of filth that infected
the present.

He turned to face it fully, but frowned at the huge, silver dial.

How the hell was he supposed to get into it? He was no safecracker. He didn't have the combination.

He turned and looked over Shinne's desk, hoping by some miracle to find it lying there, but the moment he turned around, the lights winked back out and he stumbled in the moldy darkness.

Startled, he swung his flashlight toward the giant, moldy worm, convinced that it was still right there where he left it, but it and Shinne had both vanished, along with the bones that he'd followed here. There was only a great, greasy trench leading out the door.

He frowned at the empty, black room around him. How long had he been gone? Wasn't it only a few seconds?

He shook his head. No. There was no time for speculation. The monster was gone. That was all that mattered at the moment. He turned his attention to the safe next to him.

He never would've found it if not for that glimpse of the past. All he could see in the present was a carpeting of lumpy, black slime. Grimacing, he reached out and wiped away the mold where the dial had been. It was there, just as it had always been. It was weathered and filthy, but it was here, and it still turned.

But he still needed the combination.

As he stared at it, however, he realized that he'd known the combination all along. Rupert Vashner gave it to him, along with his cryptic instructions to "look for the floating house," "find the abandoned soldier" and seek "the secret in the prophet's tomb." The last thing that hateful dead man screamed at him before shrieking the name "Evancurt" at the top of his spectral lungs was a series of numbers, which he still recalled as vividly as those other words, even after all these months had passed: twelve, thirty and twenty.

Ignoring every natural instinct that screamed at him to avoid contact with the fetid mold, he leaned close, clutched the dial in his fingers and began turning it.

Was it left, right, left…or right, left, right? He'd never had much luck with these kinds of combinations before. There was always some sort of trick. You had to go around the dial an exact number of times for each number, being sure to pass certain numbers at certain times. It might take some trial and error that he probably didn't have time for.

He and Karen had a small safe in the basement where they kept important documents safe in case of a fire. He supposed he'd try opening this one the same way he opened that one.

But after his first try, the slimy handle didn't budge. Was there a different way this one was supposed to open? Or was it only user error?

From somewhere in the next room came a wet crash as something fell over. Then the foul, gurgling voice of the thing that used to be Rutherford Shinne boiled from the festering slime all around him: "Where did you go?"

Cursing under his breath, Eric tried the combination again.

Chapter Fifty-Six

He yanked at the stubborn handle again and bit back another curse.

Something was stirring in the next room. He could hear it, a soft, liquid sort of sound sliding through the darkness, getting closer and closer.

"I know you're still here," burbled Shinne. "How are you hiding from me?"

Eric clenched his jaw tight and focused on the slimy dial. Twelve... Thirty... Twenty... Then he pulled at the stubborn handle.

Shit.

Again, this time in the other direction: Twelve... Thirty... Twenty...

Nothing.

Again, he wished he could talk to Isabelle. In her strange travels through the broken places outside of the normal flow of time, she'd absorbed the lingering knowledge and memories of a great many hopelessly insane trapped people. At least *one* of them must've known how to open a stupid safe.

She was probably screaming it at him right now. ("Twice around the dial and then back the other way, dummy! It's not brain surgery!")

Twelve... Thirty... Twenty...

Dammit!

Again, his flashlight winked out and he banged it against the palm of his hand. "*Come on!*" he hissed.

Something crashed to the floor in the next room. Had Shinne heard him? His awful imagination delighted in suggesting that the great, moldy monster was even now slithering toward him, those hideous tentacles reaching out for him, unseen in the inky darkness.

He gave the flashlight another hard shake and it flickered back to life, revealing nothing about to devour him.

But that awful, wet sound was definitely getting closer.

"What are you doing?" gurgled the Shinne thing.

Twelve... Thirty... Twenty...

Goddammit!

Twelve... Thirty... Twenty...

Please, God!

Twelve... Thirty... Twenty...

No!

Maybe this wasn't what Vashner's message meant, after all. Maybe those numbers were for something entirely different and he'd missed the real combination somewhere along the way.

An awful dread was rapidly filling him, making it harder and harder to focus. Did he try it that way already? He couldn't remember.

This couldn't be the way it ended. He'd battled blood witches and ogres and agents and wendigos. He'd faced the terrible wrath of a genie, the deadly depths of the Hedge Lake Triangle and an army of magically conjured nightmare creatures. He'd even faced off against an *evil clown*! He could not be killed by his own ineptitude at opening a damn *safe*!

Twelve...

A great, black shape bubbled up in the doorway. He could see the slimy mold glistening in the dim reflection of his flashlight.

Thirty...

The walls around the doorway rippled. The ceiling and floor seemed to warp as the mold came alive.

Twenty...

"In here..." boiled Shinne.

At last, the handle lifted. The heavy vault door opened with a hiss and a gust of strange-smelling air.

He didn't think about it. He pulled the door open and slipped inside, closing it carefully behind him as that hideous, half-serpent shape oozed into the office.

Shinne was a monstrous pile of slimy, black mold, but he wasn't an idiot. Even in the utter darkness, he was probably going to notice that the safe door was ajar. It wouldn't take long to figure out where the intruder went. Eric had managed to slip away for a few more seconds, but he was only more trapped than he was before. There was nowhere to run.

The space around him was no bigger than his hall closet at home, its interior walls lined with heavy drawers. It was as dark as the rest of Shinne's barn, but in stark contrast, there wasn't a speck of mold inside it, except of course for what he'd just tracked in with him, which was a considerable amount.

My bad.

For a single, distracted second, he wondered what sort of insulation could keep out mold that had been able to spread through solid concrete and glass, but he didn't have time to waste on questions he couldn't answer. He glanced around at the various drawers, wondering where he should start.

Then his flashlight went dark again.

Cursing under his breath, he gave it a hard shake. Then another. Then he banged it against the palm of his hand several times.

Was that something scratching at the vault door behind him?

He gave up on the light and stuffed it back into his pocket. In the darkness, he reached out with his hands and felt at the drawers. He chose the first handle he found and pulled. It slid open easily, as if the mechanism were brand new.

When he attempted to reach inside, however, he discovered that the top of the drawer was covered. Frowning in the darkness, he slid his fingers across it, trying to work out how the thing opened. There seemed to be a latch of some sort near the front of the drawer's top. He fumbled with it, blind, as the hinges of the safe door creaked menacingly behind him.

Come on...come on...

He turned the latch and lifted, revealing a soft, bluish glow from inside.

"What are you up to?" growled that sinister, gurgling voice.

He reached inside the drawer and withdrew a small, glass case by a handle on the top. Inside, there were several dozen strange, tiny, wriggling hair-like things, each one giving off that strange, bluish glow.

Worms… The scrawny, spectacled man in the woods shouted that word at him, didn't he? When he told him to starve the lines and close the streams. He'd forgotten that part until just now.

He lifted them closer to his face. These little creatures were of the same world as those monstrous, moldy things in the stalls? They weren't frightening at all. They were even sort of pretty…

But he didn't have time to think about that right now. He'd found the specimens. That was what was important. But now that he had them, what was he supposed to do with them? And how was he going to get back out of this vault?

He turned to face the door, the bluish light illuminating a boiling shape blocking the way out.

"Filthy thief…" growled the Shinne thing.

"Really? I'm offending *Dr. Frankenstein's* delicate morals?"

He tried to take a step backward, but there was nowhere to go. His back was already against the wall.

Slimy, tendrils of black mold crept into the room, little more than empty shadows in the soft, bluish glow of the alien worms inside the glass case, while the space just outside the doorway churned and boiled.

He lifted the case and held it in front of him. "Okay, little guys," he said. "You're supposed to alter reality or some crap. So do something. *Anything.*"

But the worms did nothing, just as he typically expected of worms, even glowing alien ones.

The monstrous, moldy form of the fat, psychotic scientist squeezed through the doorway, rapidly filling the vault. Cold, slithering things slipped around his ankles and wrists. Something foul and wet crept up his pants leg.

"*Little help here!*" croaked Eric.

But help didn't come to him, and soon he was enveloped in

a cold, hideous, sulfurous blackness that choked the breath from him.

Chapter Fifty-Seven

What happened next, Eric couldn't explain.

One moment, the world was turning a cold and festering black. The next moment, he was being dragged through unfathomable, icy depths and across vast distances by an unyielding current.

He'd been here before, to this endless, murky place. More than once, in fact, though he could scarcely remember when or how. It wasn't a place he should be. Not now. Not *yet*. For this, he was suddenly and absolutely certain, was the great After. This was the Beyond. This was Guinee. This was *death*.

A great despair washed over him as he began to realize that he'd failed. He didn't stop the Evancurt Machine. He didn't save Tessa or the girl in the cupcake tee shirt. Or anyone. The machine would devour them all. It would wipe them all away, from all of existence. And then it would complete its monstrous task and who knew what horrors would be unleashed upon the world because of him?

But there was something about this scene that didn't belong.

He squeezed his fist closed around the handle of the glass case.

He looked down at it, at the unearthly glow of the tiny, wriggling worms within. If he were really dead, then why did he still have this? How could he carry something physical to Guinee?

Nothing comes with you to Guinee.

He looked down at his clothes, at the filthy, stolen jacket. He felt the flashlight in his pocket. And the note that never found its way to Charlie.

It was as if a spell had been broken. He wasn't drifting help-lessly along a swift, cosmic current. He was standing on his own two feet in the dark.

Gone were the closed-in walls of the vault. Gone was the great, moldy thing that had once been Rutherford Shinne.

But then where the hell was he?

He held the softly-glowing case out in front of him, casting its soft light as far as it would reach—which wasn't far—and began to turn around, taking in his black surroundings.

He didn't seem to be outside. The floor was even beneath his feet and there weren't any snow clouds overhead. Judging by the slippery, squelching sensation in the soles of his shoes, he must still be in Shinne's barn somewhere.

When he held the box out behind him, the soft glow caught the slimy gleam of mold and revealed the familiar shape of the open door of the giant cage.

Remembering the great, moldy form of Shinne's alien ser-pent and that hideous mass of bulging, black eyeballs when he flashed back to the past, he couldn't stop himself from jumping back and very nearly slipped and fell.

At this same moment, a rumble rolled through the barn and the angry, gurgling voice of the fungus that used to be Shinne wormed its way through the fetid air: "*What is this?*"

Eric turned and made for the door through which he first entered this awful room. If he could just get past all those freaky stalls, he could leave this nest of monsters and never come back. But as he approached the doorway, he found that a large, churn-ing mass of mold was rising between it and him, like a great, grasping hand reaching out for him.

He stumbled to a stop, slipping and sliding, barely keeping his balance.

"*What are you?*" demanded Shinne.

Eric didn't have time to tell the monster he could ask the same thing of it. In the next instant, the room was filled with light again and the mold had vanished.

He stood there, blinking, confused.

A skinny, stooped old man was standing on the other side

of the doorway with a dirty push broom, staring with wide, startled eyes at the man who'd probably just popped out of thin air.

A moment passed as he tried to process the sudden change, but then he came to his senses and ran for it.

He still wasn't sure what was going on, but in this past place there were none of the obstacles of the present to slow him down. The lights were on. The floor wasn't covered in slimy mold. The farther he made it before jumping back to his own time, the less distance he'd have to travel through the slippery, festering rot.

But without the cover of darkness and mold, the horrors of Shinne's barn were in full view. As he ran between the stalls, he caught glimpses of terrible things behind the planks and the chicken wire. Great, bloated shapes. Foul piles of slimy, writhing things. Hideous, creeping appendages that didn't look like anything he'd ever seen before, many of them slithering through the gaps and wriggling at him as he passed.

He focused his attention on the floor in front of him and pushed himself to run faster.

He was almost at the end of the aisle. He could already see the door. He was almost free of this nightmare.

But then everything went black again.

Still traveling at a full sprint, his feet immediately lost traction and he went down hard onto his back. He clutched the glass box against his chest, desperate not to let it shatter, as his momentum carried him forward at a worrisome speed.

He was trying to calculate how close he was to the stall at the end of the aisle when he crashed feet-first into it, splintering the rotten planks as if they were nothing and slamming hard into a great, reeking mass of mold and slime.

In the next instant, Eric's thoughts were divided between several terrible facts about his current situation. First, that was entirely too reckless. He was lucky the glass case didn't shatter. Not to mention he could've seriously hurt himself. Second, that hideous, festering, probably-toxic mold had oozed under his jacket and shirt all the way up his back. It was cold and slimy and altogether *nasty*. His hands were covered in it. He could feel it in his hair. And the back of his pants were thoroughly soaked through. Third, he realized that he could still hear the gurgling bellows of that foul thing that had once been Rutherford Shinne, and it was growing louder by the second. And finally and most distressing of all, he was now lying in something very awful and very grotesque-smelling that was making a terrible hacking-yelping noise and slapping at him with something cold, slimy and flipper-like.

In a blind panic, he scrambled backward through the slime and the rotten remains of the stall door, desperate to get away from whatever foul abomination he'd disturbed in the hideous blackness, the whole while clinging to the glass case with its strange, tiny, glowing worms.

"Get back here!" bellowed Shinne. (Or whatever he was now.)

Slipping and sliding, he half-scooted and half-crawled back out of the hacking-yelping-slapping thing's stall, ignoring the fresh pain in his shoulder and ribs, and even somehow managed to get onto his feet.

There was a moment of disorientation in the darkness. The glow from the worms wasn't bright enough to create more than a small aura of light around him, barely enough to keep him from bumping into walls.

The hacking-yelping thing was in front of him. Shinne's in-human, gurgling curses were behind him. Cringing at the cold, slimy feel of the mold on his skin, he turned toward where the door should be and hurried forward again, far more cautiously this time.

There was a moment there, far too long for his liking, in which he was lost in the darkness again, uncertain of where he was. He took the flashlight out of his pocket and tried to make it work again, but it remained dead. Had he finally exhausted the batteries or had Evancurt's hideous machinery finally burned it out? Either way, this was an awful time to be caught blind. He stuffed it back into his pocket and held the glowing box a little higher.

Finally, he glimpsed the slimy gleam of moldy lumber, and

then a glint of rusty metal where the mold had been wiped away. That was where he'd entered the barn, where he'd put his hand while pushing the door closed behind him in his escape from the diseased wendigo.

He'd forgotten about that thing… And at this point, he didn't have the luxury of worrying about it. He was just going to have to trust that it was either gone or that it was close enough to dead that he could outrun the thing, because he couldn't stay here.

He pushed the door open, ready to defend himself, but as he peered into the somewhat brighter darkness of the rotten forest and the falling snow, he found that there was nothing waiting for him. The wendigo had wandered off again—or perhaps had been returned to its dimension of origin—and no other horrors were waiting there for him.

"Put that back!" bellowed the gurgling horror behind him.

He took off into the forest, not bothering to close the barn door behind him. Later, that would probably haunt him, he realized as he set off into the woods. Between the open door of that massive cage, the slimy thing that slammed the door in his face, the unknown horror lurking in the corner and the thing whose stall door he'd just broken, there were any number of monstrosities wandering free in there. And he'd just left the door open for them…

Shinne told him that the world those creatures came from had no concept of death. Did that mean they couldn't be destroyed? That hideous imagination of his was quick to show him a terrible picture of a not-too-distant future where these monstrosities were free and multiplying, covering the entire world in horror and mold.

He shook the thought away. That was preposterous. The things in there barely moved. If they'd really wanted out, he was sure they could've escaped at any time. The place was a rotten, decades-old barn.

He focused on where he was going, thankful for the rocky earth that allowed him more traction on the moldy forest floor. He had the worms. The only thing left was to find his way to the main house and retrieve the jewel from the core of the machine. Then this nightmare would finally be over and he could get back to his life.

But at this thought, he glanced down at his chest, where the reaper had punched its monstrous finger through him. He'd forgotten about that injury. How many times did he slip and fall in that black hell of a barn? How many times had he strained the strange, ectoplasmic patch that was allegedly all that was holding his soul in place?

He told himself it was only his imagination, but more of those wisps of smoke and black flecks of ash were sputtering through the breast of his jacket than before. He pulled it open and peered down the front of his shirt, finding that there was, indeed, a small tear in the web-like fabric.

Cursing, he pulled the jacket closed and forced himself to focus on the task at hand.

It'd be all right.

He wasn't an ordinary man, as much as he would've liked to be. He'd discovered the profound secret in the cathedral. And he'd been protected every step of the way since then. The mysterious little gas station attendant and his daughters had helped him on multiple occasions. And others, too. The shadowy Frank Lezner. The mysterious Cordelia in her strange, yellow house. Those mysterious voices that sometimes guided him. He'd even once earned the favor of the voodoo loa, Papa Ghede. At the very least he had the entirety of a powerful coven of witches at his disposal. If nothing else, he was sure Delphinium and her sisters would be able to patch him up again.

He just had to keep it together until then. Literally.

He turned and looked behind him. The ominous form of the moldy barn was fading into the blackness that surrounded it and there was still no sign of angry mold men or diseased wendigos or even any hacking-yelping-slapping horrors.

But when he looked forward again, he found that the moldy, bloated mockery of Rutherford Shinne was not confined to the walls of the barn, but extended into these dead woods with the spreading rot.

He stumbled to a stop as the thing loomed before him, a twelve-foot-high mass of writhing, festering black slime with the face of a man who ceased to exist forty-seven years ago.

"Very interesting…" it burbled as it reached out with a great, wriggling thing that couldn't even jokingly be called a hand. "I've never seen anything like *you* before."

Eric backed away, still clutching at the glass case.

"I thought it was the machine making space-time break," said the Shinne thing. "But it's *you*. *You're* the one doing it."

He stared up at the monstrosity, confused. "Huh?"

He was making time flip back and forth like that? That was ridiculous. He couldn't do something like that. It was Voltner's alien Nazi machine. And the freaky, multidimensional glow worms.

"I can't wait to take you apart and see how you work."

Eric turned and fled, uttering a not-at-all-heroic, "Nuh-uh!" as he went.

But cold and slimy mold closed around him before he could get away.

"Now stay still."

Chapter Fifty-Eight

Cold, festering blackness enveloped him again, overwhelming him, filling his nose and mouth, burning his eyes.

Then, in an instant, he was standing in brilliant sunshine, squinting up into a clear, blue sky through a myriad of early spring buds.

Then, just as quickly, it was night again, and he was staring at the black, mold-covered door of Shinne's barn.

Then that, too, was gone and he was running through a dark and snowy forest.

He stopped, gasping for air, confused. Was this earlier? He turned and looked behind him. Was he running from something? He didn't see anything. What was happening? He didn't remember starting to run. He was standing there, staring at that moldy barn door and then he was just running, with no transition whatsoever. His head was spinning. He felt dizzy.

Before he could even begin to wrap his head around it, he was suddenly standing beneath a large and brilliant full moon, surrounded by summer leaves, the air around him hot and humid.

"This…isn't on the itinerary…" he muttered.

Was he skipping through time? He clutched the glass case closer to him and turned in a circle, scanning the forest around him. This wasn't the same woods he was in a moment ago. There was something strange about it. Something beyond the mere fact that it was no longer mid-winter. These trees and ferns… It didn't look like any Wisconsin forest he'd ever been to. It looked far more jungle-like. Far more *primitive*.

Something large swept through the air overhead, startling him, and somewhere in the distance something let out a strange and terrible howl, like nothing he'd ever heard before.

Then, before he could even begin to comprehend the possibilities, the jungle foliage was gone and he was standing in a blizzard, squinting into an endless white wasteland as a dreadful wind blasted through him, threatening to freeze him solid.

But again, he was only there for a moment. Then he was back inside the coordination office, staring down the open shaft into the black cellar below. He blinked and immediately found himself on the porch of the little house with its crystal machine, his hand resting on the doorknob, preparing to enter. He snatched his hand back, confused. But before he could turn and look around again, he was standing at the front gate, staring up at the carved name of Evancurt and the lone crow perched atop it.

"Find what is lost," said a familiar voice on the wind.

Again, he turned around, but he was looking out over the railing at Lofleder's alien jungle. "What's happening?"

"Follow the bones and you will find her."

He turned *again*, but he was back in the rotten forest, surrounded by those skeletal, towering stalks that had once been trees.

Her? The bones had led him to Shinne's vault and the worms. Had he missed something?

Then he was sitting in a chair in a cluttered room that smelled of automotive grease and gasoline. He was woozy. The room was spinning. He could barely keep his eyes open. And he was in *pain*.

"I'm terribly sorry about all this," said a familiar voice. "This isn't the way things are supposed to be."

With a considerable amount of effort, he turned his head and looked at the little man as he wrapped his mangled hand in bandages.

The gas station attendant gave him a familiar smile. "But regardless of that, you have an important job to do. And I know you can do it."

"What...?" But when he blinked, he was only staring up at the falling snow.

What was that? Why was he back in the gas station attendant's office? That wasn't even the past. It was a memory from the dream that sent him to that god-awful fissure. It was the reality that never came to pass, where he'd lost half his right hand to a monstrous cat and then died an agonizing death in the strange, heavy depths of the cathedral.

He turned around, hoping it was over, only to be blinded once again by the sun. A great, thunderous fireball was erupting over the distant trees.

Then it was dark again and Tessa was telling him that this was where they broke the world.

Then, for just a moment, he was lying in the woods near the wreckage of the PT Cruiser, face down in the snow with the pungent smell of dirt, dead leaves and blood in his nose.

Then he found himself back in the spring sunshine again, watching a cloud of smoke climb high into the sky as fire rained down around him.

Finally, he was standing in the snowy forest again, staring out at the dark trees. There were crows raising a racket overhead. He waited there a moment, expecting to be hurled through time and space again, but nothing more happened.

Daring to let his guard down, he glanced around. The rotten forest was behind him. He seemed to have left Shinne's festering domain, though he wasn't entirely sure how he did so. There were no footprints leading out of that mold. Even the snow around him was undisturbed. It was as if he'd appeared out of thin air....

And as he looked down at himself, he realized that he was no longer covered in mold. His hands were clean. Even his clothes were dry. Somehow, he'd left all of it behind. Every drop.

Weird...

He looked down at the glass case and its softly glowing residents. "Was that you?" he asked them. "Or was that me?"

The worms didn't answer him, of course. But something else did. A familiar and distinctly impatient-sounding cry came from the forest floor to his right. He turned to find Spooky sitting there in the snow, staring at him.

The cat cried at him again.

"Don't yell at me," Eric snapped. "*You* didn't have to go in there."

Spooky ignored him and took off into the forest.

Eric rolled his eyes. "I don't even get a minute to catch my breath?" As he started after the bossy little beast, he lifted the glass case and examined the tiny, glowing creatures inside. For all the thrashing around they must've endured during all that, they seemed perfectly fine. They barely seemed to have been disturbed.

What really happened back there? Several times he'd seemed to jump through time, sometimes interacting with those around him, sometimes just observing and sometimes slipping into himself in the past and seeing it as he saw it before. He even once landed in the dream that first sent him exploring the weird.

It'd started way back in the treehouse, when he glimpsed the little girl, Perrine, sitting at the little table, long before he'd found the worms. But as soon as he acquired the glass case, those oddities became more wild, not merely flashing him back to 1971, but showing him what he was pretty sure were much more distant points in the past, giving him a glimpse of what might've been the ice age and even taking him all the way back to what he was fairly sure was a *prehistoric* forest.

And then there was the fact that he started returning from those weird flashbacks to entirely different places from where he left.

But what did Shinne mean when he said that it was *Eric* who was responsible for those strange happenings? He didn't have the power to do something like that. He was only a man. Not even a particularly *fit* or *heroic* man. He certainly wasn't some kind of time-traveling, teleporting *wizard*.

And yet, it must have *something* to do with him. Why else would it send him back to that dream of all places?

This was all so confusing.

From somewhere in the gloom ahead of him, Spooky cried back at him, his voice barely carrying over the cacophony of those damned birds.

"I'm coming!" he snapped, picking up his pace and following the tracks through the ever-gathering snow. It was about an inch deep now, though he felt like there should be more than that.

He looked up into the trees. There must've been hundreds of crows up there now. They were worked up into a frenzy for some reason.

Harbingers of the dead, he thought again. Why did those words kept haunting him? Was it only because the damned things were all over the place? He wished Peggy had never told him that.

The tracks merged with another pipeline and then turned to follow it.

Everette did tell him to follow the pipelines. The first one led him from the little house to the star house and the second led him from there to the barn. This one must lead from the barn to the main house. But without Spooky's help, he might never have found this third pipeline. He had no idea where he was when he was ejected from the rotten forest. He could've wandered blindly for hours looking for roads or landmarks to follow, and in the process would've likely stumbled across another wendigo or reaper or some dangerous, otherworldly predator.

At the very thought, he turned and looked around, half-convinced that something must be barreling toward him in the dark.

He withdrew the flashlight and switched it on and off again. But it seemed that the odd, alien technology of Evancurt had finally killed it.

He stuffed it back into his pocket and then looked up to find a woman dressed in hiking gear walking toward him. Her face was covered in blood and her eyes were wide with a crazed mix of disbelief, horror and fury. "He killed me..." she gasped. "The son of a bitch killed me... He just... He just...*fucking...murdered me!*"

"I'm sorry," said Eric, unsure what else to say to the woman.

She wasn't listening to him anyway. She walked right past him, still staring with those huge eyes, still saying those awful words over and over again.

Eric shuddered and pushed on, following the pawprints in the snow.

He glimpsed a confused-looking man in a highway worker's orange vest and a nervous, skittish-looking young woman with telltale bruises on her arms. There was a very pretty blonde woman in a pair of skimpy pajamas who covered herself and fled into the forest when she saw him looking at her. A middle-aged man with the logo for Vertical Logistics embroidered on his baseball cap was ranting to someone Eric couldn't see about inexcusable republican greed and the desperate need in this country for universal healthcare. And a small, hunched old woman was complaining loudly that her kids had simply stopped calling altogether now.

On one hand, he wished these people would haunt some other acre of the woods. He found the spirits of Evancurt sad at best and more often downright disturbing. He didn't want to think about what all these people had left behind and the regrets they may never be able to let go of. But on the other hand, he'd begun to notice that when the ghosts were around, other things weren't. These spirits never haunted the twisted places. And they steered well clear of the rot.

"Hey!" shouted a tall, creepy looking man with exceptionally large ears. "Hey you! Can you feel it?"

Eric looked over at him, but didn't bother responding. It probably wouldn't do any good anyway. The sight of him seemed to trigger these random interactions, but his response, reaction or even presence didn't seem to be required beyond that point. The man was going to say what he was going to say no matter what he did.

"It's the end, my friend. It's upon us! Time is almost up."

Wearily, he replied, "I'm working on it."

When he looked forward again, he found that a young woman with long, braided pigtails was walking beside him and tugging uncomfortably at her skirt. "I was just going out for a minute," she muttered. "I didn't know anything would happen." She looked up at him, her cheeks flushed red, her eyes pleading.

"Okay?" he said, unsure where she was going with this.

She pouted at him. "Now I think I'm stuck here…and I'm not wearing any panties."

Eric threw his free hand up in the air, exasperated. "*Why did I need to know that?*"

Before the woman could answer him, a rock bounced off the side of his head. He cursed and turned to see the nasty little boy in the black hoodie glaring back at him from behind a tree. Once again, the brat showed him his middle finger and then fled back into the forest.

"Getting less and less sorry you're dead," Eric grumbled after him.

When he turned to look at the distressed commando woman again, she was gone. Instead, the short-haired blonde woman was there, glaring at him.

"*Don't you*—!" he shouted, but it was too late. She slapped him hard across his face again. "Fuuuuuuuuu…" he groaned.

The woman turned and stomped off again.

Seriously, was she and that kid related? Because he was noticing some resemblances.

He moved on, picking up his pace.

Above him, the crows cawed on and on. He really wished those things would take a break. They were starting to drive him crazy.

There was an older woman leaning against the trunk of a tree, smoking a cigarette. She was wearing way too much makeup and way too little clothing for this or *any* weather. "Hey, cutie," she said as he approached. "Wanna see my tits?"

"No thank you," he replied without hesitating.

"Can you tell me how to get to Minneapolis from here?" asked a young, chubby man with a neat goatee and dark sunglasses.

"That way, I think," he replied, gesturing randomly to his left.

"I should've asked Molly on a date when I had the chance," lamented a timid-looking man with a balding head.

"Probably," agreed Eric.

"I *really* should've deleted my browsing history before I left for the hospital," worried a sickly-looking man in a robe and slippers.

"Definitely." He glanced down at the worms. "They're really coming out of the woodwork now, aren't they?"

When he looked up again, he caught sight of a familiar pair of bare, sneaker-clad legs sticking out from behind a tree. He stalked over, already knowing what he was going to find, and snatched a rusty blade from the black-haired girl's hand as she was pressing it against her wrist. He turned and flung the weapon as far out into the surrounding forest as he could and then turned and shouted, "Knock it off!"

The girl shrank away from him and vanished.

Grumbling, he walked back to the tracks, where a man in a bright yellow ski jacket stood blocking his path. He had a distressed look on his face and was wringing his hands.

"I think I might be dead!" he gasped.

"Duh," said Eric as he stepped around the man and hurried on his way.

Then a blinding light washed over everything. He stopped and squeezed his eyes shut against it, then squinted into brilliant sunshine.

"This again?" he grunted. He turned and looked around. He seemed to be in exactly the same spot as before. But back in the past. The air was warm and smelled of spring. And the crows had gone silent.

He rubbed at his burning eyes and when he opened them, he saw a streamer of fire spiraling down in front of him.

Looking up, he saw a familiar ball of smoke rising into the air, closer than he'd ever seen it before.

Then everything was dark again and the crows were screaming in the trees.

He cursed and squeezed his eyes closed. "And now I'm blind again," he grumbled. "Thanks for that."

Blinking, he turned and looked around, wondering if he was back where he started or if he'd been flung to some far corner of the estate. But there were cat tracks in front of him and cat tracks *and* human tracks behind him. It didn't seem that he'd moved a single step during that jump.

He should probably be concerned about how frequent those flashbacks were getting. He had a feeling that it was like the flushing of the tunnels and the venting of the system. It was like labor, he realized. The contractions were getting closer together.

Something was about to happen.

He was distracted by small fingers closing around his hand. The girl in the cupcake tee shirt had found him again. He looked down at her. He was growing rather fond of the girl and was glad to see her again. She helped the loneliness of this place a lot better than the angry blonde woman and that bratty kid in the hoodie. But he didn't care for the worried look on her face. She seemed troubled. She clung more closely to him than she did before.

Time was running out. He knew it was. And so did she. He could tell.

He gave her hand a gentle squeeze and then continued following the tracks in the snow.

Chapter Fifty-Nine

There were more ghosts haunting Spooky's trail as Eric and the girl continued forward. But these were considerably less chatty, thankfully. For the most part, these seemed to be lost and unsettled souls, wandering blindly through the cold, dark forest or else just sitting or standing alone in sad and thoughtful ways.

Once he saw another of the broken people. An older, well-dressed gentleman who kept alternating between sitting on a snowy log to standing beneath a great maple and staring up into its branches. It still felt weirdly like he was watching a glitching video game.

He still wasn't sure why these particular ghosts appeared this way. Was there something wrong with them? Did it have something to do with the weird physics of Evancurt?

The girl wasn't likely to tell him, even if she could, so he didn't bother asking.

He continued on in silence, following the feline tracks. A teenage boy asked him for directions, a man with a tall, colorful mohawk randomly informed him that he looked a lot like his father and a bitter-looking young man stormed out of the woods shouting, "'Eat vegan,' they said! 'You'll be so much healthier,' they said! 'Think how much longer you'll live,' they said! I could've spent the past six years eating *bacon cheeseburgers*, but *no*!"

Eric nodded. *There* was a life lesson he could get behind.

But the rest of the spirits that showed themselves didn't acknowledge him in any way. They seemed strangely distracted and nervous. Most of them kept glancing over their shoulders or up at the sky.

He walked past another row of those strange, lead pipes he found when he first arrived—or perhaps it was the same row of pipes, he couldn't be sure—and found it unsettling to see that they were now puffing out considerable amounts of steam.

The girl seemed distressed by it too, because she crowded closer to him as they walked past them.

Shortly after the pipes had vanished back into the darkness behind them, he looked up to see another row of power lines looming ahead with several noisy crows perched on them. Again, he remembered what Dora told him about electricity not working here and wondered if they were repurposed or if they were merely a remnant of whatever was here before Voltner and his Nazi hell machine.

As he passed directly beneath the power lines, he looked down to see the faint remains of another trail. Then, looking at the pipeline, he saw where the snow had been disturbed and realized that he'd been here before. This was where he'd "followed the power" to the prophet's tomb, per Vashner's posthumous orders.

He wasn't sure why, but he found himself half-surprised to find any evidence of himself left in these woods. It felt strangely as if Evancurt would find a way to wipe itself clean of him, as if he were nothing more than another of its countless dead.

Before he could think too much about this odd thought, however, the very ground beneath his feet seemed to shudder.

"The hell was that?" he asked, looking around. It wasn't just his imagination. A great many of those crows had taken flight and he could see clumps of snow falling from shuddering branches all around him.

There was a change in the air. The atmosphere seemed to have a charge to it that wasn't there before.

"Is something happening?" asked a timid-looking woman with glasses and long, brown hair falling out of her ponytail.

"I don't feel good…" said a teenage girl with bright red hair and a smattering of freckles on her face.

From somewhere in the forest came a terrible scream.

The girl buried her face against his arm.

"It's okay," he assured her. But he began to move faster. He had a bad feeling.

Ahead of him, he caught sight of a familiar flannel shirt and hat. Mr. Nicholas, Mrs. Avery had called him. As they approached, the man turned to face him, his expression grave. "Pretty sure this is it," he said. "Last call, son. Better hurry."

Eric nodded and rushed past him without pausing.

It was difficult to hear much over the damned crows, but he thought there was more screaming coming from deeper in the forest. More ghostly shapes were moving among the trees. Voices murmured all around him.

The spirits were definitely growing restless. Was it possible that they were able to sense an imminent peril?

Before he could contemplate it further, something seized his right arm and knocked against him, causing him to stumble a little and tighten his grip on the glass case. "You again?" he grunted at the confused woman as she buried her face against his shoulder.

"I thought I'd lost you again," she whimpered.

It was harder to walk with someone clinging to each arm, but he didn't dare stop walking. And he didn't try to pull his hand away from her, either. She seemed different this time. She appeared upset. He glanced down at the girl in the cupcake tee shirt, but she only stared back up at him with those big eyes.

He said nothing more and pushed forward.

No more spirits stopped to speak to him. They darted across his path and cried out in the darkness, their voices tinged with fear. Every now and then he felt one brush past him unseen. Many of them muttered and gasped. Some of them wept. And some continued to cry out in terror in the forest.

"I'm scared," said the confused woman.

"It's okay," Eric assured her. He glanced down at the case still clutched in his hand. "I can still fix this."

After a few more minutes of following Spooky's trail, lights began to show through the naked branches ahead of him and soon after he could see the outline of a house looming at the far side of an overgrown clearing. It was a large, two story colonial, long left to the elements, but again, not as far gone as forty-seven years should've allowed.

But between him and the house, the cat's prints wove through a scattering of strewn debris. Mangled scraps of charred lumber, hunks of shattered concrete and torn sheets of long-rusted tin lay everywhere. And at the very center of the mess was a crater of a broken concrete foundation.

He paused here, overlooking the obliterated ruins as the little girl clung to him on one side and the woman on the other. This was the site of the explosion he kept seeing, he realized. This was where the fireball erupted on the day the machine was turned on.

He recalled the map in Lofleder's office. "This was the shed," he realized. The one that had also been labeled "reactor" on the map. Was that what happened here? Had some sort of reactor exploded? Was that what the giant fireball in 1971 was?

But before he could consider it further, he was pulled backward by the two clingy spirits, as if something about the place were unbearable to them.

"Honey…" moaned the confused woman. "That's a bad place."

He didn't have to ask her what she meant by that. Before the words had left her ghostly lips, a foul breeze and a scorched stench gusted up from the ruined remains.

A twisted place? Out here?

Thick, black smoke began to pour from the debris at the bottom of the hole, followed quickly by the flickering of flames. As he watched, these flames grew into several separate fires that seemed to creep across the ground of their own will, each one moving independently of the wind and in different directions. Then each fire began to take the unsettling shape of a writhing body. Finally, terrible screams filled his head and at last he turned and yielded to his ghostly guardians.

No wonder they didn't want him going near there. It wasn't merely a twisted place. The people trapped there weren't just changed by Voltner's monstrous machine. They were changed at the very instant the building was blown to pieces. They were caught at the very second of their violent, fiery deaths, frozen in that hellish, agonizing instant for all time.

He wasn't entirely sure how he knew these things. It was something about those hideous screams. Some deeper and more mysterious method of communication. A psychic expulsion, perhaps. Or maybe it was something spiritual. Or something he could never hope to understand. But he knew it was true. Those poor people...

"Honey..." groaned the confused woman.

"Yeah, yeah," he breathed, too disturbed by what he'd felt to again tell the woman he wasn't her "honey." He pushed aside the awful thoughts that had filled his head and tried to drive that awful screaming from his mind.

There wasn't time. He had to stop the machine. He had to find the core and remove the jewel.

With the help of a bunch of tiny glowworms...apparently...

He turned his attention to the house in front of them. Was it only his childish imagination that made it seem that the place loomed there like a sleeping dragon? Or was that an accurate analogy for the heart of Evancurt and the home of the machine's guarded core?

He was approaching the house from the side. Between him and the front porch was a fenced-in area overgrown with naked trees and the frozen stalks of dead weeds and out-of-control hedges. And as he drew closer, he realized that he'd seen this place before. Or, more specifically, he'd seen what this place *used to be*. It was back in the green lab, in that maintenance room while he was speaking to Port. He flashed back to this place, to what seemed to be one of Port's own memories. This was the garden where Bronwen was watching the girl, Perrine, play.

But before he could step through the rotten gate, he was again halted by his companions.

This time, they didn't drag him back. They merely stopped.

"Bad place?" he asked, looking down at the confused woman.

She glanced up at him, but only quickly, as if she didn't dare take her eyes off the overgrown garden for more than a second. He didn't think she'd answer him, but she surprised him by replying, "Different kind of bad."

The girl in the cupcake tee shirt nodded agreement.

Eric looked around. There was more than one way into the house, but Spooky's pawprints didn't lead to any of those. They led through this gate and into the garden. Bad place or not, he didn't dare deviate from the tracks.

The cat knew things, after all.

From somewhere in the surrounding woods came a terrible scream. He glanced back over his shoulder. "I have to go," he said.

But the woman clung more tightly to him. "I don't want you to!"

"I don't care what you want, I have to go."

He thought the woman was going to force him to remove her from his arm or else drag her into the "bad" garden. But she let go of his arm and turned to face him. "I know," she whimpered. "But I'm scared."

"You'll be fine," he promised her.

"I'm scared you won't come back."

"You don't even know my name!" he snapped.

Before he could stop her, she stood up on her tiptoes and surprised him with another kiss.

"Stop doing that!"

"Please be careful," she begged, taking a step back.

"When this is over, you need some help," he told her as he turned and backed away from her toward the garden gate. "I don't know if it's a psychologist or an optometrist, but you need to see *one* of them. *Soon.*"

This time, he actually felt the little girl let go of his hand. She stepped away from him and took the woman's hand instead. Then the two of them stood watching him.

"Please come back," said the woman.

Eric stood there a moment, watching the both of them, a cocktail of unsettling emotions swirling inside him.

It was strange. They looked like two perfectly ordinary people. Standing there, without so much as a shiver to indicate that they felt the falling snow or the chilly wind, with only his and Spooky's footprints at their feet, it felt strangely as if they were real and it was Evancurt that was only an illusion.

Finally, he turned and walked through the garden gate, continuing alone.

Chapter Sixty

Eric stopped and looked around. This was definitely the same garden he glimpsed in that weird flashback he was dropped into while talking to Port. From here, he could see the stone bench Bronwen had been sitting on. Port was over there, kneeling in the dirt, tending to the plants. The girl was on the other side of those straggly trees, frolicking around the flower beds. But a lot of time had passed since then. Even if it wasn't the middle of winter, no flowers would have remained. The garden had been overrun with weeds and trees and invading brush.

His eyes swept the area, cautious. He wasn't the only one here. He'd felt a familiar, eerie chill almost as soon as he stepped through the gate. And as he started toward the door, an icy wind swirled through the thorny tangles.

Yet another twisted place. He wondered what it'd be this time. Killer hedge animals? Giant moles? Mutant aphids?

But he didn't have to wonder long. All around him, the trees began to twist and bend, cracking and groaning, following him as he crossed the ruined garden, shrugging off clumps of snow that rained down around them and sending angry crows flapping and cawing into the snowy sky.

As he approached the doorway that opened onto the old garden, he saw the wooden siding buckle and crack, as if something were moving around behind it.

He had time to appreciate the familiarity of the scene. This was just like what happened in the treehouse.

And just like in the treehouse, the rotten wood snapped and split, exhaling a great, dusty breath before crying out in an eerily familiar voice, "*Perrine!*"

Eric stopped walking, confused. "Bronwen?"

"Perrine?"

He ran his hand through his hair. "No..." He remembered what Port told him about the girl being gone, that she wasn't like the others, and his heart ached as he said, "Perrine's not here. I'm sorry."

"Perrine..." sighed the wall. The sadness in that voice was almost unbearable.

"It's just me again. Eric."

"Eric...?"

"Yeah. We talked earlier. In the treehouse?"

"Perrine's...treehouse...?"

"Do you remember me?"

"Eric..."

Conversations with Bronwen were considerably less creepy without the nightmare toys repeating everything she said, but it was still pretty eerie. He hated that awful, desperate tone in her voice. He'd hated it the first time he met her, and it was only worse now that he knew that the girl she was so desperately searching for wasn't here. Especially knowing that her own father had sacrificed her in order to complete the awful machine that did this to everyone. But even more bizarre was that she was here. He thought she was trapped inside the treehouse. But if she was trapped, then what was she doing here now?

"Yes..." said Bronwen. Or whatever thing this was that thought it was Bronwen. "I remember you... But... That was so long ago..."

"Was it?"

For a moment, the crack in the wall was silent as she thought about it. "It...*feels* like a long time..."

He couldn't argue with that, he supposed. It felt like at least a week had passed since that business in the treehouse. Besides, he already knew that time was messed up in this place. Maybe it *had* been a long time to her.

But he'd suspected from the condition of the property that time was running *slower* in Evancurt, not faster. Did it flow differently for the people than it did for the buildings and lawns?

"Have you seen Perrine?" asked Bronwen.

"No. I haven't. I'm sorry."

The thing in the wall moved, buckling and splintering the wood as it went. Then another board cracked open and called out with another dusty breath, "Perrine!"

"I'm sorry." He just kept saying that. He wasn't sure what *else* to say. He was just terribly sorry. He wished there was something he could do, but Perrine wasn't changed with everyone else. Perrine was gone.

"Where are you, Perrine?"

Another wave of vertigo washed over him and he closed his eyes. When he opened them again, it was daytime. But instead of blinding sunshine, the day was gloomy and gray. There were storm clouds on the horizon. He could see distant flashes of lightning and hear the soft rumble of thunder.

The garden was a garden again, instead of a dead and frozen thicket.

Bronwen was standing in front of him, the real Bronwen that she was before the Evancurt machine turned her into a thing that crawled through walls and animated toys. Her back was turned to him, her long, auburn hair blowing about her in the gusting wind. She was wearing a different dress than when he saw her in Port's flashback, but it was the same style of long, modest dress. "It's time to go inside now," she called out.

From somewhere in the garden, a girl's voice answered her: "Just a little while longer? *Please?*"

That was poor Perrine, Eric realized, though he couldn't see her from where he stood.

"It's going to rain soon," replied Bronwen.

"But it's not raining *yet*."

"It will be any minute now."

"And *then* I'll come inside! A few drops won't hurt me! *Please?*"

He didn't get to see who won the argument. Another wave of dizziness sent him stumbling back into the snowy darkness of the present.

"Perrine..." moaned the thing that lovely Bronwen had become. "Where are you, Perrine?"

That was strangely unsettling. Something about the sheer *normality* of that interaction in the face of the evil thing that happened in this place. A fleeting glimpse of the modest existence she once enjoyed. He didn't want to see any more. He turned and hurried to the door.

Like at the other house, it wasn't locked. But as he pushed the door open, he glanced down and realized that Spooky's footsteps had vanished.

He frowned. Had the cat disappeared? It wouldn't surprise him if he had, to be honest. At this point, it wouldn't surprise him if he'd sprouted wings and flown away.

But the thought had no more than crossed his mind when he heard an impatient mewl from overhead and he looked up to see Spooky staring down at him from the edge of the gabled roof above.

Or it had merely climbed to higher ground, like even normal cats were known to do.

Again, Spooky cried at him.

"I'm going!" he grumbled as he turned back to the task before him. But before he could step inside, Bronwen called out his name.

He turned and looked out at the garden. Just like at the treehouse, all the trees and bushes were reaching out for him, their skeletal branches clutching like groping claws.

"That house…" whispered the walls all around him. "Don't let it swallow you."

Eric stared out at the groping garden, unsure how to respond to such a terrible warning.

Then, before his eyes, the overgrown garden began to pull away again, returning to the way they were before he entered the gate. "Perrine…" moaned the desperate voice. "Perrine… Please come home…"

As Bronwen wailed for poor, lost Perrine and the maddening crows continued their endless noise, Eric stepped inside the house and closed the door behind him.

Chapter Sixty-One

As he took his first look around Evancurt's main residence, he found himself surrounded by more of Patelemo's strange machinery.

Like the little house with its crystal machine, both the lights and the heat were on in this building, which was nice, given that his flashlight was as dead as the people here. But there was nothing else in this room. There was no furniture, no decorations, nothing at all to indicate what sort of space this was originally meant to be. It could've been a dining room or a sitting room or a bedroom. There were only several large, blocky machines connected by vast tangles of fat, gold cables, heavy lengths of twisting, lead pipes and ribbed, copper-colored rods that ran between beachball-sized silver orbs hanging from translucent-white boxes mounted on the ceiling.

Everything was covered in a thick layer of long-undisturbed dust, but like in the other main buildings, there were hardly any cobwebs, which still left him feeling rather unsettled, as if the spiders knew something he didn't.

No one was here. Everything was silent.

He lifted the glass case and clutched it against his chest again, protecting it from whatever horrors he was certain to find here, and then crossed the floor to the door on the far side.

The next room looked less like something that should be in a rural Wisconsin house than in some sprawling New York sewer. A large pool of pungent, churning liquid took up most of the floor, surrounded by a walkway of that strange, translucent-white material. Dozens of gold cables rose up out of the liquid and disappeared into various outlets in the upper walls and ceiling of the room.

Again, he felt as if he'd wandered into some strange, alien spaceship and he found himself wondering if the plans Voltner took from that Nazi bunker at the end of the war could've originated somewhere among the stars after all.

But he didn't linger. He needed to keep moving. Somewhere in here was the machine's core. He crossed the room and walked through the nearest of the two other doors in this room, where he found himself in an old and dingy kitchen.

He paused here, surprised. It was strange to move from a room so utterly alien to a room so completely normal. And it was a strangely simple kitchen, too. The only appliances were an old-fashioned wood stove and a strange, insulated box that looked like a chest freezer, but appeared to be built into the wall. There wasn't even a toaster or a coffee maker.

But then again, what did he expect to find here? Modern amenities? Even ignoring the fact that this kitchen was at least fifty years old, Dora told him back in Lofleder's office that electrical things didn't work long in Evancurt. A functioning kitchen would've been necessary to feed everyone who worked here, but electric appliances simply wouldn't work. Everything was probably made on that stove.

There were windows on two sides of the room, looking out over the overgrown yard. An open doorway waited to his left, but a quick peek inside showed him that this only led to a mudroom and a back door. He'd have to go back and try one of the other doors leading away from the mysterious churning pool.

As he stepped back into the kitchen, however, a voice cried out, "Charles!"

Eric froze. He glanced around, but nothing was moving, neither in the walls, nor in the strewn dust. There were no impossible globs of molten concrete. Fire didn't erupt from the stove.

"Is that you, Charles?" came the voice again.

Was it coming from the window? Cautiously, he stepped toward it, listening. It was a strangely gurgling voice, eerily like Shinne's back in the barn, but this voice was distinctly less menacing. And it sounded feminine.

And was it saying "Charles"? As in, Charlie? From that strange cellar in the middle of the woods?

His hand crept toward his pocket where the undelivered letter rested. "Are you...*Millicent*?" he asked as he stepped up to the sink and peered through the dirty glass.

"Charles?"

He looked down. The voice seemed to be bubbling up from the sink. "No. I'm not Charles. I'm sorry."

"Not Charles..." bubbled the voice in the pipes.

Eric stared into the black drain. "Is your name Millicent?" he asked again.

"I am..." bubbled the voice in the drain.

He wondered suddenly if perhaps Millicent had been standing right here by this sink when the machine came online. Maybe she was washing her hands at the moment the world shattered around her...

"Charles worked in that bunker out in the woods, right? He recorded data from some sort of machine down there?"

"Charles?" bubbled Millicent, her voice rising. Inside the drain, something moved. "You know...Charles?"

Water boiled up from the black drain. It wasn't clean water. It was reddish-brown in color, sort of rusty-looking, and gave off a musty smell.

"Where is he?" gargled the voice in the drain. "Is he safe? Did he get away from here?"

He wasn't sure what to say. Should he tell her that Charlie was still here, trapped in the concrete of that bunker just as she seemed to be trapped inside the house's plumbing? Or would she be better off thinking he escaped this awful fate.

"Please tell me!" pleaded the voice from the drain.

As he watched, the water that bubbled up into the basin moved in strange ways. To him, it looked like eerie, liquid fingers grasping at the metal, as if the thing inside were trying to claw its way out.

"I tried to warn him, but he was out on an errand... I left a note... I prayed..."

Eric's hand crept toward his pocket again, to the very note

she was speaking of. It was surreal to think they were one and the same.

"I overheard them talking... Voltner and that creep, Patelemo... Heard what they said..." The drain gurgled. The sound was unnervingly like a great, wet sob. "People were going to die. The reactor shed... It was designed to explode during the first process. Like a pressure release valve. Protecting the rest of the machine."

He stared down into the darkness of that drain, horrified. He remembered the ruins of the shed. The strewn debris. The destruction. That nightmarish vision of eternally burning mockeries of human souls... Someone *knew* that was going to happen?

"And the machine that Charles was monitoring..." she went on. "It wasn't just collecting data. Something was going to happen with it, too... They called it an energy pulse. Not an explosion, like what was going to happen at the shed, but still something *awful.*"

He recalled that strange machine in the back room of the bunker, the one Charlie was monitoring. (*...broken now... ...no more data... ...nothing left to measure...*) The memory of that creepy conversation gave him a fresh chill in light of this. Did he know what happened to him? Did he have any idea?

"They were going to kill him..." said the watery thing that was once Millicent. "My Charles..." The sink bubbled and gurgled in a strangely forlorn sort of way. "What happed to him? Please tell me..."

He stared down into the basin. He'd never felt so bad for a drain before. "He's still waiting for you," he decided. It was a version of the truth he was comfortable with. After all, whatever happened when this was all over would probably happen to both of them. Maybe they'd end up there together.

Those watery fingers suddenly receded into the drain again. Everything fell silent.

Eric stood there, staring into the darkness at the bottom of the sink, wondering if that was the wrong answer.

Then, very softly: "He's...still waiting...?"

Eric nodded. "I'm here to help," he tried. "I'm going to fix everything."

"Fix…everything…?"

"That's right."

"You can…really fix it…?"

"I think so," he replied. Although he was afraid he might be lying to her. He could find the core, pull out the jewel, disable the machine and put a stop to the madness that was happening here. At least, according to the *Lady of the Murk* he could do all these things… And this *was* the sort of thing he was always doing, after all. If this turned out to be like all those other times, then he was confident he could put an end to the alien creatures and the wendigos and the reapers. He could perhaps even fix the broken space-time thing. But he wasn't sure what would happen to Millicent and the rest of the people trapped in the twisted places.

"The way things used to be…" bubbled Millicent. He'd never heard water bubble so *dreamily* before.

She had a surprising range of emotions for dingy drain water.

"Sure," said Eric, though he couldn't help but shiver a little. "As much as possible. But I need your help, Millicent."

"My…help…?"

"Can you tell me where the machine's core is?"

"You can't get there," she replied.

He looked down at the worms in the glass case. "I think I might be able to, actually. I found a way. But I have to know where it is. Can you just tell me where it's located in the house?"

"That's the problem…"

He frowned. "What?"

Water boiled up from the drain again. This time, instead of clawing fingers, a great, boiling face appeared and stared up at him. "You can't just go there…" she told him.

"Why not?"

"It's the house…" she explained. "It won't let you…"

Chapter Sixty-Two

The thing that used to be Millicent drained back down into her black prison and Eric backed away from the sink.

The house wouldn't let him go there? What did that mean?

He turned and left the kitchen the way he came, only to find that the room with the mysterious, churning pool, which should've been waiting on the other side of the doorway, had suddenly become a cramped hallway with great bundles of glass-coated, gold cables running along the ceiling.

"Wait...*what?*"

He turned and looked back through the doorway again.

The kitchen was there, just like he'd left it. He walked back through the doorway and looked around, as if he'd only made a silly mistake. But there was only the one doorway and the mud-room. There was no way he could've gotten lost.

He walked back through the doorway again and back into the cramped hallway. Okay. He was starting to understand now. The house wasn't going to let him go there. That answered that question, he supposed.

There were three doors on the right side of the hall and an opening in the middle of the left side. He made his way to the opening and peered around the corner.

There were stairs here, leading down to the floor below.

"Am I upstairs?" he asked, apparently posing the question to the worms, because no one else was here. Even after all this, he was still in the habit of talking to Isabelle and these little guys were turning out to be a fine substitute in a pinch. Unlike Isabelle, however, the worms didn't have a snarky reply for him, which wasn't all that surprising, but was, he found, a little disappointing.

He took the stairs down to the lower floor and opened the door at the bottom. Here, he stepped into a cluttered office with several tubes of thick, bubbling liquid lined against the inner wall. Two large windows took up much of the other side of the room and looked out onto the overgrown and snow-covered yard. But when he pulled the curtains back and looked out, he found that he was on the second floor, looking down over the debris from the reactor shed.

He frowned at the scene before him and then at the doorway through which he entered the room. He entered a two-story building on the ground floor, went *down* a flight of stairs and ended up on the *second* floor.

This must be that new Common Core math everyone hated so much.

He turned away from the window and left the room the way he came in, because it was the only door. Instead of the stairs that brought him here, he found himself in a room with one of those large, spirit cell battery things and three other doors. One of the doors didn't lead anywhere, but instead acted as a portal through which ran a large collection of pipes, gold cables and fat, rubber tubes that descended from the ceiling and from the various translucent-white boxes mounted to the walls.

Eric nodded and glanced down at the worms. "Well I, for one, have seen this trick before," he told them, "so I'm not exactly impressed."

This wasn't so different from the Altrusk House, where he first found Isabelle. The doors there didn't lead where they were supposed to, either. When Isabelle took his hand and led him to the exit, the path was anything but logical. But after being trapped there for thirty-six years, she knew her way around. It was the only thing that saved him from ending up as just another mad trapped person whose memories she'd absorbed.

Whether this was the same sort of place, where order could eventually be found in the chaos with enough time and practice, he'd likely never know, because time was something he simply didn't have.

He stepped through the room, careful not to touch anything, and peered through the gaps in the blocked doorway. He could see into the next room, but there weren't any lights on in there. Was it just another machine room of some sort? From what he could see, the entire space was crammed full of pipes and cables and metal boxes of varying size.

Like at the workshop, he was struck by the strangeness of the machinery with its lack of wheels and gears and belts. Only Patelemo's clockwork room had visible moving parts. And while some of it was giving off a steady, almost humming vibration when he drew very close to it, and some of it even produced an unsettling sort of rhythmic *thrumming*, it was all so unnaturally silent that he kept forgetting these things were still operating. And given what Dora told him about it all being incompatible with electricity, it wasn't any wonder it all felt so strange.

Then he saw something moving in that darkened room. A black shape was oozing between the pipes, long, bladed fingers probing every nook and cranny.

A reaper.

He backed away, his free hand instinctively reaching for the ectoplasmic patch on his chest.

He should've expected those things to be here. Tessa told him they were protecting the core. Everette told him they were Voltner's enforcers. *Of course* they'd be patrolling the building containing the machine's core.

He needed to keep moving. He wasn't going to walk away from another encounter with one of those things. He'd already used up his one extra life for this game.

He hurried to the nearest of the two remaining doors and stepped through it, where he found himself standing in a bedroom overlooking a sagging, full-size bed long covered in an extra blanket of dust.

Realizing that he'd just walked into the room not through the actual door but from the closet, he turned and looked back through the doorway again.

The room with the spirit cell was gone. Instead, he was staring into a dusty, but spacious dining room.

"Huh," he said. Then he walked over to the window and

peered out over the yard.

He was still on the upper floor, he saw, but looking out from a different angle. From here, he could see the overgrown garden.

He wondered if Bronwen was still out there looking for poor Perrine.

As he stood there, a strange, *flowy* sort of voice whispered into his ear: "Hello there."

He jumped and turned around. "Who's there?"

The fabric hanging over the sides of the bed ruffled, as if something were moving around underneath. He turned to face it, clutching tightly at the glass case and the tiny worms inside. But as he stood with his attention fixed on the bed, something brushed against the back of his thigh.

He twirled around and backed away from both the bed and the window, but the curtains, moving as if by a phantom breeze, fluttered after him, seemingly reaching out for him, trying to snatch at him.

"I'm Betty," whispered a breathy voice from behind him.

Again, he twirled and backed away. His attention diverted, the curtain wrapped itself around his leg. This time, when he tried to pull away, he was caught. He tripped and fell, barely managing to hold onto the glass case.

"What's your name?" whispered the creepy voice that called itself Betty.

He sat up and looked around. The other curtain was fluttering, seemingly struggling to reach him. And the bedclothes were flapping violently, as if a storm were brewing in the dusty darkness beneath the mattress. "Uh… I'm Eric?" he replied, unsure what else to do.

"Eric," sighed the voice of the dusty linens. "I like that name."

"Do you work here, Betty?" he asked.

"I'm the housekeeper," replied the Betty thing. "But I haven't worked in a long time. Everyone went away. And I've been so *bored*." As she said this last word, the curtain wrapped around his leg dragged him closer to the window and the other one whipped toward him and caressed his cheek.

"I'm sure it *must* get boring around here these days," he agreed, trying to lean away from the groping fabric.

"And so *lonely*," purred Betty as the fabric of the curtain brushed at his face in motions that felt eerily like ghostly kisses.

"I'm sorry to hear that," he told her.

Something reached out for him under the blanket, pushing it toward him and sliding it off the bed, sending up a cloud of dust as it thudded to the floor.

He scrambled to his feet and began prying at the curtain wrapped around his thigh. "I'm kind of in the middle of something important," he told her.

"I'm sure you can spare just a *little* bit of time," purred the shape under the blanket.

"No, no. I'm *very* busy." He managed to unwrap himself from the fabric and free himself. "*Really.*" Then he let out a startled yelp as the other curtain reached between his legs and groped him.

"Forget about all that other stuff," whispered the voice as the blanket thing brushed against his arm. "Let's have some fun, instead."

He scrambled away from the window and out of reach of the curtains, but he wasn't quick enough to avoid the blanket. It wrapped itself around his arm, pulling at him. "I'm married!" he blurted, pushing it away.

"Married?" whispered the voice as the blanket slumped back onto the floor.

He nodded. "Yep! Married. Sorry."

Then something moved on the bed. He watched as the thin sheet began to lift upward, revealing the distinct shape of a woman's body beneath it. She turned her head and looked at him. "I don't mind," she told him.

Eric stared at her. He wasn't sure which was more bizarre, the fact that he was being hit on by slutty linens or that he was talking to an *actual* ghost in a sheet.

The woman in the sheet stood up and moved toward him. There was nothing under it. He could see the empty space when it fluttered around her feet, but the fabric clung to the invisible shape, revealing every curve of her otherwise invisible body. "She doesn't have to know."

He backed away. "No, she'll know. Trust me on that."

The blanket on the floor began to slither toward him. "Then you can just tell her I tied you up and made you do it."

"Uh..." He ran his hand through his hair, flustered. Evancurt's housekeeper was kind of a freak.

"She'll understand."

He gave his head a hard shake. *"Oh no she won't."*

Betty lunged at him.

Eric turned to flee, but at the same moment, the blanket on the floor wrapped itself around his legs, tripping him again. He fell to his knees, still clutching the case, desperate not to drop it. In an instant, he was wrapped in smothering fabric.

And then there were hands all over him. Fingers crept over his entire body, far more than just one person should have. He felt them under his clothes, warm and soft. They probed and caressed him, tickled him, *clawed* at him.

"Mine now!" squealed the thing that used to be named Betty.

Eric cried out, desperate.

Then, suddenly, he was lying alone in a dusty bathtub, still clutching the glass case against his chest.

For a moment, he just lay there, staring up at the ceiling with wide, startled eyes, uncertain of what had just happened. Then, slowly, he looked down at the little, glowing worms. "Thank you?" he gasped.

And in case Isabelle was still watching on, he added, "That wasn't my fault! You tell Karen I said no! That was all the linen lady!"

Chapter Sixty-Three

Eric sat up in the bathtub and rubbed at his weary eyes. He wondered what time it was. How long had he been wandering the dark acres of Evancurt?

He needed a little break.

He rested the glass case and its tiny worms between his knees and opened his jacket to examine the ectoplasmic patch on his chest that was supposed to be holding in his soul.

There was more blackness bleeding through it than there was before. He was sure of it now. There were several tears in the web-like material. And was it any wonder? How many times had he tripped and fallen? How many times had he rolled over the hard ground?

He was a terrible patient. His doctor would be so disappointed with him. And Karen would have scolded him a dozen times by now.

Again, he imagined her and the others sitting around the table, frustrated by this unfortunate block in communication. Holly and Paige would be putting everything they had into their spells. Perhaps they'd called their sisters, too.

He was rather surprised, now that he was thinking about it, that they hadn't contacted their crystal sisters with their impressive teleportation spells to come searching for him. He hadn't thought of that until now. But he supposed if no one knew exactly where he was, it wouldn't do them any good. They needed a *location* to blip to.

Maybe that's why no one had shown up. Not even Paul.

This was beyond simple payback for leaving him stranded in the Canadian wilderness. Far too much time had passed for him to just be taking his sweet time. He should've been here well before now. Either there was something preventing Paul from finding him or... Well, he didn't care to think about the alternatives.

His awful imagination, however, was more than happy to suggest that Paul's banged-up old pickup truck was even now sitting dead somewhere on the property while its unaware owner wandered haplessly into some dark and monster-infested building.

He shook his head. No. Paul had done some stupid things like that before, but he knew how dangerous things were. And so did Isabelle. She would've stayed in contact with him and she wouldn't have let him do anything that stupid. He was sure of it.

He probed at the patch on his chest. Besides those small tears, it was starting to pull apart around the edges, too. It wasn't just tripping and falling that was damaging it. He was doing damage to it with every careless movement he made.

He watched those black wisps of smoke and flecks of ash as they sputtered through the patch. Was his soul naturally black? Or did it only look like that because those were the pieces of his soul that had died and were peeling away? It seemed an odd color for a soul to be. Wasn't a black soul typically the preferred analogy for the *villain* of the story?

He closed his jacket and pondered the idea for a moment. Hadn't he seen a soul before?

It was during that business with Aiden and the unseen places, two and a half years ago. The nameless agent he dubbed "Pink Shirt" had possessed the terrible ability to create what he'd called "aura plasma," which he claimed was a manifestation of his own soul. That stuff wasn't black. In startling contrast, it'd been a shimmering, molten gold.

But he had no idea if that stuff really had anything to do with a person's soul. He only had Pink Shirt's word on that. And Pink Shirt was, among many other horrible things, a liar.

He was distracted by the sound of bubbling water in the drain by his feet.

"Charles?" gargled the watery voice of Millicent.

"Just me again," Eric called down to her.

"Oh…" replied Millicent. "Okay…" There was a soft gurgling from the toilet and then the sink, then all went quiet again.

Being trapped in a twisted place was clearly a very lonely existence.

He stood up, rubbed absently at his aching hand as he recalled that queer, golden goo that was said to leave nothing but a stain of anyone who got in the psychotic agent's way, and then picked up the case with its tiny passengers and stepped out of old tub.

He paused at the dusty mirror to glance at his back, where more of those black wisps and flecks sputtered through his jacket and dissipated into the air.

Was it his imagination, or did that one look *worse* than the one in front?

Deciding that there was nothing more he could do about it now, he made a note to tread much more carefully in the future and then stepped from the room and into a familiar hallway with gold cables running along the ceiling.

Now *that* actually made some sense, he thought. Maybe the bathroom wasn't affected by whatever strange magic had twisted this house into an insane Altrusk-like abomination. That would be sensible, he thought. Bathrooms, more than any other kind of room, should stay put. It was just common sense. But when he glanced back through the door behind him, he found that it wasn't a bathroom anymore, but instead a cramped broom closet.

So much for common sense.

He turned and started down the hallway, wondering where he should go next. But when he reached the staircase, he saw a black shape creeping up the steps on spidery, scythe-like fingers, and he turned and fled back the other way.

He darted into the first room he found, which proved to be a little girl's room, strewn with dolls, books, crayons and old stuffed animals.

Before he had time to take these surroundings in, Bronwen's desperate voice burst from a crack in the wall in a great cloud of dust and insulation: "Perrine! Is that you, Perrine?"

"Just me again," said Eric. "I'm sorry."

"Just you again..." sighed Bronwen.

Neither she nor Millicent were doing much for his self-esteem. He'd never heard two people more disappointed to see him.

Betty would be happy to see him again, though, he supposed. He'd have to settle for that.

He looked around at the strewn toys. "This was her room, wasn't it?"

"It is..."

"Right," he said quickly. "Is. What I meant to say."

As he stood there, a little plastic doll, an old, vintage-looking Barbie, he was pretty sure, with badly frazzled hair, sat up and looked at him. "Her room..." said the doll.

"Her room..." agreed a deflated-looking stuffed bear that was too lazy or depressed to do more than roll its ragged head toward him.

"Her room..." agreed about a dozen other random previously-inanimate objects.

He couldn't help but take a step back. And as soon as he did, he was struck hard by another dizzying wave of vertigo.

"Dr. Roden!" cried Bronwen.

Eric turned and looked back through the doorway. The world on the other side of the windows was bright and sunny again. A familiar woman with long, auburn hair ran by.

"Dr. Roden!"

"What is it?" asked a man's voice.

Eric walked over and peered out into the hall. Bronwen was there, standing in the next doorway, speaking to someone within.

Dr. Roden? The fifth scientist? The expert in exotic energies and the monster who sacrificed his own daughter?

"I can't find Perrine anywhere!" gasped the woman.

"Calm down," said the unseen man. "You know how she likes to explore. Check all her usual spots."

"I *have*. She's not playing in any of her favorite places."

"I just saw her at breakfast. She couldn't have gone far. You probably just missed her. Or she's playing jokes on you again.

427

Calm yourself and take another look around."

The woman took a breath and stepped back out of the room. "Yes sir," she sighed.

Eric turned and looked around at the room. It was bright and sunny. Dust hadn't settled over all the toys yet. Everything here was much newer and brighter than it had been when he left. And yet there was something dreadfully eerie about it all.

It was all in exactly the same place it was when he first entered the room.

Perrine never set foot in here again.

Hurried footsteps approached in the hallway. "Perrine?" called Bronwen. "Are you in here?"

But before she reached the door, another blast of vertigo returned him to the present and he stood alone in the darkness.

He looked down at the scattered toys around him. The girl's room...her treehouse...and the garden where she used to play... "You're trapped in all the places you thought she should be," he realized. It was heartbreaking. Almost as much so as the hideous, awful truth of the matter.

He sacrificed his own daughter!

Did he know where his daughter was when he told her caretaker to calm down and look for her again? Had he already sacrificed her to Voltner's nightmare machine?

He remembered Shinne cursing about Voltner moving up the time. Was he trying to keep her busy until then?

"Perrine..." moaned the voice in the wall.

"Perrine..." echoed all the voices of a little girl's childhood.

These voices still didn't sound human, but now he could almost hear the voice of the woman he'd just glimpsed in the hallway buried in them somewhere, adding a whole new dimension to the tragedy as it played out before him.

Eric shivered. "Bronwen, can you tell me where the machine's core is? So I can finally turn it off?"

"You can't..." sighed the wall.

"Can't..." said a little pink bunny with a missing eye.

"Can't turn it off..." agreed two little plastic dogs.

"Can't..."

"You can't…"

"Can't do it…"

"*Maybe I can*," he said, raising his voice, trying to sound more confident than he felt. "If I can just find it."

"Can't find it…" moaned the wall.

"Can't…"

"Can't find it…"

"Just tell me where it is!" he shouted over the eerie voices. "Tell me and we'll see."

For a moment, there was a heavy silence in the room.

"Can't…" sighed Barbie.

"Can he…?" asked a stuffed panda.

"If he could…" whispered a toy horse.

"He can't…" groaned the lazy bear.

"What if he did…?" wondered a deflated-looking sheep with stuffing oozing from a loose seam.

"I just need to know where they built the core. I'll figure the rest out on my own."

There was silence as the toys pondered the matter. Then, finally, the crack in the wall creaked open and, in a dusty voice, Bronwen whispered, "The attic…"

"Attic…" agreed the toys in their myriad voices.

"Attic…"

"The attic…"

"Up in the attic…"

He nodded. The attic. That was all he needed to know. He looked down at the glass case he was holding, at those tiny, glowing worms. Everette had told him that Shinne's "abominations" would provide a way through Voltner's otherworldly defenses.

It was time to find out if that was true.

"You're going to die up there…" said the lazy bear.

Eric shot the limp creature a dirty look. "No one asked you," he informed it.

Chapter Sixty-Four

He walked out of Perrine's room and stood outside the door, contemplating the task before him. He knew now that the core of the Evancurt Machine was in the house's attic. He knew that he had to remove some kind of jewel from that core. He knew that the worms were supposed to allow him to do these things. But as he stood there, looking around him and finding that he was back in the kitchen, he realized that he had no idea how he was supposed to get to the attic when doors didn't work how they were supposed to and he still had no idea how to aim a teleporting box of alien worms.

"Charles?" splashed Millicent from the sink basin. "Is that you?"

"Just me again," Eric informed her.

"Well shit..." she bubbled, disappointed.

"Sorry." He turned and walked back through the door again, this time ending up in a linen closet.

Remembering the entirely-too-friendly sheets he encountered in that last bedroom, he quickly retreated from there—just in case—and found himself in that dining room he'd spied through Betty's closet.

He turned and looked around, running his hand through his hair.

If there was a logical way to navigate this house, he didn't have time to figure it out. The reapers would find him long before he found the attic. Clearly, that wasn't what he was supposed to do.

He was already wasting too much time. There was no way to know what was going on outside these walls. Before he arrived here, there was steam pouring from those lead pipes and Mr.

Nicholas was saying that the tunnels were flushing nonstop. Even the ghosts had begun to react to the approaching doom.

So what was he supposed to do?

He looked down at the worms. They were the key to all this. But how did he use them?

They were *worms*.

Everette told him that the creatures Shinne found altered the state of the universe around them. According to Shinne, himself, they did this because there was no concept of death in their universe and therefore they couldn't die, forcing the environment that should've killed them to change. He still wasn't sure whether that made perfect sense or no sense at all, but it was all he had to go on. Everette told him that these worms would make it possible for him to bend reality and make possible what was never possible before.

And it was right after he took them from the vault that he began teleporting away whenever things started getting dicey. Did they sense danger, perhaps? Or maybe they were psychic creatures who could sense when he felt overwhelming panic. Either way, it seemed logical that what he was supposed to do was use them to jump straight to the attic.

Except he had no idea how to make them work on command, much less how to aim them.

And he wasn't going to have time to figure it out now, either. As he stood there, contemplating the magic, teleporting worms, the door on the other side of the room creaked open and a reaper scuttled through it.

He turned and fled back through the door by which he'd entered, ending up back in the first room with all the machines and pipes and cables. With nowhere to go from there, he turned and ran back through the same doorway again, this time finding himself in a new bedroom, this one with two twin beds, two dressers and a vanity. Before he could contemplate how the sleeping arrangements might've been here in 1971, the curtains blew inward and Betty's voice cried out, "You're back!"

"Just passing through!" he gasped, and again he fled through the doorway.

This time, he ended up somewhere cold and dark that smelled of dank earth and that foul, sulfurous mold.

The basement? And another of Shinne's abominations?

He didn't attempt to explore this darkness. He simply turned around and felt his way back through the doorway. A moment later, he found himself back in the upstairs hallway where another reaper was crawling toward him from the far end, its blade-like fingers clawing at the floor and walls as it pulled itself along.

He turned and darted into the first doorway on his right, where he tripped and stumbled over clumps of overgrown vines.

One of Lofleder's plants, of course. The entire room was covered in it. Vines overran the floor, climbed the walls and clung to the ceiling. He couldn't tell where the thing began or ended. There didn't seem to be any roots. It was just an endless, creeping vine.

He turned and left again, only to find himself in a long, empty corridor lined with heavy lead pipes and winding, golden cables that seemed to go on forever without so much as a door in sight.

It looked like the sort of place where he *really* didn't want to get caught between two reapers, so he turned again and ran back through the doorway, where he discovered a room with a great, cavernous hole in the center of the floor, down which countless pipes and cables descended into a cold, distant blackness.

"Huh," he said as he peered over the edge. It was obvious at this point that not all these rooms existed in the same world. The house was clearly much larger on the inside than it was on the outside.

Everette warned him that much of the machine was built in other worlds, beyond the reach of any who might wish to shut it down. Given how many monsters had crossed over into these woods, it was safe to say there were *several* worlds intersecting in this place.

He glanced around, baffled. "We're not making much progress here," he told his tiny, glowing companions. Although it was nice being able to use the same door over and over again to explore the house, he had a feeling that this strategy wasn't ever going to lead him to the attic.

Voltner was probably making sure of that.

He needed to figure out how the worms worked. And he needed to figure it out fast. There was an anxiousness beginning to gnaw at him that he didn't like. It felt like time was running out.

But he wasn't going to figure it out here. When he glanced down into the pit again, he saw several black shapes crawling out of the darkness on long, sharp fingers.

He turned and fled back into the hallway, where he was now standing *behind* the reaper he first saw there.

The thing turned and looked at him.

He bolted across the hall and through the next doorway, where he immediately banged his head on a low-hanging pipe.

He cursed and continued on, circling around several dusty machines, ducking under another pipe and squeezing between two more big, silver orbs before slipping through the next doorway and into a closet.

He stood there a moment, confused and frustrated, then turned and went back the way he came, where he found himself descending the stairs and then exiting into another bedroom, where he again fled from the groping linens, into another closet and back out into a quiet living room generously furnished with an old-fashioned matching couch and loveseat, several ugly armchairs, two rocking chairs, an ancient television set and a well-stocked bookshelf.

He ran his hand through his hair and looked around. He felt as if he were running blind through several different movie sets that had nothing to do with each other.

He crossed the room, heading for the doorway on the other side, but before he could get there, another reaper appeared, blocking his way forward. He cursed and turned back the way he came, but again he was thwarted. Two more reapers crept through that way.

He was trapped.

He turned and backed himself against the wall. "Well," he

grumbled, "can't say I didn't see this coming." He glanced down at the glass case. "Now or never, little guys."

The reapers drew nearer, their deadly, bladed fingers closing around him like the bars of a shadowy cage.

"Any time now," he croaked. "*Really.*"

This was going to be a lousy end to his story if these stupid worms didn't wake up and do something very soon.

There was nowhere left for him to go. He'd run out of doors.

He thought of Tessa. The girl in the cupcake tee shirt. The confused woman. All those lost souls with tears in their eyes and desperate, pleading faces. And he thought of Karen. And Paul. And Isabelle. Holly and Paige.

It couldn't end like this.

"*Get me out of here!*" he cried as he slid down the wall, making himself smaller and smaller, putting off the inevitable as long as possible. "*Now!*"

The reapers lifted their hands, their scythe-like fingers hovered over him for a moment, impossibly black.

In a flash, thirty soul-shredding blades descended on him.

Chapter Sixty-Five

When Eric opened his eyes, he was sitting on the floor, his back to the wall, still clutching the glass case with its tiny, glowing worms from another dimension.

He was no longer in the dated living room. Instead, he was looking out over a long space with short walls and a low, gabled ceiling. A great, metal monstrosity of a thing took up most of the room. It seemed to rise right up from the middle of the floor and into a great, twisted, coiling mass of cables and pipes and tubes and wires.

It made no noise that he could perceive directly, but seemed to be producing a low, thrumming sort of sensation that he could feel pulsing against the inside of his skull. The entire room was charged with a strange sort of energy that made his skin feel warm in spite of the cold air and sent the hairs on his arms tingling.

This was it. This was the attic. And the thing in front of him was the core of the monstrous Evancurt Machine.

The worms had finally brought him where he needed to be.

And yet…

Wincing, he glanced down at himself. There was a black cut on the back of his left hand. Ominous wisps of smoke were rising from it. Farther up his arm, just beneath the elbow, more black smoke was wafting from a fresh tear in the jacket. There was another high on his right shoulder as well.

The worms were just a little too slow, it seemed.

Or maybe Shinne was right and it was just that *he* was a little too slow.

He watched those tendrils of black smoke and the little flecks of ash that occasionally sputtered out.

Souls don't heal, dude. Like, ever.

Not even dead. Just gone.

He closed his eyes and let himself breathe for a moment. One thing at a time. He'd found the core. It was time to finish what he was brought here to do. *Then* he could sort out this damaged soul nonsense.

Everything was going to be fine.

He rose to his feet, still clutching the glass case with its tiny, glowing worms.

It was funny how these things came together sometimes. He found himself reminded of Hedge Lake and the insatiable Conqueror Worm and those little wooden orbs that he'd carried deep into the triangle... And now these little guys. It was amazing how such colossal problems could be solved with such small things.

Of course, he hadn't solved anything yet.

He still had to figure out how to reach the jewel inside that core.

As he started toward the machine, however, the world lurched and he stumbled. The room brightened. Sunlight poured through a small window behind him.

"I'm not sure about this," said a voice he recognized. It was the same voice he heard speaking to Bronwen in his last flashback. It was the voice of Roden. He was just on the other side of the machine.

"It's necessary," replied another familiar voice. It was the voice of the tall man he'd seen speaking to Patelemo in an earlier flashback. Walter Voltner.

"If you say so."

"I *do* say so. I've cleared all the failsafe areas. Patelemo, Lofleder and Shinne are at their stations. Now is the time."

Eric crept around the machine and peered through the tangle of cables and tubes. Voltner was there, tall and pompous-looking, with his neatly-trimmed beard.

He *looked* like the sort of man who'd build a doomsday machine, he decided. He'd probably be right at home stroking that obnoxious beard while gloating about his nefarious schemes and watching James Bond being lowered into a vat of acid.

"And what about the jewel?" asked Roden.

Eric leaned out a little farther to see him. He was a much smaller man, thin and weak-looking. One of those *brainy* minions, he decided. But no less evil. This was the man who'd sacrificed his own daughter, after all.

And yet, although this was the first time he'd actually seen the man, he looked strangely familiar, as if he'd seen that face before somewhere.

Voltner gestured at the core. "In place already."

Roden turned and scowled at the machine. "I don't like last-minute changes."

"It's *necessary*," he said again. "I told you, Patelemo found an abnormality in the clock. It's a small risk, but it's worth avoiding. Are the lines flowing at full capacity or not?"

"I told you, everything's ready."

Then, with another lurch of his stomach, Eric was yanked back from the past.

This was where it happened. This was where the machine was turned on. This was where they broke the world.

Take the jewel! Starve the lines! Close the streams!

He looked down at the glass case in his hand.

Worms!

He flexed his aching hand and glanced down at the sputtering wounds on his arms. This was it. Just one last task. And with no time to spare, it seemed, because as he crept around toward the front of the machine, a soft hissing noise began down near the floor, like a pressure cooker building a full head of steam.

He expected to find both of Evancurt's evil masterminds waiting for him, probably in some monstrous, video-game-boss-like form, but there was no one there as he crept around the machine's core.

Could he possibly be so lucky to have avoided Voltner and Roden completely?

And yet, any hope he had of slipping in undetected and simply yanking out the critical piece of the machine was dashed the moment he reached the front of the core and discovered that there wasn't anything here.

He stood there staring at the machine, confused.

Everette told him to remove the jewel from the core. That was his exact instructions. And yet...the core was nothing more than a great hunk of metal at the center of a massive tangle of pipes, cables and tubes. There was no door. No access panel. Not even a porthole window to stare longingly through. There was *nothing*.

Now what was he supposed to do?

All around him, the hissing grew louder.

A strange steam was starting to roll across the floor and through the forest of cables and pipes. It had an otherworldly sort of quality about it, like the iridescent sheen on an oil-slicked surface.

Above him, strange, grayish condensation had begun to collect on the canted surface of the attic ceiling, running down the bare boards in dirty streaks.

His every instinct told him that time was up. This was the final stage of the second process. Any second now the machine would power up again and every soul on this property, including Tessa and himself, were all going to be wiped off the face of the earth, erased from existence forever. And he had no idea how to stop it.

"What a fascinating specimen."

Eric turned, startled, to find that he was no longer alone.

A large, utterly black shape with oozing streaks of bloody red flowing through it had appeared between him and the exit. It looked just like the reapers, except it was a great, bloated thing, with hundreds of those deadly scythe-like fingers protruding from its back and coiled around its bloated, blob-like body.

Only its face retained any trace of the man who found those monstrous plans and built this nightmare machine. He could still see the outline of that beard.

That was why the reaper's face looked strangely familiar when it attacked him in the bunker. It had the same face as the man he saw speaking to Patelemo in his office.

Voltner, the reapers and this thing were all one and the

same!

The thing that used to be Voltner loomed over him. He didn't step toward him so much as swell to take up more of the space between them. "What sort of thing are you anyway?"

Eric glared up at the horror before him. "Have you seen *yourself* lately, Wally?"

The thing seemed to grin at him. It was a terrible thing to see. Oozing, tar-like lips peeled back to reveal monstrous rows of foul, diseased-looking teeth. It made his stomach turn. "Or maybe the question I should be asking is this: what, exactly, do you *think* you are?"

"What?" This guy wasn't making any sense at all. Had his monstrous transformation driven him crazy?

Not that it mattered. He literally had his back to the wall. There was nowhere else to go. Voltner was the king of the reapers. He was the embodiment of death beyond death. With a single jab of any one of those many scythe-shaped, spider-like appendages, this monster could rip him open and send his charred soul dissipating forever into the ether.

He didn't know how to reach the jewel inside the core. He didn't know how he was going to escape this monstrous attic. He didn't know how much time was left before the third process would be triggered. He didn't even know how long he had before his soul bled away and he vanished forever.

He didn't know *anything* except how to keep talking and stalling for time and hoping for one last miracle.

"How did you do it?" he blurted. "How did you build something that required breaking the laws of nature?"

The Voltner monstrosity leered at him. "Do you really want to know?"

Eric stared at the monster. He hesitated. Did he? He of all people should know that there were things out there better left unknown.

"God," said the Voltner thing.

He frowned. "God?"

"Well...*a* god, anyway. One of them."

He was still on the fence when it came to his belief in actual gods. He believed in God. With a capital G. And he knew for a fact that there were other very godlike forces in this weird world. The jinn he released from its charred prison beneath the old, unseen high school in Creek Bend was practically a god. And then there was that thing they summoned last year in Chicago. Mambo Dee had described it as a minor god from a former universe. And just tonight, Tessa had described the Sprit of the Forest that twice sent him fleeing through the trees in blind panic as being something like a god.

"After Roden and I found the plans in that German bunker, I went and located those ancient desert ruins where those monsters claimed to have found it."

Ordinarily, Eric would've pointed out that this bloated shadow thing was the last one who should be calling anyone monsters, but this was the Nazis they were talking about. Besides, this was actually interesting. "You found where the plans came from?"

"Not where they came from," explained Voltner. "Where they'd been stored, since the very beginning of our universe, when they were brought here from the previous age."

He nodded. "Oh." Universes that existed before this one...entire realities that rose and fell, with humanity migrating from one to the next in an endless cycle... He'd heard this before, too.

"I took the plans back there, hoping to find a clue to deciphering them. But what I found was even better than a clue."

More vents began to hiss behind Eric, higher up, near the ceiling, reminding him that time was growing desperately short.

"*He* was there," said Voltner, his black eyes filled with an awful sort of wonder.

"You're, uh...*god*...was there?"

"He spoke to me. He showed me how to build it. He told me where to find the people who could help me make it work."

The other scientists. Patelemo, Shinne and Lofleder.

"Everything that I did here was His will. It was all according to His great plan."

"Even the part where you turned into a giant pile of crap?"

Voltner ignored this childish insult. "He told me things," he purred. "Wonderful things. Terrible things. *Amazing* things. Secrets from worlds long gone. Answers to the greatest mysteries."

Eric raised an eyebrow. "Did he say anything about that movie, *Inception*? 'Cause that one's been driving me nuts ever since I watched it."

Voltner oozed forward again and grinned that terrible grin. "And He told me about *you*."

This caught him off guard. "Me?" Voltner's dark god mentioned *him*? "I wouldn't even have been born yet."

"Do you really think something as trivial as that makes any difference to a god?"

Eric frowned. "Well that's just basic *chronology*. I mean, really..."

"He told me you'd come. He told me you'd be resourceful. He told me you'd exceed all my expectations."

"He sounds like some witches I know. 'Somebody call Eric. He can handle it. No problem.' Like, do I even get a say in any of this?"

Another vent opened and hissed. The energy of the room was growing more intense by the second. It felt like there was a static charge in the room. It crackled in his ears. Except there was no electricity here. This energy was something different.

He glanced down at the back of his hand, at the black vapors that were pouring from the cut those reapers left there.

He really wasn't sure how he was getting out of this one.

"And He told me something else, too," added Voltner. He took a step toward him. Except it wasn't exactly a step. He didn't seem to have legs. It was more of a grotesque sort of wriggling. He sort of *slithered*... Or maybe "*oozed*" was a better word. Whatever it was, it made Eric's skin crawl. "He told me that when I met you...you'd know His name."

Eric squinted at the monster, confused. "Huh?"

Again, Voltner *oozed* closer. Those deadly blades began to uncurl from around him. There were more than he first realized. Dozens more. Maybe *hundreds*.

He clutched the glass case closer to him and pressed his

back against the impenetrable core behind him. "I know the name of your god?"

"You do. I can already see it."

He shrugged. "Is it Peter?"

"His name…"

"Alfred?" There was nowhere to go. All the clocks were running out. "What about Harry? Is it Harry?"

"His name is *Altrusk*."

He stared up at the monster, confused. "Wait… *What?*"

"He said to tell you goodbye," said Voltner, and in a single, lightning-fast instant, one of those searing, shadowy blades shot forward and buried itself in Eric's flesh.

Chapter Sixty-Six

Everything was washed away in a great, sweeping tide of searing agony. The attic. The machine. The monster that once called itself Walter Voltner. Even fear, itself, seemed to melt away into the pain.

Seconds passed like untold ages, until it seemed that all he'd ever known must have turned to dust.

And yet he was still here. The pain, itself, was proof enough of that.

Eventually, the world returned, slowly winding itself back up to its proper speed, and he opened his eyes.

Voltner's reaper blade sizzled in his left shoulder. Great, black plumes poured out around it.

Break either of those wounds open, or let one of those shadow dudes stab you again, and it'll all come spilling out.

Definitely not a good sign.

Voltner leaned over him, his hideous reaper face grinning madly. "You never had a chance against Him. You should know that by now."

Eric barely heard him. An inferno was raging through his shoulder. And his skin felt like it was on fire. It crackled and burned. His hair tingled with it.

Was this what ultimate death felt like? Was this what it meant for a soul to die?

From somewhere in the pain-filled world, a whistle began to blow.

Voltner looked up, that grotesque grin spreading ever wider, exposing even more of those hideous teeth. "Do you hear it? The third process is beginning. It's over. *He* wins."

Another wave of all-consuming agony swept him away as

the monster yanked out the blade. He dropped to his knees and cried out in agony. Black smoke and ash gushed from both sides of his shoulder.

Somehow he was still clinging to the glass case. He looked down at those tiny, glowing worms. They did their job. They brought him to the attic. They brought him to the core. It was *he* who failed. Everything that happened after this was all his fault.

Voltner turned his hideous face back to him. Those soul-piercing appendages drew back. "Goodbye," he growled.

The crackling sensation on his skin became a flickering, white flame. It rippled across his body, electrifying his every nerve.

For just an instant, he saw Voltner's hideous face contort with confusion. Then a great, white blast knocked the black, bloated beast backward.

"Go, Eric!" cried a new voice. "Use the worms! Enter the void! Take the jewel!"

Eric stared, amazed, as a human shape formed from the blazing energy.

He knew that voice. But it was so weak last time he heard it. It could barely form words. It was almost maddening to listen to.

"Everette?"

"Roden!" growled Voltner.

Eric stared at the two monstrous forms before him. Darkness and light standing against each other. Roden? Wait... *Everette Roden?*

He saw it now. That was why Roden had looked so familiar in the flashback. He looked like the reflection in the crystals.

But Roden was one of the bad guys. Wasn't he?

"What are you doing?" snarled Voltner.

"Did you think I wouldn't find out?"

Voltner glared back at him.

"The 'jewel' you claimed to have found in that haunted desert... The spiritual power source that would start the machine... You bastard."

Eric stared at the two of them, an awful realization dawning on him.

"A meager price, really," growled Voltner. "A single soul. Pure. Untouched."

"*She was my daughter!*" screamed Roden.

"Perrine..." breathed Eric. He remembered those flashbacks. Bronwen searching for her, unable to find her anywhere.

Port had it all wrong. Roden didn't sacrifice his daughter. Roden never knew what Voltner was planning. Not until it was far too late. It was probably the real reason he moved up the starting time. So no one would have a chance to save her.

His head was spinning. There *was* no jewel. There never was. The power source Voltner claimed to have found and hidden away, refusing to reveal to anyone until the machine was built... It was all a lie. What he really found in those ancient ruins was an evil plan to steal an old colleague's child and sacrifice her to his dark god to kickstart his evil doomsday machine.

What a *dick*!

"Go, Eric!" shouted Roden. "She's still in there! I've felt her! Only *you* can pull her from the void!"

Voltner lurched forward, those black blades tearing at the white form before him.

"Tell her I'm sorry!" said Everette Roden. And with a terrible bolt of white energy, both forms exploded in a blinding flash and were gone.

Eric was alone again, but he dared not linger another moment. He stood up, grunting against the pain, and turned to face the machine.

His head was spinning. Roden wasn't a heartless monster who built a doomsday machine and sacrificed his own daughter to make it work. Perrine wasn't gone forever. And everything that had happened here was the fault of some dark and obscure god who shared a name with the perverted con-man who built the insane mansion that swallowed Isabelle.

It was a lot to take in. And he simply didn't have time to sort it all out.

Time was running short in a great many ways.

He reached out with both hands and held the glass case against the metal side of the machine. "Come on, little guys," he groaned. "Just once more."

He didn't think he could do it. He didn't know how. He was making this stuff up as he went along. But as if responding to his words, the worms began to glow brighter.

Then everything changed.

The pain disappeared.

He wasn't adrift in the murky depths of that icy ocean again. That, he realized, was merely death. This, however…*this was different*. This was nothing. There was no light in this place. No sound. No feeling. He couldn't move. He was adrift in this nothingness. Helpless.

It was exactly what Roden said it was. It was a void. And he'd been here before…

He tried to call out, but his voice never made it to his lips.

Hours seemed to pass. Days. Weeks. *Years*. Until he felt he would go mad.

Then, suddenly, he wasn't alone anymore.

He couldn't see anyone. He couldn't feel anyone. But he knew someone was there, floating in the same empty darkness, their noses almost touching.

"You finally came."

He knew that voice!

From out of the emptiness came two slender arms. They wrapped around him and held him tightly.

"I knew you would," whispered Perrine.

Then a great, bluish glow blossomed in the darkness of the void and he realized that he was still holding the glass case with its tiny worms.

It wasn't anything as simple as a realization. He simply knew what he was supposed to do next.

He reached out into the void and let go of the case. For a moment, he watched it float away.

Then reality took hold of him again and he fell backward, into a world of searing agony, and fell crashing onto the hard, wooden floor of the attic.

That ominous whistling noise died away, followed by the desperate hissing of the vents.

One by one, the rushing steam relaxed under the rapidly diving pressure.

It was over.

He grunted and sat up, lifting the motionless form still clinging to him and looking at her for the first time with his own eyes.

She wasn't remarkably beautiful, but she was pretty, with blonde hair and a spattering of freckles across her cheeks and nose, just the way he knew she looked each time he'd met her in his weird travels, even though it had always been dark and he could never actually see her.

She looked to be about Holly's age, maybe twenty-one, but she was still wearing the same dress she was wearing when Voltner placed a twelve-year-old girl inside the machine. It didn't fit her older body, leaving her barely covered. Her hair and nails had grown impractically long as well during her time in the void. She looked too thin and too pale, but she was *alive*.

He brushed her hair out of her face, marveling at the fact that the little girl trapped in this machine had somehow aged at most a decade in the almost five that had passed in this world. And as he gazed down at her, she slowly opened her eyes and looked up at him. They were two different colors. One was dark brown. The other was pale blue. And he felt as if he'd looked into them a million times before.

"I knew you'd save me," she sighed.

Then she closed her eyes and drifted off to sleep again.

He frowned down at her, worried. Was she okay? Did he need to get her to a hospital? Was she dehydrated and malnourished after her extended stay in that freaky limbo?

But he didn't have time to fret over her now. Somewhere beneath him, something gave a hard shudder, shaking the entire house around him.

"Get out of there, Eric!" whispered the mysterious voice that had been warning him of danger all night.

Again, he didn't have time to ponder over who the voice belonged to. He understood in an instant that he still had work to do. He'd stopped the machine, but it wasn't over yet. The system was failing. Evancurt was falling apart.

Grunting through the pain, he shrugged out of the jacket he stole from Patelemo's office, wrapped it around Perrine's shoulders and buttoned her into it. Then he scooped her frail form up into his arms and carried her down the attic steps, all too aware of the smoke and ash that was pouring from his otherworldly wounds.

Chapter Sixty-Seven

With the machine broken and its monstrous master blown apart by Roden's vengeful energy form, the house seemed to have been cured of its insanity. (Although he was keenly aware that none of that sounded even remotely sane.) The doors now led where they were supposed to lead, allowing him to descend to the second-floor hallway and then down to the foyer and straight to the front door without any unexpected detours through mournful children's rooms, sorrowful bathrooms or kinky linen closets.

Nothing tried to stop him. The reapers had vanished along with Voltner and none of the spirits of Evancurt had dared approach the house. But deep down below the building, something gave another shudder and shook the very foundation beneath him, threatening to bring the whole place down on him if he didn't hurry.

Without the "jewel" that held it together, the machine was coming apart. And without the machine, all of Evancurt was unraveling. Spread across and throughout any number of worlds, it was going to tear itself to pieces.

This was another of those things he had no business knowing, but somehow did. Perhaps he'd shared a brief psychic connection at some point during his ordeals in the main house, not unlike the one he shared with Isabelle. Or perhaps it was something he somehow learned while jumping through time and space with those tiny, alien worms. Or maybe it was just because this was the way things like this always seemed to work. Because nothing finished off an exhausting, night-long marathon like an epic, cross-country *sprint* while carrying an unconscious woman.

He'd stopped Voltner's monstrous machine from unleashing whatever hell it was intended for. He'd saved the souls trapped on this property from being devoured. He'd even found the woman with the mismatched eyes who'd been calling out to him to save her for two and a half years. But if he wasn't quick, both he and Perrine were going to perish in these dark woods regardless of all that.

There was a lot of distance to cover between here and the front gate. He focused on the front door and tried to ignore the ominous shaking, the rapidly dimming lights and the unsettling *sinking* sensation that he felt beneath his feet.

The door opened on its own as he approached it. Even a few hours ago, this might've given him pause, but he was well beyond that at this point. He wasn't sure if it was a helpful ghost or one of the people trapped here or if it was the house, itself, perhaps apologizing for its rude behavior, and he didn't care. He didn't stop to ponder it. It didn't matter. He simply shouted, "Thank you!" And hurried through it, happy to be free of another insane house.

As he ran out into the snowy night, however, he thought he heard Bronwen's voice calling out one last time for Perrine and *this* was nearly enough to make him want to pause.

This wasn't how he wanted to leave. But he had no choice. He pushed on into the night, praying that the poor woman would finally find some peace after all these years. She deserved it. They all did. Bronwen. Port. Millicent and Charlie. Lonely Betty. Everette. All those poor, miserable, suffering souls trapped all over the property.

He hoped they all found their peace.

(Except Voltner, of course. Fuck him.)

(And his three psycho "geniuses" too.)

But as he crossed the lawn, he forgot about the evil scientists and the poor, trapped souls of the twisted places. Chaos had broken out over the grounds. Otherworldly creatures stampeded through the forest. Ghostly, half-seen forms darted back and forth, many of them screaming and crying. There were shrieking crows everywhere. And somewhere in the forest, an explosion sent ribbons of fire streaming through the air.

The house behind him gave off a loud, echoing crack as something gave way, followed by a thunderous crash of splintering wood and shattering glass.

"Keep moving!" shouted someone he didn't see, but was pretty sure was Mr. Nicholas.

He didn't look back. With no idea which way he should go, he headed straight down the driveway. It wasn't a straight line, but it would eventually take him back to the front gate and to the road that waited there without risk of getting lost. He only had to keep moving until he reached the property line, after all. Then he could find help.

But he didn't make it far before he caught sight of the hideous, naked form of a wendigo loping across the road in pursuit of what looked like another of those ugly, furry toad things and he decided to take a chance and cut through the forest, instead.

Almost immediately, however, he found himself dodging a great, bloated, wasp-like thing that emerged like a nightmare from the darkness and sailed over his head, almost close enough for it to snatch at his hair with its giant insect feet.

Then something long and scaly slithered across his path, carving a long, winding track through the snow.

Something much faster darted behind them. Eric turned in time to see just a glimpse of disturbed branches and a set of tracks that looked unsettlingly like something from a *Jurasic Park* set that had crossed his own tracks only a few steps behind him.

Other, much larger things tore through the brush on either side of him, invisible in the gloom of the forest without his light or even the dull glow of the alien worms to aid him.

He was just beginning to realize that all these things were running from the same general direction when a great flume of smoke and fire belched from the ground somewhere nearby, illuminating a familiar, towering silhouette tearing through the trees, raining down broken branches in its wake.

It was like a scene from some apocalyptic disaster movie. And he was going to have to run through every horrifying element of it before he was going to be allowed to escape this awful forest.

Clutching Perrine tighter against him, he set a course safely *away* from the fireballs and the fleeing giant and prayed that the monsters of Evancurt were too preoccupied with the rapidly approaching end times to be interested in two exhausted and mostly helpless humans.

He climbed up a rocky hillside and then stumbled down the other side, past a screaming woman with spiky, purple hair and a strange, fat, furry bird that hissed at him as it waddled from his path. A muscular man in a sleeveless shirt and a cowboy hat ran sobbing past him, nearly knocking him down. Another of those freaky, winged centipedes slithered through the air overhead, making his skin crawl. And all the while, the crows seemed to shriek at him from every branch of every tree.

Then, without any warning, the chaos abruptly ended.

Eric stumbled to a stop, his heart suddenly pounding. Those distant explosions and the cries of the dead faded into the distance. The snow and wind had stopped. Even the crows vanished. The forest was as silent as a tomb.

No! Not now!

Beware the Spirit of the Forest, he thought, remembering the warning Tessa passed to him from the Lady of the Murk.

But he was the one who fixed this mess! He was the one who broke the machine! Why was the Spirit of the Forest angry with *him*?

He clutched Perrine's limp body closer to him and hurried forward. Every instinct he had was screaming at him to run, to flee from this place as fast as he possibly could, but he couldn't risk tripping. He had to protect her. He'd gone through hell to rescue her from that nightmare void and he wasn't about to let anything happen to her now.

But he could already hear that awful buzzing sensation that was both all around him and inside his head.

"It's not real…" he groaned. "None of it is real… It's all in your head…"

It was a lie of course. If it was only in his head, why would Tessa have told him to "beware the Spirit of the Forest"? She would've told him instead to "be brave in the face of the *irrational fear* of the forest." Or to "man up and don't freak out over the *stupid, harmless buzzing sound* in the forest." But he didn't have a lot of options at his disposal, and if lying to himself about the danger he was in was all he could do, then that was what he was going to do.

Everything seemed a little hazy. Was that the Spirit of the Forest, too? Or was he just weary from an exhausting night of fleeing from monsters and conversing with lunatics? Or was it merely that his soul was rapidly bleeding into the ether? He was oozing black stuff at an alarming rate, after all. If it were blood, he was sure he would've been dead long ago.

As the awful panic built up inside him, he pushed himself to run faster. He couldn't help it. He couldn't control himself. He had to run! He had to get out of these terrible woods!

But then he tripped and stumbled. He dropped to his knees, barely managing to hold onto Perrine's unconscious form.

The hellish buzzing was all around him now. It seemed to descend upon him like a tidal wave, washing away all rationality. He felt a mad urge to forget everything else and run, to simply toss aside this cumbersome weight that he was clinging to for some unrecalled reason and flee screaming before it was too late, before the true horrors of the forest came crashing down on him.

No!

He set his jaw and cradled Perrine against his chest.

She'd suffered in that void for forty-seven long years waiting for him to rescue her. He wouldn't abandon her now. He'd risked his life and soul for this girl. He'd nearly died. He might *still* die. But he wasn't going to let anything else happen to her while he was still alive.

If this "Spirit of the Forest" intended to harm her, it would have to wrench her from his cold, dead arms.

He closed his eyes and took a ragged, shuddering breath.

And as every unspeakable horror he'd ever dreamed of in dreams too terrible to remember descended on him in those silent, nightmarish woods, he lifted his head and screamed at the sky above.

Chapter Sixty-Eight

He had no idea how much time passed after that.

It felt like he spent days kneeling there on the frozen ground, his soul bleeding into oblivion, his head full of nightmares and his heart pounding until he felt sure it would burst.

But it could have been minutes at most.

Then, as suddenly as it all started, it was over. The snow was falling. The icy wind gusted over him, making him shiver. The damned crows were screaming down a him again.

He blinked hard. He couldn't seem to focus on the forest around him. He was so tired. He couldn't remember ever feeling so weary in his entire life.

He looked down at Perrine as she slept in his arms. Then he looked down at the black fumes that were still pouring from his shoulder. How much time did he have left? How long before he was bled dry and vanished from not only this but *all* worlds?

He closed his eyes for a moment, squeezing them shut, willing his head to clear. Then he opened them and gazed out at the snowy forest.

That haze was growing thicker, as if a fog were rolling in, closing in around him. It made the world feel *smaller*, as if it were shrinking.

Something caught his attention to his right. There was a person over there, half-hidden in that encroaching haze. Or...he *thought* it was a person. A woman? With long, dark hair blowing strangely about her head?

As he squinted at her, he realized that she was moving away from him. Not walking, exactly, but sort of *floating* away, gliding through the trees, slowly disappearing into the mist.

Somehow, he understood that he was supposed to follow

her.

With a considerable amount of effort and plenty of *grunting*, he rose to his feet, still cradling the girl against his chest, and began to stumble after the figure in the forest.

For a long time he followed the mysterious woman. He wove through the trees, staggered through brush and over rocks, climbing hillsides and crossing gullies.

All the while, the crows followed him. Thousands of them, it seemed. Maybe tens of thousands. They were everywhere.

He was just beginning to wonder if he was chasing nothing more than a hallucination when he caught sight of something familiar emerging from the trees.

It was the ruined PT Cruiser, just as he'd left it, but now covered in a thin blanket of snow.

Three crows were perched on top of it, their beady eyes fixed on him. Even over the din of the other crows, he thought that he could hear them cawing at him in a strange, almost *chanting* rhythm.

Or maybe that part was all in his head. He was so tired. The strength ran out of him and he dropped to his knees again, still clinging to the girl who'd become a woman in the untold depths of the void.

He closed his eyes, exhausted. And when he opened them again, there was a beautiful woman with long, black, flowing hair standing before him.

No... Not standing. *Floating*. As if she were adrift in the shadowy depths of a great, murky ocean...

And she was naked...which probably should've seemed odd to him in this weather, but at this point he was too exhausted to be concerned with such trivial things.

"I know you..." he realized.

The woman smiled at him.

"You saved me once..." Way back in Hedge Lake, after he was knocked into the water and nearly swallowed by that great, undead fish. She'd appeared to him then and frightened away the monster.

Then a pair of skeleton mermaid women dragged him into

the shallows where he had a major emotional breakdown in front of a couple of local fishermen. (True story.)

"And again...earlier tonight...in that bunker. You're the one Tessa told me about..." He squinted at her. "*You're* the Lady of the Murk?"

The woman nodded. She kept smiling, but there was something unsettlingly sad about her smile. He wished she'd stop smiling at him like that. It was making him uneasy.

"Tessa said you were the protector of the dead... A guardian angel, she called you."

"I wouldn't say 'guardian angel,'" said the woman. Her voice was soft and soothing. She had a strange accent, like nothing he'd ever heard before.

And that was even more weird because he shouldn't have been able to hear it over the noise of those shrieking crows.

They were so loud...

He stared at her for a moment, then he looked down at the girl in his arms. "Is she going to be okay?"

"She'll be fine, now," promised the Lady of the Murk. "She only needs rest."

He nodded. "Good. That's good." Then he looked up at her again. "And the spirits trapped in Evancurt?"

"They're now free to go, thanks to you. Most of them are moving on to where they belong."

"Most of them?"

She smiled. "Some have other business to attend to first."

He nodded again. That happened. Maybe they were like Tessa. Maybe they had things to do before they moved on. Or maybe they just didn't want to move on just yet. "And the people in the twisted places? Bronwen? Port? Millicent and Charlie?"

At this, the Lady of the Murk's smile faltered. "I can't say for certain. Their souls became a part of Evancurt when that remnant of the Black World was activated. And as we speak, Evancurt is ceasing to exist. The worlds that were forced together are being torn apart. The remains of the machine are being pulled from this dimension forever."

That wasn't the answer Eric was hoping for. He kept thinking about poor Bronwen. Did she know that he'd found Perrine? That she was safe at last?

"By the time the sun rises," said the Lady of the Murk, "there will remain no trace that Evancurt ever existed in this world. And for that, you have my eternal thanks."

Eric shrugged. "It's what I do. I guess. I mean, apparently..."

She smiled. "You even managed to impress *him*."

He frowned. "'Him'?"

"The Spirit of the Forest."

He looked out into the forest, a little skittish at the mere mention after what he'd endured. "I did?"

"I don't think he believed that there were still humans who could endure his wrath for the sake of protecting someone else."

He looked down at Perrine again. Was that why the fear ended? Had he proved his worth in some way? Had he won the Spirit of the Forest's approval while he knelt in the snow, screaming like a terrified child? Just because he'd refused to let go of her in that blinding moment of terror?

The Lady of the Murk smiled. "I *told* him you were special."

He glanced up at her again, embarrassed. He wasn't special. He couldn't even keep himself in one piece this time around. He glanced down at the black smoke and ash that was still pouring from his wounded shoulder and from the cuts on his hand and arms. "I don't suppose you can patch me up again, can you?"

But at this, her smile melted away completely. "I'm sorry. I can't."

He stared up at her, surprised. "You...?"

"I was able to put off the inevitable only long enough for you to finish your job. But there are some injuries that can never be healed. Not even by me."

An icy dread had filled him. No. This wasn't the way things worked. He did the terrifying things the weird asked of him and then the universe took care of him. He stepped in front of the insane witch's knife to save a teenage orphan and the universe magically healed his wound. He locked himself inside a rat de-mon's lair for all eternity to save a bunch of sugared-up children at a birthday party and a ghostly clown pushed him out and took his place. The universe looked out for him. It *always* looked out for him.

Delphinium once told him he'd always make it home as long as he remained true to himself. What did he do so wrong this time?

He laid the unconscious girl in the snow in front of him. She looked so fragile there. He wished he could do more for her.

"So… I'm really going to die?"

The look the woman gave him was heartbreaking. "Haven't you figured it out yet?"

He stared at her. "Figured what out?"

"You've been dead this whole time."

He stared at her. Those words didn't compute at all. He'd been dead this whole time? What the hell did that mean?

The woman turned and gazed out over the ruined Chrysler. But it wasn't the wreckage that drew his attention. It was the motionless form lying on the ground.

Chapter Sixty-Nine

Eric stared at the motionless body. That was *him* lying there... "But...?" He shook his head. A terrible dread had already filled his heart and now he felt as if he were drowning in it. "No... That's not possible..."

"It's the only reason *any* of this was possible. No living soul could reach inside the core of the Evancurt Machine. It had to be this way. For *her* sake."

He looked down at Perrine. "The only way...?" he sighed. "The only way to save her was to die in a car crash?"

She smiled that sad smile again. "You didn't die in the crash," she explained. "You died three and a half years ago. At the bottom of the cathedral."

He looked up at her again, confused. "What?"

"Two of you set off on that journey. One on the first day. One on the third day. Two timelines converged at the bottom of that hole, where time and space were compressed. You..." She bowed her head, but those dark, beautiful eyes never left his. "You were the *first* to arrive."

The one who left first... "The dream..." he recalled.

"Not a dream. A warning. From you to your other self."

He stared at her for a moment as her words sank in. She was saying that...*he* was Dream Eric?

Very slowly, he lifted his right hand, the one that had been aching all night, and looked at it.

It was wrapped in blood-soaked bandages, half the size it should've been.

He let out a strangled gasp.

It all came flooding back to him. The dreams. The fissure. The *village of the crumbling people*! How did he forget about that?

No. His hand didn't look like this before. He was sure of it. He had full use of his hand. He held the flashlight with it. He opened Shinne's safe with it. He held the little girl in the cupcake teeshirt's hand with it.

And yet, he also remembered that awful day in the fissure. The way everything began going to hell... Starting with that little village...

Numb with terror, he pulled up his sleeve and looked at the burning wound on his arm, the swollen, crescent-shaped gashes of a nearly-human bite mark.

He squeezed his eyes closed. "No..." he groaned. That wasn't real. He never went to that place. He went to Father Billy's church, instead. Just like he went into the Altrusk house where he met... He frowned. Where he met...*who*?

What was he thinking? He never went inside that house. He never had to. He arrived before the foggy man. He was never attacked by those...what were they called? Those monsters that were waiting for him there...? What did they look like again?

He reached up and pulled down the collar of his shirt, revealing his left shoulder. For some reason, he thought he had three long scars there, claw marks from some unremembered monster. But there were no scars. Because there was no monster. The foggy man never... Wait... Who was the foggy man?

He was so confused.

Memories were slipping away from him. *Three and a half years' worth of memories.* It was like waking from a dream. Everything was fading, being swallowed up...as if by a vast, murky ocean....

Empty names floated through his head. Did he know someone named Holly? It felt like he used to know someone by that name... She was someone close to him. A friend. Someone he was quite fond of. Her name was... It was...

What was it again?

Somewhere deep down, he almost understood what was happening. If he never made it back from the cathedral, then he never did any of the things that came after.

Except...*nothing* came after... Nothing at all. He remem-

bered reaching for the lid on the clay pot with the red ribbon…
He remembered unspeakable pain… And then…

He shook his head. And then nothing. Not until a few
hours ago, when he woke up face-down in the dirt.

"Now that you're aware, your two souls are finally pulling
apart," explained the Lady of the Murk. "The parts of you that
were him are disappearing with the fragments of your soul."

He shook his head. No. He just had to clear his mind. That
was all. He tried to remember…

He awoke one morning from a dream. It felt like a long
time ago, but it couldn't have been that long. It was only a few
hours ago…wasn't it? It was just this morning. He went for a
drive to clear his head. He ended up in that fissure, where he
followed the path. He found that barn. The rope bridge. The
abandoned resort that turned into a mansion. The boat that he
took across the lake that turned into a swamp that then turned
into a field. Then that horrible village and those nightmare things
that walked like people but were monsters. How could he ever
have forgotten those awful faces, even for a moment.?

He shook his head. No…

But these memories went on, clearer than they'd ever been
before. He made his way through the abandoned factory in spite
of the wound on his arm, all the way into that narrow canyon
where the monstrous cat found him.

He stared down at his ruined hand, horrified.

It wasn't real.

It didn't happen that way.

But it *did* happen that way. He drove the beast off with a
well-placed jab from a sharp rock and staggered on, bloody and
in shock. He found the old gas station. The little attendant there
patched him up. Gave him drugs. Sent him on his way.

"I'm terribly sorry about all this," the little man had said.
"This isn't the way things are supposed to be. But regardless of
that, you have an important job to do. And I know you can do
it."

Was he talking about the cathedral? Or was he talking about
Evancurt? Did he know this would happen? Even way back

then?

The rest was a blur. There was an old man in a junk yard. A great, gaping hole in the ground. A room full of clay pots.

And then...

He lifted his face and stared at the woman. "I really...*died*...down there?"

She kept smiling that gentle smile. "You did."

He shook his head. "No... I'm not like any of the others here. I...I was *real*. I was *hurt*. I *bled*. I..." He turned and pointed behind him. "I left *footprints!*"

"Spirits manifest in many ways," she said in that patient, gentle voice. "Some mimic life much more than others. You already know this."

It was true. He'd encountered a number of ghosts in his weird travels that were indistinguishable from the living.

"And on extremely rare occasions, a spirit can be so strong that it becomes entirely physical in every way except one."

One difference... He looked down at the black fumes and ash that were spewing from his body, understanding at once. Such a spirit wouldn't contain a soul, he realized. It *was* a soul.

That was why the other ghosts felt so alive? Why Tessa's touch felt so warm when it always felt so cold before? Because he was one of them all along?

"But then...?" His gaze drifted past her, to that other him who was lying face-down in the snow.

"The strange gravity of the cathedral mashes the timelines together. You died, but you didn't remain there. You fused with your other self, who was in the very same place. In essence, you possessed yourself. Two souls shared one body. You merged and became one. It's why you've had such a powerful connection to the spirit world. It's why the dead were drawn to you."

Eric stared at that other him, a storm of emotions raging in his heart.

Was this really it? Was this really the way it was going to end?

"I'm sorry," said the Lady of the Murk. She held her hand out to him. "But it's time to go."

He stared at that lovely hand. She wasn't offering to take him away, he realized. That wasn't how this was going to work. It was never how it was going to work. She was only here so he wouldn't have to be alone.

Those crows were so loud…

He looked around at them all and frowned. He watched the three that were perched on the remains of the mangled PT Cruiser.

Why did he ever think those things were crows?

Harbingers of death, he thought.

He closed his eyes. He took a deep breath. Then he looked up at the Lady of the Murk again. He reached out and took her hand.

She squeezed it. She smiled that gentle smile. A tear streaked down her face. "I'm sorry," she said.

He looked out at the other him lying in the snow. They weren't even dressed the same, he realized. That Eric was wearing the sweater and pants he was wearing when he left the house that morning and he was wearing the same clothes he set off in that early Monday morning three and a half years ago. Funny how he never noticed that this whole time…

Finally, he looked up at her again. He gazed into her gentle eyes. "It's okay," he said. And he found that he meant it. "I think… I think I understand."

As the countless things that were never crows carried on all around him, he felt the last of his soul bleed away.

It didn't hurt.

In fact…it almost felt nice. It was a little bit like floating away on a gentle breeze. He even managed a smile as he blew away in the January wind and disappeared forever.

Chapter Seventy

Everything was darkness, pain and fog. Eric drifted through an icy, black void, lost in the crushing depths of a vast, stinging ocean, his thoughts tossed in the strange currents, scattered and broken, grasping at desperate fragments of confused questions churning in the murky waves.

What happened to him? Where was he? Why was he in so much pain? And what was that terrible noise?

Slowly, he clawed his way back to consciousness and struggled to open his eyes. He was lying on the cold, snow-covered ground, his face pressed against the bare earth, the smell of dirt, dead leaves and blood filling his nose.

Why did he feel like this had happened to him before?

His head was pounding. There was a throbbing in his left knee. It even hurt to breathe. And he was so *cold*. His fingers and toes felt numb. His teeth were chattering.

How long had he been lying here?

With a painful grunt, he lifted his head and blinked away the tears in his eyes. It sounded as if a hundred crows were all crying out in those branches, drilling at his aching head.

Then he saw that he wasn't alone.

There were people over there. A man and two women. The man was kneeling in the snow. One of the two women was lying on the ground in front of the man. The other woman seemed almost to be floating over them. She was holding the man's hand and appeared to be naked for some unfathomable reason. But the strangest thing of all about the scene was that the man looked just like *him*.

He squeezed his eyes closed and rubbed at his aching head. What an odd thing to see. Did he have a concussion? When he opened them again, the floating woman and the other him were gone.

And the crows had suddenly gone silent.

But the other woman, the one lying on the frozen ground, remained.

Shivering, he rose to his feet and stumbled toward her, concerned. Her legs were bare and her skin looked frightfully pale.

What the hell happened here?

He remembered driving home from the teacher's conference. It was a dreary, drizzly sort of day. Then Tessa appeared without warning in the seat beside him and said, "The dead have business with you, Eric." It was the same words Ari spoke to him more than a year ago. The combination of those haunting words and her sudden appearance startled him quite a bit. He nearly swerved onto the shoulder of the interstate. "She's called for you. It's time."

"Who?" he asked her.

"The Lady of the Murk," replied Tessa, as if that made any more sense than just "she."

She then instructed him to get off the highway and drive for eleven miles.

Isabelle informed Karen and Paul right away. And Karen immediately contacted Holly and Paige. They knew the drill by now.

He remembered Tessa telling him to pull onto a narrow, rural road. He remembered continuing on for several more miles. Then, without warning, a dense fog closed around him, blinding him, and then the pavement abruptly vanished from under him. He plowed into the trees almost before he had time to stomp on the brake.

Dazed by the jarring impact and the exploding airbags, he staggered from the vehicle and stumbled off into the forest, where he collapsed onto the ground.

And that was all he remembered until just now.

Except...

He knelt down over the woman, a deep frown overtaking his features. The memories of the night began trickling back to him. Slowly at first, then picking up speed. His eyes washed over her. She was wrapped in an old coat that looked strangely familiar.

The forest... The crows... Evancurt...

The floodgates seemed to open somewhere in his mind and the memories began to rush back to him. The broken girl dancing in the snow. The wendigos. The twisted places. The wandering spirits. The girl in the cupcake tee shirt. The night tree.

He looked over at the mangled PT Cruiser with its open door. His jacket was in the seat when he stumbled out of the wreckage. Now it was gone, stolen first by a ghost who thought he was Eric Fortrell and then by a monstrous tree in a black space inside a madman's workshop.

But he didn't have time to dwell on it.

He remembered Voltner.

The machine.

The reapers.

Death.

It was a little fuzzy, like a dream, but it was all there. Every moment of it. And the weight of those memories nearly took his breath away.

In the heavy silence, his cell phone began to ring. He fumbled it out of his pocket, half-surprised to find it there, and accepted the call without looking at the screen.

"Are you okay?" asked Isabelle.

"I think so," he replied, although he wasn't actually sure about that.

"Those memories..."

"I know." It was so overwhelming... Could it be real? He stared at the woman. Her name was Perrine Roden. And if she were to open her eyes and gaze up at him right now, he'd see that they were two different colors.

"You weren't gone that long," marveled Isabelle. "I only lost you for half an hour. Forty minutes at the most."

He frowned. That was more than long enough to explain the chill. But that other Eric had definitely been out here longer than that. Those memories must've spanned almost until sunrise.

But Tessa *did* warn him that time was broken in this place. Or...she'd warned *one of them* about that, anyway...

He was so confused...

"You scared the hell out of me, by the way."

"Sorry."

"It's okay. I'm just happy you're safe. That place is weird. There's a tremendous amount of exotic energies, especially spiritual. But it's draining rapidly."

"Sounds about right."

"My god, Eric... The things that other you saw in there..." She was still taking it all in. There was *so much*.

"I know..." He looked out over the forest again. "What Voltner said in the attic. About his 'god' that gave him the secrets to building that machine..."

"Altrusk... Yeah."

"That can't just be a coincidence."

"I agree."

He ran his hand through his hair as he tried to process this. "But what could Altrusk possibly have to do with Evancurt? Isn't he trapped in that mansion on the flip side of Gold Sunshine Resort?"

"Isaac Altrusk was a fake name, remember. He was nothing but a con-artist and a closet pedophile. But he must've taken the name from somewhere... Possibly from someone who taught him how to build an insane mansion where doors don't lead where they're supposed to..."

He nodded. "Just like Voltner's house..."

"Yeah... I'm not going to lie. That's kind of unsettling."

It *was* unsettling. And he couldn't stop thinking about what Voltner said about his "god" speaking of him decades before he was born. Was it possible that it really was a god?

"But Eric... If that *was* Altrusk... Or...the *real* Altrusk...or whatever... Then that girl..."

He looked down at Perrine again.

"She's like me."

He stared at the woman lying before him. She was right. They weren't exactly the same, obviously. But there were too many similarities to ignore.

"And if you could get *her* out of the void…"

"…then maybe I can still get you out, too," he finished, his eyes widening at the thought. Was it really possible? Could there still be a way?

"Something to think about," said Isabelle. "But right now, you need to get that poor girl out of the cold. Paul should be there any minute."

"Right. We'll talk later."

He started to put the phone away, but she called out to him once more: "Eric!"

"Yeah?"

She paused for a moment, thoughtful. Then she said, "Something seems different about you."

"Different?" He glanced down at himself. If these memories were real, then he supposed he *was* different. He was one soul *lighter*, for one thing.

"Don't worry about it," she said. "We'll sort it out once you get home."

He nodded. "Yeah. Later." He stared at his phone for a moment before returning it to his pocket. He didn't lose it, after all. It was right there all along, just like his wallet. Instead, it was *Eric* who was misplaced.

And Isabelle… She was never there with that other Eric. All those times he'd talked to her, assuming she was there and that he just couldn't hear her…but he really was alone that whole time. There was something unsettling about that.

He pushed the thought away and stuffed his phone into his pocket. Then he looked down at Perrine again. His eyes washed over her pale, naked legs as she lay there in the snow. He couldn't bear it. He scooped her up and carried her to the PT Cruiser, where he wrapped her in the blanket that Karen kept in the back for emergencies.

He considered taking the stolen jacket off of her. The blanket would probably be enough to keep her warm. But he didn't want to risk it. Isabelle already told him that Paul would be there soon. He'd be okay until then. But for all he knew, Perrine could already be succumbing to the elements.

"She'll be okay," said a very familiar, warbling voice from behind him as he lifted her into his arms again. "She just needs some rest."

He turned to find Tessa standing there. She was smiling. "I know," he replied. "She told me so. Or…she told *him* so?"

"So you remember it?"

He nodded. "All of it." He looked down at Perrine.

"He and you shared a body and a mind. It created a powerful psychic connection. It's not surprising that your memories were entwined."

"That probably explains it," he muttered. Although it was strange that *he* remembered everything that had happened tonight when that *other him* began to forget everything that'd happened these past three and a half years the moment he realized who he was. "I was a little worried I wouldn't be able to talk to you anymore."

Tessa smiled. "It was because of him that you developed such a strong connection with the dead, but that won't change now that he's gone. You're still bound to the spirit world."

Suddenly, someone was hugging his hip. He looked down to see the girl in the cupcake tee shirt. She didn't look afraid anymore. She was smiling up at him with those brilliant blue eyes.

He glanced around, feeling awkward, and found that the confused woman was there, too, standing next to him. She didn't grab his arm and cling to him this time. She was rubbing her elbow and staring down at the ground, looking awkward and embarrassed. "I'm sorry I caused you so much trouble," she said.

He stared at her, surprised. "No trouble at all," he replied. And it really wasn't. That wasn't even really him back there, after all. It was the *other* Eric. This was technically the first time they'd met.

She gave him a sweet smile and then turned away and vanished.

"You did it," said Peggy, who was suddenly there beside him. "You said you'd fix everything and you did. You really *are* profound."

"It wasn't really me, though…"

But she, too, disappeared.

"You did great back there!" said Dora, who appeared on his other side.

This was getting a little awkward. "I literally didn't…"

"You and he were the same person," explained Tessa. "It made no difference which one of you entered Evancurt. The result would've been the same. And now, thanks to you, we're *all* going to be okay."

"Dude!" said the pierced man from where Peggy had been standing a moment before. "That was totally awesome!"

"*So* cool!" agreed Dora.

"Listen," said the pierced man. "A lot of people are splitting as quick as they can. Places to go, you know? Mr. Nicholas already took off, but he wanted me to tell you thanks and good-bye."

"Thank you so much!" gushed Dora.

"We've got to go too," said the pierced man. "See you on the other side, dude!"

"Bye!" chirped Dora.

Then they, too, were gone.

Eric couldn't help feeling like a fraud. He didn't deserve the praise. He didn't do anything. That was all the other him. It was all *Dream Eric*. Shouldn't they have thanked *him*? Before he…melted away?

Someone behind him sniffled. He turned to find the miserable girl standing there, wiping at her smeared makeup. She was still crying, but she was no longer sobbing. She even managed a pained sort of smile for him. Then, with a shuddery sort of hiccup, she, too, turned and vanished.

Looking around, he spotted the suicidal girl staring back at him from the forest, looking shy. She gave him an embarrassed smile and a bashful wave, then faded away.

Then everyone was gone but Tessa and the little girl still clinging to his hip. He looked down at her, into those big, blue eyes.

"Thank you," she said. She let go of him and turned away.

Then she stopped and looked back again. "Oh yeah... My name's Eva." Then she turned away again and ran off into the woods.

Eric watched her. For just an instant, she wasn't alone. Someone was standing there, arms open to catch her.

Then they were both gone.

He stared after her, his head spinning.

What a night it'd been.... And he'd *slept* through all of it...

"Take her home," said Tessa.

"What?"

"She still needs you," she explained. "She has nowhere else to go."

He looked down at Perrine. She was right, he realized. Her only home was forty-seven years in the past. Her family was gone. Bronwen and her father... Everyone she ever knew, probably. Even her home was gone.

"And one day," added Tessa. "*You'll* need *her.*"

He stared at the sleeping form in his arms.

Tessa turned and looked out into the forest. "The last traces of Evancurt are vanishing."

He followed her gaze into the wilderness. Was it only his imagination, or was there an unsettling sort of vibration coming from somewhere over there?

When he looked back, Tessa was gone. So was the PT Cruiser.

He was standing by the side of a dark, narrow road, the same one he was driving down when he suddenly shifted into whatever neighboring universe Evancurt had been hiding in all these years.

The snow still falling, his body shivering, his heart heavy, he cradled Perrine's body closer to him, shielding her as well as he could from the cold, and then he set off down the road.

"Thank you, Eric. I'll never forget what you did here tonight."

He paused and looked back. That whispered voice, carried on the wind. It was the same voice that had been helping him all night, ever since it told him to "find what was lost." It definitely

471

wasn't Tessa's voice. Or any of the ghosts he remembered during the night. And he didn't think it belonged to the Lady of the Murk, either. But he had the strangest feeling that it belonged to someone he knew...

He held Perrine a little closer and then turned and walked on into the quiet night.

Chapter Seventy-One

It was only about twenty minutes before a pair of headlights bore down on him and a familiar, old pickup truck pulled up beside him.

"Finally found you!" exclaimed Paul as he leaned over and pushed the door open. "I've been up and down this stretch of road at least a hundred times."

Probably looking for a mangled vehicle instead of a much-harder-to-see, unconscious body lying face-down on the side of the road, reasoned Eric. That was why Dream Eric couldn't find the road and never saw the other him lying there until the Lady of the Murk revealed him. They were in two different worlds. The road existed in one and Evancurt in the other. It was probably why the buildings hadn't fallen into utter disrepair and how no one had stumbled across such a bizarre setting in forty-seven years.

"Now maybe Karen will get off my ass about it," Paul went on. "Where the hell's your coat? And who is *she*?"

Eric carefully placed Perrine in the middle seat and buckled her in. "Lost it," he replied, "and she's a friend."

"*Another* friend?"

"Yep."

"Huh."

"What?"

"Nothing." Paul turned and looked out the window, making a show of minding his own business.

Eric ignored him and climbed into the seat next to Perrine. As he reached back to close the door, Spooky jumped up into his lap and promptly began making himself comfortable.

Paul stared at the cat, surprised. "I'm gonna just go ahead

and guess you didn't take him with you when you left the house this morning."

"Nope." He closed the door and began warming his hands in front of the heating vents. This was the first he'd seen of Spooky since leaving him in the garden. He hadn't noticed anything following him as he walked down the road. It was as if he'd just appeared out of thin air. But he thought nothing of it. After all, he wasn't really even a cat. He was something else. Something *profound.*

Paul shook his head and then pressed his foot down on the accelerator and pulled away. "So...what're we up against this time? Giant worm? Agents? Clowns?" He glanced at Perrine again, "Fairy tale witch?"

Eric shook his head. "All taken care of."

"You're done?"

He nodded.

"*Already?*"

"Uh huh."

"So we're just...going home?"

"Yep."

"Damn. That was fast."

"Was it?" He really couldn't tell anymore. How long had he lain there in the snow while his double from another timeline gave everything he had to stop Voltner's nightmare machine?

Isabelle said she'd only lost him for about half an hour, but there was no way that all those things he remembered had taken place in such a small amount of time. It had to be the broken physics of Evancurt. Perhaps the same time rupture that kept returning him to the past to witness that explosion had thrown him back to the beginning of the night when it was all over.

Paul glanced over at him, his hairy eyebrows furrowed. "Hey, uh...where's your car?"

"Gone," he replied. He felt so fuzzy and distracted. He felt like he could sleep for a week. Was it the accident that left him feeling so worn out? Or was it that half of him had disappeared forever?

"Gone?"

"Gone."

"As in totaled?"

Eric nodded. "Totaled. Definitely."

"Ah."

"Also gone. Another world somewhere. Probably."

Paul frowned and nodded, clearly not understanding. "Sounds like a nightmare of an insurance claim…"

Eric grunted. It did indeed. But he simply couldn't think about that right now. Just like he couldn't think about the fact that he was pretty sure his keys were still in it… That was probably going to be a pain in the ass, too.

Silence fell over the cab of the truck.

He just wanted to close his eyes and rest for a while, but every time he did, he found himself back in that forest, kneeling in the snow, his soul pouring out of him, the Lady of the Murk weeping over him. And each time he remembered it, the weight resting on his heart grew heavier.

A part of him disappeared forever back there… How did he go about processing something like that?

Paul kept looking over at Eric, studying him. Finally, he said, "You okay? You look like shit."

"Thanks."

"No. Like… *Really* like shit."

"You really know how to butter someone up, you know that?"

"I'm *serious*. You look…" He struggled with the words for a moment, then said, "You look *haunted*. What the hell happened back there?"

Before Eric could answer, Paul's cell phone alerted him to a text message. He pulled it from his pocket and scowled at the screen, but he said nothing more on the subject. (Isabelle had obviously just told him to shut up about it.)

For the next few minutes, he drove on in silence, but he kept glancing at Perrine in the seat between them.

"Don't say it," said Eric without looking over at him.

"Oh, I'm gonna say it."

"Don't."

"I'm gonna."

"Just don't."

"You can't stop me."

He sighed. "Fine. Get it over with."

"Karen's gonna kill you if you don't stop bringin' home chicks."